PRAISE FOR *This Used to Be Us*

"I devoured this book, which is hilarious, unnervingly relatable, romantic, and heartbreaking in the best way. Renée Carlino has that rare ability to utterly transport you, and to create deeply human characters you won't soon forget."

—JULIA STILES

"*This Used to Be Us* is a real and heartfelt portrayal of the roller-coaster ride that is our time on this planet. It made me laugh, it made me weep, and it made me so grateful for each small moment of beauty in my life. This book will stay with me for a long time to come."

—JILL SANTOPOLO, *New York Times* bestselling author of *The Light We Lost*

"*This Used to Be Us* is a sharply penned, wincingly funny, jabbingly poignant examination of a marriage in shambles: Alex and Danielle snipe and snarl their way through a divorce, aware that they have become the worst possible versions of themselves, wondering where exactly they went wrong. The answers are complicated and painful, as they navigate coparenting, new romance, and old wounds around the memories of what they used to have. Renée Carlino's knack for answering the hard questions of the human heart is masterful."

—KATE QUINN, *New York Times* bestselling author of *The Diamond Eye*

BY RENÉE CARLINO

This Used to Be Us

The Last Post

Blind Kiss

Shopping for Love

Wish You Were Here

Lucian Divine

After the Rain

Sweet Thing

Sweet Little Thing

Nowhere but Here

Before We Were Strangers

Swear on This Life

this
used
to be
us

this
used
to be
us

a novel

Renée Carlino

THE DIAL PRESS
NEW YORK

A Dial Press Trade Paperback Original

Published in the United States by The Dial Press, an imprint of Random House, a division of Penguin Random House LLC, New York.

THE DIAL PRESS is a registered trademark and the colophon is a trademark of Penguin Random House LLC.

LIBRARY OF CONGRESS CATALOGING-IN-PUBLICATION DATA
Names: Carlino, Renée, author.
Title: This used to be us: a novel / Renée Carlino.
Description: New York: The Dial Press, 2024.
Identifiers: LCCN 2023031324 (print) | LCCN 2023031325 (ebook) |
ISBN 9780593729281 (trade paperback; acid-free paper) |
ISBN 9780593729298 (ebook)
Subjects: LCSH: Married people—Fiction. | LCGFT: Romance fiction. |
Novels.
Classification: LCC PS3603.A75255 T55 2024 (print) |
LCC PS3603.A75255 (ebook) | DDC 813/.6—dc23/eng/20230714
LC record available at https://lccn.loc.gov/2023031324
LC ebook record available at https://lccn.loc.gov/2023031325

Printed in the United States of America on acid-free paper

randomhousebooks.com

9 8 7 6 5 4 3 2 1

Book design by Caroline Cunningham

For Anthony

I think it's okay to workshop this forever.

Amidst the rush of worldly comings and goings,
observe how endings become beginnings.

—*TAO TE CHING*

this
used
to be
us

1

are you listening?

2002

ALEXANDER

"I love you," I whisper to Dani. We're lying in bed . . . her back is to me. I can tell by the rhythm of her breath that she's sleeping. It's early twilight. The room is bathed in just enough light for me to see the curve of her bare hip. I run my finger down her side. She shivers so I pull her to my chest. She relaxes into me and makes a small, satisfied "mmm," sound, but I'm sure she's asleep.

Chet Baker is crooning quietly from Dani's record player in the corner, something about "it's always you." This was the first time I said "I love you" to her and I was too much of a coward to say it while she was awake. I think I'm just testing the words on my lips. I already know it's true.

It was a long day, but a beautiful one. After weeks of uncharacteristic rain, we woke up this morning to blaring sunshine. The outdoors were calling. We hiked up to a waterfall at Eaton Canyon near Dani's apartment. It was maybe an hour or so into the hike when we had to climb down a steep, muddy hill. I got to the bottom first, then looked back up at her to lend a hand if she needed one. She was up to her calves in mud and struggling a tiny bit to navigate the terrain, but still . . . she shot me the biggest smile. I thought instantly, *Oh my god, I love her.*

We came back to her apartment and have been lounging around the last few hours, mostly naked, talking about everything from our childhoods to our futures. There was a hint in her tone that I might be in her vision for the future. Nothing specific, I just wasn't excluded. We've been dating for a while . . . I know I need to tell her.

She stirs then relaxes again. I begin to doze off.

It's morning now and Dani is up already. She's dressed and sitting at her desk with a cup of coffee, writing something on the Chet Baker album sleeve.

"Good morning."

She looks back at me where I'm still lying in her bed. "We slept for like four hundred hours," she says, smiling.

I chuckle at the exaggeration. "What are you writing?"

"It's personal." She winks. "Maybe someday I'll let you read this."

I love everything about her: the way she sees the world, the language she uses to describe things and feelings, her kindness, her quirkiness, her energy, her exaggerations . . . everything! I want to marry her and I need to tell her I love her.

2

i see you

2007

DANIELLE

We've been doing renovations on the house for what feels like forever, but I can't stop thinking about how beautiful it will be when it's finished. I'm proud we're doing it all on our own. After we got married and bought the house, we had less than a hundred dollars in the bank but Alex was determined and so was I.

The day the agent gave us the keys, Alex said to me, "We've got this, Dani. We'll figure it out and do it on our own." That's what I love about him. He just gets it done.

Now we're almost there. We just scraped the popcorn off the ceiling in the kitchen and the wall started crumbling so we had to pay for new drywall on a credit card. No money for a hotel or even a campsite so I'm sleeping on a mattress in the garage. It's cold and dirty in here. I've pulled the string of my hoody so only my eyes and nose are exposed, hoping my breath will warm me up. I'm in a sleeping bag on a dilapidated mattress on the floor of a garage built in 1908 but I just can't stop imagining the house completed and how happy we will be, so I'm still smiling . . . internally anyway.

Alex is at the side door, about to come and get into "bed." He's looking at me and smiling. "You are so cute," he says. "Such a trooper."

"Get your ass in here, I'm freezing."

He looks to his left and casually walks behind where I'm lying, then hurriedly grabs a bucket.

"What are you doing?" I ask.

"Nothing." He sounds panicked.

"Tell me!" I'm looking back at him now. The bucket is on the floor upside down behind him.

He's standing with his hands on his hips, looking a bit disheveled. "I'm about to get in there with you, so get ready."

"What did you just do with the bucket?"

"Nothing," he says. I start to get up to look at it. "No, Dani, don't."

"What is it?" Now *I'm* panicked. "Is it a spider? What is it?"

"No, it's not a spider, Dani. Just lie down."

"Tell me," I demand.

"It's like a little June bug."

"Liar! You used that name because it sounds cute. But I know it's not cute, and now my imagination is going wild. What is under there?"

"It's a little roach."

"Why didn't you step on it if it's so little?"

I start to get up. "Okay," he says. "It's a *big* roach. I'm going to get it outta here, okay?"

I watch most of the spectacle. Imagine a man trying his damnedest to collect an apocalyptic-sized roach into a dustpan to then re-home it.

"Are you kidding, Alex. Kill it! That thing is gigantic. It's had a long life. It's probably at least two thousand years old."

Deciding not to look, I bury my head in the covers and remind myself that living in the garage is only temporary.

It's been a minute. I know he's gotten rid of it. He's bringing the record player in. He puts on Fleetwood Mac, "Everywhere," and starts to strip down to his boxers. I'm watching him and laughing inside. He's trying *so* hard to make this situation pleasant. He mouths the lyrics, "I wanna be with you everywhere," while simultaneously pointing at me.

Once he's in bed he says, "It's true, Dani. I want to be with you everywhere. Even a roach-infested garage."

I perk up. "Infested?"

"No, just one really old guy, and I put him out to pasture."

"Not funny," I say.

He laughs then pulls me onto his chest, wrapping his arms around me. I relax. I'm dozing off. Everything is exactly the way it should be. I need to remember to write a note on the Fleetwood Mac album sleeve that Alex couldn't kill a cockroach . . . and that I'm starting to think it's the sexiest thing ever.

3

whisper these words to me

2011

ALEXANDER

We're in bed. Dani rolls over to face me and has to lift her belly with her hands to shift her body to the other side. Today is her due date. Our first child. Dani is beautiful, glowing, truly gorgeous, but her stomach is so huge, it has to be painful.

"Alex?" she whispers. It's early and she's still groggy. She's wearing just a tank top that only covers half her belly and a pair of tattered floral underwear. It's adorable. I run my hand over her stomach and feel our baby kick. It's one of the best and oddest feelings in the world. Dani is all belly. It almost seems like the rest of her body is actually thinner, like the baby is taking everything she's got. If she didn't still have such a vibrant energy, I might actually be concerned. The baby moves and turns dramatically, it's hard not think there is at least a three-year-old in there.

"Yes, my love."

"I want to ask you something." Her eyes are still half-closed. She maneuvers to get closer to my ear. I can feel her breath.

Now my mind is on other things. I think she's going to kiss my neck when she very quietly says, "I think we should insulate the attic today."

My eyes shoot open. "What?"

Taking a deep breath, she sits up. "This house is cold and the insulation sucks. We should go rent one of those machines that shoots insulation into the attic."

"How do you know about that?"

"I saw it on an episode of *This Old House*. We can get it all at Home Depot."

Dani is nesting at the moment . . . quite literally. She wants to blow tons of insulation material into our attic, like an actual nest, and I can't tell her no.

"I think it's like a two- or three-man job," I say.

"*Man?*" she snaps.

"Person," I reply, a little exasperated. "You know what I mean."

"You and I can do it," she argues.

"No, Dani! No way. You're not going up in the attic right now."

She takes a deep breath and calms down. "You go in the attic and I will put the insulation into the machine outside. It runs through a big hose and you'll just shoot it all around up there."

It's now the afternoon and I cannot believe I agreed to do this, but I knew Dani wouldn't take *no* for an answer—and honestly, how could I refuse her? She is smiling as she stands in the side yard preparing to dump giant bales of insulation into the hopper machine down below. I'm watching her from the attic opening and through the kitchen window. She has the radio blaring "Eye of the Tiger," and she's bobbing her head to the beat. She's ready. "Go ahead," I yell and then prepare myself for the onslaught. The insultation comes shooting out with the force of a fire hose.

It's not slowing down and now I'm about knee high in the stuff. I wonder if Dani will ever stop throwing the bales in. "Stop," I yell, but she keeps going. The music and sound of the machine are drowning me out.

I finally set the hose down and go over to the opening. The hose is flailing around wildly, but I need to get her attention. She's covered in sweat and insulation particles and she's frantically cutting the bales open and tossing them in. I pause for a moment to take it all in. It's hilarious. She's so determined.

Finally, I have to scream, "Stop, Dani!"

She looks up, still smiling. "Oh, sorry!" she yells.

When I get down from the attic, I check my phone and see there is a message from our neighbor, Carl. It says:

Monica and I are very concerned, Alex. We see your wife across the street frantically throwing stuff around. Isn't she very pregnant?

I laugh to myself and reply:

Yes. Today is her due date and she decided she wanted to insulate the attic. I love her so much.

4

i haven't heard your voice in years

present day

DANIELLE

It's 4:32 in the morning and he's walking down the hall toward the stairs. I know the time without looking at the clock. The springtime light isn't yet piercing the horizon. There are no cars on the road; his will be the first. It's quiet out, but loud in my head, loud in this house.

He's shifting his 170 pounds from one foot to the other, down the stairs . . . loudly. It feels intentional. He clears his throat. It feels intentional. I can hear him from my bed, far away in my bedroom. What used to be *our* bedroom. *Our* bed.

No one is awake at this time in the morning. No one in this house, no one in this neighborhood, no one else in my life. He must know he's waking the whole house as he shuffles his feet across the travertine floors, down the hall, past the dining room, and into the kitchen, where he presses the button on the coffee grinder. We're up now! *You've made your point, asshole.*

This is how it has been for years. After 3,008 complaints, it hasn't occurred to him that he should grind the beans the night before? It's not evident to him that no one else in this house needs to be awake for another three hours? Not me, not our twelve-year-old son, not our thirteen-year-old son, not even the damn dog. After so many years of tolerating his inconsideration for the sake of marriage, it no longer feels like a sacrifice . . . It feels like a crime, one in which I'm victimizing myself by staying.

In the last several years, there hasn't been a single morning I've woken up on my own, or even by an alarm I had set myself. No mornings lying naked, languid, exposed . . . wrapped up in a lover. Wrapped up in him. I have entertained such phenomenon, I have revisited that life in my mind many times. The life I used to know. I shimmy out of my tattered sweats and T-shirt at dawn. I run my hands across my breasts, my stomach. I feel what I might feel like to someone else . . . someone who isn't in such a hurry.

I imagine a man being awestruck, telling me he doesn't want to leave. I remember that feeling, which is now so far away. He asks me to stay . . . in bed . . . I imagine sleepy morning sex while listening to Chet Baker croon quietly from the speaker in the corner. Later we amble directionless around the room until we're dressed, teeth brushed. Strolling to a café, sharing a meal, drinking our coffee, kissing, and saying goodbye. Realities I no longer experience.

I'm alone. I feel the scars he calls "marks" like they're tattoos chosen from a wall off the retail store of my youth. Drunken mistakes? A tramp stamp, as it is so terribly referred to? No! These are stretch marks from pregnancy . . . scars. Four pregnancies in all. My two beautiful sons and the two horrific second-trimester miscarriages I endured alone . . . my daughters. He doesn't see them every day the way I do. He doesn't imagine the women they would've become every time he looks at his own body in the mirror.

The grass isn't greener, it's gravel on the other side. This is what I have told myself for years and this is why I've stayed, but now my imagination has become too wild. The grass isn't greener, it's a vitamin-rich waterfall oasis with magical, golden baby goats and Adonis angels feeding me calorie-free chocolate ice cream.

It's Sunday and I'm awake at 4:45 in the morning, but I won't go downstairs until at least seven. I will not give him the satisfaction of knowing he woke me up, yet again.

He's completely deaf in his left ear, according to the world-renowned audiologist he saw—his words, not mine. He can hear a mere twenty percent in his right ear, but it's enough, and it's why I automatically walk and sit and eat and instinctively move to a person's right side when interacting with them, regardless of their aural-apparatus capabilities. You evolve after twenty-two years of adjusting your frustration levels, speaking up, enunciating, shouting, "How was your day?" Eventually, you just move to the right side.

I'd think it contemptuous to be annoyed by his deafness if I didn't believe it was partially selective on my behalf. He seems to have much better hearing when anyone besides myself is speaking. It's that insolent wife joke about how obnoxious her voice is. I can't believe I used to laugh along to jokes like that, as if to say *I'm too cool, too easygoing to be offended by a joke about how women in general are annoying and my own voice is grating or off-putting*. The voice I used to soothe our children, night after night, the *only* voice that could soothe our children, is somehow raucous to Alex and to others? Is that what I'm supposed to believe?

He had just gone deaf the year I met him and was monumentally struggling with his balance, among other issues that present when your hearing in one ear suddenly goes out. It was an inner-ear infection, the first world-renowned audiologist had said just before closing the book on Alexander—no amplification possible. He'd have to get a cochlear implant, which at the time was a devastating idea, even to me. Yet now, after twenty-two years of people shouting at him, he still refuses to look into cochlear implants? Part of me thinks it could have saved our marriage.

In the beginning . . . I pitied him, and I know it doesn't make sense to resent a person for pitying them . . . but it is possible.

I tap the screen on my phone. It's now seven-fifteen in the morning. Today is a big day. Moving day. I realize I've been lying in bed, awake, listening to the clanking, tinkering, shuffling, shifting for almost three hours. In my head I imagine making three tally marks on top of an old chalkboard. The screeching chalk in my mind coincides with the sound of Alexander slamming the vitamin cabinet above the trash can. He'll take the trash out next and when he does, he'll lift the trash bag out and let the heavy plastic trash can liner slam back down into our overpriced simplehuman stainless steel trash can. It's made for simple humans after all.

I glance at the clock and add another tally mark to the chalkboard. The thousands of lines represent the hours I've wasted being unhappy.

Regardless of how many aspects of my life are predictable to the point of soul-murdering boredom, one thing is, ironically, predictably unpredictable, and that's the fact that I never know when Alex is going to leave the house or return. Even though he wakes up at the same time every day, some days he says he has to be at work at 7 A.M. Some days he's home at two or four, and others not until 8 P.M. He's a physical therapist with his own practice, and his hours vary greatly. If you ask him to try and give you a heads-up, he'll act like you're somehow taking away his autonomy, when the reality is, by virtue of his own recalci-trance, he has eliminated any autonomy *I* could possibly have.

And so I am the default parent . . . the mother. He is the man who deserves autonomy.

Cases in point, more than a thousand times over the years we will be headed to a destination we've both agreed upon, Alex driving, of course, because I'm a woman, when, without warn-ing, he will turn in the opposite direction from the agreed-upon destination, at which point I will say, "Where are we going?"

In the more recent years this question has become increas-ingly agitating to him. "I'm stopping at the gas station to get a Lotto ticket. Is that okay with you?"

I'll usually respond with something like, "Sure, it's just nice to know where my body is being driven."

Almost every time he looks at me and rolls his eyes.

Just last week, many months after we had already decided to file for divorce, we chose to ride together to the mediator's of-fice. We were naively optimistic, and also . . . we pretend we're progressive. On the way there, Alex decided to take a different route.

"Where are we going?"

"To. The. Mediator's. Office."

"Why are we going this way?"

"Because I decided to go this way and I'm driving."

"Well, then let me drive," I said without condescension.

"No, this is my car, I'm driving, and I am going this way be-cause I want to go this way."

"Alex, do you see how this conversation started as a simple question and now it's turned into a battle over whose damn cookie it is?"

He glanced at my crotch. "Well, it's not yours; we know that."

Shocked, I said, "Now that we're getting a divorce, you're a sex-crazed, deluded, misogynist man from 1805, calling my vagina a cookie? Well, that definitely makes things easy for me."

"Lighten up."

"No, I will not lighten up. You lighten up. I just asked where we were going, and now you act like I was the one overreacting. If you're not stonewalling me, you're blatantly gaslighting me."

"Well, I'm glad the thousands of dollars we spent on therapy has improved your vocabulary. Anyway, it's never just a simple question with you, Danielle. I can always hear something in the underlying tone."

"You're projecting."

"According to you, I'm everything in the goddamn psychiatric bible!" he yelled.

"You said it. In this instance, I really did just want to know where I was going. I'm not your property, not along for the ride. You've been doing that to me for what feels like a millennium . . . And by the way, Alex, I've always had a stellar vocabulary."

"Leave it to the writer to exaggerate everything and then to brag about her word prowess on top of it."

"Let me explain something to you—"

"Dani, just stop talking."

"No, I'm pissed now."

"You're always pissed."

"Listen to me, there is a difference between exaggerating, like 'My dress was nine hundred dollars' when it was really seven hundred, and 'My dress was a million dollars.' It's beyond the scope of possibility or likelihood and it's simply for effect.

Furthermore, I haven't written in a year. For some reason I am no longer inspired to write."

"Don't blame me for your writer's block."

"Stop saying everything I do is because I'm a writer. You always do that. You knew me before I was a writer."

"You said yourself you were a born writer, a storyteller, which makes you a born liar."

"Oh, screw you."

"You won't let me."

"You're a pig. Why would I? Your jealousy about my career has made the fact that I am a writer the enemy of this marriage."

At this point, we looked up to realize we were in the parking lot of the mediator's office. "I don't know what you're talking about. I'm not jealous of you. I have my own career. Are we gonna go into Kevin's office yelling and screaming at each other like last time?"

"I'm not yelling. I have to talk this loudly so you can hear me, remember? How come when you yell, you say it's because you can't hear, but when I yell, I'm a bitch?"

"Are you ever going to *shut up,* Dani?"

"Are you going to start showing me some base-level respect by telling me when you decide to take a different route, or stop at a convenience store while I am the passenger?"

He sighed. "This is ridiculous. It doesn't matter because you'll never have to be the passenger again."

"Fine by me. I can't believe we thought we could actually ride together. And for the record, Alex, this cookie is closed—to you anyway."

"Well, that's settled. Let's head in. Now get the hell out of my car."

Under my breath I said, "Your car that I paid for," which isn't entirely true, but I do know how to push his buttons.

That was exactly three seconds before I unbuckled my seat-belt and got out. It was exactly five seconds before Alex jammed the car into Reverse, backed up, almost running over my foot, and took off down the road while I looked on from the parking lot, completely dumbfounded.

5

because i have nothing
to say

ALEXANDER

For a moment, I wondered how long my prison sentence would be if I backed over her in the parking lot of the divorce mediator's office. Kevin always liked me more. Maybe he would testify in my defense. Say it was in response to the years of Dani's berating, emasculating bullshit.

When I pulled into the driveway of our house, I knocked around the idea of a world without Danielle. Somehow, it still seemed unbearable even though I despise her. I mean, I literally cannot stand her.

I walked into the kitchen to make a sandwich and immediately felt I was doing something wrong even though I was alone in my own house. There will be crumbs on the counter. I'll use the wrong cheese. I'll spoil some imaginary meal I will never actually eat.

My phone buzzed with a call from Kevin, the mediator.

"Hey, buddy. I have Dani here. You guys had an appointment. You know she's crying—"

"I am not crying because of him," I could hear Dani say in the background. "I'm crying because my foot hurts!"

"She said you ran over her foot, Alex."

"Nonstop drama. I didn't run over her foot. Listen, I feel like Dani and I should only communicate via email or something. It's just too volatile."

"Alex, would you mind if I put you on speaker? We can address the bullet points here and just call it a day. I'll mediate. That's my job."

"Fine, whatever," I said with a mouth full of turkey and lettuce.

Kevin put the phone on speaker, so I did the same on my iPhone. I was sitting at the kitchen bar eating my sandwich, fully intent on listening, abiding, and pleasantly arriving at some conclusions or agreements with Danielle. I guess I will never learn.

"So guys, I have to say, this is our fourth meeting and I still have not gathered all the information I'll need to put a plan together. I'm still waiting on those documents, Alex. And Dani, I need you to fill out the schedule form and let us know what your workday will look like."

Before I could even respond, Danielle started in. "Alex, we can hear you chewing over the speakerphone. Can you postpone your lunch, or mute your phone when you're not talking?"

I threw the sandwich across the kitchen. I mean, I really chucked it hard against the Shaker cabinets. I couldn't help myself. Little bits of shredded lettuce went all over the counter and floor and I had no intention of cleaning it up.

"I'm done with the sandwich," I said calmly. "Kevin, I'll have my assistant drop off the insurance docs later today."

"Who the hell is your assistant?" Dani blurted out.

"It's Jenna, Dani. You know that."

"Jenna is not an assistant and she'd vomit knowing you called her that. Jenna is a supervisor. She runs your entire clinic and she has more schooling than you in her big toe."

"Are you done, Danielle?" I said. "And is this you mediating, Kevin?"

I could hear muffled talking before Kevin took me off speaker and came onto the line.

"Let's reschedule. Tempers are flaring and I'm not sure we'll get much accomplished today," he said.

"You just need to mediate, Kevin. That's the idea."

"Dani stormed out. She's gone. And for propriety, I don't think we should talk any further."

"So are you billing us?" I asked.

"Alex, this is my time too," he said.

"Dani—"

"You left, Alex. You drove away."

"I'll call you back. This is still our hour." I hung up the phone and immediately called Danielle.

"What?" is how she answered the phone.

"Are you coming straight home? We need to have a discussion since mediation was completely pointless."

She stayed quiet for several moments. I could hear her breathing heavily. "I'm in an Uber. I'll be there in ten minutes." She hung up.

I looked around to see what I could do to avoid being yelled at when she got home. I cleaned up the sandwich, wiped down the counter, and got the mail. Despite my desire to stand up to her, it's not worth enduring five minutes of her wrath.

She used to be my best friend, my confidant, my cheerleader, my teacher, my lover. Now it's like she was my tyrannical boss.

I heard the familiar clacking of her heels as she walked down the long hall from the front door to the kitchen. "Alex!" she yelled.

"I'm in the kitchen," I said.

She hesitated in the doorway of the kitchen for a moment. I saw her eyes dart around the room. Looking for something, I imagine. Something to complain about. I was standing, relaxed against the kitchen sink, my feet crossed at the ankles and arms crossed over my chest.

We glared at each other.

"I didn't run over your foot," I said.

"When you decided to gun-it in reverse, nearly running me over, I stumbled back and rolled my ankle. Would you like to see how swollen it is?"

"Why don't you take your shoes off?"

Silence.

Danielle is not a malicious liar, at least not that I can tell. She actually prides herself on being morally sound, a do-gooder. However, she is a habitual exaggerator. There's a difference. Her melodrama makes her stories sometimes appear unlikely, which, to people who don't know her, makes her seem erratic or unstable. Danielle is the most stable person I know. She's just emotional and has a flair for telling a story. Her emotions are exhausting to me now after so many years. She's just . . . *a lot.* Not high-maintenance, just a walking broken tooth, exposed nerves, sensitive to even the slightest breeze. Your mere existence in a room, shifting the air, can aggravate her. If you blink for one second longer than you normally do, she will instantaneously come up with three scenarios for why your blink was unusual, and most of them have to do with her being personally attacked.

Ironically, despite Dani being so hypersensitive, she has no problem serving her own assaults up to me on a platter of sarcasm and snark, sometimes blatant cruelty. But . . . the majority of the time, when it comes to other people, her exaggerations and energy are completely appropriate and will turn an otherwise boring conversation or activity into a theatrical presentation. Her friends welcome this side of her. It breathes air into a room. Sometimes, calling her a liar is all I have to match her quick-wittedness. It's the one thing I know for a fact that she's insecure about.

"Are you just going to stand there and stare, Dani?"

"My shoes aren't the problem."

"So you told lies to the mediator thinking it would help us? You were basically accusing me of trying to kill you?"

"Who's telling lies now?"

She was unwavering. Stoic. This is how I knew she was really pissed.

"All I'm saying is, when you dishonestly say or even just insinuate that I'm trying to hurt you to our divorce mediator, it doesn't look good."

She blinked, then set her purse down on the counter and walked to the refrigerator as I watched. She took a half-empty bottle of chardonnay out of the door, popped the cork out with her teeth, and drank directly from the bottle.

"It's two in the afternoon. Are you not picking the boys up?"

She turned on her heels. Daggers! Slowly and deliberately she said, "Are you not picking up the boys?"

"I'm saying it because you always pick them up."

"Yeah, I do!" she sneered. "Maybe you can today. How about that?"

"You're so bitter, Dani."

"So obtuse, Alex. We're getting divorced because we are *both* bitter. Resentment has festered like a plague."

"How poetic. You deliver your word diarrhea with such great panache that it sounds like a Broadway musical. *Panache,* there's a word for you, smarty-pants."

"We can no longer fake it till we make it. There is nothing funny about this situation." That's when the waterworks began. Her face scrunched up, tears rolled down her cheeks. I couldn't help but smile. It was a knee-jerk reaction. "You're smiling? You condescending, fucking ego-monster. Look at you. Nothing. Emotionless, heartless vessel," she said.

I laughed out loud even though I knew things were escalating for Dani. By this point, she was sobbing. She shook her head, tears pouring from her eyes.

"We didn't make it," she said, barely able to speak. And that's when I actually . . . finally . . . felt a modicum of sadness. I could see the despair on her face, yet I still didn't react. "We didn't fucking make it, Alex!" she cried and then stormed out of the kitchen with the bottle in hand.

"Does this mean I'm picking up the boys?" I said to the empty kitchen.

I liked to end arguments with moronic statements like that because that's the way she makes me feel. Like a moron.

6

you've murdered the
best parts of me

DANIELLE

Inside my large walk-in closet, I slithered down the wall, gripping the chardonnay to my chest like it was a dying friend. Alex always gave me a hard time for hanging out in my closet even though it was the size of a small apartment. I would joke that I was a closet drinker because I liked the peace and quiet inside the closet while enjoying a glass of wine here or there, on the floor no less. For years, it was simply a mommy break, and then it became a safe place. A place to imagine. A place to explore myself. A place I didn't feel judged or critiqued by everyone in my life, including the strangers who saw the television shows I wrote.

When you begin the divorce process, which for us started years ago, you immediately look for the answers. In the beginning of the disintegration all you have is "why?" No *because*. At the stage we are at, everything is a *because*. Because he exists and I am stuck co-parenting with him until the end of time. That's how it feels. Because he has brown hair and sharp toenails. Because his mom smoked while she was pregnant with him.

In the safe haven of my closet, I checked my phone and found a text from my agent to call her. It had been a year since I was fired as a staff writer on the religious family drama *Happiness Road*. Who came up with that title anyway? I'll never know. The creators had all quit by the time I signed on. I got fired for telling the new, much younger head writer that I thought the show presented a sense of false moralism. I was fired on the spot and I didn't even care. My career was a towering inferno by that point anyway, and writing a religious drama was a last-ditch effort to salvage it and save face after being accused of pandering to the male showrunner on a different series.

It was the popular streaming series *Litigators*. And by *pandering to,* I mean sleeping with. I hadn't done anything of the sort. Lars was a fan of my writing before I even started working for him. We were great friends, but that was all. *Litigators* was a dramedy about a fabulously dysfunctional family of lawyers in Seattle, which happens to describe my best friend's family. I also grew up in Seattle. I had a lot of material. Lars assigned many of the episodes to me, which won us both three Emmys. Lars didn't deserve the slimy reputation he got because of it. He was always all about the work and he got blacklisted too.

The accusations were made by Beth Zinn, a jealous female co-writer who couldn't pitch the idea of water to people on fire. Every episode pitch she gave involved someone stealing a dog. It just became a stupid joke. No one wanted her ideas or writing, so of course she found a way to ruin everyone else's career because of her wounded ego. I wasn't the only one who didn't want to research court cases involving K-9 theft in Seattle, but I got the brunt of her wrath because we were the only two female writers on the show, and exactly the same age. In retrospect, the whole dog-theft thing could have made for some much-needed funny moments on the show, but it didn't happen, and it wasn't entirely my fault. If I could go back, maybe I would have fought harder for her.

I can't believe I actually feel sorry for a person who was so vindictive and terrible to me, but that's the thing . . . pity can make you have unreasonable feelings. In my mind she is the scum, desperate at the bottom of the sludge, trying to claw her way up. It's more heartbreaking than unnerving. Once my back-to-back miscarriages were public knowledge at work, I overheard Beth telling another co-worker that I was full of dead babies and spiders. Maybe if she could have written with the same zest and detail of her shitty comments, she would have had some success.

I stared at the phone for another beat, then dialed my agent, Connie.

"Dani, hi."

"Hi."

"I haven't heard from you," she said in a concerned voice.

I jerked my head back. Was I supposed to call her to remind her I still didn't have a job? "Well, nothing is new really, so—"

"What happened to the pilot?"

I had told her a year ago I was going to create a show and write a pilot that no one could take away from me. I had basically given Connie and the agency a *Braveheart* speech. It was very dramatic. I yelled over a conference call, "They may take my Emmys, but they will never take my pride!" No one actually took Emmys away from me, but it felt like it when the accusations were swirling.

I had said I planned to write a new, better dramedy that was going to be like *Parenthood* meets *The Ice Storm* with a sprinkle of *Thirtysomething*. Connie was totally behind me on it and said she would sell the shit out of it. That was a year ago, and so far I had only written twelve nonsensical pages.

"The pilot is happening. I just went in and tweaked it a bit yesterday." That wasn't a lie. I deleted a comma the day before, then instantly shut the document down.

"Meaning you still only have twelve pages?" She took a deep breath and went on. "You told me in the beginning, eight years ago when I became your agent, that you never wanted me to do the rah-rah bit."

"Yeah, I don't need an ego boost."

"About five years ago, Dani, you told me you don't respond whatsoever to tough love either."

"Exactly, I want a straight shooter, but I don't need to be reminded that I am broken-down, unemployed, almost divorced, and aging at hyper-speed."

"Is that all you are?"

"Connie, are you serious?"

"What are you doing right now at this very moment?"

I looked down at myself. I had taken off my blouse to blow my nose into it, so I was sitting in my slacks and a bra only, on the floor of my dark closet drinking chardonnay from the bottle at two in the afternoon.

"I'm talking to you. That's what I'm doing," I said.

"What were you doing just before you called me?"

"What's your point?"

"You've told me many times not to agent you, but I think it's time to agent you."

"I meant I didn't want you overwhelming me with your endless idioms."

"Your behavior is beyond the pale, Dani."

"Oh my god!"

"Listen to me, you are the most talented writer I know. You're prolific, brilliant, clever. Do not waste it. You are not a dime a dozen. I feel like I'm beating a dead horse here, so I'll stop beating around the bush—"

"No more horses, no more beating bushes, no more cats and dogs!"

"You're sitting in your closet, aren't you, Dani?"

"So what?"

"Danielle?" came Alex's voice from outside the closet door.

"Hold on, Connie. What is it, Alex?"

"I'm going to pick up the boys." His voice was quiet . . . worried. I wished for a moment I could see the expression on his face. It had been a long time since he showed concern for me.

"Okay," I said. I felt the tightening up of my throat and welling tears in my eyes. Whenever Alex acted like he cared even just an ounce, it made me emotional.

Connie spoke up. "Dani, I have to jump on another call. Listen, I'm going to a luncheon thingy tomorrow for one of my clients and Eli Abrams is going to be there."

"Okay," I said, not sure what she was getting at.

"Eli is working for Gina Edwards, who has that big overall deal with Apple right now. They're looking for an episodic dramedy."

"Wow. I know Eli. We had a great working relationship."

"Well, he's producing content for her now. Why don't you shoot me over the twelve pages tonight so I can talk about it tomorrow with him?"

"Okay," I said in a much higher voice. I instantly had the simultaneous thoughts, very common among writers, where you hear your own voice say, "I can write award-winning television in my sleep. I'm going to write the whole pilot tonight," and "I'm a fraud, a hack, a talentless impostor."

"We have a plan, then, Dani?"

"Yeah, I'll send the pages over tonight."

It wasn't until an hour later and a half a bottle of ten-dollar chardonnay in my gut that I decided to actually leave the closet. I threw on a pair of sweats, twisted my hair up in a bun, and made my way downstairs to the recycling bin, passing my thirteen-year-old son, Noah, as he sat at the kitchen counter reading. He's the brainy one whose curiosity and interests over-shadow the turmoil going on around him, thank god.

"Hi, Mom. I just read that Elon Musk developed a video game at the age of twelve and was paid five hundred thousand dollars for it."

"Wow. I guess that explains why billions to him now must feel normal." I paused and looked over Noah's shoulder at the iPad he was holding. "What site are you reading?"

"An article in *Popular Mechanics*. I could probably develop that same game, except so could half the kids I know."

"Innovation and skill are different things."

He smiled and looked up at me. "Are you saying I'm not in-novative?"

"You are innovative, the most innovative person I know. You just have to figure out how to develop that thing that no one has created but that everybody wants or needs." I bent and kissed the top of his head. "How was school?" Noah was growing up. I noticed for the first time he had peach fuzz on his upper lip. Alex and I were too swept up in our drama to notice that our boys were becoming men right before our eyes.

"Do you think I'm more innovative than Ethan?"

I blinked, contemplating how to answer. The boys were too old now to pull one over on them. I instantly regretted using the superlative "most," even though it was true. Noah was the most innovative person I knew, but he was still a kid with normal sib-ling rivalry tendencies.

"Ethan is innovative, but his strengths are different than yours."

"Explain."

"Noah, you and your brother are different. I'm actually surprised at how different you are, considering you are brothers so close in age." My voice was starting to rise with irritation. "Ethan has that flexible kind of brain that makes it possible for him to adapt to any situation."

"I'm flexible," Noah said.

Ethan walked into the kitchen as we were talking about him and it didn't even faze him. He glanced at the empty yogurt container in front of Noah and said, "Did you really eat the last yogurt even though I told you I wanted it?"

"I thought there was another one in there."

"No, you didn't. Whatever."

"Hi, Ethan, nice to see you," I said, trying to divert his attention.

"Hi, Mom. Why did Dad pick us up today?"

It took great self-restraint to not blurt out something snarky, like "*Because he's your father, for god's sake—and furthermore, I just argued about how adaptable you are, Ethan.*"

"Because he was here and . . . I asked him to," is what I actually said.

"He made a scene at school because he didn't want to park in the parking lot, so he just waited for us in the drive-through area, holding up the line. People were honking, it was embarrassing. Why didn't you tell him that on Wednesdays we walk all the way from the other side of campus?"

Even when I'm not involved, everything is my fault.

"Well, now he knows, doesn't he? He didn't intentionally make a scene. He probably just thought you'd be looking for my car." I was still always defending him. "Where is he, by the way?

I have a lot of writing to do and I need to get back up there," I said, referring to my desk upstairs.

"He went back to work," Noah said without looking up from the iPad.

I shook my head and tried desperately to hide my disappointment. He avoided me even though he told me we needed to discuss things. He couldn't even give me an hour to cool off.

"I'm making salmon tonight. I'll start dinner around five-thirty. Can you guys get your homework done, clean up your rooms, and throw the ball for Louie Louie before dinner? I need to go upstairs and write."

"Sure, Mom, no problem," Noah said.

Ethan looked at him and rolled his eyes.

"Ethan, don't antagonize. For being a punk, you can pick up dog poop in the backyard."

Noah smirked at him. Ethan didn't have much impulse control. When he felt slighted, hurt, or irritated, he let it be known. "That's so unfair. Just because I'm not kissing your—"

"Stop, Ethan, before you get yourself into actual trouble. Noah picked up the dog poop last time. It's your turn. I'm going upstairs. I have to focus."

When I got to my computer at the desk in my room, I opened the twelve-page script document and stared at a blinking cursor. Writer's block is a tricky beast. To overcome it, you have to actually write, which seems obvious, but the block isn't an easily definable state of mind where words and ideas escape you. The block, and succumbing to it, is more like an exaggerated form of attention deficit disorder, where everything is a distraction.

Plucking your eyebrows or getting the mail takes precedence over your work in progress. It's also cyclical in that it feeds and starves itself. You subconsciously look for diversions. You convince yourself that learning to make a key lime cheesecake from scratch is a pressing matter.

I could feel myself slipping into avoidance. My focus had shifted from writing the script to writing Alex an email, but I knew I had to redirect my attention. For several minutes, I chanted over and over: *Avoiding this script, Danielle, will only make the state of your life worse. Finish it, then write Alex the email.*

It would be my reward. I would allow myself to tell him exactly how I felt, but only once I finished. I knew writing an entire script in one sitting was probably impossible, therefore telling Alex how I really felt would be successfully avoided, but I lied to myself anyway.

Against all my internal will, I shut the twelve-page heap-of-crap writing down and opened a new blank document. Ditching even that small amount of material to a writer is painful, but I knew it was trash. I began writing the script from the beginning. After twenty minutes, I had twelve new pages. Page twelve represented some kind of mile marker in my head, like it was the beginning of that last grueling five-mile climb of the Tour de France. It's just the beginning of the climb, but your position is still everything.

I set my alarm for five-thirty on the off chance that I would actually get into a writing groove and need reminding that the kids were hungry. I opened Spotify to a writing playlist and put it on random. It only took thirty seconds of the loud music to push me over the giant block of procrastination. Finally, I was in the story.

Writing can be like a coma, a blackout, or a time suck, where you produce very little, yet still feel emotionally and mentally drained. But when it's good, there's just enough light for awareness. You're aware that you're writing, that words are flowing. You're telling a story, watching it happen while your fingers are recording it. It's euphoric . . . better than any other high.

"Mom? It's seven-thirty. I'm gonna make grilled cheese for me and Noah."

I looked up at Ethan as tears were steadily streaming down my cheeks. He looked over my shoulder and read the last words I had typed . . . *The End.*

My smile was an obvious tell for him. "You finished it?" For me, finishing a story is equal parts relief, pride, and sadness. It's the final coming down.

"Yeah. I did. I'm sorry I forgot about dinner. I got caught up. Dad's not home?"

"Don't worry about it, Mom. We didn't really want salmon anyway. Dad texted us and said he'd be home around nine. I'll make a grilled cheese, it's no big deal."

I nodded.

"Good job, Mom. I'm proud of you."

"Thanks, E."

What I didn't . . . *couldn't* tell Noah earlier was that while his younger brother may not be the innovator of the two, he was definitely the feeler. He had a greater emotional intelligence than most adults I knew. He possessed a true empathy and emotional maturity that is so uncommon in boys his age. Though Noah had the accolades, I somehow knew Ethan would also do well in life. You can't be that aware of the world and the workings of interpersonal relationships at age twelve and not do something good for mankind.

Ethan put his hand on my shoulder. "Love you," he said.

"I love you too."

He smiled. "Want me to make you a grilled cheese?"

"No thanks, buddy. You know, you remind me so much your uncle when you smile like that?"

"I wish I could have met him," he said.

"Yeah, me too," I replied, as the tears welled up again.

Ethan looks and acts just like Ben, my younger brother, who died at nineteen in a car accident. Ethan has Ben's crooked smile that was almost always a smirk, and eyes the exact color of a perfectly cloudless sky. Ethan is beautiful, cherubic, but his baby face is fading fast, being replaced by sharp edges and peach fuzz. He's growing up, but not out—yet—but when he does, I'm going to have to pry girls off of him. Ben was the same.

I was twenty-four years old when Ben died. It was six months after I had met Alex. Only a short time into our relationship, Alex and I were forced together by the seriousness of life. I hadn't thought about that fact in a long time. What if Ben hadn't died? Or what if he had died before I met Alex? Would Alex and I have been glued together so tightly from the beginning? I doubt it. "Enduring hardships side by side," or is it "overcoming adversity"? Maybe it's "experiencing tragedy" . . . whatever that saying is, it's not true. Alex and I have had it all and we couldn't be further apart.

I was still thinking about Ben as I stared at Ethan. Ben was a bright light, lit from within by some otherworldly source . . . something off-limits to the rest of us. He was an easy son and good brother to me. My goofy baby brother for so long and then it was as though he hit sixteen and instantly became a man, wise beyond his years, but somehow still seraphic. He skipped the awkward phase overnight and . . . at nineteen, Ben became who he would always ever be. Perfectly frozen in time.

I wonder if that's how it works . . . if the brevity or expansiveness of our lives is predetermined and we grow emotionally at a relative rate. I stared at Ethan with this thought in mind. *That can't be how it works. I won't allow it.*

Ben died alone, driving to meet one of his college professors. He was killed instantly, hit head-on by a drunk driver who walked away from the accident. Ben never had a girlfriend. I wondered sometimes if he had even kissed a girl. He was quiet about that side of his life. These things, experiences that seemed to be delayed for him, didn't have any effect on his emotional literacy. He was brilliant and well-rounded. I know he would have been the kind of person who waited for the exact right partner, and then made it all the way to the end with them. I obviously wasn't that kind of person. I didn't. We, Alex and I, didn't make it.

When Ben died, it was the most tragic event in all of our lives, and would forever be . . . I hope. I think about him daily and miss him desperately. I miss who he was, but I also miss the idea of him . . . the idea of having someone to walk beside me in life whose love is unquestionably unconditional. Not having anyone to share my childhood memories with makes them feel obscure and fictive. Losing Ben made me feel utterly alone. I've had a sense of vague loneliness looming over me since he died.

I could feel myself weakening again at the reminder of him. It had already been a rough day, but I needed to write the email to Alex. I needed to say what I had wanted to say in mediation.

Finally snapping out of my trance, I noticed Ethan was trying to read my script. "You need to go eat, babe," I said to him. "Will you make sure you clean up your mess down there? I'll be down in a bit."

"Sure, Mom."

Once Ethan left the room, I opened a new email and began typing.

7

you struck first

ALEXANDER

When I started my own practice fifteen years ago, I was committed to making it successful. I had the full support of my wife, her encouragement to stay late and put the time in, which I did. But the funny thing is, back then, when my business needed my attention in order to grow, all I wanted to do was get back home to Dani. Our nightly dinners, our alone time, playing house, falling deeper and deeper in love. Now I do everything I can to avoid our house, stay late at work, create new projects that have nothing to do with my practice.

When you build a life with someone, there are reminders everywhere. Even at work: vacation photos, picture mugs, homemade elementary school paperweights, the couch in the corner where Dani and I would sit, eat lunch . . . make out like teenagers. She hadn't come to my work during a lunch break in years. She'd pop into the office now and then to drop something off, but our relationship had long since been reduced to an arrangement.

The office was empty and dark. The other physical therapist, supervisor, and front office staff had all gone home for the day. I sat at my desk trying to dream up some reason to avoid going home even though I was exhausted. It had already been a long and grueling day after the mediation debacle, holding up the line at the boys' school, and listening to Dani sob in her closet.

Glancing at the clock, I made a deal with myself to suck it up and head home in ten minutes. That would put me at the house around 8 P.M. Hopefully, everyone would be settling in and I wouldn't have to face Dani or the boys.

From my office window, I looked out at the glowing red lights spreading out on the 5 freeway. The traffic was letting up, finally. My office was a mere three miles from our home in Los Feliz, but if traffic was bad enough, it could take me forty-five minutes to get across the 5 freeway from Glendale. Dani was well aware of the Los Angeles traffic norms, which meant she knew that unless there was an accident, getting home at eight meant I had been in the office for at least two hours after the clinic had closed.

I don't think she ever suspected an affair, and she would be right not to, but there was no doubt that Dani knew I avoided her.

When my email dinged, I smiled, excited at the prospect of possibly having work to do, a client to respond to, or a colleague checking in that would force me to stay in the office longer. But that wasn't the case. As soon as I saw Dani's name on the email, my stomach dropped. *What now?*

Alex,

The vitriol, anger, and constant arguing is spilling over into every aspect of our lives. We always talked about avoiding divorce to protect the children, now it's about completing the divorce to protect the children. I never thought this would be us, Alex! But it is, despite the dreams we both had about family and growing old together. They were idealistic dreams, but we were both in it, weren't we? Maybe that relationship hubris came back to bite us in the ass. We thought we were so much better than everyone else and now we're a cliché.

It was supposed to be you and me, my friend, growing old and gray, and older, and older until the end.

Instead you behave as though you wish I were dead. Maybe so you can start a new life. Do you? Wish I were dead?

I know you're sitting in your office, probably staring out the window, wishing you didn't have to come home.

Soon, Alex, soon!

I'm writing to you to tell you that I'm putting a deadline on this nonsense. No more marriage counseling, there's no point. We can still use Kevin to work out the financial logistics and co-parenting, but there is no "us" to talk about. We're getting a divorce.

I don't want to move the boys back and forth between two broken homes. I think we should get a bird-nesting apartment.

That is my request. In two weeks, by the end of the month, we have an apartment we share to use on our days without the boys. Hopefully we can both be grown-ups about sharing a space. I sent Kevin a schedule and looked at your request to be with the boys Sundays, Mondays, and Tuesdays. I wanted to argue about how convenient that would be for you to have your freedom on Wednesdays, Thursdays, Fridays, and Saturdays, but I don't care anymore. Freedom isn't being away from the kids. I hope that's not how you're looking at it.

I won't be available to you as a babysitter or bus driver on your days at the house with the boys, so you'll have to figure that out. I don't want to know about it, or be a part of it, unless it's an emergency.

That's it. That's all I have. We have two weeks to get a place. It's time.

-Dani

I sat still, quiet, my mind swirling, contemplating how to respond to her. I typed . . .

Dani,
You know what? Go fuck yourself.

I was hovering the little arrow over the Send button when I heard a knock on the door.

"Knock, knock," Mark said as he pushed the door open to my office. I startled and then settled back into my chair. I moved my hand away from the computer mouse, leaving Dani's message unanswered.

"Hey man, come in," I said.

"The front door was unlocked. I just pushed it open."

Mark and Alicia were our best friends. Alicia was Dani's childhood friend. They had always been inseparable, even moving to LA from Seattle together during college. I met Dani and Alicia before Mark was in the picture. I knew it would take a rare breed to be married to bullheaded, tough as nails Alicia, and Mark is just that . . . rare. He and I fell into an easy friendship from the start. He's a calm and cool person, which makes him a brilliant lawyer as well as a perfect match for Alicia's intensity. She comes from a long family line of judges and lawyers who make an Olympic sport out of suing people. What is undeniable about Alicia, though, is that she is loyal and genuine to the core. She represents good people who are suing bad people, and she always wins. Mark and Alicia are partners in life and at the firm, but they don't have any children, so our boys are as close as they'll come to parenting.

Mark and Alicia are major factors in why Dani and I have struggled to commit to divorce, but they know everything that's going on. It's ironic that now the commitment is in the divorce and not the marriage.

"Yeah, I was just about to leave, but come in, sit down," I told him.

He smiled, glanced down at my empty desk and back up again. "I was picking up take-out and had to park three blocks away. Walking by, I saw your light on." He held up a bag of Chinese food. "Hungry?"

"Starving." I lied.

Mark pulled a chair out and sat down, leaving the takeout in a bag on the floor. "Well?" he said.

"Well what?" I chuckled. He wasn't just in the neighborhood. "Was Alicia talking about us or something?"

"Honestly, Alex, Alicia doesn't stop talking about you guys." He smirked. I always thought of Mark as a salt-of-the-earth kind of guy. He didn't have sneaky ulterior motives when he decided to stop in my office late on a Wednesday, but he also wasn't walking by. He was checking in on me.

"What did she say?"

"Just the usual. If Dani and Alex can't make it work, how can anyone else?"

I laughed, flippantly. "That ship has sailed. Alicia's probably just scared. She's been watching the death of a marriage for years now."

"She's also worried about what it means for us, Alex."

"You guys are solid."

"No," he said. "Not *our* marriage. Our couples marriage to you guys." He laughed.

"Everything will be fine with us," I said, though I wasn't convinced myself.

"The last thing Alicia wants is for us to have to choose sides."

"No one is asking you to, Mark," I said with a hint of irritation in my tone.

"It's been years with threats flying between you and Dani. You've both asked us for names of lawyers, mediators, financial advisors. Alicia and I made a pact that we wouldn't get in the middle of things, but it's hard to see you like this, and it's hard to see it affecting Alicia too."

"Well, I'm sorry it's affecting Alicia, but jeez, it's like the last thing we have on our minds, I'm sorry to say."

"I'm trying to be honest with you. It's for everyone's sake, not just Alicia's. The weeble-wobbling, the emotional motion sickness, the back and forth, the ups and downs—"

"I get the point. No more weeble-wobbling," I said and then laughed a little to try to lighten the mood.

"It's for your kids too, man. You guys got lucky with a couple of rad kids, but aren't you worried this will eventually take a toll?"

"Of course. We worry about that every day." I felt like he was crossing a line even though I couldn't deny what he was saying was true. "It's hard to know what's better for everyone. The amount of thought we've put into divorce is exponentially greater than the amount of thought we put into getting married in the first place."

"That's how it always is, because divorce is final and everyone knows marriage is not," he said.

The statement struck me. It was true. Something no one likes to admit. We claim it's forever as we stand up and take our vows, but in our subconscious we're saying forever . . . unless x, y, or z happens. Some might say divorce doesn't have to be final either, but there is no divorced unless x, y, z happens. We're getting a divorce, not making a promise to each other. It's final. It's the end of a promise, a union. It's a death.

I was trying to shuffle the seriousness of the conversation to the bottom of the deck, but Mark wasn't letting me. "We're trying to do the right thing for the kids," I said finally.

"But in the process, you're all putting everyone in limbo, including yourselves. Shit or get off the pot, you know?"

I laughed lightly. "God, I hate that saying. Can't we just talk about golf or something?" I really wanted to change the subject but knew I wouldn't get off that easy.

"Alicia wants her friend back. We miss you guys, the vacations . . . everything. What's going on right now? Are you working on things? Now that Danielle's mom is gone, is it better? Or are you ready to file the papers and sign that shit and be done with it?"

"We're getting a divorce, Mark. There's not going to be couples vacations and hanging out."

"There hasn't been in a long time. At least everyone will understand the boundaries though. You and I will always be friends. Alicia is not going to make you a pariah, okay? She knows Dani too well. She knows it was a culmination of things. No one blames either one of you—or your mother-in-law, for that matter."

It felt easy for me to blame Danielle's mom for the demise of our marriage. Dani and I had barely addressed the fact that, four years ago, the day we moved my mother-in-law into our house to take care of her, basically marked what I viewed as the beginning of the end for us. But Irene has been gone for a year now and things haven't gotten better.

"It wasn't just Irene, though I don't think you could possibly understand what it was like to live with her. Her toxicity," I scoffed.

"She had Alzheimer's, man," he said.

But he wasn't there to see her nastiness, her disdain for me. I don't think it was all the disease talking.

I also took Irene's criticism while Dani looked the other way and it was just too much. After having Irene in our house for six months, I was a shell emotionally. I couldn't take it. Dani was swept up in work . . . swept up in Lars. She would start fights with me every night over how heartless she thought I was. She *actually* called me heartless while I was at home caring for her mother and reading on celebrity websites about how Dani was screwing her boss.

They're not even celebrities.

Dani can deny it, but she was always going into the office when she didn't have to, and she defended Lars. I know *something* was going on. Constant late-night calls. The giddiness in her voice when she would talk to him. I couldn't trust her, and so I stopped needing to trust her. That's when, mentally, I left the marriage.

Mark was staring at me waiting for me to respond. He had the same look of disappointment Dani would get when she thought I was being insensitive. "I know she was sick," I said finally. "It was sad and brutal to watch, but it's the reason all our problems came to the surface. If we were meant to be, wouldn't we have survived that?"

Mark shrugged, then picked up the food and started taking it out of the bag. "I think you guys should have worked through your mother-in-law issues with a good therapist. Taking care of an ailing parent is hard on any relationship. It's been, what, a year since Irene passed?" I nodded. "And you guys are still constantly spiking serves at each other? You do know that kind of petty back-and-forth means you still love each other? You're still fighting like kids on a playground."

I paused, contemplating his statement. "Of course I love Dani. You can love someone and not want to be married to them anymore. We're done. It's over." I glanced down at the email I had almost sent. "I promise we won't drag you guys into it. I'm getting an apartment this week. Dani and I are gonna try the bird-nesting thing and I'm going to sign the papers."

He looked up, surprised. "You think you guys can handle that . . . sharing an apartment?"

"Well, we live in the same house. And we won't ever be at the apartment at the same time."

"You've been in the same house but separate bedrooms, right? For how long?"

I glanced out the window, remembering the day I came home to Dani filling the guest room closet with my clothes. That was three years ago.

"Yeah, it'll be different though. It's the next step. The pettiness is prolonging the inevitable. I'm signing the docs tomorrow. The paperwork is done. We'll get the apartment and stick a fork in it, okay? It's what she wants too."

"I'm not trying to push you in that direction—"

"No, but you're right. You can tell Alicia everything. I'm going to email Dani in a minute."

Mark stood up and pushed a carton of food toward me. "You know this is gonna look like I prodded you."

"No, it really won't. It's been a long time coming."

"Okay, man." Mark turned around in the doorway. "I'm here for you."

"Thanks. Hey Mark, can we grab a drink this weekend?"

"Yeah. Don't the boys have baseball?" he said. He knew we

always went to dinner with other baseball families on Saturday nights. I guess that was going to change too.

"I'll be free after five."

"Okay. Call me."

As soon as I heard the door to the clinic close, I looked at the email to Dani and deleted what I had written earlier. I kept the new message short and to the point.

Dani,
    All of that is fine and I agree. I'll look for an apartment and send you the options so we can make a decision.
    -Alex

I'm not a crier. I'm sure Dani could count on one hand the number of times I have almost cried, but never did. Of course, when her brother died, I didn't even know him, but seeing her pain and her parents' pain made me emotional. Still, I never shed an actual tear over it. There was the death of our beloved first dog, Sparty, who took his last breath in my arms as Dani wailed next to me in the vet's office fifteen years ago. I felt sad but didn't cry; he died of old age, and honestly it was a relief. There were Dani's two miscarriages, when I almost cried, but not from the loss as much as from seeing Dani's pain, physical and emotional. And then the birth of our two boys, where again, watching Dani labor, unmedicated, through excruciating pain, the relief and joy I could see on her face when they plopped our screaming babies on her chest—that's what actually moved me the most, but not to tears. Never to tears.

Sometimes, I wondered what was wrong with me. Why I didn't often get emotional. Dani sure as hell made a point of bringing to my attention that I was likely made of stone. I didn't take it seriously, though, because it was coming from her, a person who cried when someone sang the freakin' "Star-Spangled Banner." I always found that one particularly confounding because Dani wasn't patriotic at all. She said she was moved by togetherness. A group of people sharing a moment. An evocative song. Someone or an animal in pain. A dog with a limp could literally make Dani spiral into a deep sorrow. To say I didn't get it would be an understatement. I didn't actually believe it was real. I thought she was an Academy Award–winning actress in life.

In the twenty-two years we had been together, I had never cried. Not in front of Dani and not alone. But that night, a minute after I sent Dani the email, and thirty seconds after I sent the lawyer an email to complete the divorce paperwork, I closed my computer down, looked out the window, across the freeway to where we lived for so many years, and the tears finally came. I sobbed. And I understood it . . . finally. It was the finality of it. The death in it. The mourning of something *I* actually loved.

8

i was screaming for help

DANIELLE

We no longer have to pretend in front of friends and family that we're trying to stay together. I can stop feeling like I'm victimizing myself, and I can put an end to the internal dialogue about a possible divorce. It's the reality now.

Today is moving day and I'm the first to go, take my things, spend the night in the nesting apartment . . . alone. Secretly, I made a deal with myself to avoid calling it the "nesting apartment" out loud, it gives the implication that we are expecting a baby, and boy if that's not off the mark. I don't completely understand why sharing an apartment and going to and from the family home during the divorce process is called "bird nesting," but I bet there's some anthropological reason for the name, one I don't even care to look up.

The idea was the first suggestion our therapist had proposed that actually made sense to me. Up until that point, she was always pushing us more toward staying together than divorcing. She had gotten irritated with me at our last counseling session four months ago, telling me, "Dani, I'm a marriage counselor, not a divorce counselor. You guys need to get a mediator. Try separating physically—get an apartment and go from there."

It was the moment when both Alex and I finally showed some sign of surrender. We looked at each other, he blinked, and I said, "I guess that's what we'll do." Of course we found ways to prolong that process as well, but here we are now, finally.

As I get dressed to head downstairs, I can hear the boys chatting with their dad in the kitchen. I'm dreading walking into the scene and interrupting their conversation, but I'm also anxious to get this whole process over with.

We had sat down with Noah and Ethan numerous times over the last two weeks to explain the looming divorce, to discuss their feelings, and to reassure them that it was not their fault, that we would always be a team for them. Throughout those conversations, I had done most of the talking, of course, while Alex sat back and nodded in agreement.

Noah's reaction was expected. "Does this mean I get my own room now? I mean, you and Dad will share the master bedroom again, right? Just at different times? So the guest room or Nana's old room . . ."

"No one is moving into Nana's room," I had said.

It was barricaded with boxes anyway. I normally didn't have hoarder tendencies but when you watch a parent die in front of your eyes, it's not an image easily erased from your psyche. You don't want to continually have to revisit the room where it happened, so I made it off-limits. I intentionally filled it with junk to stuff the void of grief I felt, which was just another thing that irritated Alex.

"This is a four-bedroom house, Dani," he had said in response to Noah's comment. At that point Alex looked to Noah and said, "We'll make it work. You'll get your own room."

Ethan's reaction to the news was different. He was quiet. He came up to me later in my bedroom and said, "Did you want this too . . . the divorce?"

I wondered what his perception was. We kept a lot from the kids but they were no strangers to our trivial arguments and the general sense of unrest in our house. Still, I felt they were too young to understand that the marriage type of love is not always forever and it's not unconditional.

"Yes, I do, Ethan," I had told him. He simply nodded and looked down. Was he looking for a hero and a villain? "There's no bad guy in this story, babe." I could barely choke the words out.

He had looked up at me, blinked, tears in his own eyes, and said, "Okay."

I had hurt him by telling him the truth. Another parenting decision I would go on to question endlessly. Would it have been better to lie? To give him a narrative that would make the pill easier to swallow?

The conversation currently happening in the kitchen sounds light, so I take it as a cue to go down and get some coffee.

When I get to the bottom of the stairs, I look off to the left and notice the blinds in the front room are open. I try to remember if I left them that way the night before. It was one of my pet peeves that Alex would be seemingly oblivious to the blinds open at night on the front-facing windows. It made our house feel like a fishbowl to the neighborhood. I always closed them when it got dark and opened them in the morning, but they were open already.

As Ethan passes me on the stairs I turn to him and say, "Did you open the blinds in the front?"

"No, Dad did. Are you leaving soon?"

"In about an hour," I say. "Why, you trying to get rid of me?"

He laughs once and heads up the rest of the stairs. In the kitchen, Noah is wrapping up a conversation with Alex about space junk as I walk in. Noah looks up and scatters like a startled animal. Our kids are, understandably, in a constant state of avoidance when Alex and I are in the same room.

"Has he actually talked to you about what's going on?" I say to Alex after I'm sure Noah is in his bedroom.

"Yeah, he asked me if the rules were going to be different when I was here alone with them," Alex says without looking up.

He's buttering an English muffin directly on the countertop. It's disgusting and quickly forming a crumb-covered grease smudge on the granite.

I breathe deeply in and out of my nose. He glances up, "What?" he says.

"Nothing. Did you open the blinds?"

"Is that okay?" he snaps.

"You know it's okay. I was just asking."

With a mouth full of muffin he says, "Noah's fine. He isn't melodramatic, thank god."

"What is that supposed to mean?" Without waiting for an answer, I continue, "Avoiding his feelings is not healthy for him."

"Moping around can't be any better."

"This conversation is pointless."

"As are many of our conversations."

I choose to ignore him as I pour myself a cup of coffee. With the mug in one hand, I open the cabinet under the sink and reach for the Windex to clean Alex's grease smudge. Then I hesitate.

I don't have to worry about this shit anymore. I'm leaving, going to a place where there are no grease smudges, no crumbs on the counter, no derisive looks.

Alex is watching me. "You don't have to worry about the grease and crumbs on the counter anymore, Dani."

The gift of mind reading comes with the long-term relationship territory. "Well, I will on Wednesday, won't I?" I say.

"I'm sending the cleaning company from the clinic here every Wednesday morning to do a once-over before your scheduled noon arrival. They'll also go to the apartment every Sunday morning to pretty up the place up for you, your highness."

"How much is that costing?"

"Who cares, if it means I never have to hear you bitch at me again?"

Resigned, I say, "Great. I'm going to pack up the rest of my stuff and head to the apartment, then."

As I leave the kitchen I glance back at Alex, who is happily chomping away on his muffin and staring at his phone, completely indifferent.

Once Alex agreed to get an apartment to share, things happened fast. He found one a block away from his office. I agreed based on the pictures and the next day it was a done deal. The apartment is a small one-bedroom, furnished in sterile grays . . . not exactly my style, but I would do my best to make it comfortable.

It's been hours of packing and organizing when I finally shove the last suitcase and laundry basket into the back of my Jeep and head back into the house for one last box. It holds my record player and a stack of LPs I grabbed randomly from my collection. Alex and the boys are still upstairs as I head to the front door carrying the box.

"Danielle!" Alex yells from upstairs.

"What?"

"Was just checking to see if you were still here," he says as he makes his way to the landing and looks down at me standing near the front door.

"I'm leaving in a few minutes. I'll say goodbye," I say, struggling to hold on to the heavy box.

"Wait a minute." Alex comes down the stairs and approaches me. I set the box down.

"What?" I say, impatient.

"You're taking the record player?"

"You're kidding, right? I'm the only one who uses it. It's mine. Yes, I'm taking it."

He reaches down and flips through the stack of LPs in the box.

"And these records? The boys listen to these."

"No they don't. No one has used this thing for years. I want to get back into collecting. This was *my* collection. I had it before I even knew you."

He holds up Bruce Springsteen, *Born in the U.S.A.* "This is mine. You hate Bruce," he says.

"I do not hate him. Fine, take it out. Whatever."

It's true. That album is Alex's, but the stunt he's pulling right now has nothing to do with the record player or the albums, or goddamn Bruce Springsteen.

"What are you holding on to, Alex?" I say quietly. "It's definitely not me."

He looks up, a seriousness that is void of anger washes over him. "That room is not your mother's, it wasn't before she got sick and it's not now that she has passed."

"You're seriously lacking a sensitivity chip. I don't want to talk about that room right now." I haven't yet started crying, thankfully. "I'm taking the record player to the apartment. It's not like I'm donating it. You will be there too, and you're welcome to use it then." A few beats of silence sit heavy between us. "I used to write on these LP sleeves, remember?"

"I remember."

Part of the collection was my father's. He had started the tradition when he and my mom first got married. He would write a few sentences about what was going on in his life on the white LP sleeves. Every time he would play a song from that album, it brought the memory to the surface. Many of his notes were about Ben and me growing up. Things like, "Ben took his first steps today. Irene caught him just before he tumbled into the coffee table. Supermom!"

The year Ben died, my parents divorced. They couldn't recover from the loss. My mother became hardened and bitter . . . mean. She was verbally abusive toward my father, toward everyone. But my father had been checked out completely at that point anyway. He's existed in some alternate universe ever since. It's a place where there is no love and therefore no chance to lose it. Even though ten years ago he moved less than a half an hour away from us, I only see him once or twice a year, on a holiday or birthday, where he'll stop in, have a meal, leave a gift, and go home. He barely knows my children, but every month he deposits two hundred dollars into their college funds. It's too hard for him to be close to us. He never remarried, he's just alone, going to his job as an insurance adjuster, punching the clock, eating, and sleeping. Barely existing. Even music is too strong of a reminder for him, so he gave me his entire record collection.

I continued the tradition for years, making little notes on the LP covers about what was going on in my life. Those memories are forever attached to the songs. Most notes naturally involved Alex or the boys. It was *my* thing and *my* collection and Alex knows that.

"This is how I fell in love with writing," I tell him. "By making these notes on the inside covers, remember?"

"Yeah, I remember, Danielle. You did that for a few years. So you think it's gonna help you get over your writer's block?"

"I don't have writer's block anymore. I wrote a pilot script in one day two weeks ago."

"I'm sure we'll hear about it endlessly until you write something else."

"You have no limit, no governor, do you? By the way, I wrote the notes in the LP covers for more than *a few* years. This holds meaning for me. I'm sorry you are a shell and have no feelings and that makes you incapable of understanding mine."

"Dani, I do have feelings. I'm mainly irritated about something else and this is just adding to it."

"Please, do share, I'm all ears."

"That room, Danielle! We have to do something with your mother's things."

"Go ahead. Knock yourself out. By the way, I won't let you buy me out of this house. I love this house."

"So do I," he says.

"Are we gonna go to war over it?"

"We can afford to split the mortgage for now. Let's cross that bridge when the boys go to college."

"The nesting apartment is temporary," I say.

"We'll figure it out!" he snaps.

I pick up the box and open the door to head to the car.

"Stop! So you're gonna be okay with me clearing out that room so Noah can have it? You're not gonna be pissed?"

"It's fine," I say quietly, momentarily forgetting that Alex can barely hear.

"What?"

"It's fine!" I scream.

"Why are you shouting?"

Here come the tears. "I'm leaving, okay? Do whatever you

want. Put my mother's stuff in boxes in the garage and I'll go through them when I'm back."

"Now you're crying?"

"Of course I'm crying." I set the box down on the porch. Alex is standing in the doorway. "You act as though I shouldn't mourn her because you two didn't get along."

"She didn't get along with anyone, including you! She was a monster, Danielle. She was horrible to you, to the boys, to your father. I put up with it for so long while you made excuses for her."

Alex is leaning against the wall with his hands in his pockets. His body language and lack of expression on his face makes him seem like a sociopath.

"Can you imagine what her life was like? Her only son dies suddenly, then her husband leaves her a month later? I was all she had." I wipe tears from my face and pull it together.

"She should have treated you that way, but she didn't. She hit you, threw food at you, called you stupid. She called our sons pussies, Danielle. Her own grandsons. She said they would be weak like their father . . . me! She told me that you settled for me, that you never loved me, and that you cheated on me all the time. What kind of mother does that?"

"One with *early onset Alzheimer's,* Alex. One who is swept away in her own delusions. It wasn't long after those outbursts that she didn't even know her own name, let alone who the hell we were. Have you no compassion?"

"Each time I defended you. 'She wouldn't cheat on me,' I'd tell her when she was on one of her kicks, but she wouldn't stop there. Do you know how many times she told me that you and Lars belonged together? That he was your 'intellectual equal'? I mean, it wasn't enough that *Entertainment Weekly* was saying you two were sleeping together. I had to have your mother rub it in my face too, all while I was helping take care of her physically and financially."

"I didn't cheat on you! We've been over this. She was sick and Hollywood gossip isn't real. You know that!"

"One time she actually told me Lars had a bigger dick than me." He laughs maniacally while I cringe.

"That was less than three months before she died," I say.

"Does he?"

"What?"

"Have a bigger dick than me?"

"How would I know? How would my mother know that? You're being ridiculous. You know all that Hollywood stuff is bullshit!"

"Maybe I don't know that. Maybe I'm not smart enough. Not your *intellectual equal*."

Emotionally spent, I say, "Maybe you aren't. Lars never even made a pass at me. He thought I was happily married because that is how I acted. I could have won an award for that performance."

Alex rolls his eyes. "Now you're defending his virtue?"

"His virtue? His career was trashed. He was accused of being a misogynist at the height of the Me Too movement and he's literally the most fair and progressive person I know."

"He sounds great. Anyway, it was you that was being accused of being unprofessional, remember?" He smirks, arrogantly satisfied with his comeback. He knows how sensitive I am to the topic.

"Let's get something straight. My professional reputation . . . his career, they were torched to the ground and smeared all over the internet because of one woman's jealous accusations and her own harebrained imagination. We were stripped of our dignity. I was strong enough to fight back and that's why I'm still treading water in this business, but Lars was not. He's now a shut-in at some hippy freaking commune in Northern California! *Because of me, Alex! Me!* I feel a tremendous amount of guilt for something I'm not even responsible for."

"You never think about us. It's always *your* career, *his* career, *your* mother, *her* feelings, and on and on . . ."

"I could easily say the same about you and the fact that you avoid this house. At least I'm here."

I can't believe the day is already coming to an end. It's getting dark out and I'm still fighting with Alex on the porch.

"You took care of her despite her endless criticism, her abuse, and her unyielding cynicism. She was toxic, Dani. And you still defend Lars despite being accused of having an affair with him. It's disgusting."

"I defended Lars and I took care of my mother because it was the right thing to do. Is this why we're still fighting? You need me to apologize . . . again? For something out of my control? Okay, fine. I'm sorry about my mother. And I'm sorry I wasn't more considerate of your feelings with the Lars thing. It's confusing because you don't appear to have any feelings."

With that he turns on his heel and heads back into the house. Just before shutting the door, he says, "It's exhausting, Dani. I can't wait for this to be over."

"Same!" I grab the box and head down the steps to the driveway. I'm holding it together all the way to the car. I drive away as the picture of strength and resolve, but I get exactly one block down the road before I pull over and start sobbing.

It's hard to pinpoint how I feel. I don't understand why Alex is pushing back now after weeks of being seemingly detached. I thought he would have been shoving me out the door.

I look down at my phone to see a text from him only a minute after I left. The argument continues . . .

Alex: What about dating, Dani?

Me: Dating? You're kidding me? What are you asking me?

Alex: Are we gonna set some ground rules?

Me: You in a big hurry to jump back in the deep end?

Alex: I'm asking to avoid another huge fight.

Me: Do whatever you want. The apartment is off-limits though. OFF-LIMITS! I don't want to see or hear about it either. You're a piece of work. The ink isn't yet dry. Twenty-two goddamn years!

9

i tuned you out

ALEXANDER

No one mentions how you're jettisoned into an unknown abyss once you separate. You're forced to relinquish this control you've had for so long . . . this right to respect, or loyalty, or something I can't quite put my finger on. I guess it's simply the knowledge of knowing what the other person is doing at all times.

Asking her in a text what the dating rules were created a pit in my stomach as I stood in the entryway waiting for her response. She was pissed and thought it was too soon. She thought it was absurd. I took a deep breath . . . relieved we finally agreed on something. Yet, despite that fact, I still couldn't bring myself to respond. I would leave *her* to wonder.

I'm folding clothes in the bedroom Dani and I used to share. I haven't spent much time in here over the last few years. I look around and notice it's unusually tidy. *Does she sit in here and organize in her spare time?*

"Are you going to move back into this room now?" I hear Noah say from the doorway.

I turn to face him. "No. I think I'm going to stay in the guest room. I like the bed in there better," I say without emotion.

"So you're gonna stay in the guest room and leave this for Mom when she's here and then I'm going to move into Nana's old room?"

"That room actually used to be the office," I say and then immediately wonder why I had to clarify that. The woman is dead, for Christ's sake.

"Do you guys even need an office? Mom writes in here and you work at the clinic and no one has used that room since Nana died."

I'm staring at him and noticing the hair on his upper lip. He looks like a completely different person just in the span of a few months. He's taller, lanky, awkward, but it's not the braces that make him seem awkward. He's in that couple of years where your body isn't quite in proportion. Almost like his arms are longer than they should be. His hair cannot decide if it's long or short and it looks oily from where I'm at, even though I know he showers every day.

He's looking back at me, expressionless, waiting for me to respond. I seem to be at a loss, just examining him and how different he looks to me in this moment. If Dani were here she might say it's a good time to have *the talk* with Noah.

"Yeah, you can have that room, Noah," I say, completely ignoring my train of thought. Dani can have *the talk* with him if she thinks it's so necessary. "I need to move your grandmother's stuff out of there and put it in the garage."

"Do you want me to do that?"

"Yeah, I'm just gonna finish folding these clothes and I'll come in and help you in a bit."

"Why are you in here?" he asks. "If it's just basically Mom's room now and you're folding your own clothes?"

"I don't know. It's closer to the laundry room. It just seemed more convenient."

He shrugs as if he doesn't buy my excuse. It's true there really isn't any reason for me to be in this room. It's just where Dani always folded the clothes. I glance at her desk and notice the computer is gone but there are handwritten notes on a yellow legal pad. This is how Dani has always brainstormed for whatever she's writing. Early in her career, I was so fascinated by her process. When I had asked her once if she outlined, or plotted, or jotted down notes on bar napkins to bring home and turn into magnificent stories, she laughed and said, "That's not exactly how it works, for me anyway."

She had been writing since I'd known her, but didn't really call herself a writer until she got paid for it. That was not long after we met. Our first date, though, she told me she was an assistant producer. I remember the day she completed her first episodic series script. We were still in our early months, not yet living together, so I hadn't ever seen her actually sit down and write.

We were in this tiny Thai restaurant somewhere near Warner Bros. Studio, where she was working with an all-female team developing a *Cagney & Lacey* type of TV show. She hated the idea of how women making shows about women had to be a thing people would ask her about. She said, "It's like asking Anthony Yerkovich and Michael Mann how they felt about creating *Miami Vice* about two male detectives. It's just a stupid question that perpetuates sexism."

That night we were celebrating the episode she had written, which was about to be filmed. We weren't even exclusive, but I remember asking her, "How do you write this stuff? Do you have a bulletin board with a bunch of scenes written on four-by-five cards?"

She laughed, "Sometimes I scribble little notes."

"Well, how do you keep it straight in your head? Like, organized?"

"I just do. It's kind of intuitive. The stories are three-dimensional in my mind."

"Is every writer like that?" I had asked.

"I have no idea. Probably to a degree. Think of it like this . . . You know Clare?"

"Yeah, what about her?" I had said. Clare was a girlfriend of Brian's. Brian was a writer friend of Dani's from work who I actually hit it off with, and who I am friends with now. He's my only single friend. We mainly just golf together once a month. Clare and Brian broke up long ago, but at the time I was dating Dani, Brian was dating Clare and we used to all go out together.

"You know how she's *shit* at telling a story? Like you never know when it's over, so you're not sure when to react or respond and it always makes for a weird conversation with her? You feel like you're patronizing her all the time?"

"Yes, it's totally like that."

"She wouldn't make a very good writer. Like, no sense of timing, no intrinsic understanding of beginning, middle, and end, you know? Like climax and resolution? When you hear her talk you're always wondering if it's the end, if it's time to force a laugh, and then she just continues on and on like a toddler giving a foreigner driving directions. When she doesn't get the reaction she's hoping for, she adds another layer to the story and it becomes this convoluted mess. Horrible writing."

I laughed so hard. I remember thinking back then about how much I liked Dani's brain. Now all I can think about is how much I hate it.

"That's so funny, Dani, and so true about Clare. I never really thought about writing that way."

"Storytelling has to be inside of you, and then you have to be able to write it down in a way that makes sense. That's it! It's simple. Those two things make a writer, I think. If you're creative on top of it, and you can imagine well, it's a bonus. You've got all the parts needed for fiction writing. That's how I see it. I could be wrong. I mean, I know some writers who obsessively outline and plot, but I bet they have it in their head already. I usually just take a notepad and scribble down words or scenes that I don't want to forget. I don't think anyone else could decipher my notes. It's nonsensical chicken scratch."

I smiled, then said, "There's this guy I work with and he's always saying he's got the next great American novel in his head. He's really passionate about it. He talks incessantly about going on vacation so he can write the book."

"That's the thing though," she said, "I don't want to squish his dreams or anything but he'll probably never write it. Writers don't sit around thinking about writing. My favorite thing is the guy on a first date who says he's an aspiring writer because he has a clever idea about a casino heist or something. I tell him I'm a writer, and then he insists on telling me the whole fucking casino story over tapas, while I nod, smile, and ply myself with alcohol. Then I suggest he sit down and write it and he either says he will someday, or he says something even more idiotic, like 'You can write it if you want. I'd give you half credit.' We *all* have a story in our head, you know? But you have to *write* it to actually be a writer. You have to want to write it, and you have to like it, the same way a person likes roller skating. Have you ever heard a person say, 'I hate roller skating but I think I could choreograph it really well?' It's not the idea, or inception, it's the execution. Believe me . . . there's no shortage of casino heists up here." She tapped her temple and winked.

I think that was the moment I fell in love with Dani. I also simultaneously prayed she would never go on another first date again. It's too bad we couldn't have held on to that thing we had. I was so impressed by her, so enamored, even though she was never trying to impress me. She was literally just being in the moment. She was authentic and that's what I loved.

"I like you a lot, Dani," I had told her.

She laughed. "I like you too, Alex."

"I don't want to date anyone else."

"I don't either," she had said before leaning over and kissing me softly, slowly . . . right smack in the center of that restaurant. She'd never do that now. Neither would I, I guess.

All good things . . . blah, blah, blah.

The memory sort of pushed me toward her desk to look at the legal pad. I realized I had never really looked at her nonsensical chicken scratch before. Not in the entire twenty-two years we were together.

I glance down at it, not wanting to actually touch it, and I see, for the first time, her thoughts. In order from the top down it says, *Rick; Jarren; bear in liquid; thirties pickle-ball instructor; Valentino; adjustments; bagels, wheatgrass; engineer; rat on porch.* Some of it I can't make out. It is, truly, nonsensical chicken scratch.

It isn't much to read, so I flip the page where there is more of the same, and then halfway down the scribbling stops and what looks like a poem starts. I never knew Dani to write poetry. Intrigued, I read on.

Love Me Still.
Was that your pound of flesh?
I've been here for so long.

The furniture has moved,
covered the stains, all the traces of you,
there's nothing left but here, in my mind, my body, my time,
wasted, thinking about you. Wondering if you love me still.

Is this about me? Is this about Lars, that granola-eating tree-fucker? No, it has to be about me. It has to. I spilled wine on the carpet. The stain has been there for years. This must be about me.

I feel tormented wondering what this poem is about. I'm tempted to call her but I have no idea what I would say. I want to ask her why I didn't know she was a poet too. Instead, I gather myself. I shouldn't be reading her notepad anyway. This could mean nothing and I'm not sure why I even care. It's hard to imagine a world where I don't care even just a modicum, but I decide I better figure that out soon.

The sound of yelling from the other room breaks me out of my trance.

"Shut up and get out!" I hear Noah shout.

I storm into the boys' room. "What's going on?" Both are giving the other dirty looks.

"Ethan is treating me like I'm stupid because I tried making slime in the bathroom. I wanted to see if it would make a decent conductor."

"Excuse me, *what*? I thought you were moving Nana's stuff?" I say to Noah, but he buttons up, sits down on his bed, and crosses his arms over his chest, pouting.

I look to Ethan next. "I told him he was making a mess. He just kept blabbering about electric slime," Ethan says.

"Electric slime?" I turn and look into the doorway of their bathroom, where I see a purple powdery substance all over the floor, along with some purple slime, I'm guessing. "What the hell, Noah? You're playing with water and electricity? Are you insane? Get in there and clean it up."

Noah begins crying. He curls into a ball on his bed. Ethan looks up at me and shrugs. "Well, that went well," he says.

"Noah, get your ass up and go clean that mess. Have you lost your mind? Why aren't you using that big brain of yours?" That was harsh. I instantly regret saying it.

Noah is in hysterics now. He can't even speak. He's beginning to hyperventilate.

"What the hell is going on here?" I ask. Ethan stands and walks out into the hallway. I'm staring at Noah in shock. "I haven't seen you cry since you were like six." Noah says nothing. "Get up and go clean it, now!"

"Okay!" he yells. He gets up and starts walking to the bathroom.

"What is your problem?" Ethan asks him.

"Nothing, leave me alone," Noah says. Ethan is watching from the end of the hall.

I walk toward Ethan, shaking my head. "All of the sudden he cries now?" I say to him.

"Mom talks to him differently."

"What?" I snap.

I walk past Ethan. He follows me into the living room, where I sit on the couch to put my shoes on.

Ethan sits next to me. "He doesn't cry because Mom doesn't really talk to him like that."

"He made a huge mess. And it was dangerous!" I argue. Ethan just shrugs.

"Okay, so what would mom have done, then, Ethan . . . if you know everything?"

"Why are you mad at me, Dad? I'm just telling you. Mom likes that kind of stuff, she's like a science nerd."

"Your mother is far from a science nerd."

"I mean, she would have asked him what exactly he was trying to do. Noah *is* smart. He sometimes does some cool stuff. He's made that slime before and tried to make conductors with other things."

"Then why were you calling him stupid?"

Ethan stares at me for several seconds. "Because I knew you would get mad at him and make him feel dumb for doing it." I could feel the heat behind my face getting more intense. My anger was escalating, but Ethan was right. "He's crying in our room," Ethan says again, glancing down the hall.

"What?" I say.

I gage Ethan's expression. "Noah is in there crying. Can't you hear him?"

The boys' bedroom is at the end of the hall but our house is not gigantic. "You know I can't hear that well. Is he crying loudly?" I genuinely do not know what to do in this moment. I feel inadequate. I've always prided myself on being a good father. If Dani ever even hinted to me that she thought I wasn't holding up my end of the deal, I would get extremely angry. I knew dozens of men who spent zero time alone with their kids. I was always hands-on, from diapers to coaching their sports teams. I didn't understand why I found myself stumped now when they were basically old enough to take care of themselves.

"No, it's not loud, but I can hear him. You should go talk to him," Ethan says.

I hold back the urge to scold Ethan for telling me what to do. Instead, I stand and head down the hall. As I get closer, I can hear Noah sort of whimpering. I knock once and open the door. Noah is sitting on his bed; he's not hysterical, just likely feeling sorry for himself.

"I cleaned it up," he says in a clear voice.

"What exactly were you trying to do?"

He looks up and stares, nonplussed, before finally saying, "Now you're interested?"

"Don't be a smart-ass."

"I thought I was the opposite of a smart-ass?"

"Noah! Watch your mouth!"

He shrugs.

I know I'm shooting myself in the foot. If there was one thing Dani always said about the way I parented, it was that I was constantly shooting myself in the foot. Noah picks up his phone and starts scrolling through it as if I'm not even standing there. It's the first time I realize I don't really know him at all. Kids are not our clones. They grow and change and we have to get to know them all over again at every new juncture.

"Noah, can we talk?"

"Do I have a choice?"

"Look at me." Noah looks up and sets his phone aside. "I'm sorry," I say.

"I was going to clean it up. I didn't plan on leaving it there. Why can't you trust that we're not little kids anymore?"

"I know you're not." I gestured toward the end of the bed. "Can I sit?"

"Sure," he says.

"I'm under a lot of pressure right now, and I took it out on you. I didn't really assess the situation. What were you trying to do anyway?" I laugh a little to lighten the mood and he laughs with me.

"I don't know. There's a lot of water in that slime we make with the Borax. The charged ions, like the salt in the water, make for a good conductor. It was just fun to make glowing, electrical slime."

I jerk my head back, not expecting that answer. At the same

time, I notice the boys no longer have Star Wars bedspreads, and there is a picture of Noah with a girl from school on his bookshelf. It's from one of those picture booths. It's not romantic, just kind of goofy, but I've never seen it before.

"Wow, Noah, you actually knew what you were doing with the slime?"

"Yeah, what did you think, I was just gonna go squirting water into a light socket? Fork in the toaster?" He raises his eyebrows humorously. "Blow-dryer in the bathtub?"

I laugh loudly. "You are so much like your mom."

"Do you think that's a good thing?"

I'm immediately jolted out of the moment. How do I answer this? "Of course it's a good thing. Your mom is great. She's funny, clever. She's a wonderful mother. You have her snarky sense of humor." I wasn't lying.

"She's just not a good wife?"

"What? No. We've been over this. Your mom and I just don't get along anymore. That's it. Look, I'm sorry, Noah. Pretty lame of me to treat you like a little kid about the slime thing. You did cry, though, because I yelled at you." I elbow him lovingly.

"I didn't cry because you yelled at me."

"Why were you crying, then?"

"Because I thought you would think the slime was cool. Instead, the whole thing just made me feel dumb."

I'm struck with guilt; this is how Dani has made me feel countless times.

For a moment, the silence is heavy in the room. He doesn't realize the impact his statement will have on me from here on out. How do kids break our hearts, put them back together, and then teach us how to be good human beings again just by virtue of their own virtue?

"I do think the slime thing is cool. I didn't understand it. It's my fault. I should have listened. I'll be a better listener. I want to know everything, Noah. Everything going on in your life. Everything about school and you and . . ." I walk to the bookshelf and pick up the photo, "Is this Zoe Bennett, all grown up?"

"She's not my girlfriend, we're just friends," he says quickly and defensively.

"No, I know. I like Zoe. She's a sweetheart. Her parents are good people too. Let me finish up some things around here and then we'll go get a late dinner and keep talking, okay?"

"Sounds good," he says, smiling.

I walk over and hug him. "I love you, Noah."

"Love you too, Dad."

First fire as a solo parent . . . extinguished!

10

you could hear me whisper then

DANIELLE

It's almost completely dark out as I pull up to the complex. I glance at the clock: six-fifteen. I told Alicia I'd meet her at the salon at seven-thirty. She got me an appointment last minute with her hairdresser. She said I needed a "drastic physical change" so I'm going blond. Well, blond-ish. My hair has been dark brown, almost black, since I was born. I've entertained the idea of going lighter as I've gotten older, something softer, but Alex always said he liked my striking dark hair.

Divorce is always a good time to bleach your hair, I figure.

I'm cursing myself inside for fighting for so long with Alex on the porch. I'll hardly have any time to settle in with this last load of things I've brought to the apartment. I park in the front fire lane, turn on my hazards, and jump out. As I'm unloading my suitcases and a couple of boxes to the front of the building, a woman walks out. She looks to be in her sixties, wearing pink scrubs.

"Hi, girlie."

I laugh out loud. "Hardly," I say. I know I'm going to like this woman already.

"I'm Candy, let me help. I have a few minutes. The manager told me you were moving in today—2A, right? Danielle and Alex?"

"You can call me 'Dani.'"

"Dani and Candy, how cute," she says, and I laugh.

I hope she's not nosy. Candy seems like one of those humming-bird type of people, so she probably is. Always in motion, talking, chewing gum, fidgeting constantly, to the point where you think if she stops moving, she'll die. She's thin. I notice her pink scrubs have little tiny bananas on them and her badge says, CANDY LEE, RN above the emblem for Verdugo Hills Hospital.

I point to her badge. "Ah, my husband does one day a week there." It immediately hits me that I called him "my husband" and she is never going to see us together. Do I explain this weird situation to her? Do I call him my ex, or soon-to-be ex?

"Oh yeah? What department?" she asks.

"He's a physical therapist."

She winks. "I'm in the ER. I probably never see him."

Of course she is, the ER requires her kind of energy.

We put the last of the boxes at the bottom of the stairs going up to my new apartment. "Well, it was nice to meet you. I know you have to run . . ."

"Same to you. I'll give you my number in case you guys need anything. They keep this place real nice, and it's safe too. By the way, where is the fella?"

I guess I'm not getting out of this one so easily. "He's . . . um." I don't have it in me right now. "He'll be here later." *Dammit, why didn't I tell her?*

"Well, good luck with unpacking." And she's off, humming along.

Once in the apartment I flip on all the lights. LEDs every-where. It's stark. I hate the lighting, I hate the gray furniture, and I hate the gray wood floors. This place definitely needs some life—plants, art, music, macramé. No one will drop dead from a little splash of color and a few tchotchkes.

I take a deep breath and plop onto the sofa, which looks and feels like a solid granite slab. There isn't much I can do at this moment. It's too late to go out looking for furnishings, so I get up and begin unpacking. The record player fits perfectly on the built-in shelves in the corner. I manage to rig the speaker with my MacGyver skills, which I know Alex will criticize if he no-tices I didn't use the proper hooks or a stud finder to hang the speaker. There are no babies here, we can operate like college kids, so unless it falls on his head, it should be fine.

I start putting the records on the bottom shelf, when one of the sleeves pops out. It's a Mazzy Star record. Not exactly a clas-sic passed down from generation to generation, but I guess it will be now. I laugh to myself at the memory of buying that rec-ord. Alicia had made fun of me, saying it wasn't the type of band you got on vinyl. She had bought the CD, but look now, I doubt she'd be able to find her old CD collection, and here I have this little time machine to take me back to the late nineties. Music and smells are the senses that evoke memories for me more than anything else.

I started to continue my father's tradition around the time I bought this album. The white sleeves on the inside of some of my father's records would be covered with his notes. Some were just lists of things happening around that time, and some were in the form of short narratives. I had done the same for many years after he passed them down to me.

I put the Mazzy Star album on and set it to the song "Fade Into You." As I read the note on the sleeve, I'm instantly back, twenty-two-plus years ago, to the first night Alex and I were together. I was so light then, in every way emotionally. Nothing was serious to me yet. Ben was still alive, my parents were together, and I was breaking in as a writer. I was living a dream.

On top of all the good things happening, I was also dating Alex. We had met at a mutual friend's house party, exchanged phone numbers, talked on the phone, and gone on a couple of group dates, both of which concluded over a pile of cocaine on a picture frame and drinking until we passed out. Those two nights, Alex and I ended up chatting on the friend's porch into the early hours of the morning. We didn't even kiss, but looking back, I credit those two nights to the solid foundation we formed as friends. We hadn't gone on a proper date at that point, but somehow the cocaine-fueled evenings had led to some intense conversation. We knew a lot about each other from those talks. We knew for sure that we liked each other and agreed on practically everything in the world news.

In messy blue ink, the Mazzy Star album sleeve reads:

Alex was here last night. Alex was everywhere.

I remember writing it. It was after our first real date. We had gone to dinner and my roommate was out of town, so Alex had come back to my apartment. We didn't sleep . . . and there was no cocaine. I guess when I wrote the phrase on the sleeve, I wasn't thinking about handing the record down to my children. It wouldn't matter if they saw it anyway, even at their age now; they've been exposed enough to the inner workings of my mind from watching the shows I've written. They wouldn't be surprised I wrote something like this on a record sleeve twenty-something years ago.

That night, so many years ago at my apartment, I saw Alex's

vulnerability for the first time . . . he was a little insecure, unsure of himself. Prior to that night, he'd been nothing but confident. He had that kind of confidence that's never mistaken for arrogance. It was the thing that attracted me to him from the start. He was funny and kind with me, and with our mutual friends. He moved in a way that made him seem coordinated and smooth, but not slimy. He had spatial awareness and self-awareness, and he was intelligent but not immodest. Physically, he was by far the most universally attractive person I had ever dated. He still is, after all these years, a man who turns heads but doesn't really know it.

But that first night we were alone at my apartment was different. He was softer, more timid. I had put the Mazzy Star album on, poured two glasses of wine, and sat next to him on the couch.

"So your roommate is in Europe?" he asked. Something unspoken was lingering between us. We were either going to have sex or we were going to be friends. I don't think he knew with any kind of certainty which it would be, but I definitely had a clue.

"Yeah, she's in Spain for a month visiting an aunt." He watched me closely, which made me uncomfortable. I was fidgeting. He put his hand over mine and smiled.

"I can't believe we haven't kissed yet," he said, before laughing. Instantly the mood lightened. He had pointed out the elephant in the room and things felt easier. He was staring at my mouth.

"I guess that is weird," I said. "Not attracted to me, or what?" I teased, knowing that wasn't the case.

"You're beautiful and I'm very attracted to you. The most attracted to someone I've ever been, I think. I just don't want to blow it." He was sincere, but cautious.

"Do you date a lot?"

"Not really. I had a girlfriend for four years."

I don't know why that surprised me. "You did?" I said, and then laughed.

He smiled. "Why do you think that's so funny?"

"Just because we're so young," I said.

"I'm twenty-five. A little older than you. I guess that's still young-ish." He shrugged. "Maybe I'm kind of a relationship person?"

"Why'd you break up?"

"I'm afraid if I tell you, you'll think I'm shallow"

I remember in that moment thinking, *Oh no, this guy's gonna tell me his girlfriend gained ten pounds and I'm gonna have to punch him in the face and tell him to get out.* "Try me," I said. It was important for me to know if he was, in fact, shallow.

"She called me 'bro.' I have no idea why. I mean . . . I spent four years with her calling me that, and for a long time it didn't bother me. She did it from the very beginning. Anyway, we weren't really a great match. It wasn't totally about that. We were nothing alike. Toward the end she became obsessed with Beanie Babies. You know those little stuffed animals?"

"Yeah. I have a few my mom gave me. Is there something wrong with them?"

"When I say obsessed, I mean she had *hundreds*. She spent all her money on them and then she started dragging me to Beanie Baby conventions." He laughed and looked away. "I just couldn't get into it. She's a nice person. She's already moved on to a fellow Beanie Baby collector." His delicacy about the subject was charming, as if he felt guilty for not liking her.

"I don't think it was shallow of you. Did you break her heart though?"

"Not at all. It was unemotional, like she expected it or wanted it. I went to her house and told her I thought we should take a break. She told me she had been wanting to call it off for a long time. That was that. I called her on her birthday four months ago and she said she was getting married."

"To the Beanie Baby guy?"

"Of course."

"It was meant to be this way," I told him.

He leaned in and kissed me then. It was not a long, passionate, crazy kiss. It was like a testing-the-waters kind of kiss, but I could tell just from those three seconds connected to him that he was going to be good in bed. When he pulled away he was searching my eyes . . . hesitant. "What about you? Do you date a lot?" he asked.

"I've never really had much of a substantial relationship, other than this guy Jacob, who I dated my first year in college. But no, I don't date a lot. I've made it very clear to my friends to stop trying to set me up. I went on like eight stupid setup dates last year."

"I wonder why they didn't set us up?" he said.

Alicia had told me that Brandon, a guy she was dating, had a friend, Alex, but that he was into blondes. In the beginning I thought a lot about the "blondes" thing. At the time it was strange for Brandon to try to thwart Alex and me getting together, but years later, Brandon revealed to us that he was gay, and had always had a thing for Alex, so it all eventually made sense. I loved the way Alex handled the situation when Brandon came out and told him. Alex was flattered, gracious, and forgiving of the whole thing. He didn't make Brandon feel bad, even though I know when we were first dating he was pretty pissed at him.

"Brandon told Alicia that you were into blondes."

"He did what?" Alex seemed genuinely confused, and a little pissed.

"Yeah, that you wouldn't be into me."

"I never said I was into blondes or that I wouldn't be into you. The opposite actually. Yeah, my last girlfriend was blond, but we know how that ended." It was quiet for several moments. "Honestly, when I first saw you, your dark hair . . . I mean, you're so striking, Dani, I could barely take my eyes off you. You have this thing, it's like a transcendent beauty."

It felt like all of the air in the room had suddenly dropped to the floor. Time had stopped. We were in our own atmosphere. He leaned in to kiss me again, but then hesitated. "Brandon knew I thought that. I don't know why he told Alicia—"

I put my hand to his lips to quiet him. "Never mind."

Every detail of that night is still a sharp memory. Later, when things really got going in the bedroom, he asked me if I liked what he was doing. I could barely speak when I told him yes. He wanted to please me then. He cared.

Nothing lasts forever, I guess.

⁓

My phone is buzzing in my pocket. It's Alicia.

"Hello?"

"I'm on my way to the salon. Are you there yet?"

"No, I'll leave in a minute." I had lost time. Floating around in a dream of what used to be.

"Is that Mazzy Star I hear playing in the background?"

I laugh. "Yes."

"Why?" she said.

"I love this album," I whine.

"You're such a dork. Meet me there in ten."

"Bye."

As I'm walking out, I glance at my laptop screen on the desk. There is a Facebook notification. I look closer. It's just a reminder of an old high school friend's birthday. After wishing her a happy birthday, I decide to type *Jacob Powell* into the search bar for some reason I can't explain. His profile immediately pops up. Even though I know I'm running late, I can't help myself. He looks exactly the same. Jacob was my longest relationship before Alex and it was only a year, my freshman year in college. He had actually, legitimately broken my young, tender heart. Jacob was just one of those people who couldn't be pinned down, but he was so much fun and unbelievably sexy. When we were together, he made me feel amazing, but he was too wild. I wanted him in my life forever, but relationship commitment was just not in his DNA. And we were so young.

His profile says he's single, of course. Then something catches my eye: We have two mutual "friends," Alicia and Mark. Alicia had definitely met Jacob a few times while he and I were dating many years ago, but Mark never did. *Why are they Facebook friends?*

I change my status from married to single and then immediately go back and try to return my status to married, but it won't let me. The computer is frozen, displaying an endless spinning pinwheel. "Ugh." I don't know why I did it to begin with. Frustrated, I shut it down and grab my purse to leave for the salon. I make a mental note to ask Alicia why she and Mark are friends with Jacob on Facebook. Then I wonder if this moment officially marks the beginning of my divorcée status.

11

you don't have to say it

ALEXANDER

Through this whole separation process, every couple of days I get a wave of emotion that I don't know what to do with. It's fear. It's like my stomach drops to the ground, I start shaking, my brain turns to mush, and the only thing I can think to do is go for a run. But I'm on kid duty now so I can't go charging for the hills. Dani would hate that I'm thinking of this single parenting thing as a chore. I'm really not, I'm just not used to it. What is this new life I'm supposed to live? The unknown is giving me unrelenting anxiety.

Some single friends I know act like being single is a personality trait. Maybe I even used to think that. There are relationship people and then there are the people who can't be tied down. Now where do I fall?

Am I really still folding clothes?

Noah walks past the doorway. "Are we going to dinner?"

"Yeah, give me ten minutes," I tell him.

"I'm starving."

I turn around and glare at him. "Go jump on the trampoline."

"We haven't jumped on that thing in forever," he says.

"Why?"

From the other room Ethan answers, "Mom said not to! She said the gardeners messed it up or something."

Why didn't she tell me? I walk to the window of Dani's bedroom . . . our bedroom . . . and look out into the backyard. "It's fine!" I say, irritated. "I can't believe I'm still doing laundry!" I yell. "Give me ten minutes. Go jump and let me finish this up."

Noah shrugs. "Okay. Yeah, Mom always complains about the laundry too."

"You guys should be doing your own laundry," I snap back.

"She says that too."

"Then why don't you?" I say as I sift through a pile of mismatched socks.

He shrugs again. Ethan enters the room. "We'll start doing it, okay?" He pulls on Noah, "Let's go jump."

Because Dani was often home with the boys, she always did the laundry. Even before we had kids, it was her thing. She never asked me to do it and she'd fly off the handle when I'd start a load and not finish it, or forget clothes in the dryer. She'd say, "Either do it right, or just leave it and I'll do it." She always folded the clothes when they were still warm, and I thought she was an anal-retentive maniac because of it. Now, as I'm hanging wrinkled clothes on hangers and unable to find a single matching pair of socks, I get it.

I can hear the boys arguing again about something. For a moment it occurs to me that they sound like Oscar and Felix from *The Odd Couple,* and then I realize, no, they sound like me and Dani.

"Shut up, Noah," I hear Ethan say. A moment later there's a very loud, piercing scream but I can't tell who it's coming from.

Running as fast as I can, I make it downstairs, then go sliding through a puddle of water on the kitchen floor before falling on my ass. It's Noah; I can now hear him screaming, "Ow, ow, ow!"

I pick myself up and dart into the backyard, where Noah is lying on the ground and Ethan is kneeling next to him.

Ethan looks up. "I think he broke his arm," he says. I notice the trampoline, including the safety net, is on its side. "See, Dad, Mom was right. The leg is unhinged on the trampoline or something."

"Oh my god," I say under my breath. Noah is crying on the ground. "What is it, Noah? What hurts?"

"My arm," he cries.

I'm frozen. *What do I do?* I'm examining his arm and trying not to move it. Ethan is staring at me, waiting for me to save the day. His eyebrows are arched like he's just asked me a question and is waiting for the answer.

"What, Ethan? Jesus!"

"Want me to call Mom?"

"No!" I bark. "Sit up, Noah."

Noah sits up while I hold his arm in place. I move it just a little and he screams, "Ow!"

"Calm down." Just by looking at it I know that it's broken, somewhere around his elbow, but I won't tell him that. I'm a physical therapist, for god's sake, and I'm kneeling on the ground looking like a deer in headlights.

"It hurts," he whines.

"I know, Noah, I'm sorry. Ethan, go get the ACE bandage. I'll wrap it up and we'll take him to the ER. So, what actually happened?"

Noah stops crying abruptly and looks up at me, "Obviously, the trampoline is broken!" He looks exactly like Dani in this moment. His expression derisive and demeaning. The implication is that I'm a *fucking moron,* clearly.

"I'm sorry." I do feel horrible. Ethan returns with the bandage. I wrap up Noah's arm to stabilize it to his chest. We stand and I guide Noah inside onto the couch. "Where's the insurance cards and stuff?" They both look at me like I'm speaking a foreign language. "I need to call your doctor. I need to figure out where to take you. Where did Mom take you, Ethan, when you got the stitches on your ear?"

"Verdugo. Remember, you were there?"

When you don't *have to* remember things, you don't try to. Dani is going to blow a gasket. "Ethan, call your mom and ask her where the insurance cards are."

"She's gonna freak out!"

"I know, just call her," I say.

"There goes baseball," Noah says to himself. He's calmed down a lot. It looks like he's not in as much pain, so much as he's just disappointed in me.

I can hear Ethan talking in the kitchen, but there's a wall blocking him, so it's difficult to understand what he's saying. Lip-reading has become a talent of mine since I lost my hearing in one ear. If Dani knew how much I relied on lip-reading . . . Who am I kidding? Dani knows. When we were still together, she told me once that intimacy between us was hard because she felt like she couldn't speak softly, be soft, when she was talking to me. I wonder for a second if that's true or if she just liked pouring salt in my wounds. The deafness isn't my fault anyway, and it's just cruel of her to criticize it.

"Dad!"

"What?" I say to Ethan, who has come into the room.

"Mom wants to talk to you." He holds the phone out.

I hesitate. "Hello?"

"How bad is it? Ethan said Noah's stopped crying," she says. "I'm at the hair salon currently, sitting with bleach in my hair. Do I really need to come home?"

"No . . ." I'm at a loss for words. I want to ask her why she has bleach in her beautiful dark hair.

"Hello? So he's okay?" she says. Several seconds pass. My mind is spinning. "Oh my god, hello, Alex? Just let me talk to Noah."

"I'm here. I'm sorry. I need to know where the insurance cards are."

"They're in the drawer under the toaster. I'm so pissed at those boys. I told them not to jump on the trampoline until we got it fixed," she says.

"Why didn't you tell me?"

"I did. Remember when I was writing the gardener a check and I made the joke about deducting the trampoline cost from it?"

It hit me. The whole conversation came back to me. *Shit.*

"I told them to go jump on it. I forgot it was broken," I say. I know my voice is weak . . . and penitent.

Silence.

"It's not your fault," she says, but it is precisely my fault. "Can I just talk to Noah?"

I look at Noah on the couch, staring at me. He's completely calm but his elbow is swollen. I know I need to take him to the ER.

"Alex!" she yells. "Let. Me. Talk. To. Noah!"

I hand Noah the phone.

"I'm fine, but it still hurts," he says to Dani. "Okay. Okay. Love you too. I'll call you from the ER. Okay. Bye."

He pushes End on the phone and looks up at me. "She said to tell you if the wait is too long at the ER, then to just wrap it well and she'll take me in the morning. She also said to remind you that the ER gets crowded late at night and to park in the south parking lot, because the front entrance will be closed."

Even though I work at that hospital, teaching a class one day a week, I would never remember those details about the ER. Again, when you don't have to remember the minutiae, you don't try to.

I'm confident everything will be fine. Looking at Noah now, I'm guessing it's probably just a very small fracture, maybe even a sprain. The level of anxiety I felt has diminished, but the one thing still nagging at me is why Dani is bleaching her gorgeous hair, and why she decided after so long to finally show me some grace by telling me it wasn't my fault, when it unequivocally was.

12

you wouldn't listen anyway

DANIELLE

Time exists to provide a framework for our lives. We invented it. It's subjective. You can't measure half of something if you don't know how much the whole is, and everyone's number is different. This day has felt like ten days for me. It's nine-fifteen and I'm exhausted. I feel like I haven't slept in two weeks, but at least I'm here now, at the salon, getting some much-needed pampering and friend time in.

I hit End on my phone and look at Alicia, who is staring at me with concern from the chair next to me. Her hairstylist, Laura, a generous friend who has opened the salon late on a Sunday for me, had lathered my hair in bleach and was currently in the back room pouring champagne into flutes.

Earlier, Alicia had come dancing through the door of the salon with champagne, singing, "Happy divorce to you. Happy divorce to you. No more tears and no more fights. No more sad and sleepless nights. Happy divorce to you!"

It wasn't exactly the joy I was feeling, but I appreciated her effort. Now she's staring, waiting for me to tell her what the phone call was all about.

"Noah fell off the trampoline and maybe fractured his elbow. Everything's fine. Alex might take him to the ER tonight, but Noah's gonna be all right," I say.

"Well, why'd they call, just to ruin your first night of freedom?"

"I wouldn't exactly call it freedom. Alex needed to know where the insurance cards were."

Alicia lives in a pantsuit and expensive shoes. Her blond hair is always pulled back into a tight, low ponytail. No bangs. She looks like a badass, but she is currently spinning around in the salon chair like a seven-year-old. I've known her since we were seven and really not much has changed between us. We're best friends, but more like sisters, actually.

Laura hands us each a flute of champagne. Alicia holds hers up, "Cheers to single and ready to mingle."

We clink glasses, I take a massive gulp and say, "I appreciate you trying to lift my spirits, but I think this celebration is a little premature." And then I say what I've been saying to her for years: "It can't always be coke and threesomes, Lish."

"You're such a buzz kill," she says. We both know it's a joke. Alicia hates platitudes or trite sayings, she's actually a pretty buttoned-up and realistic person. Her wedding involved me, Alex, her and Mark, a justice of the peace, and the courthouse. She's not about fanfare or party-girl culture. And anyway, we're in our forties.

Laura stands over me and examines my hair. "It's lifting. You're gonna be a blonde soon."

"Really?" I say, getting excited.

"Not really a blonde. Someday, if you want," Laura says. "It'll probably take a year to get you there without frying your hair.

You will be lighter after this though. We're going for a yummy honey."

"I have no idea what that means, but it sounds delicious," I tell her. "Oh, Alicia, I almost forgot to ask you . . . why are you and Mark friends with Jacob Powell on Facebook?"

"Jacob? Oh yeah, we work with Jacob. I always forget you dated him."

"What? Wait a minute, he's a lawyer? And how could you forget I dated him? He broke my heart."

"I was going to tell you awhile back. He's a financial analyst we use for certain cases. It was completely coincidental that we hired him. I didn't even realize it was him until we met face-to-face. We've been using him for a couple of years."

I'm in shock. I can't believe she didn't tell me. "What? A couple of years? Well, did you guys discuss the fact that he dated your best friend?"

"Yeah, Dani, in the beginning, but I forgot to tell you. It was right around the time your mom got really sick. It didn't exactly seem like a priority."

In rapid-fire speak, I ask, "What's he like? What did he say about me? Did you tell him I'm getting divorced?"

She rolls her eyes. "Calm down, jeez. He's exactly the same. He looks the same too."

It's terrible but I instantly recall an image of us having sex. My face flushes.

Alicia continues. "He's always off somewhere, here or there, surfing in Costa Rica, building houses in Haiti. The type of work he does gives him the freedom to be anywhere. He does well for himself. Never got married though. No kids."

"I'm not surprised. But what did he say about me? About our relationship? Did he ask how I was?"

"About your one-year, semi-relationship nearly three decades ago? Hmm . . . let me think how that conversation went, though I'm surprised you even care," she says.

It's not subhuman to wonder if people think about you. There are moments and experiences I had with Jacob that stuck with me. I often thought about Jacob when Alex would be in serious mode, when he'd be all business, no pleasure. I associated Jacob with fun intensity. It wasn't often, but when I would think about him, I would instantly get a rush of adrenaline. Alex, on the other hand, was security and logic to me. He was there physically, but so often non-participatory on an emotional or psychological level, and it had nothing to do with his intellect. I could be laughing to the point of tears while telling Alex a joke and he would just stare at me. On the other hand, I could be crying hysterically, and he'd just look at me like he didn't understand why I was upset. I still resent that about Alex. He never seemed to understand how to *be* toward me, and he never tried to.

When you're married, even after so many years, you still want to be your spouse's number one in everything, but is that even a reality? To be the good, fun, nonjudgmental friend, while also being the lover, parenting and financial partner, and the person you want to cut loose with? Can we desire our spouse enough to reach that level of excitement, lust, passion after years of ups and downs? How can you want something you already have? Alex and I were both at that place when we decided to split. We no longer wanted one another . . . on any level.

In the beginning of our marriage, I constantly compared Alex to Jacob. While Alex enjoyed being active, getting out and exploring, he insisted on details being meticulously planned out. It was a point of contention for a while, but after a few years I learned to accept it. Every vacation we took was over-researched to the point where there was no surprise in it, no novelty . . . just an anticlimactic trip that, as a writer, I had already fully imagined in my mind. Jacob represented the opposite to me. Spontaneity, freedom, the thrill of the unknown.

"The memory is a little hazy at this point," Alicia says. "He mentioned you a couple of years ago, right when we started working with him. He asked how you were and I told him your mother had moved in and was sick. He said to send thoughts and good wishes from him, and I'm sorry, but I forgot."

"That's it?"

"Yeah, I mean, he knows you're married. I'm sure he knows you're a writer. He can look you up."

Laura checks my hair again. "Let's go rinse you," she says.

We make our way to the shampoo bowl; Alicia follows. I'm still hung up on the Jacob news.

"Does he have a girlfriend?"

"I don't know. I don't ask him stuff like that," she says. She's humorously frustrated.

"So he's still hot?"

Resigned, she huffs and then smiles wide. "Yes, he's still hot. Don't go getting any ideas though."

"Single and ready to mingle," I say, joking.

"Coke and threesomes," she pings back. I love her.

After Laura blows my hair out, she spins me around for the reveal. It's shocking at first. It's nowhere near blond, but I realize now that if I had gone for blond I would have had a coronary at the sight of it. I'm practically having one now.

"It looks great!" Laura says. "Do you like it?"

I smile. "I'm . . . Yeah, I like it."

Alicia is standing behind me, next to Laura, looking at me in the mirror. "Bombshell. You look like J.Lo."

I don't look anything like J.Lo. My hair color is more Jennifer

Aniston anyway, but it's totally shocking against my face, at least for me.

"You'll get used to it," Laura says. "It's an adjustment, but the warmth looks great with your skin tone."

Laura has blown out my hair in soft waves. I do look younger. I know that was the goal even if I could barely admit it to myself.

"I do like it. And I need this change," I say finally. "I'll get used to it."

"Next time we can get you even lighter," Laura says.

"We'll see . . ."

I'm so exhausted I can barely think and Alicia is looking at me, as perky as ever. "Wanna go find a bar?"

"On a Sunday night? No. I need to get back to the apartment and finish unpacking."

We leave each other on a good note. As I walk to my car, I call Noah. A while ago, Alex and I decided to get the boys phones, and now I'm so grateful that we did. I can't imagine the days when divorcing couples had to ask each other to talk to their teenage children.

"Hi, Mom."

"How's your arm?" I say.

"It's just a hairline fracture in the upper part of my ulna. They gave me a brace. I can't do baseball this season."

"I'm sorry, Noah. That is a bummer. What's an ulna?" I ask.

"Really, Mom? Did you ditch math *and* science all the way through high school?"

"Funny. Now tell me what it is?"

I knew what an ulna was, I just liked to hear the boys explain things they had learned.

"It's one of your two forearm bones, Mom. You have one."

"I know, I was just testing you. You need to get to bed. I love you. I'll call you guys tomorrow."

I say good night over speakerphone to Ethan and Noah and get ready to leave the salon parking lot. It's late. Before I start my car, it hits me that I will frequently be saying good night to my children over the phone. How strange. I've been there since they were born. Even when I was working, I'd write from home and go into the office once or twice a week for a few hours. I've always been there to kiss them good night.

Back in the apartment, I put some things away and collapse onto the bed. It has that stiff, new feeling, and it smells like chemicals. It occurs to me that Alex bought the sheets the same day he bought the bed and just put them on without washing them first. They're white. He's always hated that I bought white sheets. He says it makes him feel like he's in a hotel room. I like to be able to bleach them when I need to, so for twenty-plus years we've had plain white sheets. The first time he actually gets to buy sheets on his own and he buys plain white. I wonder what's changed for him. Did he get them to please me? Or are we both just conditioned to operate on autopilot at this point?

I'm falling asleep with my clothes on. While still lying down I peel everything off and throw it on the floor. How liberating. I crawl under the stiff covers and take a deep breath. As I reach over to set my alarm, I realize that I have nowhere to go tomorrow morning. I skip the alarm and stretch out, basking in the feeling of being naked. It's been eons. Without thinking, I open Facebook on my phone and look up Jacob Powell. His profile is public, and it basically looks like a travel log. He is still very good-looking and in amazing shape. Surfing all over the world will do that for you, I guess.

I send him a friend request and continue scrolling through his pictures. In this moment I am free. I feel alone, but not lonely . . . yet.

A second later my Facebook pings with a notification that Jacob accepted my friend request. A second after that I see a direct message from him. I close the app, set my phone on the nightstand, and shut off the light.

I won't read the message from Jacob . . . not tonight anyway.

13

flipping the script

ALEXANDER

Somehow, I managed to make it to Wednesday. I spent the last three days juggling pickups for the boys, afterschool activities, homework, meals, laundry, everything. It's a small miracle I was able to get into the clinic and work at all. My mom came through for me in a big way, even though she still works full-time as a kindergarten teacher, she was able to swing over, pick the boys up from school, do homework with them, and then start dinner. If Dani knew I had enlisted my mom, I'd never hear the end of it.

Dani loves my mom, and she knows I wasn't coddled by my parents. Still, she'd have to make a comment about how I can't do it on my own. Anyway, I feel like Dani has the boys over-booked. She's constantly telling me they need more, but they rarely spend any time being bored.

It's Wednesday now, time to swap houses, I guess. I got out of the clinic early and was able to bring the boys to baseball practice; poor Noah sitting on the bench in a sling. I feel terrible. I also feel tired and generally irritated today.

Is this going to be my life? Picking up, dropping off, cooking, folding clothes nonstop, while juggling clinic calls? It's insanity.

Movement in my periphery catches my eye. Dani is walking down the ramp toward the baseball field bleachers, except that it doesn't look like her at all. Her dark hair is gone. The only Dani I've known is gone. I can only recognize her from the way she walks. It's a fast saunter, her hips swaying rhythmically, and she has a heel-to-toe motion that's more dramatic than most people's, like her feet are rolling a stamp over the outside of someone's hand. Even in her most casual attire, she always has a splash of her eccentricity on display. Today she's in jeans and a T-shirt, a rather soccer-mom-ish outfit for her, except that she has a bright orange belt on. It's impossible for her to look plain. She's carrying a travel coffee mug and a pile of sheets. They're our bedsheets.

Oh god.

I get up and meet her at the bottom of the bleachers.

"Hey," I say.

"Hey."

"Are those the bedsheets from the apartment?" It wasn't meant to be a snide comment.

"Yeah, Alex, they are. I went to a laundromat and washed them for you this morning because they were stiff. I haven't been to a laundromat in a hundred years; I forgot how it all worked, so that was interesting. It took way longer than I imagined, so I figured I would bring them here since you're going to the apartment straightaway and I would've had to drive thirty minutes—"

"Fine, whatever," I tell her. I get the logistics. She doesn't have to write a goddamn novel about it. "You know they have a laundry room in the apartment complex?"

"All the machines were taken. Are you mad that I did you a favor?" she asks with a deeply furrowed brow.

"No, just had an irritating day. Sorry."

As I take the sheets from her left arm, she simultaneously drops the mug of coffee in her right hand. It doesn't have a lid. The mug hits the ground and coffee splashes up all over the sheets.

"Oh no, dammit!" she says. "I'm sorry. Oh shoot, now you're going to have to wash them again."

She bends to pick up the mug and drops it again. She's frazzled and for a moment I actually feel sorry for her, watching her fumbling around. "You okay there, butterfingers?"

"I don't know what's wrong with me today, just completely out of sorts," she says.

"Don't worry about it. I am too. I'm gonna take these to my car," I say, holding up the sheets. "Your hair looks nice, Danielle," I say, even though I'm still shocked. I would never tell her this, but she looks better with dark hair.

"Thanks. I don't know if I'll keep it. It's kinda weird . . . like not me."

"How was your alone time?" I ask.

"Fine."

She isn't going to tell me what she's been doing over the last three days. I need to get used to that.

"And the apartment?"

"It's great. It's all good."

We're just looking at each other in awkward silence. I shrug and say, "Well—"

"I didn't do much. Just shopped, got things for the apartment to make it feel more like home. I slept a lot. I got some writing in and started organizing the records and going through them. I left them near the cabinet on the floor. Will you just leave them alone? I'm putting them in order."

"Sure." I know there is more to it, something she's not telling me.

"I met the neighbor just across from us." There it is, that word, *us*. Danielle pauses, then goes on. "Her name is Candy. I think she might be preparing to become our Mrs. Kravitz."

"Great." It's the last thing we need. "Did you explain our situation?"

"No, I caught her running out the other day. I didn't have time. You can tell her if you want."

"I'm not telling her anything."

I catch a minuscule huff from Dani. I am an avoider; it irks her.

"I'm gonna go say hi to the boys," she says.

As she walks away I head to my car to deposit the coffee-splattered sheets. On my way back she's walking toward me with her phone in hand. "Alex, I need to call Connie. She has news for me. Can you stay a bit longer?"

"Yeah, sure," I say, even though I know I don't need to stay if she's just going to be on the phone.

"By the way, did you remember to give your mom that soup pot she left last time? It's so big, it takes up half the cabinet."

"When would I have given it to her?"

"When she was at our house the last three days," she says, not irritated, more matter-of-fact.

"How did you know?"

She takes a deep breath. "Alex, I talk to our children every day. I'm glad you didn't ask them to lie for you. I don't care at all that your mom was helping you out. To be honest, it was a comfort knowing she was there. Until you get your feet wet, I do worry about you juggling it all."

"I've juggled it all before," I snap back.

Calmly she says, "You're a good dad. I'm just saying it's a lot to handle, and no, you are not used to doing it one hundred percent on your own, if that's what you're implying. I could tell from twenty feet away that you're exhausted. Your hair is going in every direction; you clearly haven't shaved in three days, the boys look like ragamuffins, and . . ." She doesn't take her eyes off mine when she says, "You have an enormous green stain on the bottom of your shirt. What is that? Pesto sauce?"

I start laughing uncontrollably then. She smiles as I laugh like a lunatic. "You're right, Dani," I say between hysterical bursts of laughter. "You're right!"

"You'll get used to it," she shoots back. "I need to call Connie. I guess you can go. You don't need to stay."

It occurs to me that I'm going to have the apartment to myself for four days . . . no kids. I glance at the boys and then back to Dani, who looks impatient. Her eyebrows are arched, waiting for me to reply. I've always wanted to be at their practices, not just their games, but Dani always had that covered. "No, I want to stay. Go ahead and call Connie."

Dani walks away and stands in the shade of a massive jacaranda tree. If she didn't have a phone to her ear, it would look like a painting. The huge violet bunches of flowers almost appeared to be floating around her.

Making my way back up the bleachers, I position myself so I can still see her out of the corner of my eye. Across from her, through the chain-link fence I spot Noah glaring at me. He looks down at his arm and back up. I mouth, "I'm sorry." He shrugs and then focuses on the field, where Ethan is practicing with the team.

From my periphery I notice an abrupt movement. I look over to see Dani jumping up and down with excitement. She puts her hand to her face, over her eyes. From twenty yards away that's how I know she's crying. I'm watching her as she continues talking excitedly. She glances up and catches me staring. I look away quickly and pretend I'm not interested.

I'm watching the baseball practice, but my mind is somewhere else. I notice Dani is walking up on my right side. I look over. She's scrolling through something on her phone. Her cheeks are red and she's wearing an expression that is not quite a smile, but not a frown either. It's the flattened lips that convey satisfaction. When she looks up at me finally, I say nonchalantly, "Good news?"

"We'll see. You know how dizzying the ups and downs of this business are."

Tell me, Dani. Tell me everything.

I'm scolding myself inside for caring. This is exactly the kind of thing that wore me out and pushed me away. Her job *was* dizzying, for everyone. The constant highs and lows; all the good offers that fell through, the colleague drama, and worst of all, the inadequacy she always felt as a writer, which she took out on me. Asking me day after day for years to read early drafts she had written . . . drafts of just about anything, from the three books she had started but never finished, to silly short stories, spec scripts, even personal letters. Sometimes it was just convoluted pages that merely constituted her stream of consciousness the night before, after having too many glasses of wine.

If I said anything to Dani that remotely resembled criticism, she would fly off the handle, even if it was meant to be constructive, so I learned to say nothing at all.

Still, like it was muscle memory, I wanted to ask her what

Connie had told her that had her jumping under jacarandas at the kids' baseball practice.

She continues scrolling through her phone as she takes a seat next to me. I look over at her and she looks up. "What, are we supposed to sit on opposite sides of the bleachers now? That's weird," she says.

"Nobody said that," I tell her.

"You gave me a look."

A second later her phone buzzes. "Hello?" she says. "Yeah, yeah." Her voice is getting higher and higher. I have no idea who she's talking to. "Yes, I'll be there!"

She's more excited than I've seen her in a long time. She hangs up and turns to me. For a moment, I think she's going to tell me her good news and then she says, "What's your mom's schedule like tomorrow . . . or can you just stay until tomorrow night and we'll switch then?"

"Why?"

"Because I have an important meeting, Alex."

"I have patients all day tomorrow. I'll be at work."

"They go to school at seven-thirty in the morning, as you know, and their school is five minutes from the clinic. It's just this once. I'll be with them four days a week from here on out and you'll only be doing three. Do you even have clients that early?"

"Patients, not clients, and their school is more like twenty minutes from the clinic."

"Whatever . . . do you?"

"No, but who's going to pick them up? I have patients at two-thirty in the afternoon, back-to-back until eight o'clock at night to make up for my limited schedule the last three days. As it is, you were supposed to pick them up today from school and I covered that. Remember, it was promised that this arrangement would only affect my schedule two days a week."

She's staring at me, her eyes are as big as sand dollars. "Are you serious, Alex? Throw me a fucking bone. You could hear me on the phone with Connie."

"You didn't tell me anything," I say, but instantly regret saying it.

She's very calm. I can tell she's mad, even though she's not hysterical. Noah is watching us from ten yards away in the dugout. He looks sullen.

Dani smiles at him and he smiles back. "You know what?" she says. "I'll figure it out, though I think you should consider this . . . I also work and have a job, and sometimes I have to show up for it. Not very often . . . but sometimes . . . like tomorrow, when there is a meeting that could potentially bring my career back to life. Do you feel that canceling one afternoon appointment and bringing the boys to your office will be detrimental to your entire career?" She cocks her head to the side. This is classic Dani, trying to make me feel like an idiot.

"Dani, I'll stay with the boys again tonight. I'll cancel my appointments and take them and pick them up tomorrow, but remember you were the one who said you wouldn't be there to help me out, and now you're the one asking for help."

She takes a deep breath and very calmly says, "Honestly, forget I asked. You're right! It's my problem. I can pay a babysitter. That's what you are anyway. Actually, you're worse. You're a babysitter who outsources his work to his seventy-year-old mother."

Ouch. Why did I let this conversation happen?

She stands, turns on her heel, and heads for the dugout. I consider stopping her and insisting that I go back to the house with the boys. I also consider wishing her good luck and asking what the news is. There is so much resignation in her. This is a Dani I have only seen in the last few months. A Dani who doesn't care enough to fight.

I sit, contemplating what to do. The practice is wrapping up. Dani is still standing near the dugout with her back to me. She looks thinner. Her hair is different. Her personality seems different too. She's moving on, I guess.

As I get up from the bleachers, I look up and see that both boys are watching me. I wave goodbye to them. When Dani turns around to see what they're waving at, I instantly look down to avoid eye contact. I make my way to the car and don't look back. I'm so tired, mentally and physically. I don't have the energy to antagonize her, but I want to. I want to rile her up. I want to scream, *Why aren't you burning up inside like me?*

14

par for the course

DANIELLE

A couple of years ago we were seeing a therapist who was also a psychologist. We thought we could doctor our relationship back into bliss. Dr. Gray was his name. Gloomy from the start. He also had taxidermy in his office, which I thought was bizarre and inappropriate.

Every time we were there, an image would flash through my mind of my and Alex's heads stuffed and mounted on the wall, next to a largemouth bass. But Dr. Gray had come highly recommended, regarded for his unique approaches to solving marital unrest, so we gave it a try.

For the first twenty minutes of the appointments, we would do regular talk therapy and then the last part would be an exercise. He had us practice and work up to doing headstands side by side, against one wall of his office. The pure absurdity of it would make Alex and me laugh every time. Other sessions included us doing small jigsaw puzzles without being able to talk, and one time he even had us feed each other. It was all very strange and new wave, but for a while, the distractive nature of it helped us get along better. So maybe Dr. Gray was on to something.

What eventually happened, though, was that we would do his silly exercises and then get into the car and fight.

At our last meeting he took on a more traditional approach. He talked about John Gottman's Four Horsemen. Basically, a theory that names four relationship characteristics that inevitably will lead to divorce. Alex and I had them all.

The memory is still vivid in my mind, not only because it was our last session with Dr. Gray, but also because that same morning was the last time Alex and I slept together. By that point we were already living in separate bedrooms of the house, so sex was few and far between and never involved any sort of rapturous passion. It was basically a quickie every couple of weeks. But that morning was different, or so it could have been. The boys were on spring break and had stayed overnight at a friend's house. My mother had already been gone for six months so the topic of her abuse was rarely coming to the surface anymore. I had passed Alex in the hallway. He was dressed in running clothes.

I said, "We have Dr. Gray in an hour."

He seemed irritated and rolled his eyes. "I know, I'm going on a short run. I'll be back by the time we have to leave."

I looked down at my toes and up my own body. It was supposed to be subtle. The implication was, *Look at me, I'm wearing a short, lace nightgown.* At that time I was still hopeful. I believed if we stuck with Dr. Gray, it would all work itself out. We enjoyed his weird little exercises. But beyond the silliness of it, and laughing for a moment, it wasn't actually bringing Alex and me any closer together.

"I just thought—"

"What? What did you think?" he said, not rudely. Obtuse.

Alex's body language was telling me he was in a hurry. Always in a hurry. He stood there blinking, eyebrows arched.

"No one is here," I said.

"Keen sense of the obvious," he said, and smiled like he thought he was clever.

"Jesus, Alex." He wasn't getting it. "Uh . . . do you want to do me?"

"Danielle," he scoffed.

"Well, why do you think I'm wearing this skimpy nightgown and blocking your way in the hallway and pointing out that we're alone?" So many things I wish I didn't have to say. So many times I felt we were in the same theater watching a different movie.

"Okay, let's do it," he said.

He walked past me into my bedroom and stood near the bed, still fully clothed. In a way, I was on autopilot as I walked up next to him, pulled my nightgown up to my waist, and bent over the bed. I could see him in the closet mirror. He pulled his shorts and underwear down to about mid-thigh and took one arm out of his shirt so half of his shirt was bunched on his shoulder. This was something I recognized. He did it so his shirt wouldn't get in the way, but so that he wouldn't have to take it off completely and put it back on afterward. He still had his running shoes on when he started thrusting. It hurt.

I closed my eyes and tried to pretend we were young again, that we were in love. I tried to go somewhere else.

"Can you get down lower? Your legs are too long," he said between breaths.

My legs are disproportionately long, so Alex does have to sort of stand on the balls of his feet when we're having sex standing up. I shimmied down and spread my legs wider so the entire upper half of my body was flush with the top of the bed. My face and chest were rubbing back-and-forth against the comforter with every plunge. Idly, I thought that I was getting some much-needed exfoliation for my face.

Why did I want this? What do I look like back there?

I was trying desperately to stay in the moment, or at least the moment I imagined in my mind.

It was taking longer than usual and the sex was getting rougher and harder to tolerate. He wasn't intentionally hurting me, I just wasn't into it. Apparently, neither was he.

Finally, after what felt like forever, he stopped and said, "This can't feel good to you."

"What's wrong? Do I not turn you on?"

"I'm not the one who's not turned-on; do you realize that?" he barked.

"Then what is the problem?" I said.

"I don't know, Dani. Let's just forget it," he said.

"But . . . can we just lie down and talk about this for a second?"

"I wanted to get a run in." His tone was not mean or rude, it was almost apologetic, but it didn't matter.

"Go, then. I'll see you at Dr. Gray's. I have errands to run after, so we can drive separately."

"Okay, bye. I'm sorry," he said as he kissed me on the forehead.

After he left I cried for twenty minutes. Then Alex was fifteen minutes late to our appointment. During that time, Dr. Gray tried to make small talk with me. When I acted aloof about his idle chatter, he said, "Danielle, do you want to talk one-on-one until Alex gets here and then I can schedule a separate appointment with him? I don't normally do that, but it could be beneficial."

"No," I said. I truly had no interest.

Alex finally got there, sat down next to me, and said, "Sorry, I needed to shower and time got away from me." He glanced over at me quickly and then looked back at Dr. Gray.

"What are you saying, Alex? That it's my fault you're late, or that you were masturbating in the shower because you couldn't get off with me?"

It had been building in my chest, getting bigger and bigger. I had hit my edge and couldn't hold back.

"Whoa, whoa, whoa," Dr. Gray said.

"Oh my god, Danielle! What is wrong with you? I went running and had to take a quick shower. That's it. I ran farther than I should have. *That's it!*"

I took a deep, cleansing breath. "Let's just get on with it."

"What would you like to talk about or work on today? Did you guys have a good week?" Dr. Gray was looking at me because I was usually the one who spoke up first.

"I just feel myself giving up," I said. Alex stayed quiet as I went on. "I tried to initiate sex this morning and it was terrible all-around."

Alex made a noise like he was exasperated.

"Alex," Dr. Gray said, "do you have anything to add?"

"I can't turn her on. Maybe Lars can," Alex said.

"Just stop that," I sneered. I looked at Dr. Gray. "I need intimacy. Not quickies."

"I try to kiss you all the time, Dani. You turn your head away. You act like you don't want me to."

"Not that kind of intimacy, Alex. You don't get it."

"Danielle," Dr. Gray said, "let's reframe and rephrase. Come on. What is intimacy to you and what do you need to feel turned on? But before you answer that, Alex—remember men and women are different. I'm not talking about physically. I'm talk-

ing about the foreplay that happens from the moment you're
done having sex the time before."

"I'm not following," Alex said. "I give her attention. I tell her
she's beautiful again and again. I try foreplay all the time, but
she pushes me away then rushes into sex—"

I couldn't help myself. "See! He doesn't get it."

Dr. Gray looked at me pointedly. "Danielle, tell him specifically what *it* is." When I started to speak, Dr. Gray said, "No!
Tell Alex directly. Use the pronouns *you* and *I*, not *him*."

"Fine." I shifted on the cold, uncomfortable leather couch.
Before I even opened my mouth to speak, I glanced up at the
stuffed deer corpse mounted on the wall. My breath hitched. I
shook my head diminutively.

"Focus," Dr. Gray said.

It's hard to keep your thoughts straight and quell your emotions when a dead animal is glaring at you. I tried to imagine
being at home, on our bed. The bed we used to share.

Speaking directly to Alex, I said, "Okay. Can you face me?"

He turned his head only. "I'm looking right at you."

"Tell him, Danielle," Dr. Gray said.

I was crying before the first words came out of my mouth. My
voice was shaky and weak, but as I went on, and despite the fact
that I was hysterical, my conviction got stronger.

"Alex, I want you to be proud of me . . . and proud to *be with
me*. I want you to be fascinated by me, and by my brain, like you
used to be. Enchanted by who I am, captivated by how I see the
world, mystified by how someone like me can exist and by how
you are the one who gets to hold me in your arms. I want you to
be enamored, Alex! Even if it's not true—I want you to pretend
it is . . . and I want to believe the lie."

I was sobbing. Hyperventilating.

Alex sat there, stunned into silence. The image is still a bloody razor in my mind. Alex on the leather couch, two feet away, hugging the armrest to get as far from me as possible, his head turned toward me and cocked slightly to the right, while his rigid body stayed facing the door, I assume so he could be ready to flee at any moment. He was staring at me . . . nonplussed. And directly behind him was the dead deer, looking equally bewildered.

I was blinking and wiping tears away. Nothing. He said nothing.

"Alex," came Dr. Gray's voice. I had almost forgotten Dr. Gray was there. Alex turned to look at him. "Do you have a response?"

Alex shook his head.

"Say something," I said through tears.

"I don't know what to say," he whispered.

"Anything," I said in a voice that sounded like a mewling cat.

"I think I do all of those things," he said with no emotion whatsoever. "You don't exactly act like I'm the bee's knees, Danielle."

After that, I became the quiet one. Dr. Gray leaned forward in his leather wingback chair, resting his elbows on his knees, clasped his hands together, and said, "Are you guys familiar with the Gottman Institute?"

Alex shook his head while I nodded.

Dr. Gray went on. "They refer to the Four Horsemen—"

"Of the apocalypse?" Alex laughed. It was insensitive. Not so much what he said, but the fact that the mood was intensely serious and he tried to make a joke.

"That's right, Alex," Dr. Gray said. "So the four horsemen in a relationship refer to contempt, criticism, defensiveness, and stonewalling. When these four behaviors are involved, it's really difficult to make any progress at all. You might be wondering why I'm bringing this up now instead of doing one of my silly exercises?"

My eyes shot open. Was he admitting the exercises were trivial and just a waste of time?

"Go on," I said.

"The exercises are to give you an insignificant topic to conversate about when you leave. It's not team building, like people think. These dead animals mounted all over the room, they're not mine. I got them from a Hollywood prop house. They're just conversation starters. I've stopped our sessions ten minutes early and neither of you have said a thing about it. My hope was that every day you would leave here and talk about me or this office, or the silly exercises. Most people do, then realize they have a lot more in common than they thought. It leads to other, deeper conversations in private. You see?"

"This whole thing is just a made-up game? This is complete insanity," I said.

"Not really. I think today you should go home and contemplate why this method that has helped so many people who want to stay together has proved useless with you guys. Can you think of a reason why?"

"Because we're stubborn," Alex said.

"Maybe," Dr. Gray replied.

I didn't say it out loud . . . I couldn't, but in my head, I knew it was because we didn't *want* to stay together.

Alex huffed and then said, "Well, now that you've blown your cover—"

"We can still do talk therapy, but that involves talking. I don't think you guys are hopeless. I brought up the four horsemen because I see a lot of contempt from you, Danielle; and Alex, you are constantly stonewalling her. Eighty-five percent of stonewallers are men. This isn't uncommon. I'm guessing, Alex, you think that if you speak up you'll make things worse?"

Alex shrugged.

Dr. Gray continued, "Staying quiet actually makes things worse. The frustration that you cause Danielle by not saying anything is instantaneous and obvious."

I was shocked. Dr. Gray wasn't holding back. At first it felt like he was taking my side. A shit-eating smile spread across my face, which I later regretted.

Alex winced. "I feel like I'm being crucified now."

"No," Dr. Gray replied, "not at all. I'm telling you, point-blank, what you two need to do to heal this marriage. Danielle, you're a writer, for Christ's sake. You need to learn how to use the proper language when you're talking to Alex so he doesn't want to go running for the hills. Do you guys see how it all boils down to communication? Danielle, you are constantly pouring fuel on the fire, while Alex is hiding in the corner, shooting himself in the foot and wondering why his goddamn foot hurts."

Dr. Gray took a deep breath. Now there were three deer in headlights—me, Alex, and the stuffed one behind us. It was beyond unprofessional and un-therapist-like, but I appreciated Dr. Gray's candor that day.

"Listen," he went on, "stonewalling is a very common behavior in men. I promise there's hope for you guys. If Danielle were stonewalling, I might not think so. When the woman does it, it's very indicative of divorce. You can just stop doing it, Alex, it's not that complicated. All you have to do is start telling Danielle how you feel. And Danielle, I have learned over the course of this therapy that you are a very forgiving person. *Forgive him* for shutting down. Listen to him communicate with the beautiful language you are so familiar with."

Alex turned his whole body this time and looked at me. "Well?" he said.

"Time's up," Dr. Gray blurted out.

"What?" I barked. Finally making some progress and then time's up? I looked at the clock, he was right. We were actually twenty minutes over.

Alex stood and reached out his hand to help me stand. "Well, Dr. Gray, I guess we'll let you know what the plan is," Alex said.

"Okay. You guys take care."

We walked to the parking lot in silence. As Alex started the car, he looked over at me and said, "That guy's a quack." I didn't respond. "Right?" he said.

"I guess."

"We'll find someone better, Dani."

But we didn't. Instead, we muscled through four more bad experiences with different therapists. We continued to be miserable because neither one of us wanted to make the effort. Now it's too late. Now I'm the one avoiding. Sitting in my house, stuck in the past when what I should be doing is finding someone to pick up the boys tomorrow. I should be planning my pitch. I need to sell myself as a showrunner.

Ethan walks into the kitchen. I'm in a daze. He puts his hand on my shoulder and says, "Jose's mom can pick us up and take us to their house until you're done with your meeting."

I look up at him. He appears sympathetic. "Did you call her and ask for me?"

"I just texted Jose and he asked her. It's no big deal, Mom. A lot of kids walk or ride their bikes and then go home to an empty house until their parents get home from work."

Inside I feel appalled, but on the outside I'm trying to stay cool. "That road is not safe for you guys to ride your bikes on."

"I know. That's why I asked Jose if we could go to his house."

I nod. He's trying to help, and he *is* helping. It's also becoming clear to me that I need to cool it with the helicopter parenting. I need to prepare myself for the days when Alex and I will be legally divorced. He'll be taking the boys places I've never been, with people I don't know, and I will have absolutely no knowledge of it. Maybe there will even be a new woman there. She'll wish the boys called *her* "Mom" instead of me. She'll want them to tell her they love her, or that they like her more than me. My boys never will. They will never betray me.

"Mom!"

I shake my head back to planet Earth.

"Yeah, I'm sorry."

"Your face is bright red, you look like a tomato. What is wrong?" Ethan says, his eyeballs darting back and forth.

"Do you think I'm a good mom?" Never before have I stooped this low. "I mean, do you ever wish I was different?"

"Like a mom who doesn't make us do chores?" He smiled. He was teasing. "No. I don't wish you were someone else, that's ridiculous." It's equal parts pride-inducing and humbling to be put in your place by your twelve-year-old son.

"When Dad and I divorce officially, which is going to happen very soon . . ." I stop myself and yell for Noah. "Noah, get down here. Family meeting!"

Ethan is watching me like he thinks I might be clinically insane.

"Coming," I hear Noah say from upstairs.

"You and Dad have never said the words *family meeting*," Ethan says in a low voice.

"Well, I'm having one now."

"What's up?" Noah says as he enters the kitchen. It seems like the boys have grown a whole foot in one year.

"Sit down." I gesture to the barstools.

I begin calmly. "I know Dad's not here . . ." I pause. They look around the kitchen and both arch their eyebrows, indicating that I am stating the obvious. "It's not really a family meeting, but I think he'll agree with everything I'm about to tell you. He'll probably have a similar discussion with you in his own way."

Who am I kidding? No, he won't. He's a steel trap.

"What's up, Mom," Noah says.

"Your father and I are getting a divorce."

"We know," Ethan says. "You guys have told us like ten thousand times."

Noah says, "It's about time."

"You want us to get divorced?" I say.

"No, we want you to stop talking about it," Noah blurts out.

I realize in that moment how hard it is to see the scales anymore, let alone keep them balanced.

"I'm sorry," I say. "There is something specific I want to talk to you about."

The boys are staring at me, Ethan with his light hair, blue eyes, and Noah, all dark hair, dark eyes like me. One is stubborn, one is brainy, one is loving, one is more independent . . . but together they are perfect. Right now Ethan is about an inch taller, which infuriates Noah. Sometimes the two of them are warring nations, but right now they are a united force.

They are their own people and I've just realized in this moment that my marriage has nothing to do with them. Having two parents who get along is important, much more important than a piece of paper that is simply a declaration between me and their father.

"Mom!"

"I know, I know." I'm changing course in my mind. "So we've talked about how there are going to be some logistical changes, but I think it's important to point out that we are getting a divorce so we can be *happier,* not just divorced. We have unlearned how to be happy together."

"And can't you relearn it?" Noah asks.

"No. You can't teach an old dog new tricks." *Why did I just say that? I'm flailing.*

"But it's not a new trick, and are you comparing Dad to a dog?" Ethan asks.

"No, not at all. I'm saying we both are." I take a deep breath and collect myself. "Your dad is a great person. He is kind, generous, loving, smart, so many wonderful things. Someday, he will likely get a girlfriend." They're still staring at me like I'm spewing the obvious. "I want you to know that unless she's a total train wreck, mean or ignorant, materialistic or shallow, or she's a fan of shitty music, you *must* be nice to her. As long as she's nice to you."

"Oh, it's this talk," Noah says. "Yeah, Dad gave us this talk while we were waiting in the ER a couple days ago."

"Huh?" I'm flabbergasted. "What did he say?"

"Essentially the same thing you just said in reverse," Ethan says.

"He told you to be nice to his future girlfriend?"

"Noooo, Mom, are you serious? This is when you would call someone 'obtuse,'" Noah says playfully.

Jesus, when did my kids become smarter than me?

"He said you were great. He said you're a great mom and person and that someday you might date. His criteria was a little different though. He mentioned all that mean and shallow stuff, but at the end he said, 'If the guy is a Giants fan, you have my permission to be a dick to him.'" Both the boys chuckle.

I'm laughing and crying at the same time. I can't believe he had this talk with them, and I'm shocked that he said those nice things about me. This feels like the true marker of the end.

"Well, I guess I agree. No Giants fans." We laugh for another moment and then I stop abruptly. "I'm curious. I need to know. What did he say exactly? Like word for word?" Now the boys look exasperated.

"I don't remember word for word, Mom. He was basically saying not to make you feel guilty about being happy."

"Yes, that's right," I say, almost in a whisper. *From the mouths of babes* . . .

"Anyway, Dad would never date someone with bad taste in music," Noah says, laughing.

I shrug. "I'd never date a Giants fan."

"Can I order a pizza now?" Ethan says.

Just like that, they're kids again.

Everything is taken care of. The boys barely need me anymore. I walk upstairs thinking how insane the day has been. I still have to hunker down and get organized for tomorrow. When Connie called and said four executives from Apple TV wanted me to come in and pitch my show, I was over the moon. Before this, I really thought my career was done for. I should feel reinvigorated, or happier about the news. I was jumping up and down on the phone with Connie, but as soon as I hung up, reality came rushing in.

I wished I had someone to tell, to bounce things around with. When I was twenty years old, one of my childhood friends went to Spain to study abroad. She would send me postcards of all her fabulous travels. She ventured across Europe alone. Every weekend she went to a new country. I was envious of her independence and bravery. I planned a trip to go see her over the holidays that year. When she met me at the airport in Madrid, she was crying hysterically, hugging me as tightly as she could. She was so lonely. I kept asking her about all the places she went and she just kept saying, "It's like it didn't even happen. I'm so glad you're here." Later that week, we traveled to Portugal. It's such a vivid memory still and I love that it has stuck with me. We were staring out at the Tagus river from Belém Tower, just in awe of the country, when she turned to me and said, "None of those other places felt real because I knew I wouldn't have anyone to share the memory with."

15

where have i been?

ALEXANDER

The apartment is dark, cold, empty. What did I expect? I'm the one who found it. I flip on all the lights, set my bag down, and look around. Dani added white linen curtains, some hanging plants in macramé slings, and a bunch of tchotchkes on the shelves. Some I've never seen. She must have gone to a thrift store. It's definitely more inviting than it was, but the décor is random . . . eclectic. Very Dani. I'm much more of a symmetrical, organized, matching person. She'd call it "sterile."

I go to the small bedroom off the living room, where I start to put the coffee-splattered sheets on the bed. I don't care enough to rewash them. When the cleaning people come on Sunday, I'll have them do it. I lie on the bed and start to doze off in my clothes. I need to get the coffee ready for tomorrow. I drag my feet to the kitchen and notice Dani stocked it with some basics. I pick up a porcelain jar and open it. Ground coffee. I usually always grind the beans, but this will do. I'm relieved I don't have to go out to the store right now.

In the refrigerator I spot a takeout container. I open it to find what looks like fettuccine with some sort of creamy marinara sauce. It's not like Dani is going to eat this in four days when she's here next. I don't think she'll mind. I find a bowl, dump it in, and put it in the microwave. While the food is warming I wonder where she got the pasta. Did she go to dinner with someone? There's a pit in my stomach. *What if I'm eating his leftovers?* I briefly look around the apartment to see if there is evidence of another person here. Dani said the apartment is off-limits. She acted like it was too soon.

The microwave dings, startling me. I was headed straight down the rabbit hole. She probably went to dinner with Alicia or just got takeout alone, but I want to know. I look in the trash for a clue, but it's empty. As I'm eating the mystery pasta, I'm looking around the apartment, in drawers and cabinets, under couch cushions. In the corner I spot her record player and a stack of albums on the floor under the shelf. There are several records organized in what looks like chronological order, starting with thirties jazz, all the way through the decades to about the early two-thousands. I remember that's when she stopped collecting and writing in them. I never looked at what was written. She always said it was just for her, so I treated them like a personal diary, and out of respect, I didn't read them.

I can tell by the stack on the floor that she's still going through the albums. Several of them were her dad's. She told me not to touch them, but I can't help myself. I had forgotten just how unique the collection was.

The first one I pick up is Loggins and Messina's *Gator Creek* album. I search my memory wondering if we had ever listened to it. As I take the record out, the sleeve cover comes with it. Instantly, I see old handwriting that must be Dani's father's, and then Dani's undeniable chicken scratch, a combination of standard and cursive slanted dramatically to the right.

I know I shouldn't read it, it's not mine and it's private and she made it very clear not to touch them. But did she actually say don't *read* them? I've already touched one. If she were in my shoes, would she read them? Probably. I always said Dani's curiosity would get her in trouble one day.

I take my pasta and the record and sit down on the new, rock-hard couch. *Why did I buy this uncomfortable thing?* I set the bowl on the coffee table and pull the sleeve and record all the way out. Her father's note reads:

> Song 2, "Danny's Song." If it's a boy, Danny, if it's a girl, Dani.
> I love you so much, Irene. We have everything we need right
> here. We earned what lovers own.

I'm stunned. It's from Dani's dad to her mom. I've never known him to be emotional, or romantic. In fact, he's the opposite. He's truly a shell of a man. I had no idea he was like this. Irene must have been pregnant with Dani when he wrote it. I look over to Dani's writing.

> Song 2 was a song Kenny Loggins gifted to his brother,
> Danny, for the birth of his son. I wish I could write something
> to you now, Ben, and gift it to you. I'm glad you only ever
> knew Mom and Dad happy and in love.

When did she write this? I have a lump in my throat like I just swallowed a wad of Silly Putty. I take a deep breath and stand. I'm contemplating taking the bowl of pasta to the sink and rinsing it, but then I realize only the cleaners will see the dirty dish. I'm leaving it.

I put the record back and pick up the next one, it's Chet Baker. Standing next to the record player, I take the album out of the sleeve. We had listened to it many times but I had never looked to see if there was writing. I take it out and read only Dani's handwriting this time:

Song 2. "It's Always You." Last night you said I love you for the first time. You thought I was sleeping. Now you're sleeping . . . in my apartment, and I want it to be our apartment. I love you too.

My throat tightens up. I remember. I didn't think she had heard me. I know I have to get a grip right now. I'm mad at myself for not reading these sooner.

I flip through to find something lighter, if that's even possible. I find Van Morrison's *Moondance*. I remember her getting this album. We had just bought our house, but we hadn't had the boys yet. She'd written:

Song 5 then 3.

I put the record on to song five. Without even looking, I know it's the song "Into the Mystic." Dani used to play this album all the time. I look down and read the rest of the paragraph.

You're building the garden boxes I asked for. I'm watching you through the window. You've been out there all morning. You want them to be perfect. I can't take my eyes off you. I'm going to tell you it's time for a shower . . .

Instantly I'm right back to almost twenty years ago. The music is bringing the memory sharp into focus, almost tangible.

Dani asked for garden boxes on the side of the house to plant tomatoes. I spent one whole Saturday morning building them. I remember the moment when this song was playing. Dani was standing in the doorway out to the backyard. I could see her in my peripheral vision, watching me hammer nails into the wood.

We had just finished renovations on the house, and we were in those early years of our life where we felt like we could conquer anything together. No kids, new house, we were naked a lot.

"Are you hungry?" she asked.

I looked up and then froze. She was wearing a sheer white sundress, meant to be worn with a slip or swimsuit or something, but she had nothing on underneath. I could see everything.

"Well?" she said.

"I'm . . . I think I'm done for the day."

"Hmm, you look pretty dirty." She walked over to the spicket and hose. I wasn't wearing a shirt, just a pair of shorts, work gloves, and sneakers. I kicked the shoes off and threw the gloves to the side as I watched her proceed to pull the hose out of the bin it was coiled inside.

I remember her dark hair was long and wavy over her shoulders. It contrasted beautifully against the thin white fabric. It was before the trees in the backyard had matured, so the neighbors on both sides could look out their windows and see our yard, see us, being so in love.

"What are you going to do? Hose me down, you little naked sprite?"

"I'm not naked," she said with feigned seriousness.

"Dani, I feel like adding water to this scenario would not be in your best interest, considering your attire."

She quickly spun around to face me, armed with the hose.

She squeezed the nozzle and sprayed before I could even make a move toward her.

"You're going to regret that!" I shouted.

She dropped the hose and ran across the yard toward the door to the house. I chased her, grabbed her arm in the doorway, spun her around, and kissed her, pressing her against the open door. My hands were all over her while she kissed me frantically. I touched her between her legs, over the thin fabric. Her knees buckled. "Alex," she whispered near my ear.

The memory is heavy and vivid. Too vivid. I take a deep breath and shake my head, trying to get the image out. I pick the needle up off the record and move it to the third song. It's "Crazy Love." Just hearing the first three seconds propels me right back to that day again.

We didn't care if the whole neighborhood saw us. We were against the wall in the kitchen, on the counter, on the floor. All the doors and windows were open. We were loud and unconscious, swept away with each other. Whatever that thing was that Dani and I felt, that passion, lust, infatuation, respect . . . it was there for so many years. It was unspoken and easy, but once it was gone, we could never get it back. It wasn't newness, it wasn't puppy love or crazy love—it was just simply being in love.

My whole body is heating up thinking about that day. I have to stop.

I close my eyes and picture Dani now, her new light hair, her ridiculing expressions, the pain and misery we've experienced the last few years. Reality is back. I turn everything off, set up the coffeepot for tomorrow, do the one dish I dirtied, just out of habit, and head for the bedroom.

As I lie in bed, exhausted from my time juggling the boys and work and partially moving into the apartment, I hear my phone buzz. It's Brian, my golfing buddy whom I had met through Dani years ago.

> BRIAN: Yo! I know I told you this already, but I wanted to remind you that you're getting me in the divorce.

It was a given. Even though he was a writer friend of Dani's from a long time ago, they didn't really talk anymore and were never that close to begin with. Actually, Dani didn't like him much, thought he was arrogant, but I chalked that up to Dani not wanting me to have single friends.

> ME: Better be. T-Time Saturday?
> BRIAN: Yeah. Anywhere, anytime. We should go out afterward too.

What do men my age even do when they "go out"? I mean, it's not like I'm going to show up at a club.

> ME: What, like dinner?
> BRIAN: Yeah. Why not? What else do you have to do?

That's true.

> ME: Sure. You plan it, I'll be there.

I set my phone on the nightstand and turn the light off. But I can't fall asleep. All I can think about is how Dani should dye her hair back to her natural dark brown. How beautiful she'd looked in that white see-through sundress.

16

surprise me for a change

DANIELLE

"Hold the door!" The elevator is closing. I'm already five minutes late. I didn't even know this building existed on the Warner Bros. lot. That's how long it's been since I've come here. I'm off my game. A person in the elevator peeks around the closing doors as I'm running down the hall yelling, "Hold it!"

She's hitting something frantically. "I'm pressing the button," she whines. I shove my hand through the doors, stopping them and triggering the mechanism that opens them back up.

"You've got to be kidding me!" I say loudly. It's Beth Zinn. *Where is the hidden camera?* "Have you never stopped elevator doors from closing before?" Whatever kind of cosmic glitch is happening right now, it's not deterring my attention from the fact that she doesn't know how to stop elevator doors from closing.

"You," she says in a scolding tone. Her scowl is a canyon between her eyes.

"Me?" I say in the highest voice I've ever heard come out of my mouth. "Why are you in my magical dream-job opportunity meeting? Why? Why are *you* here?"

"I work here!"

We're alone in the elevator now. I press the fourth-floor button and notice that 3 is already lit. Good, she's not going to my meeting.

"Is that what you call it? Do not talk to me," I say.

"Why would I, except maybe to tell you about the giant sweat marks under your armpits."

Dammit, why did I wear silk? It's so not my style at all, but I wanted to seem professional. Now I just look like a middle-aged wreck.

"I can't believe you haven't been blacklisted from this business."

"You mean like you are?" She raises one eyebrow and smirks. I'm seeing red.

My rage overtakes me. I pull the emergency stop button, bringing the elevator to a standstill somewhere between the second and third floors. At this moment I don't care if I'm late, I know I'm getting the job. I know they wouldn't ask me to come in and do a presentation at this stage in my career unless they planned on green-lighting the show. I know this meeting is for protocol. It's literally just to meet the people who will be working for me, producing the show *I* have written. Those people on the fourth floor will happily wait ten more minutes so that I can murder Beth Zinn in the elevator.

I didn't get a single minute of sleep last night, and the boys were running late this morning, Alex had put their clothes in all the wrong places. Ethan forgot his math book, which we had to backtrack to get, and Noah wouldn't stop blabbering about Elon Musk. I haven't eaten a crumb in twenty-four hours, my armpits are individual humid swamplands with their own ecosystems . . .

and I've got a wonky contact in my left eye. Still, none of that can stop me. I'm operating on caffeine, bitterness, and retribution.

I take one giant breath, close my eyes, open them again, and glare across to the other side of the small elevator. Beth looks terrified . . . as she should. For the first time, I notice her age. It has not been a graceful process. I think she might be too skinny for a 45-year-old. She has mousy hair that used to be strawberry blond but is now dirtier than the dishwater in a third world country. Her skin is not only wrinkly, it's ruddy. She has the kind of nose where you can see halfway up her nostrils. I used to think it was regal looking, but right now I can see a gray nose hair and it's giving me an unreasonable amount of satisfaction, followed by shame for thinking about how terrible she looks.

I'm not letting her off the hook, even though it does seem like life has swallowed her up, partially digested her, and then puked her back out into a garbage bin. I cannot believe the nerve she has. But ultimately, I know that getting mad and screaming at her, or stabbing her to death, will get me nowhere.

I calmly and quietly say, "Why'd you *do it,* Beth?"

Her breath hitches. "I—"

"Why? You know how this business is. For the first ten years of my career, I lost jobs—gave up jobs because I wouldn't kiss ass or sleep around. I didn't even fake a smile or stroke an ego, let alone . . . God knows what. I clawed my way here with worn-out nails. I wrote, I typed, I bled into everything I created, Beth. I hired women . . . hell, I hired you. I kept you around, on the payroll, even though I wouldn't trust you to write my goddamn grocery list." I pause, shake my head. "I don't get it. Why?"

She's just staring at me, periodically glancing at the buttons as if she is trying to will the elevator back into motion.

"I don't know what I expected from you," I say. "Like, is there a thought in there and you just can't unscramble the words? Why would someone like you aspire to be a writer? There are so many other jobs. In this business alone, there are hundreds! Why a writer? It's such a lonely and tall order. Most *writers* don't even want to be writers."

She's exasperated. "I . . . I . . . Everyone loved you, Dani. Even though you were a hard-ass about the episodes. The other writers still loved you despite the fact that you were a bitch to everyone."

"They didn't love me, they respected me. I wasn't a bitch at all. Somehow everyone else knew Lars and I were trying to create something we could all be proud of. You included. Apparently, you didn't get that memo. But I guess you figured out how to get what you want anyway, right?"

I push the Stop button back in, starting the elevator up to the third floor. A moment later the doors are opening to production offices. I see a sign that says, GRACELESS. *How appropriate! How totally inspiring in this moment.* She must be writing for that show now. I've never seen it, but I hear it's terrible. She's holding the door open with one foot in and one foot out. It looks like she's searching for something to say. I can't believe she's not sprinting away from me.

"Surprise me," I say. After all, having Beth Zinn on a woman-hating rampage around town is not going to help anyone.

"Huh?" she says. She's truly dumbstruck

"Surprise me, Beth. Go pitch a good episode." With my foot, I nudge *her* foot out the door. "I gotta go, okay?" I say with a genuine and humble smile. "Good luck."

The doors close. The last image of Beth's face will forever be ingrained in my memory. She wasn't just shocked. Her brow was furrowed, her mouth was open slightly and frozen into shape. It was a slightly rueful expression. She was ashamed.

The moment I exit the elevator on the fourth floor, I'm greeted by Eli Ross. Eli and I had worked together years ago on a pilot that never made it.

"Danielle," he says as he's walking toward me. I knew Eli was the person Connie had spoken to, the one who said execs at Apple were high on my pilot and wanting to meet and get things fast-tracked.

"Hi, Eli." I greet him with a touchless side-cheek kiss. Eli is a very short man whose personality makes him seem much taller. He talks extremely fast but he's not a *fast talker* per se. He's well respected and viewed as someone in the business who puts integrity first. I'm surprised he's interested in heading up the production of my pilot, considering my tabloid run. "Sorry I'm a little late. I just ran into Beth Zinn in the elevator."

"You're kidding? What are the odds?" Obviously, he knows the story. Everyone does. "Don't let that get to you. What a crock of shit that whole thing was, right?" I nod. "No one even thinks about that anymore, it's ancient news." He pats my back.

I'm walking beside him down a long hall with small makeshift cubicles on each side.

"For the record—"

He stops abruptly and turns to me. "It doesn't matter. I know you, and I know Lars very well . . ." There is something implied in his statement that I can't quite put my finger on. I nod and he continues, "I never thought the rumors were true, but even if they were . . . even if you and Lars had a mutual relationship that was more than work, it shouldn't have mattered. It's nobody else's business. *Litigators* was a great show. It ran its course though. The reason it didn't get re-upped is because there was already something else in the hopper for that network . . . and it was time."

I take a deep breath. "You think so?"

"I know so. Listen, these people you're about to meet are putty in your hands. They *love* the pilot, Dani. They're going to greenlight it. They just want to meet you. How long have you been working on this anyway?"

"I wrote it a few weeks ago in one sitting. It took me about four hours."

"Wow." He arches his eyebrows and smiles. "Well, maybe don't mention that part. Let's go."

I follow him toward the end of the hall. "Hey, how's your wife and kids? I haven't seen you in forever," I say to him.

"She's now a rich divorcée with too much Botox and my two daughters are lazy, entitled Insta-models, or so they think. How about yours?" I burst out laughing. Eli pauses at the very end of the hallway. "I'm glad you find it so funny." He's being sarcastic.

"I'm sorry," I say, still laughing.

"Don't be, I wanted to divorce her. I couldn't stand her. The girls will be fine, eventually, if they ever put their phones down."

"If it's any consolation, I'm headed for D-town myself."

He smiles knowingly. "Oh yeah? Well, my dear, everything is better in dick town," he says with a wink.

Say what? I meant divorce town.

"Oh?" I say quietly. I'm not sure if he's saying I'll be happier single or that he likes being in dick town. I'm so confused. "You're gay . . ." I say more like a question than a statement.

He smiles. "Welcome back, Dani darling, you've been gone for so long." He takes my hand gently and pulls me along. "Come on, let's go get our money from these suits."

I'm still processing Eli being gay and the fact that I had been so far out of the loop, drowning in my own little sea of drama.

In the boardroom, I'm greeted by four people I've never seen in my life. Two men and two women. Despite the moniker, none of them are actually wearing suits. They're all dressed expressively. Expressively and expensively. They're inarguably cool, but I don't let it fool me. These people are here to represent the money. The moment I walked in the door, I was already in the red, so to speak. I have to convince them I'm worth the investment.

All they are doing is a risk assessment. I have to remind myself they've probably already made a decision, and their hipster outsides are just a ruse. These aren't creatives, they don't care about the story. They care about the people paying to subscribe to Apple TV and what *they* think of the story. I've already forgotten their names. I'm wondering where Gina is. It's her overall deal with Apple to develop content. She should be here. Eli works for her, she's going to produce this with me and she and I still haven't spoken. I met her one time ten years ago at a party, but I doubt she remembers me.

Eli pulls the chair out at the head of the table and gestures for me to sit. "Where's Gina?" I whisper.

Eli says, "She'll be here."

Literally a second later, the door swings open. I recognize her right away. She's taller and thinner than I remember, short black hair, attractive in a model-esque kind of way, with an overly pronounced masculine jawline.

She walks directly toward me. I stand. "No, no," she says. "Don't get up for me. I'm sorry I'm late. It's good to see you." She sits next to me and whispers, "I loved our conversation that night, what was that . . . ten years ago?"

"Yeah, that sounds about right."

"You were going off about how much better the movie *Waterworld* would have been if it was made into a musical."

"Ha! That sounds like something I'd be passionate about while drinking." Oh my god, I was filleted that night. I can't believe she remembered our conversation. I can't believe *I* even remember talking to her.

She looks to the group of Apple execs plus Eli. "Hi, everyone. We're so excited about this show!"

Unintentionally, I take a very deep and audible breath. Everyone's eyes are on me. Eli, seeing the terror on my face, clears his throat and takes the lead. "Everyone at Tin Roof is so unbelievably high on this." He's referring to Gina's company.

"All right, well," Gina says, "I think we've all done our homework. Dani's résumé speaks for itself and we've read the pilot. Eli's handing out the deck now. You can look that over. I think we can all agree this is just for propriety. You guys know what we're looking for budget-wise, and Bradley, you mentioned all systems were go? Lawyers have paperwork, et cetera, et cetera."

Up until this moment, I knew none of this. They're essentially in development and preproduction already. *Is this really happening?*

"I guess we let Dani give the obligatory pitch then hit the ground running?" Eli says.

Everyone is nodding.

I had planned an elaborate presentation, but I decide to go with my gut. "This is *Parenthood* meets *The Ice Storm* with a sprinkle of *Thirtysomething*. Ensemble cast, four couples, seasons of material centered around the premise that eight very different people decide to swap spouses once a week. The group is exclusive and they'll do anything to protect their secret. In their eyes, they're not being swingers, that's sort of below them. Each coupling has a unique relationship, for some it's sexual, for others just friendship or a common interest. One couple doesn't even like each other." Everyone in the room is silent. I get nervous for a second and then recover. "Playing on the fact that one person can't be your everything. Your lover, your best friend, your financial partner, your parenting partner, your confidant, your rock, your buddy, the person who won't judge you for dipping your toes in. Which friends in your life, other men or women, fill the voids in your marriage . . . and how?" I pause. They are all just giant, glaring eyes in the room. My anxiety is in overdrive. Am I being too long-winded? "Sooo, that's the question this show is answering. The second season would take the audience back to the beginning. How the arrangement was formed."

For a moment I try to read the room. *Are these people married? Do they get it? Does it even matter?* They've read the pilot, they know exactly what the show is about, so I don't go any further. One exec, whom I assume is the head guy, finally speaks. "We love it. We all really love it, Dani. It's a yes. Let's get to work."

Not only have I never experienced a yes in the room, I've never even known someone to get a yes on the table like that. Eli claps his hands together and says, "Okay, then. We'll get the documents rolling . . . as long as you're ready, Dani?"

I am so thrilled and electrified, it feels intoxicating. I'm afraid that if I speak it will be complete gibberish. Eli is staring at me. I'm assuming he's waiting for me to thank everyone or give a speech, but I'm still tongue-tied, thoughts swirling.

An image of my mother pops into my mind, as it often does in moments like these. Before my brother died, my mom was seemingly normal. She was always a little eccentric, but not mean, not cruel the way she became. She was actually quite thoughtful, and at times ruminative. My dad sometimes referred jokingly to my mother's musings as "esoteric LSD flashbacks," but she would laugh it off and say she had never touched the stuff. There's a memory of her I always think about when something good happens: It was my graduation from UCLA and my parents and Ben had come down from Seattle. We were all driving to the ceremony, and I was in the backseat with my mom because she said she wanted to talk to me. Ben sat in front while my dad drove. She was holding my hand and smiling at me.

"Danielle?"

"Yes, Mother." I laughed at our formalities.

"Be serious for a moment." She smiled tersely.

"Okay." I laughed once more. "Okay, okay."

She scooted closer to me in the car so my father and brother couldn't hear her. In a low voice, she said, "When you walk across that stage this afternoon, I want you to pause and look out into the crowd. Your inclination will be to think about where I, or your father or Ben are sitting, but I don't want you to do that. I want you to take a deep breath and consider this . . . your education is not an object to frame or a memory to look back on fondly. Your education is a tiny seed. It's a gift and if you water it, it will continue to grow . . . forever. The degree, the name of this fancy college printed on a piece of paper, or the job that may come along with it . . . those things are *not* evidence of a good education. Being self-aware, compassionate, humble, being able to see the world and the others in it through an unselfish lens, that's what an *educated* person does. They remind themselves that they have a choice, not just to do the right thing but also to *think* the right thing." She tapped the graduation cap I was holding in my lap and said, "You were an educated person long before this came along and I couldn't be prouder of that fact."

My mother had no formal education herself, but still she was hell-bent on Ben and me graduating from college. My parents even took out a second mortgage to pay for it. My mom worked for the Seattle City Clerk's Office for forty-two years, pushing paper. No one ever asked her about her job and she never talked about it. That day in the car she wasn't giving me the advice because she regretted her own life. She was preparing me for the realities of *any* life. At the time, I found it ironic that the person who was insistent on us going to college was essentially telling me that a degree, in and of itself, was meaningless. But I get it now. Before Ben died and before she got sick, my mother was the most educated and compassionate woman I knew. That version of her would have been proud of how I handled Beth today, even more than she'd be of me landing the show. Whenever I think about my mother before my brother died, it pains me knowing Alex and the boys never got to know her in that light.

Finally, I stand from my chair. The room goes quiet. "Thank you. It goes without saying that I am over the moon excited, but I'm also humbled and grateful."

Everyone stands, we shake hands, and the execs leave. Gina and Eli are standing over the table in the corner that was set up with coffee and pastries. I approach them once the execs are completely out of the room.

"I told you," Eli says.

Gina turns toward me and smiles. "I'm not blowing smoke, Dani—out of all the shows we're developing, this is the one I have the most faith in and the one I think I'll most enjoy myself."

"Thank you so much. That's never happened to me before. You guys must have sold it to them before this meeting was even planned."

"It was a no-brainer. Exactly the type of show we needed," Gina says.

"So, how do we start?" In the back of my mind I know I have to pick up the boys from Jose's house before it looks like I'm abandoning them.

"Go home," Eli says. I'm relieved. "I'll get the offices set up the rest of this week, hire a couple of interns, and get things going. Why don't you work from home, Dani, maybe get us a breakdown of episodes and some names so we can put together your writing dream team."

I suddenly realize that I don't have anything written beyond the pilot, and that I will need a group to work out a season of writing with me. "How many episodes did they order?"

Gina laughs. "Thirteen, Dani. They want the whole season. They'll probably want a second season too, considering how jazzed they were, but let's take this one step at a time. You have to choose some writers and then interview them."

"This makes me so happy."

"Did you think we'd ask for anything less?" Eli says, smirking. "We're thrilled to have you running this show."

"So I'm the showrunner?" What a dumb question.

"Yes, Dani, you're the creator and showrunner." Gina is laughing still. "I can't believe you're asking that. We're honored to have you. Now go celebrate!"

This is who I am. I'm not a fraud, not an imposter, I'm the real thing. At least for today, until the doubt creeps in again.

"All right," I say. "I'll get to work at home this week and see you guys here on Monday."

"Yep, your offices will be on the third floor. *Graceless* is going down, we're gonna take that space."

I'm spooning irony into my mouth right now and it's delicious.

"Okay," I say.

I reach out for a hug from Gina and then realize it's an awkward thing to do so I pull back. She smiles and then pulls me in for a huge embrace.

"Congratulations," she whispers. My eyes are welling up.

"I'll walk you out," Eli says.

We make our way down the hall toward the elevator. "I can't believe it," I say in a low voice.

Eli presses the down button on the elevator. "Believe it, it's happening and it's happening fast. I know you wrote the pilot in the time it takes me to brush my teeth, but you're not going to be able to pull off thirteen episodes all on your lonesome."

"I know that." We get into the elevator.

"Who are you thinking?" He's asking which writers I'm going to hire.

"To be honest, I'm thinking about Lars. He's brilliant and has such a good feel for it. It's too bad Beth Zinn poured gasoline all over his soul."

"I'm absolutely on board with that idea. Who else?"

"Are you suggesting I call him?"

"I'll call him if you won't. For god's sake, the man can't hide out in Northern California for the rest of his life."

We're walking into the dark parking structure. "I'm right here." I point to my 1987 Jeep Wagoneer.

"You still drive that thing?"

"Yeah, all my TV show money has gone to lawyers, mediators, and therapists." It actually went more to my mother's caretaking in the end, but I don't say that. "I am kidding a little. I love this car."

"It suits you," he says.

"Why? It's a gross polluter."

"Dani," he playfully scolds, "come here." He pulls me in for a hug and when he lets go, he looks me in the eyes and smiles, then takes a deep breath and says, "Lars is getting married . . . soon he's going to have to put this whole thing to bed . . . right alongside his husband."

My brain is lagging. Like that twirling pinwheel, just spinning and spinning.

"Wait. Lars is gay too? But we were so close, I would have known that." Oh my god, it's all coming together. "You are gay?" I point my index finger in Eli's face. "And Lars is gay, and you guys are getting married?"

"No, no, no, Dani. Yes, I am gay, and yes, he is too, but he's not marrying me," he says with a smirk.

"Lars talked about women," I argue. "He had a girlfriend. What was her name, Cara, Carla—"

"Keira," Eli says. "It didn't work out because Lars and I were, at the time . . . well, um . . . anyway . . . she found out. Around the same time my wife did." He sucks air in through his teeth. "Let's just say it wasn't pretty. Honestly, Dani, it's not my style to come out for other people, but I know Lars planned on telling you soon. Do me a favor, act surprised."

"So you two were together?"

"For a minute," he says. "He's too broody for me."

"Ha! He is very broody, isn't he?" I laugh.

My mouth is still open in shock and it feels like I haven't blinked in an hour. Eli is searching my eyes like he's tracking a tiny minnow in a pond.

"Breathe, Dani. Jesus. It's kind of his fault all that crap went down with you two and the affair rumors. He should have just come out and put an end to it . . . I guess he wasn't ready. Now he's getting married to some French vigneron in Napa who is insisting on a Page Six spread. I know he feels guilty about what happened with *Litigators,* like he could have prevented it, but we wouldn't be here now, would we?"

No! I would be on a tropical island somewhere, sunbathing alongside my twelve Emmys.

"I'm so confused," I say. "Also, how did you two know the other was—"

"It's a takes-one-to-know-one kind of thing. We got drunk the night you guys won your second Emmy. Remember that HBO after-party?"

"What? Did you guys do it in the bathroom?"

"No, Dani, we didn't do it in the bathroom. My wife left early. Lars and I ended up in an Uber together . . . I woke up the next morning in his bed. It wasn't weird at all. We kind of asked each other the history, and then both of us admitted we had been in denial for years. That was the beginning. We snuck around for a while, I got divorced, he dumped Keira, and then after all of that, we decided we liked being friends more. That's the story. It's not even worthy of its own episode, you know?"

"I'm going to call him. He'll tell me—he owes me."

"You should. He needs someone to put his feet to the fire anyway. He will tell you everything . . . and I know he'll write you the best episode of the season, after yours of course."

"All right, then. I gotta get going," I say. "I need to pick up my kids."

"So what happened with Alex?"

I shrug. "It's impossible for one person to be your every-thing."

"Touché," he says, smiling. "Let's hug it up, babe." We hug for a long time. "Welcome to D-land, my darling. It really is more fun. I'll be your wingman any day of the week."

"I don't think I'll be ready for that anytime soon, but I'll keep you in mind when I am."

As soon as I'm in the car, my phone rings. It's my divorce lawyer, Lisbeth. I've spoken to her a total of four times. Everything was cut-and-dried. Unbelievably, Alex and I didn't argue about any logistical or financial aspects of the divorce.

"Hi, Lisbeth."

"Hi, Dani. I just wanted to let you know Alex's lawyer said there was nothing else he wanted to contest. We got the papers you signed to the judge and he signed off on them. It was by far one of the easiest processes I've experienced."

I'm driving in the parking structure, totally confused at where to turn to exit. I end up at the top and just pull into a parking space.

"Well, it wasn't always easy with Alex."

"I know, of course, this is never easy, but you both seem to be on the same page with the kids. The finances are a simple fifty-fifty split. You both have your own retirement that's fairly equal, and when it comes time to sell the house, if you decide to buy one another out, it should be relatively straightforward. There's really nothing else."

I can't imagine selling that house. "What are you saying?"

"Your divorce is final, Dani. Once you sign, at least."

My mouth drops open. I can't breathe. Everything is whirling around—thoughts, memories, emotions. The last few months seem like a blur now that it's final. I'm stumbling over words in my head when I say, "I just landed my own TV show." The moment is awkward.

"Oh," she says.

"I mean, I'm telling you because I was going to celebrate tonight."

"Well, you can celebrate being single too?" Her voice gets

high at the end like she's trying to persuade a toddler to do something.

I'm reeling from mental exhaustion. "Okay, Lisbeth, thank you for everything." I pause and finally breathe. The finality is jarring. "One last thing . . . what did Alex say?"

"I don't talk to Alex, Dani. I talk to his lawyer."

"But he knows? That's what I'm asking. Alex knows it's final?"

"Yes." Her tone seems apologetic.

As I leave the parking lot and turn onto the main street, I feel confused and disoriented. Somehow, I make it home, but I don't remember driving there. *I need to get the boys.*

I pull out of our shallow, steep driveway and head to Jose's. I reach down for my phone and text Noah and Ethan, telling them to be outside and ready in five minutes. When I look up, it's too late. I hit my brakes, but I've already rolled into the car in front of me. It's a glossy, pearl-colored Infinity sports car.

FUCK.

It was just a bumper kiss, but I know I have to pull over. We're in the left turning lane. There are cars behind us, but the man in the car I hit decides to get out of his car while the light is green. People are honking behind me. He's walking toward my car.

I lean out the window. "Pull over into that strip mall. I'll follow you," I tell him.

It's obvious I have hit the wrong person. "What were you thinking?" He's yelling as he continues walking toward me. "Were you on your phone, damn teenager texting?"

Wow, I don't know if I should be gloating right now over the fact that he thinks I'm a teenager. I do have big sunglasses on. He looks to be in his sixties, maybe early seventies, well dressed. He's pissed. "You need to pull off and get your car out of the road," I say. "I'm not going to flee the scene, for Christ's sake. Not many people have 1987 Jeep Wagoneers in this town. Go park over there!" I point to the strip mall. A woman steps out of the passenger side. I didn't see her before because the back windows are heavily tinted.

"Get in the car, Bob, she's not going anywhere." The woman pulls her phone out and snaps a photo of me.

Bob walks back toward the driver's side. Just before he bends to get in, he yells, "You better follow me."

From where I'm at, I do not see any damage to his car, but by the time I pull into a space in the strip mall across the street, I am crying.

I get out and walk toward his car. He and the woman are bent over, staring at the back bumper. There's a black streak, which is weird, since I have a chrome bumper, and then I remember: *the bumper guards.* On my front bumper there are two black rubber rectangle guards . . . thank god! I love my car, even if it does leave a Sasquatch-sized carbon footprint. I don't drive much. That's my justification.

"Look at that!" He points to the streak. I'm still crying, but not making much sound. "You're gonna have to pay for that. Give me your insurance, missy."

Missy? I take a deep breath and pull myself together. "It's just a rubber smear."

"No, this is a brand-new car and now it's ruined 'cause you were on your phone, probably texting your boyfriend."

"Excuse me, sir." I pull my sunglasses down to reveal my well-earned wrinkles and puffy face from crying. "I am a grown woman, a mother of two. Please stop yelling at me."

I lick my thumb, bend, and start to wipe the smudge off his bumper. The woman, who I assume is his wife, says, "Well, would you look at that. It's coming off."

Meanwhile, Bob is still berating me, "You're gonna kill somebody someday . . ."

"Voilà! Good as new," I say as I stand and take a step back to inspect my work.

"I don't think so," Bob yells. I'm ignoring him as I take pictures of both his car and mine in case he reports me. "What if there is frame damage that we can't see?"

I look him straight in the eyes. Stray tears are still running down my face, but I'm breathing and speaking normally. "You're kidding me, right? I'm sorry I hit you. I barely bumped you. I know you hardly felt it. I am sorry though. There is no damage on your car or mine and everyone is good," I say, and then start to walk away. I'm secretly recording the whole thing on my phone.

"This is bullshit! I'm calling the police," he yells.

I look back and see the woman rolling her eyes. She opens the passenger-side door. "Get in the car, Bob. The poor girl apologized. She's crying. You're making a big stink about this—just get in the car!"

Bob does get in the car. He drives off, cutting into traffic and almost causing a far worse accident. Three cars honk at him as he speeds along down the road. I leave and head for Jose's, grateful again for my bumper guards. When I pull up to Jose's house, Noah and Ethan are sitting on the curb, looking bored and irritated. Noah gets in the front seat and Ethan in the back.

"Jeez, what took so long? I thought you were right down the street. I was about to order an Uber," Noah says with a snort laugh.

I glance at Ethan in the rearview mirror and see that he's smiling at Noah's comment.

"As if you could order an Uber," I say.

"It's a simple app, Mom." He does something on his phone and a second later he holds it up to me. "See."

"Yeah, but you need a credit card—"

We're at a stoplight. "Look," he says.

I'm familiar with the app. I see that within a few minutes he's ordered an Uber to head to our house.

"Are you kidding! Cancel that, Noah!"

"Okay, okay," He cancels it and then says, "You were the one who linked a credit card to our phones."

Right. I forgot about that.

"Yeah, we should have ordered an XL—like, you know, a black Escalade. We could've gone cruisin', yo!" Ethan says, chuckling from the backseat.

"No, yo! You could not have. I would have killed you myself. Do not ever order an Uber unless I explicitly instruct you to. God, I really am becoming useless, aren't I?"

"No, Mom, we're just messing with you," Noah says and then looks out the window. "Why were you late though?" I don't know why he won't look in my direction.

"I got into a little fender bender. Everything is fine, I just had to pull over and let this old curmudgeon of a man yell at me for a bit."

"That sucks," Ethan says. "Other than that, how was your day? What happened at the meeting?"

"You guys, despite the ornery old guy"—*and the divorce being final,* I think, but don't mention—"I had the best day *ever,* and now that I'm with my two favorite people in the world, it's even better."

Noah looks over and smiles at me. It's a serene smile. A mature one, like he senses the unspoken irony in my words.

"Tell us, Mom!" Ethan barks.

"I got my own TV show. It's all mine! I can't believe it."

"You did?" Ethan says. "That's awesome."

"Are we going to be rich now?" Noah asks.

"We're already rich, Noah. Compared to the rest of the

world, we're rich. And we're rich in ways that have nothing to do with money." My tone is authoritative.

"I know. I didn't mean it that way. I meant like really rich," he says.

"I feel like you're digging a deeper and deeper hole right now," I say to him with a laugh.

He laughs too and says, "Okay, okay."

I pull into our driveway, get the mail, and thumb through it. The boys have already scattered. "Do your homework!" I yell from the empty kitchen.

"Okay," they say in unison from somewhere down the hall.

After cleaning the house from top to bottom, finishing the laundry, and paying a few bills, I order a pizza and crack open a bottle of champagne. I make a to-do list for the next day. I will call Lars and grill him until he tells me everything.

I'm sitting at the breakfast bar sipping my bubbly in silence. *Is this celebrating? Is this what celebrating looks like now as a divorcée?*

I go through a mental list of whom I could call to come over and drink with me. I dial Alicia first.

"Hi, what's up?" She's curt.

"I got the show! Apple TV."

"Are you serious? Congratulations!" she says. "I wish I could chat with you right now but I'm about to go into a deposition."

"That's okay, I just wanted to tell you."

"You are a killer, babe. I knew you'd get it."

The moment I hang up, the doorbell rings. I get the pizza from the scrawny, young delivery boy, shut the door, drag my feet to the kitchen, and throw it on the counter. "Dinner!" I yell.

Ethan walks into the kitchen. "Jeez, why are you screaming?"

"Oh, I'm sorry. I thought you guys were in the backyard," I say.

"Is everything all right. I mean, you're happy, aren't you?"

"Yes, I am."

For some reason, it feels like a lie, and he can see right through me. Noah comes in and gets a slice and takes it back to his room without saying a word to anyone. "Do you want to eat on the couch with me and watch *The Walking Dead*?" I say to Ethan.

He loves that show but I'd never let them watch it—only Alex had.

"I thought—"

"It's okay," I say. "We're celebrating." I pour myself another glass of champagne and follow Ethan into the living room.

Two episodes of *The Walking Dead* in, and I have no idea what's going on in the show. My mind is somewhere else. Ethan and Noah go to bed a half hour earlier than usual and without me telling them to. *Are they avoiding me?*

I kiss them good night, head back to the kitchen, and pour the last of the champagne into my glass. One bottle down, all alone, with two children in the house. I know I have to stop after this glass, definitely shouldn't open another bottle, but . . . I'm *celebrating*. Still, I've always promised myself not to drink alone like this. I should just go to bed.

There's a text from Alex.

ALEX: Congratulations, Dani. Noah told me you got the show when I called the boys to say goodnight. I know how much this means to you. It's a really big deal. A game-changer for you.

I'm not sure how to respond. If I just say "Thank you," it will seem like I'm mad, which I actually am, but not really at Alex. I'm more irritated that Lars could have prevented the hell we went through. I'm sad that Alex and the boys only ever knew the sick and wicked side of my mother. I'm pissed at that old man for giving me a panic attack in the middle of the street. And I'm pissed at myself for a failed marriage . . . or I guess now it's a dead marriage. It's really over and it's all finally hitting me. When the good things happen, no matter how grateful you pretend to be, sometimes it's still not enough to get that small sip of air you need to not drown in the bad things. The waves crashing over me are just too big for the small boat that the show represents. I'm still getting pummeled by wave after wave.

> ME: Thank you, Alex. It's so very bittersweet that it happened today, the day our divorce was final.

I am crying now, sobbing. Tears are flooding my phone screen.

> ME: So, so bittersweet. I would be celebrating with you. That's the one thing we were NOT horrible at. Celebrating together.

I see the bubbles next to the text, indicating Alex is responding.

Then nothing.

17

untying your knots

ALEXANDER

I can hear the derision in her words, but there's also something else. Is it resignation or exhaustion, or just raw emotion? I don't know, but I feel it too. I know her like I know myself. I know that whether she's resentful, mad, or sad, no matter what, she is definitely crying right now.

There's a resounding silence in the apartment. It's deafening, constant. Dani always put music on. Twenty-four/seven there was music playing in our house. I got used to it. Now the quiet sounds like noise.

My thumb is hovering over the letters. I don't know exactly how to respond to her.

My first text was a big step for me. I was trying to be the bigger person, but now it feels like she's guilting me. There is no question that I am happy for Dani. Our turmoil does not take away from the fact that she is a talented writer. And even more than that, she's a workhorse. She will be the hardest worker on the show, like she has been on every other show, except now she'll get the well-deserved recognition.

Thirty minutes have gone by now and I have not responded. I know I need to say something.

> ME: I agree, Dani, it is bittersweet. I'm sorry the cards fell this way. No one planned for it all to happen on this day.

I can hear her snarky response . . . *I didn't say anyone did, Alex.*

I decide to add another text. I'm not just playing nice. It's true, she deserved the show.

> Me: I wish you the best nonetheless. I know more than anyone how much you deserve this show.

The next thing I know, my alarm is going off. I had fallen asleep, fully clothed, with my phone in hand. It's four-thirty in the morning, the usual time I wake up. Most days I go for a run, or hit the gym near the clinic for a quick workout, but today I hit Snooze. I hit it over and over again until I am running late for my 9 A.M. patient. This is so unlike me.

For twenty minutes I scramble around, frantically getting ready. Somehow, I make it out the door at ten minutes to nine. Normally ten minutes would be enough time to get to the clinic, but it's rush hour. I'm parking twenty minutes after nine.

Jenna, my very pregnant clinical supervisor, greets me at the back door. She's due any day now and I still need to fill her position. Jenna was the one person who was pretty shocked and disappointed when she found out Dani and I were getting divorced. I think she always looked up to Dani. In a strong and beautiful way, they respected each other, and they complimented each other often. I marveled at that display of confidence and mutual admiration. Jenna's been running the clinic for six years. I don't know what I'll do when she goes on maternity leave.

"Wow, this is a first. You have Ms. Olstein in room two."

"Is she pissed?" I whisper.

"She's always pissed. Don't sweat it. Oh, you do know that there are four people waiting to be interviewed by you at ten, right?"

"Interviewed by me?" I say.

"Yes, temps for my position."

"Oh . . . don't you just want to choose the person?"

She reaches up and straightens my collar. She's scowling. "Have you been drinking?"

"No!" I'm marginally offended.

"Alex, you have to pick someone from that lot out there today. They're all qualified, I've vetted them, it's just up to you now. Get a feel for their personalities. Before you do anything, though, grab a breath mint from my desk. Also, you have a smudge on the back of your pants." She looks dumbfounded as she says this. Dani did not take care of me that way. I'm meticulous about grooming and looking professional, but I've been way off lately. It's obviously because of the divorce. For the record, though, aside from washing my clothes, Dani didn't iron or pick out my clothes and she certainly didn't groom me, for god's sake. Still, I know what Jenna is thinking. "What is going on with you?" she says. "I've never even seen a day's worth of growth on your face like this before."

"My divorce was final yesterday. I'm not implying Dani did these things for me, just that I've been going through a lot. Missing a day of shaving does not make me a bum."

"I'm sorry, Alex," she says, but she doesn't seem truly apologetic or compassionate. "Maybe you don't realize this, but sometimes marriage is like two fruit trees. It might appear they're doing their own thing, but take one away and the other won't produce."

Oh no, no marriage analogies, please.

"I'm going to produce, Jenna!" I say a little too loud.

She starts laughing. "Oh my god, Alex. Be quiet. Go get in there before Ms. Olstein files a complaint."

I throw my backpack in my office and scurry down the hall to room 2. When I'm finished looking at Ms. Olstein's foot for the thousandth time, I head back toward my office. Jenna has spotted me and is now following me down the hall. "Okay, should I send the first temp in?" she says.

"Sure."

Taking a look in the mirror on the wall, I try to pull myself together. I'm not exactly the picture of an upstanding boss at the moment. I know I only have about thirty minutes with all of these people before my next patient appointment.

In walks a young woman, attractive, wearing glasses, her dark hair up in a loose bun. There's a hint of Dani from her twenties in there somewhere.

"This is Kate Littlefield," Jenna says.

She reaches out and shakes my hand. I'm not sure what to say, I'm a little out of it. I haven't interviewed anyone in years.

"Nice to meet you," I say. "You can have a seat."

"Thank you," she says, and sits.

Jenna hands me a folder with some handwritten notes on it.

Graduated from Berkeley. Business degree. Wants to start a free clinic. Nice. Not a criminal. References all checked out.

"Hmm," I say and look up at her. She's poised, eyebrows arched, waiting for me to say something. "So why do you want to start a free clinic? You a masochist or something?" I smile. It was a terrible joke.

She just blinks at me and then starts nervously laughing. "Um . . . um—" she says before I cut her off.

"You're hired, okay? Let's not torture the rest of the people out in the waiting room. I mean, this is just a temp job."

"Okay. Thank you," she says. She's very nice.

"You're welcome. When can you start training with Jenna?"

"Now?" She shrugs her shoulders.

"Perfect. Jenna!" I yell as I see her walking by the door.

She pops her head and giant belly into the room. "How's it going?"

"Jenna, I hired Kate. Can you start training her now?"

"Wow, okay. You don't want to see the others?"

"No sense in putting them through the ringer."

"Great, I'll let them know," Jenna says. "Kate, follow me."

Hours go by, patients are in and out. Kate is already manning the front desk of our small clinic while Jenna and I are going over patient files in my office.

"I left a few folders in the front, let me go grab them," I say to Jenna.

I'm in the hall looking through a stack of folders. I can see the back of Kate's head from where I am, but I can't see the other side of the front desk. I hear the door jingle.

That's weird, I don't have any more patients today.

"Hello, do you have an appointment to see the doctor?"

"The doctor?" It's Dani's voice. "Yeah, tell him his five o'clock is here."

I dart around the corner and come face-to-face with Dani.

"You have them calling you 'doctor' now?" she says with her signature condescending humor.

"Kate is new, as of today, Dani. She's filling in for Jenna, who is about to pop, if you recall." I look at Kate, who appears confused. "Kate, this is Dani, my . . . my . . ."

"Baby mama," Dani says with a laugh. She seems chipper, which is odd.

"What are you doing here?" I ask.

"Nice to see you too, Alex. Am I not allowed here now?"

"Let's go talk in my office." Dani is carrying a large Target bag. I take in her appearance as I follow her down the long hall. From behind, I barely recognize her. She's thinner, with the light brown hair that I don't think I'll ever get used to.

"Jenna!" she says exuberantly as she enters my office. Her arms are outstretched. Jenna stands and approaches Dani for a hug.

"Hi, oh my god, you look amazing! Your hair looks fantastic!"

Dani shrugs with feigned humility. "I don't know if I'm gonna keep it, but it's fun for now."

Fun. Why would she say it's fun?

"So is it true what they say? Blondes have more fun?"

"Enough with the love fest, ladies," I say.

Dani looks at me and scowls, "What's your problem?"

I just stare. She turns her attention back to Jenna. "Not sure I would call this blonde, but anyway, I've always thought that redheads have the most fun. But look at you! You are *glowing*."

Jenna has red hair and she isn't glowing, she's perspiring. I'm exasperated. This is exhausting. "Jenna, will you give us a minute? Actually, you can head out, we can finish this training tomorrow," I say.

Dani and Jenna hug one last time. "I want to hold that baby soon," Dani says.

"Of course. Good night, guys."

"She's such a pro," Dani says to me.

"Yeah," I say. "She acts like she's not even pregnant. By your third, I guess it's old news." I catch myself, realizing that Dani's third pregnancy ended with a second-term miscarriage. She's staring at me, her smile fallen. "I'm sorry, Dani. I wasn't thinking when I said that."

"Thinking about what?"

This is where I start to lose my footing with her. I can't read her expression and I don't know how to tread. Is she testing me? Or did she really not get the connection? For so many years I have held my tongue. In this situation, I would normally shrug and change the subject, but I'm no longer trying to avoid her wrath. I don't need to anymore. I can leave, or tell her to leave if she gets pissed.

"About your third pregnancy," I say. She's still just looking at me, her expression inscrutable. "The little girl we lost." My tone is sympathetic but still guarded.

Her eyes well up. "It's nice to hear you acknowledge her." Dani starts to break down a little, but I can tell she's fighting it viciously. We didn't name the babies we lost. Our girls. For some reason, it never felt right. I don't know what to do with myself. For a moment, I take stock of my own feelings. I imagine having a daughter. Dani is so close to our boys, sometimes I find myself envious of her connection to them. I wonder if having a daughter would feel like having someone in my corner. A strange, empty feeling comes over me. My heart races, the blood drains from my face. I feel tears start to come, but I shake them away.

Is this grief?

She sees me swallow in a slightly exaggerated way, which is something I do when I'm nervous or emotional. She cocks her head to the side. I think she's surprised. Finally, she sniffles and breaks the silence. "I brought you another set of sheets. In case the others were ruined."

"They're not ruined. Maybe stained."

"Well, it might be easier to have two sets. We can just replace them every time we trade places."

"Why would we need to do that? Seems like a lot of sheet-washing."

"I guess it doesn't matter. Just throw them in the cabinet at the apartment. They were on sale and I was right down the street. The boys are at practice. I have to get back. Have a good weekend." She sets the bag down and heads for the door. "Bye, Alex," she says without turning around.

My stomach tightens. The pain of our history is too much for either of us to tolerate.

Later, I find myself dozing off in my clothes again, in the lonely, quiet apartment, my phone in hand, waiting for something . . . or someone . . . to break this deafening silence. If anyone ever asks me when it was that I realized I was truly alone in the world, I will tell them it was this moment right now.

~

Getting to the eighteenth hole of the golf course was a complete blur. I barely remember waking up this morning, but here I am, on a Saturday, finishing up a round of golf with Brian. I do know he's been talking incessantly about inflation trends in the twenty-first century. It's easily the most somniferous topic I can think of, so maybe that's why I don't feel awake.

"You should record yourself talking about this and then sell it as a cure for insomnia," I say.

We get into the golf cart and head down the fairway looking for our drives. Mine is somewhere out of bounds. At this point, I'm over golfing. Brian's perfect two-hundred-yard drive is right in the middle of the beautifully manicured fairway.

"You don't think it's interesting how wildly unstable inflation is?" he asks.

"No, but that's okay. Are you going to write about that in something?" We're at Brian's ball. I drop a ball next to it. He gives me a look. I roll my eyes and say, "I'm not going looking for my ball. Just add one million to my score, I've already broken a hundred."

"That's no fun, man." He swings the club, laying his ball up about two feet from the hole. I shake my head. Brian is one of those people who is good at everything but too scatterbrained to care. "No, I'm not going to write about it. It would be pretty boring, wouldn't it?" he says.

I swing. The ball floats into a small pond to the left of the green. It's far enough away from the hole to be odd. "What the—" I say.

"It's amazing. You will find water no matter where it is," Brian says.

I let Brian finish the round. I don't think I've ever given up like this before, but I've lost two sleeves of balls and I'm calling it a day. We head back to the clubhouse in the golf cart.

"You want to get dinner here?" I say.

"No way. Let's go home and change and go somewhere good. This place is stuffy."

He's right, it is. "Where do you want to go?" I ask.

"You have a bunch of cool restaurants right by the apartment, right?"

There is a bit of a bar scene a couple blocks away, but I don't really want to mention that. I'm afraid Brian's "being single" rhetoric will make its way back into our conversation.

"Commerce and G? Is that place cool?"

He's referring to a trendy American foodie haven by the apartment, where the bartenders are those extremely hip know-it-alls with mustaches and suspenders, who describe in great detail the molecular weight and peaty undertones of some cheap Tennessee whiskey they charge thirty-five dollars a shot for. That's how cool it is.

"A little too cool," I say.

"Let's try it. Who cares if we're the oldest guys there?" he says.

We won't be if we go early enough. It does turn into quite a scene after ten, but I plan on being in bed by then, so I agree to meet him there.

Back at the apartment, I shower and get dressed, but don't bother shaving. I throw on a gray sweater, pants, and some light blue Vans slip-ons. I look in the mirror at my two days of growth and intentionally casual attire and realize that I'm just the older version of those tool bags with mustaches. I'm the Silicon Valley hipster circa 2010, trying way too hard to look like I'm not trying.

I head out the door before I drive myself crazy. Walking on the street feels good. When I get to the restaurant, Brian is already seated at the bar, nibbling on Marcona almonds and sipping something that looks expensive.

"Hey, buddy. I ordered some apps," he says. "Have a seat. Whaddya want to drink?" He motions for the female bartender to come over. She looks pissed, but I know she's not, it's just part of the style here.

"Can I just get a vodka soda?" I say to the bartender.

She stares at me for too long.

"They don't have vodka here," Brian says.

"Why?" I say directly to the girl.

"Because we only serve food and liquor that tastes good." She will not crack a smile.

"Oh, okay. Why don't you make me your specialty, then?" I say.

"Great," she hums a vague tune as she turns around and gets to work.

"Don't be intimidated," Brian says.

"Me? I'm not. I just think this whole act is stupid."

"Try to enjoy yourself." Brian is looking past me in shock as he says, "Holy shit."

"What?" I turn to see what he's staring at. There's a group of five people mulling around the hostess stand.

"That woman. She goes to my gym. She's Puerto Rican. She's so hot. Her name is Valeria. I can't believe she's here. I asked her out a few weeks ago. She said yes and then stood me up."

Brian is an average-looking dude, but he seems to be a successful serial dater, so I'm surprised. I don't think he gets stood up very often.

Valeria spots Brian and then looks at me and smiles. She holds one finger up, gesturing she'll be over in a minute to talk to us. She's speaking with a distinguished-looking older man, but she seems distracted. She is a striking beauty; I can see why Brian would want to date her.

Brian says, "Good, she's coming over. I can give her a little piece of my mind."

We wait for what seems like forever. I put in an order for an overpriced, fancy cheeseburger and slug my second twenty-five-dollar cocktail while Brian silently watches Valeria chatting.

Finally, she makes her way to us. She really is gorgeous. A dead ringer for Rosario Dawson.

"Brian, hi." He doesn't get up, so she leans down and gives him an awkward hug. She turns to me and sticks her hand out. "Hi, I'm Valeria."

I shake her hand. "Alex. Nice to meet you."

Brian is giving her the death stare. Completely deadpan he

says, "Would you like a drink, Valeria? How 'bout a pint of *thanks for the phone call?*"

I nearly spit out my gin-absinthe concoction. I'm laughing while Valeria is smiling apologetically toward Brian.

"I am sorry, Brian. I was going to text you. Something came up at work and I've been slammed for the last few weeks. This is the first time I've been out in a long time."

"The last few weeks? What are you, an astronaut? You work for the Secret Service? KGB? What could it possibly be?" he says, chuckling.

"I'm actually a pediatric oncologist. Those are some of my colleagues over there." That definitely silenced the room, so to speak.

"Oh," Brian says. "Kids with . . ."

She nods. "Cancer. Yes, Brian, I am a doctor for kids with cancer."

"Ah, I see," he says.

"Gin?" I hand her my drink, which was served in a crystal pink antique glass. I'm surprised she takes it. It was sort of a joke.

She takes a tiny sip and hands it back to me. "Mmm, that's good. I think I'll have that; what is it?"

"It's called a 'Lip-reader,'" I say.

She glances at the menu on the bar and laughs. "It's an homage to *Seinfeld*. They're all named after episodes."

"Yeah, it's clever," I say. I'm extremely attracted to her.

She smiles at me and says to the bartender, "I'll take three more of these," then to me, "Mind if I sit with you gentlemen for a bit? I've been with those people all day."

"Of course," I say. I scoot one stool over so she can have mine. She's dressed in a white silk blouse and black slacks; it's classy, but not stuffy. There's something elegant and refined about her. I can't help but compare her energy to Dani's. She's calm and seemingly grounded, compared to Dani's ceaseless buzzing. Dani's personality shifts from one extreme to the other. Either she's mentally absent and floating around in her own headspace, imagining her stories, or she's a busy bee fueled by nervous energy. It's exhausting.

"So," Valeria says, "how do you two know each other?"

I take the lead because Brian is pouting. "Brian used to work with my wife, a long time ago."

Valeria glances at my ringless left hand.

Brian corrects me, "Ex-wife."

"Right," I say.

"So, you guys are just getting out for a drink and some food?"

"Yep," I say, and hand her the menu. "Do you want something?"

A moment later the bartender sets my burger down in front of me. "That looks delicious," she says.

"I'll share," I tell her.

There is something happening. It's easy with her. She's not fussy. I cut the burger in half and she unabashedly grabs her portion and takes a giant bite.

"Mmm, this is heaven. I was starving." She's charming and delightful.

"Are you two having fun over there?" Brian says. Valeria shifts to create more of a semicircle so we can all talk to each other at the bar.

The three of us continue ordering drinks and fall into an easy conversation about everything from the Dodgers to the healthcare industry to having children. She's in her forties, was divorced several years ago . . . no kids of her own. Her work keeps her busy and she considers her patients her kids. It feels like a friendship is forming. I like this woman, but I don't really feel like flirting with her. I'm not ready for that, even though I can tell she's more attracted to me than to Brian. He's clearly given up and switched to water anyway.

The restaurant bar is closing and they're basically shooing us out the door. On the street, Valeria is looking at her phone.

"I need to order an Uber," she says.

Brian makes one last attempt. "I can take you."

"Where do you live?" she asks.

"I'm like two miles away."

"I live all the way down in Redondo," she says.

Brian squints. "But the gym—"

"Yeah, I work in the medical building next to that gym a couple days a week. My house and regular practice are in Redondo though. It's okay, I can get an Uber. I planned on it anyway. I just have to pee so badly. I'm gonna go back in and use the restroom."

"Okay," Brian says. "Nice seeing you." He hugs her. I stand there, not really knowing what to do.

Without hesitation, she walks up to me and reaches out for a hug. "It was nice meeting you, Alex." I can feel her slip something into my back pocket. "There's my business card. If you ever want to chat over drinks again."

"Oh, yes, thanks," I say. "It was nice meeting you too." I point down the street. "My apartment is a couple of blocks away, so I'm off. Bye, guys."

Valeria heads back into the restaurant, Brian to his car, and I start my stroll for home. Well, the apartment.

About one minute into my walk, I hear, "Alex!"

It's Valeria. She's walking toward me. "Hey," I say.

"The bar's closed, they won't let me in, and my Uber is still twenty minutes away."

She's staring at me, waiting for me to respond. "Okay," I say, a little dumbfounded.

"Do you have a bathroom I can use?"

"Oh my god, sorry, yes, I do. I didn't know what you were asking me."

She laughs lightly. "Yeah, I'm about to pee my pants."

"Sorry, let's go, it's right up here."

We walk briskly to the stairs that go up to my apartment. I hesitate, wondering if this is okay. Would Dani be fine with it?

"Hey there, Dani and Alex," comes a voice. "Off to do the graveyard shift. Have fun, kiddos!" It must be Candy. She's walking by. *Shit.*

"Bye, Candy," I say weakly as Valeria and I head up the stairs. I turn to her, "I'll explain."

She laughs again. "You don't have to explain anything to me."

She's easygoing. Inside, I lead her to the bathroom and then walk back down the hallway toward the kitchen. She comes out a couple of minutes later and stops to look at the pictures Dani has put up.

"Have you heard of a nesting apartment?" I say.

"Yes, I have. I figured it was something like that. It's cool you guys get along well enough to do this for the kids."

She's intuitive and observant.

"Well, it's still in its trial phase."

I want to know everything about this woman, but I'm uncomfortable and it's showing with my awkward silences. She holds her phone up.

"Oh no, what is going on? Damn. My Uber was canceled. Another twenty minutes. I'm tempted to start walking." She laughs.

"No, it's okay. You can wait here."

She glances at the bottle of red wine Dani left on the counter. "That's a good wine, a good year for a pinot."

"Yes," I say. I am frozen. The bottle is open, still has three-quarters left. "Would you like a glass?"

"Wow, for moment there I thought I was going to have to send smoke signals."

I laugh, then walk over, pour two glasses, and hand one to her. We're still standing near the kitchen counter.

"Yeah, this is a good wine," I say, though I have no clue what I'm talking about.

"Well, let's enjoy it. I'll get the Uber in a few minutes."

I glance at the clock on the wall. It's 12:45. I don't think I've been up this late since the nineties, but strangely, I'm not tired.

She walks toward the record collection, and I quickly move into gear. "I'll put some music on." I'm trying to distract her from the records. I turn on the Bluetooth speaker to an old jazz station. "Have a seat." I gesture toward the couch and take a seat myself.

She walks to the front of the couch to sit next to me so I instinctively stand to be polite. We're face-to-face. She moves an inch closer. "Good manners," she says in a low voice as she bends to set her wine down on the table.

She's so close to me now. We're standing still and quiet in front of the couch. It will be weird if I don't kiss her, but I cannot bring myself to make the move. She leans up and kisses me instead. In the moment it feels normal, just a little different than Dani, but I can hardly remember kissing Dani anymore anyway.

I move my hand to cup the back of her neck. She makes a small, satisfied sound. She's getting more into it, her hands squeeze my biceps tightly.

Pulling away, I take a breath and say, "That was nice." I don't know what possesses me to do this, but I pause for a moment and look down at her feet. She's wearing sandaled heels and she has the *weirdest* toes I've ever seen. They look like my ninety-year-old grandmother's fingers.

Why did I look? She takes a step forward, closing the last little bit of distance between us. The toes keep flashing in my mind. Candy breezing by thinking Valeria was Dani keeps flashing in my mind. My kids keep flashing in my mind.

I kiss her again. She's pressing her body against me, but suddenly I'm entirely not in the mood. When she realizes this, she moves her hand down to touch me.

Oh my god! It's not going to work.

All I can think about is that if her toes look like old fingers, what do her hands look like? When she realizes nothing is happening, she stops.

I step back and breathe in and out dramatically. "You are stunning," I say, out of breath.

"You think?" she says with a half smile, a condescending look.

"I'm sorry. I am so in my head right now. I just got out of a twenty-two-year-long relationship." I search for something else to say, but I've got nothing.

Valeria seems to be contemplating something. I watch her thinking for a moment. She *is* gorgeous. If I wanted to, I could make this all happen right now.

"Alex, I'm established, in my forties . . . and I've been divorced. I'm not looking for that. In fact, I probably wouldn't have even returned your call after tonight."

I jerk my head back, feeling oddly wounded. Despite what she said, she's closing the distance between us again.

"Uh-huh," I say. It finally hits me. It's just sex. I'm going to have sex with this woman and then never see her again. I bend and kiss her again, this time for a long time. I'm thinking about where I'm going to do this. On the bed Dani will sleep in tomorrow? On the sheets she washed for me? In the apartment she told me was off-limits?

Pulling away again, I say, "I'm sorry." But now I am turned on and she knows it.

She smiles with compassion. "I understand, Alex. I really do." She cups my cheek with her hand. "You'll get there. Just not tonight." She reaches down to the table and picks up her phone.

"You don't have to—"

"Oh perfect! There's an Uber right here," she says as she picks up her purse and starts walking toward the door.

This is like my dream woman. I can't believe I'm letting her go. She is so understanding, easygoing, calm, beautiful, sexy, and she doesn't want a relationship, but I cannot get out of my headspace enough to sleep with her.

She opens the door to leave, then turns around. She's looking back at a photo on the table by the door. "I remind you of her, don't I?"

"No, no, that's not it." *Dani has much prettier toes than you.* Valeria doesn't remind me of Dani. The only similarity is that she's witty and intelligent and has dark hair. Valeria's demeanor is completely different, but I can see why she would think that after seeing the picture of Dani and the boys hiking the Zion Narrows. It was taken from far away and it just shows Dani's figure and dark hair, but you can't really see her face. I don't want Valeria to take my behavior the wrong way. "Maybe we can try to get together—"

"No thank you, Alex. It really isn't you. You're charming, a blast to be around, and I'm clearly attracted to you, but I just do not have time to date and it's not fair of me to lead anyone on."

I smile, strangely relieved. "Okay. Well, again, nice meeting you."

We hug, she leaves, and I go straight to bed. It's been a long day. For the first time in many years the smell of Dani on the pillow is comforting.

18

you're kidding me

DANIELLE

It's 9 A.M. Sunday morning and I'm packed and eager to go to the apartment. It's not that I want to get away from the kids, it's that I don't want to wait on Alex. I don't want him to dictate what time the whole switcheroo is going to happen, so I text him first.

> ME: I'm leaving the boys alone for a bit. Gonna go to Sprouts then the apartment. Are you close?
>
> ALEX: I'm two minutes away but the cleaning people are on their way to the apartment. They'll probably be there for a while.
>
> ME: It's fine. Leaving now.
>
> ALEX: Copy.

I hate when he texts *copy*. The boys aren't even phased by me leaving, so I kiss them and leave the house. Instead of going to Sprouts first, I head to the apartment to see what food is left in the cabinets. When I arrive, Candy is walking into the complex at the same time. It looks like she's returning from working a night shift.

"Hi," she says cheerily.

"Hi," I say, and slow down to walk beside her.

"Geez, girlie, you change your hair color like I change my underwear."

"Hmm?" I say absently, not really paying attention.

"Light last week, then dark, now light again. Must cost you a fortune."

"No, just once," I say with a smile.

"Doggone it, really? I could swear your hair was dark last night when I saw you two."

My stomach drops. I stop walking. My heart is beating out of my chest. I feel like I'm going to pass out. Candy stops next to me on the walkway.

I can barely get the words out. My body is weak. "That wasn't me last night, Candy."

She's staring, trance-like. She cocks her head to the side. Her voice gets quieter and slower, "I'm not following you, honey."

I take a deep breath in and exhale audibly. "God, this is hard. Alex and I are divorced. We share this apartment on the days we aren't with the kids. They stay at our family home. I haven't been here for four days, Candy. He and I won't ever be here at the same time."

"Oh," she says, wearing a penitent look. "Oh, honey, I'm—"

"It's okay. You didn't know." I'm having some weird crisis. There's still hope in me that it wasn't Alex she saw. I hope the first days he was at the apartment he didn't break the one rule we made. "Are you sure it was him? I mean, I don't care, but are you sure?"

"Yeah, sweetie, I'm sure. They went up the stairs to your apartment. I'm sorry."

"It's his business, it's just that he's not supposed to have women here." I start crying quietly. I can't stop the tears.

"It's hard, sweets. I've been divorced twice. Would have been three times, but the last asshole dropped dead in line at the supermarket. But the first, that was the hardest. I really loved him."

"Then why'd you get a divorce?" I'm sniffling, but genuinely curious to hear her answer.

"You don't always stop loving 'em just 'cause you can't stand 'em."

She's right. "Ain't that the truth," I whisper. In this moment, I decide that I'm going to have to adopt a different persona if I'm going to be a divorcée. I stand up straighter and put my shoulders back. "Thanks, Candy. I'm gonna be fine."

We hug and then I head up to my apartment, wondering what went on in there the night before. I'm hoping he just hung out with someone. I don't want to think about his sexual escapades in the bed I sleep in, or the couch I sit on. I would never have pinned Alex for a guy who picks someone up and then screws them the same night, but I guess I don't really know him anymore. Who knows, maybe he's been seeing her for a while. We've essentially been divorced for a long time.

I notice the cleaning people are arriving and walking toward the stairs, so I go inside and leave the door open. It's not messy. There aren't bras hanging from the ceiling fan. I doubt it even needs cleaning. I walk into the bedroom and notice Alex has taken the sheets off the bed and left the new sheets folded for the cleaning people to put on.

Wasn't he the one who said we didn't need to change the

sheets? I guess when you're boinking some woman all night in the bed I said was off-limits, it's the least you can do.

The dirty sheets are piled in the laundry basket. I can't believe he left them for the cleaning people to wash. He should have taken them and washed them himself. I hate him.

"Hello, ma'am?" says one of the cleaning women.

"Hi, yes, actually, there's nothing really to do here," I tell her. "You can go." I have time on my hands to clean the tiny apartment. It'll keep my mind off things.

About every three seconds I get an overwhelmingly nauseous feeling like a relentless set of waves. I shouldn't care. I'm divorced. The cleaning crew is gone. I close the door and head back into the bedroom. I'm just staring at the bed, furious.

Whenever I get down about anything, I throw myself into something else as a distraction. I cannot waste this day crying, so I walk over to the laundry basket. I'm going to take the sheets to the washers and go to Sprouts. I can handle this. I don't want to see the dirty sheets and imagine what might have happened on them. I want to wash them and put them away.

As I reach in, I notice Alex has also left his pants. I'm sure it's a mistake. He wouldn't leave this for me, but he did have a late night, so maybe he was counting on the cleaning people to take care of it.

When I pull out the pants, something falls onto the floor. *What is that? A business card?*

It belongs to a Dr. Valeria Rivera, a pediatric oncologist in Redondo Beach. This has to be her from last night, or maybe not. Maybe he met her at the hospital? He does know a lot of doctors. I turn the card around and see she has scribbled, *Call me, Alex. I had a great time tonight.*

I've always had visceral, emotional reactions, but I didn't expect to vomit on the floor. My head is spinning with scenarios. I clean up the mess while chanting in my head, *Do not sleuth. Do not look her up, Dani. Do not do it unless you want to cry all day. You already know she's a doctor. That's enough. Why couldn't she be a bimbo? Uneducated? A barfly?*

It's not so much that I am jealous of the woman or mad about him bringing her to the apartment, though that does piss me off; I'm more jealous of Alex, on a competitive level. Why is he finding someone first? Why does it seem easy for him? Oh right, because men look distinguished as they age and women just look old.

As if I'm being controlled like a marionette, I walk over to the desk in the corner, sit down, and open my computer. I can't help it.

I google *Dr. Valeria Rivera.*

I hate what I am seeing so much that I'm squeezing my hands into fists so tightly, my nails are piercing my skin. She's not just a doctor for kids with cancer, she's a highly revered doctor . . . and she's *beautiful.* I click on her picture to zoom in.

Why am I doing this to myself?

There is something innately sexy about her. She has long dark hair, big full lips, and flawless skin. Surprisingly, I'm not crying. I just feel sick to my stomach. I zoom in more and notice she has fairly large ears. *That's what I'll focus on.*

I dial Alicia.

"Hello, babe."

"Do you have a minute?" I say in a dull tone.

"Yeah, I'm at the office, shoving food in my face. Working on a freakin' Sunday. I can take a break for a bit, though. What's up?" she says.

Everything spills out at lightning speed, "Alex fucked a hot doctor at the apartment that was supposed to be off-limits. In our bed."

Alicia is silent. She's never silent. "Dani . . ." she says cautiously, but I stop her.

"Is this what he was waiting for?"

"It's going to be hard at first. Be clear with him that it can't happen at the apartment anymore. That is basic respect. Alex can afford a hotel room."

My eyes start to water. I'm feeling sorry for myself. "It *is* basic respect."

"How did you find out?" she asks.

"The neighbor thought she was me and mentioned seeing me with him last night and then I found the woman's business card in the pocket of his pants. I googled her."

"Dani, why were you looking through his clothes?"

"I wasn't. His pants were in the laundry. The card fell out. Her writing was on it, saying she had fun and to call her."

"Ouch."

"Yeah," I say as tears finally escape my eyes. I can tell Alicia has stopped eating.

"He's going to get a girlfriend, Dani. Alex isn't the hookup type."

"Apparently, he is," I say. "She has massive ears though. You know what? She's not hot at all. I mean, her ears are like a deformity, they're so big. I have an image running through my mind on a constant loop. She's standing on a building ledge with a fucking feather on her nose, about to take flight."

"I think that's an okay image to have on a loop, if you have to have one right now," Alicia says.

I know what she's hinting at, and of course she's right that I'm *actually* picturing Alex having sex with Doctor Dumbo.

"She's a pediatric oncologist, Alicia. She's a goddamn saint and I'm over here making up piddling stories for a living."

"Stop it. You have an important job."

"No, I really don't. It's inconsequential and trivial in the big scheme of things. I'm paid to lie! It's so juvenile, it's embarrassing."

"Dani, you guys are divorced. He's going to date. He's going to probably get serious with someone else and she will meet the boys, and who knows, you might even like her."

I can't handle any of this.

"Lars is gay. Isn't that weird?"

"Really? Well, I guess now there's no question that you weren't cheating."

"Did you think I was?" I say.

"Not really."

I'm offended that she had even a small doubt. "I have to go. I need to wash the sex sheets. I know he's going to date, Lish. I just didn't want him to do it here."

"Be clear with him, but don't berate him. Call me tomorrow."

I hang up and open Facebook on my computer to find two new messages. Both are from Jacob Powell.

Jacob: Hey, Dani! How are you? You look great! I see Alicia and Mark once in a while. Hope you're doing well.

A few days later, he wrote again.

Jacob: I saw Alicia today. Sorry to hear about the divorce. Feel free to call or text anytime if you need an ear or shoulder.

That's not exactly what I need right now, but I'm sure he's flexible. He's attached his contact info, so I text him before I can give myself a moment to hesitate.

Me: Hi, Jacob. Thanks for the message on FB. Shot in the
    dark, but care to get a drink?

He replies almost instantly.

Jacob: Yeah, definitely. Tonight?
Me: Why not?
Jacob: Want to meet me on the Westside? I'm about to jump
    in the water to surf for a bit.

I haven't even seen him yet and I already want to lick salt
water off his chest. It's been a while.

Me: Sounds good. 5 pm? Water Grill?
Jacob: It's gonna be a nice sunset. See you at 5.

What just happened? That was too easy. I'm already nervous.
I contemplate calling Alicia, but I don't want her to know.
Despite the nerves, I have a new jolt of energy.

~

I'm running twenty minutes late, but that's normal for me. I
texted Jacob, letting him know, and he said he was sitting at the
bar. I'm relieved. I don't want to have a romantic dinner with
him, don't want to sit and stare at him from the other side of a
little quaint table overlooking the ocean. This is just a drink. No
different than a friend or colleague.

As I speed down the street, I think about the day Jacob broke
up with me so many years ago. He told me I was too serious, and
we were too young. He said he liked me so much that it scared
him because he wasn't ready to settle down. I thought about

him for years after that, even after I had started dating Alex. I was heartbroken because the relationship with Jacob was meaningful to me and he'd acted the same way in the beginning. But in the end, he didn't really care. It made him seem duplicitous. He seemed madly in love one day but had no problem breaking up with me the next. We never talked again after we split. It's been a gazillion years.

I walk into the restaurant and head for the bar. Even from behind, I recognize him. He looks the same.

"Jacob?"

He spins around on the stool, smiling broadly. He's attractive in a sun-kissed Southern California average-man way, and his resting face is a closed-mouth smile. The guy is just happy to breathe.

"Dani, oh my god! You're even more beautiful."

He was always good with compliments. I'm blushing. "Thank you."

He stands up, throws his arms out, and scoops me into a bear hug. "It's good to see you. I'm so glad you texted!" he says.

All the butterflies are coming back. "It's good to see you too."

"Sit, sit. What do you want? I'll wave her over," he says, gesturing toward the bartender. I'm contemplating what to drink. "Still a margarita girl?" he asks.

He remembered. In this moment, I want nothing more than to be that young margarita girl. "That sounds great!" I say.

We get our drinks and settle in. He orders appetizers, and just like when we were young, we fall into a light, fun, playful but somehow still intimate conversation. We talk about everything, even the serious stuff, but we both find a way to spin it toward a positive light. That's what I remember about Jacob. He's always happy, smiling . . . hopeful. I'm starting to get tipsy, and even though I'm working from the apartment tomorrow, I realize I still have to drive all the way back there tonight.

The sun has officially gone down. I'm on my third drink and decide to leave my car and take an Uber back to the apartment.

"Remember going to Hollywood on Saturday nights? All the bars on Sunset? We had a blast."

"Yes, yes! I remember! Remember that girl who followed us for three blocks because she thought you were Ethan Hawke? That was hilarious!"

The laughing dies down. There's finally a hitch in the chatter, but unlike with Alex, it's not because one of us is mad or offended, it's because I think we both realize how much we are enjoying each other.

"Did you plan on driving home tonight? I'm gonna order another drink—do you want one?"

"I was going to Uber home."

"Great." He gestures toward the bartender. "Two more, please, thanks."

"How are *you* getting home?" I ask.

"I live three blocks away."

"Well, I picked the right spot, then, didn't I?" The giddiness is gone. There's a subtle seriousness in the atmosphere.

"I wasn't lying when I said you're more beautiful now." PDA is not my thing, but I can feel myself leaning toward him. He touches his thumb to my bottom lip. "Pretty lips," he says. "Beautiful." My mouth is just slightly open, there is so much going on in my body right now that I can barely breathe.

"You look really good too," I say, clearly out of breath.

He smiles and then leans in and kisses me softly. "Stay with me tonight," he whispers near my ear.

"Okay."

19

you're over me

ALEXANDER

It's Wednesday. I never thought I'd say this, but Dani was right. I didn't know what it was like to juggle work, the kids, and the household on my own. I'm exhausted once again and ready to swap, but the boys are playing their first game of the season and I'm not missing it. I texted Dani earlier, letting her know I'd get them from school and bring them to the game, and we could just switch there.

Noah is sitting on the bench with a sling on and I still feel terrible, but the boys and I had a good few days. I managed to devise a system at work where I put all my patients back-to-back in the mornings right after I drop off the boys. Kate actually came up with the plan and organized the appointments for me. It's intense not taking a break for several hours, but by two-thirty, I'm out of there. I go pick up the boys and bring them back to the clinic for a couple of hours. They do their homework while I wrap up patient notes and the clerical business I would normally sprinkle throughout the day.

I miss Jenna and how well we worked together—she could basically read my mind. But Kate is being a superstar and picking up the job quickly. She's punctual, nice to the clients and staff, bright and professional. She's also levelheaded. Nothing seems to bother her. Things definitely feel like they're looking up for me in my transition to part-time single parent, but there's no question that it was a rocky adjustment.

It's already the seventh inning and I'm surprised Danielle is not here. She never misses games, but she did mention she had to go to the studio today and check out the new offices.

Finally, in the bottom of the eighth, I see her coming down the ramp toward the baseball field. Her hair is back to dark brown. She seems chipper, not overtly so, but there's a little bounce in her step.

Once we make eye contact she smiles with a tight, closed mouth, and walks toward me.

"Hey," she says. "What's the score?"

"Tied three–three."

She looks over toward the dugout. "Poor Noah, benched all year."

I feel bad enough without her pointing it out, but I don't think she's being antagonistic. "Yeah, it sucks," I say, as she sits down next to me.

"He's being a good sport about it. How were the last few days?"

"They were good. Smooth sailing. They're itching for summer though. Do we have a plan for that?"

"I don't see why we would need to change our days, if that's what you're asking. I'll come to the house Wednesday mornings and go to the apartment Sunday mornings."

"I know, but—"

"I signed them up for camps all summer, Alex. They'll have one camp every day for most of the summer."

"Oh, you did that?"

"Of course I did. I've always done that. They'll be busy. It'll be just like school. They have baseball camp, golf camp, surf camp, and Noah is taking an astronomy class at Glendale Community College on Thursday nights, but that'll be my day, so you don't have to worry about it."

"Surf camp?"

"Yeah, they both want to learn. It's good exercise. Maybe I'll learn too, who knows."

"Well, okay, then. That makes things easy. I've got a good system at work now so I can do drop-off and pickup on my days."

"Good. So no more Grandma?" she asks with a smirk.

"It was temporary, Dani. Speaking of, why'd you change your hair back?"

"It was fading into an awful, brassy orange color. I looked like Chewbacca," she says with a laugh.

I laugh with her. Things feel light. The summer conversation is easy. I have the urge to pinch myself because it feels like she and I are getting along, and after so many years of fighting, that sensation is pretty surreal. I want to tell her that her hair looks amazing, but it just doesn't seem right to say it out loud.

Ethan is up to bat. Both boys are good baseball players, but Ethan usually struggles with hitting.

"Let's go, E!" Dani yells.

Ethan looks at us as he walks from the batter's circle to home plate. We're sitting close to each other. Both of us are smiling. It must feel encouraging to him, because it looks like he shifts into a more poised posture.

"Jeez," Dani says. "Bottom of the ninth, two outs, and tied

up? No pressure. Poor Ethan. He's so hard on himself about hitting."

"He's been practicing a lot though."

Ethan swings. It's a strike. Noah stands in the dugout and grasps the fence with his good hand. "Let's go, E. Eye on the ball!" he yells.

Strike two.

"Bummer," Dani says. Ethan looks nervous, but he hasn't given up.

The next pitch comes barreling right down the middle. Ethan swings. It's a fly ball to right field. For a moment I think it's going to clear the wall but it hits the foul pole and bounces back to the field.

"Fair ball," Noah yells. "Run, E!"

Ethan turns first, zips to second, and heads for third while the right fielder heaves the ball across the field. "Down!" the third base coach yells.

"Slide!" Dani screams.

Ethan slides just as the third baseman is jumping for the ball. It's overthrown. The coach is yelling to Ethan, "Get up! Go! Go! Go!"

He gets up and runs for home plate. It's going to be close. He dives, and he's safe, just barely. We are jumping up and down, screaming. Ethan just won the game with an inside-the-park home run. Dani and I head over to the dugout. Everyone is going crazy, hugging and celebrating. Things feel normal. Great, even.

I don't think I've seen Ethan more elated in his life. He can't stop smiling. Noah is also happier than I've seen him in a long time.

Everyone congratulates Ethan. The coach declares him the MVP of the game and the boys start gathering their stuff. Dani is mingling with the other moms. I'm waiting for them to head to the parking lot when I realize I'm going to a different place. I don't need to wait.

Dani looks up at me from about twenty feet away. I walk over toward her and she says, "It's gonna be a while. The coach wants to work on something with Ethan and another kid."

"Okay," I say. I don't know what to do with myself.

I go over to the boys and hug and congratulate them again. "I'm going to the apartment, guys," I say.

"We know," Noah says. "We'll see you in a few days." They're acting like it's no big deal. I shouldn't want them to care, but it feels so strange to leave the baseball field alone . . . again. They all seem adjusted, but I don't feel used to this at all.

"Okay, love you guys," I say and turn to leave. I'm walking by Dani, who is swept up in a conversation with two other moms. "Bye, Dani."

She looks up, nods, then throws up a half-assed wave, so I wave back and head for my car.

"Alex, wait a sec!" Dani jogs toward me. She reaches into her back pocket and hands me a business card. It's Valeria's. My stomach drops. I feel dizzy. Very quietly and calmly, Dani says, "This fell out of the laundry basket. Not at the apartment, okay?" She's wearing a small, tight smile. Her eyes look almost sympathetic.

I'm speechless. I start fumbling for words. I would feel terrible if I hurt her this way, but I don't think I did. I have been plenty mad at Dani, but I've never been maliciously careless. The weird thing is that she doesn't seem pissed or sad, it's like she . . . feels nothing about it. "Listen, I—" She shakes her head as if to indicate that I don't need to respond.

I flip the card over and read, *Call me, Alex. I had a great time tonight.*

Oh my god, this looks so bad. "Dani . . . nothing—"

"It's fine," she says, shaking her head minutely. She's preoc-cupied, looking over her shoulder like she wants to get back to her conversation.

She starts to turn toward the moms. "Dani, listen to me." I grab her arm. She looks down at my hand like I'm a stranger. "I met her at Commerce and G. She's a friend of Brian's. I was with him . . . we all talked at the bar. She gave me her card at the restaurant. It was just friendly."

An enigmatic Dani is staring at me now. She blinks a couple of times like she's internally deciphering my thoughts . . . my lies. "Alex . . ." she says. She's stoic. "Not at the apartment, okay? It's gross, and if for no other reason, it's confusing to the neigh-bors. You can afford a hotel."

I feel so stupid in this moment. Candy must have told her. God, Dani has a way of making me feel like the biggest moron on the planet. "I didn't sleep with her," I whisper, but it's loud enough for the other women to hear. They all turn and look at us.

"I gotta go. I was in the middle of talking to Lisa. I'm being rude. We'll get separate places eventually, but for now, let's just have some respect for each other. See you Sunday." She turns on her heel and walks away. She wasn't even angry.

I'm standing there with my hands at my sides, stupefied. I must look like an ape. Why isn't she mad? It's like she doesn't even care. Maybe she doesn't.

Driving to the apartment feels like a dream. I'm running a million scenarios in my head. I wonder what Dani is thinking and I just want to tell her over and over that Valeria and I didn't sleep together, but why do I feel the need to do that? We're di-vorced. It's none of Dani's business. I feel bad that she found the card, and that she had to explain things to Candy, but something like this was eventually going to happen.

For a few minutes I walk around the apartment in circles. My hands feel numb. Every thirty seconds I look at my text messages. I'm waiting for something. Dani's wrath, maybe? Nothing happens.

There's a welling mass in my chest so I sit on the couch to catch my breath. All the windows and curtains are open . . . it's the one benefit of having a second-story apartment. There's a serene breeze moving across the living room and into the dark bedroom. I haven't turned on any lights. The ambient light is disintegrating by the moment. It's hard to see the details of things in the room, but it's not completely dark. I notice how quiet the street is during this time of day. It's magic hour, which is actually much shorter than an hour. It's that twenty minutes after the sun has dipped below the horizon, but before the sky has darkened. The glow left over is fading, but it's enough to still give the apartment a peaceful contexture. I'm calming down.

What had felt like a witching hour has mollified. The tone in the room is a combination of surrender and exhaustion and the peace one feels in that. I fall asleep with my head resting on the back of the couch.

When I wake an hour later, it's dark outside, and in the apartment as well. The one outdoor light on the walkway below is giving off a small orange glow that's just enough to guide my way to the kitchen light switch.

I flip on the lights. It's nine-thirty. I'm tired, but I know I won't be able to go back to sleep for a while. It's still eerily quiet and I'm hungry. These are the moments when loneliness starts to seep in. This is bedtime for the boys. If we were still together,

Dani and I would be finishing up dishes, getting the kids situated, reading before heading to bed.

There are four books on the shelf in the apartment. Two John Irvings, *A Son of the Circus* and, my personal favorite, *The Fourth Hand*. There's one long, boring Salman Rushdie, *The Ground Beneath Her Feet*, which Dani raved about for years but I could never get into it. And then a random historical romance novel, *The Bronze Horseman*, by Paullina Simons. This one I remembered Dani also sung praises about. I never cracked it, using the excuse that the category was too schmaltzy for me. I mocked her love of romance novels and, internally, I even degraded her as a writer because of it. Looking back now, it seems infantile that I would dismiss an entire genre when I couldn't even muscle through a Rushdie.

That's the thing: Dani read every type of book, listened to every kind of music, and appreciated every difference in every human being she came across. I used to wish I was more like her . . . more receptive and loving. It's hard to see that in her anymore though. That side of Dani has been replaced by a malevolent dictator. *Dictator* might be a little harsh, actually. I pick up *The Bronze Horseman* and set it on the couch-back table to remind myself to give it a go. I need to open myself up to the world more.

After heating up a chicken dish Dani had left in the refrigerator, I take my plate back into the living room, sit down, and start eating. I'm getting used to this weird routine of reheating and eating her old food. I wonder if she knows I'm eating it and not just tossing it out.

It's too quiet in here. My phone will not link to the Bluetooth player so I get up and walk over to the turntable and LP collection.

Eeny, meeny, miney, mo. I don't even care, I just don't want to hear my cynical, sad-boy inner dialogue any longer.

It's The Velvet Underground *Loaded* album. I turn it around and look at the songs on the back of the cover. "Sweet Jane."

I let out a laugh, remembering an argument I had gotten into with Dani about this song. I take the record out of the cardboard, leaving the sleeve inside. It wasn't exactly an argument, more like a little glimpse of Dani's passion, which I now refer to as her bitchiness. But back then it didn't feel bitchy, self-righteous, or braggy. It was charming.

The song starts and I'm back to twenty years ago.

"Standin' on a corner
Suitcase in my hand . . . Oh, sweet Jane."

We had finished the hardwood floors and paint in the house and were finally moving furniture in. Dani and I had done everything ourselves. We had to. We had thirty-five dollars left in our bank account when we closed on the house. Those days were wild. I think we were still high from the lacquer fumes, because we were unreasonably giddy about spending our first night in the house even though we couldn't even afford groceries.

It was late and the rooms were cluttered with boxes and furniture in odd places, but we managed to get everything out of the moving truck so we could return it.

"Let's call it a day," Dani said, plopping onto the green velour couch my mother had given me in college.

"I feel disgusting," I said as I sat down next to her.

"I don't even know where my clothes are."

"I found some of mine in a box you must have packed, because it was only five of my T-shirts and your wedding dress. You can wear one of my shirts."

She got up to go take a shower. "Thanks, I will."

We had gotten married a year and half before we bought the house. Our wedding was small. At the time, it was still hard for Dani and her parents to celebrate anything because of Ben's death. It sounds sad, considering it was our wedding and it was hard for them to celebrate, but it was enough for me and Dani. The size of our wedding was never an issue. Neither of us are flashy people. We sort of fell into being engaged after a long conversation one night and marriage felt like an easy next step. We picked out the rings together, planned a small wedding at a little outdoor venue in Pasadena, and that was it. I wouldn't have done it differently and I don't think she would have either. Well, except for the getting married part, I guess? It's pretty hard to regret the marriage, though, when it gave us Noah and Ethan.

Almost immediately after the wedding, we started looking for a house. There was a specific street in Los Feliz that we wanted to live on. We would drive up and down it looking for FOR SALE signs until finally there it was . . . our house. It needed a lot of work and we paid an inordinate amount of money for a Spanish revival that basically needed the entire interior redone, but we *loved* it.

We spent months sleeping in the garage while we were remodeling. Dani was a trooper and I worked tirelessly to make the house exactly what she wanted.

I had showered, was sitting on the couch in the fume-filled unpacked room. I was too tired to do anything more. I had been swept up in a house design magazine when Dani came sauntering out in one of my T-shirts and nothing else.

I arched my eyebrows.

"Well, I wasn't gonna put my wedding dress on," she said with a laugh.

"No, you look adorable in my shirt. I like it."

She made her way over to a tall, built-in bookshelf where we had stacked her records and the record player. She put on "Sweet Jane."

"Is this the Cowboy Junkies song redone?" I asked.

She spun around quickly like she had been stung by something. "This?" she said as she started to dance around to the music. She was so sexy with no makeup, wet hair. Her nipples were hard through the thin T-shirt fabric. "This, Alex, is not the Cowboy Junkies," she said with mock indignation.

"I know it's not, but it's their song, right?"

"Oh, Alex, Alex, Alex, you are so wrong. This, my friend, is the original. You don't know who this is?"

I shrugged.

"Well, you have to guess, then," she said. "And every time you're wrong, you have to take off an article of clothing."

I laughed and looked down at myself. I was wearing a T-shirt and basketball shorts over boxers. I didn't have too many wrong answers to spare. "Okay," I said. "But what about you? What do you have to do?"

"Obviously if you get it right, then I will have to strip something off."

"You mean *when* I get it right?" I said.

She was still dancing around to the music while I was seated on the couch. "You have a lot of confidence for a guy who thought this was the Cowboy Junkies," she said.

"I didn't think it was—"

"Time to guess, Alex. The song will be over soon."

"The Rolling Stones?"

"Off with your shirt!" she yelled.

I ditched my shirt and then searched my mind. "The Animals?"

"Bye-bye, shorts," she said cutely with a wave toward me.

I stripped them off quickly. I couldn't place the voice. My parents were not music people. Dani's were. She could recognize any artist from their voice even if she hadn't heard the song.

"Rod Stewart?"

She buckled over, laughing. "Rod Stewart? Are you kidding me?"

"It sounds like him," I argued.

"Take them off!" she said, pointing to my boxers.

I shimmied out of my boxers and sat buck naked on the couch as she twirled in circles. I was extraordinarily turned-on when she finally looked back at me.

Her mouth fell open. "Oh," she said.

"How do I even out this playing field?" I asked.

She came toward me and straddled me. We were kissing. I started to pull her shirt up. She whispered near my ear, "Nope. You haven't guessed the right answer." She was grinding on me, naked under the shirt. It was torture. "I'll give you a hint . . . it's Lou Reed's band."

"The Velvet Underground. Now take this fucking thing off."

I pulled the shirt over her head and tossed it onto a stack of boxes.

I shake my head now, to get out of the memory that feels almost *too* good.

I'm standing in the apartment, staring at the wall, feeling lonely. What we'd had was so good. What happened? I realize I hadn't taken the white sleeve out to see if she had written something on it. Maybe she wrote about that day.

The sleeve sticks to the cardboard like it had been wet at some point. Tears? I take it out and read her writing over and over again, trying to place the memory. It's not that first night in our house at all . . . It's horribly sad.

Song 2: "Sweet Jane"
I'm wondering if you remember our game about this song when we moved into this house. Things have changed a little. All good things though. I'm watching you hold Ethan. He dozes off as you're feeding him in your arms. He's just over a year old—beautiful blond curls. Noah is climbing on the back of the couch, wrapping his arms around your neck, choking you, but you don't care. You're still smiling as you look up at me. Noah is giggling. It sounds like the music you would hear in heaven. This is the moment that represents exactly what love is to me. You look up and smile again. We found out three days ago that we're having a girl. I haven't told you this yet . . . but I want to name her Jane.

I never knew. Why didn't I ever read these? A tear streams down my cheek. It feels like a foreign invader. I do the math; Dani miscarried the week after she'd written this. She was nineteen weeks pregnant . . . almost halfway. We'd heard the heartbeat already three times and had seen the tiny baby on the screen twice. She was far enough along for them to know the sex. Dani had a small baby bump that didn't go away for several days after the miscarriage. It was hard for me to see, so I can't even imagine how it felt for her.

She never told me she had thought of names. After it happened, we didn't talk about it . . . about her, the baby, or who she might have been. I didn't want to make it worse for Dani. That day she had been writing at home while the boys were toddling around her feet. I was at the clinic. She said she had felt crampy in the morning, and by the afternoon, she was bleeding.

Her mother came over and took her to the hospital. I met them there. At that time, Irene still acted like a grandmother, but she wasn't as sympathetic toward Dani's pain as I thought she should have been. Maybe she was comparing it to losing a child that had already grown into a man. She took the boys back to our house and told me to go in and be with Dani.

The hospital room was dark when I walked in. Dani was lying on her side, facing the window.

"Dani?" I said softly.

She sniffled. I could see her body start to shake. She was crying. When I came around to the other side of the bed, she broke down.

All I could think to do was simply hug her. I lay down next to her on top of the blankets and took her in my arms. She cried. Her body shook. She sobbed. Tears drenched her gown and my shirt. I rocked her back and forth until she fell asleep. We said nothing.

20

getting to know me

DANIELLE

It's been two months since we got the apartment. Things have been getting better every day with Alex and the boys. It's not uncomfortable doing the swap or seeing him at the kids' functions. He's been respectful, leaving the apartment clean and organized. I trust that he's no longer using it as a bachelor pad, so we stopped insisting the sheets be washed every five minutes.

I threw myself into work. Now I go into the offices nearly every moment I'm not with the boys. Lars declined my offer to write for the show this season, but he promised he'll come on board for the second season. He said he had too much on his plate, planning his wedding and honeymoon. I don't buy it. I think he's cowering out of guilt for not putting all the rumors to rest.

He did finally come out to me over the phone in a very nonchalant way, sort of implying that he thought I always knew. I wish I *had* known. It could have extinguished many of the fires in our house, with both Alex and with my mother. I know it was just one catalyst, but had it not all been for Lars, the rumor, Beth . . . would Alex and I be divorced?

I've seen Jacob for the last several Sundays. I go to the Westside and stay at his condo with him. It's easy and familiar. He's energetic . . . happy. We cook dinners or swim in the ocean, paddleboard, go for bike rides. It's freeing to be with someone who doesn't talk to me about finances, or college funds, parent duties, household chores, or neglected needs.

At first, I was nervous about being vulnerable and physically close with Jacob, but then I remembered what sex had felt like with him when we were young. I could tell he remembered me too. I hadn't felt sexy in a long time, almost like that part of me had gone dormant. Now it's alive and my skin looks better, my hair is thicker and healthier, and I've lost the flab around my stomach, which I thought would never go away.

I haven't told anyone about Jacob, but I think Alicia has suspicions because she's basically clairvoyant when it comes to me.

I don't want to get ahead of myself, but things feel *good* right now. I'm finding our stride. Eli fast-tracked the show. They've already started shooting the pilot episode. The cast and crew are amazing, everything I could have dreamed for and more.

When we were married, Alex and I had a rhythm. As a team, we were effective, especially in the beginning. He was building his career; I was building mine. We shared all of the household responsibilities. When we had the boys, it felt like I was shouldering more as far as domestic and parenting duties, but Alex had the consistent income that offset the monetary fluctuation of my volatile profession. So it still never felt unequal.

We prided ourselves on how productive we were together, but when things started going downhill, all of that energy was transferred to fighting. Each of our focus was on winning the argument, no matter what it was about. And my mother dying in the other room only exacerbated the turbulence.

Now I feel that camaraderie coming back, but in a different form. Alex and I are compromising. We're communicating, "You do this, I'll do that. Okay, great! Let's get it done." It's not a competition and it's not adversarial. The house and apartment are running smoothly, the boys are happy and no one is fighting. All of this had felt impossible before the divorce.

It's Sunday morning and I've just gotten to the apartment. I haven't made concrete plans with Jacob tonight, but I've been seeing him on Sundays, so I assume we'll get in touch later today.

Flipping through my records, I come across another one of Alex's Bruce Springsteen albums, *Devils & Dust*. He must have missed this one when he was taking his albums out. Of course I never played this record or wrote anything in it, but I heard it enough in the car. He was obsessed with the song "Devils & Dust." He overplayed it, and as a result, I have so many memories attached to it. Alex once told me that he had listened to it on his way home from work every day for a solid year. He said it calmed him. He felt like Bruce was his friend telling him a story. Personally, I thought the song was a downer.

I put it on just for kicks. As far as I can tell, Alex hasn't played my records or snooped through my things since he's been here. He's always been respectful in that way, though sometimes that respect could feel like indifference. Maybe I wanted him to be curious enough to snoop, to read what I had written inside the covers? It doesn't matter now.

The music comes on and the first memory tied to it begins floating through my mind. We were driving through Cape Cod, on our way to Provincetown. It was the year before we had

Noah, so it felt like a last-hoorah vacation. I had gone off birth control. We were actively trying to get pregnant. There is something innately sexy about knowing you might be getting pregnant when you're having sex. Well, I guess maybe only if you *want* to be pregnant, and if you haven't experienced infertility or tragedy.

Everything felt new and exciting. We were headed to a quaint bed-and-breakfast we had been to a few years before. Alex was driving our rental car, a generic gray sedan of some kind, with black faux-leather seats. The air conditioner wasn't working properly. The heat was radiating off the seats, our legs were sticking and sweating, but we were still laughing . . . still having fun. Alex was teasing me about how I had spent two hours on the phone with the rental car company trying to get a better deal. He used to flirtatiously pick on me for being practical. Now he calls me "cheap." I call it "pragmatic." The windows were down, I had my seat laid back. It was the middle of June, but the Atlantic Coast air was warmer than usual. Lying down, I was marveling at how angular and perfect his jawline was. He didn't know I was staring at him.

He was wearing black Ray-Ban Wayfarer sunglasses and bobbing his head to the music. He hadn't had a haircut in a while so his hair was what I liked to call "messy hot." He never lets it get that way now. He books his haircuts months in advance, and it's always the same, clean-cut style. He thinks it looks professional, I think it's boring. I guess we're pragmatic in different ways now.

A Flock of Seagulls song was playing as we were driving down the Cape. Then "Devils & Dust" came on. I wasn't yet sick of the song.

The windows were down; the crisp, delicious wind was rushing through the car. Alex looked youthful. He was so transparent then . . . in the best way possible. I could tell he was happy and at peace.

At one point during the song, he looked at me. I had taken my shirt off and was wearing a bikini top, shorts, hair up in a chaotic topknot, and that kind of serene smile that would take effort to turn to a frown.

"You're so beautiful, Dani," he had said.

"Oh yeah? Like this? All disheveled?"

"Especially like that." He put his eyes back on the road and said, "Sometimes I can't believe I'm married to you. I look at you and think, 'Holy shit, I can't believe I get to spend the rest of my life with a hot, funny, smart wife. I'm so lucky.'"

I started to get choked-up then. "Thank you," I said, voice trembling.

"I mean, Dani, you have to know, you're a grand piano in a room with a bunch of toy pianos."

I laughed and cried simultaneously. "I don't know what to say."

"You don't have to say anything; just know I know how lucky I am."

"I'm lucky too," I whispered.

Naturally, we spent the next two days mostly naked. We were making the ultimate commitment, starting a family. It felt more permanent than saying "I do."

I turn the record player off and look at my phone. I'm obsessively checking it, waiting for Jacob to text me. Instead there's a text from Alicia asking me to call her.

"Hello," I say when she picks up.

"Hey, I've been working so much, I need to get out. Let's go to dinner and get drinks tonight?"

"Um—"

"Are you gonna tell me that you're busy sitting in the apartment alone?"

"Well, I was writing . . ." It wasn't a total lie, I wrote a little bit, first thing in the morning when I was still at the house, before I came to the apartment.

"You have to write all night long? What's going on with the show, by the way?"

"It's going superfast. They're shooting the pilot episode."

"That's amazing! But I know you, you need a break. Let's go out."

"Alicia . . .

"Oh my god, you're about to tell me something. You're seeing someone?"

"Yeah, I knew you would know. Not just seeing him, we're, like, getting serious."

"Oh no, Dani." She sounds disappointed.

"What?"

"Getting serious? You *just*—"

It's irking me that she's not happy for me.

"Don't, Alicia!"

"How did you meet him?"

Very quietly I say, "It's Jacob."

"*What?*" She literally hangs up the phone, then immediately texts me.

Alicia: I'm coming over. Be prepared.
Me: No, I have plans. We'll talk later.
Alicia: Whatever.

Still no text from Jacob. I text him . . .

Me: Hey, what's on the agenda?

No response. An hour later . . .

Me: Hello?

An hour after that . . .

Me: Everything okay, Jacob?

No response. I sit on the couch and wait for what feels like forever.

It's getting dark and I'm frustrated, but I'm also getting worried about Jacob. I can't help it; I open up Instagram and look at his profile. There's a picture from *twenty* minutes ago.

It's a beach. It looks different than here. It looks tropical. The caption says: *Nosara, Costa Rica, never lets us down. This perfection all day.*

He went to Costa Rica and didn't even tell me? He obviously has cell service and he's not responding to my texts. I text again . . .

Me: Now I'm getting really worried, Jacob. Why aren't you responding?

Three profiles are tagged in his beachscape photo. I click on the first one; it looks like a surf buddy. I thoroughly sleuth and put together that the guy is married. The second profile is another guy, same thing, married with kids. The third profile is a woman. She's younger, very athletic looking. Most of her first photos are of what I'm assuming is Costa Rica. Then I come across one where she's sitting on Jacob's lap. It's from a year ago. My stomach drops. They look like they're sitting at a beach bar in some exotic location. There are other people sitting at the table with them. She and Jacob are both laughing, seemingly unaware that a picture is being taken. He's shirtless, she's in a bikini, and his hand is on her thigh. One minute later, I get a text . . .

Jacob: Hey, sorry, just saw this. Let's catch up sometime.

What?

Me: Catch up? Sometime?
Jacob: I'll be in town next weekend. Drinks Friday?
Me: You know I can't. I have my kids on Fridays.

No response. I wait. I know I told him which days I would be at the apartment. I'm so confused. I hesitate over Alicia's number but I don't call her; instead, I drag my feet into the kitchen, feeling bewildered and a bit unhinged.

Is this what being single is like? You go out with someone multiple times, think you have a connection, spend several consecutives Sundays with that person playing house, and then they disappear and behave as though you don't exist? In this moment I feel expendable . . . easily replaced. Casual dating is only a temporary reprieve from our feelings of low self-worth. When reality sets in and the commitment is nowhere to be found, our self-worth plumets to an even darker depth of misery than before.

I fish a full bottle of chardonnay out of the refrigerator, then reach for a glass and an opener. After popping the cork, I fill the glass only halfway, as if I'm holding on to some attempt at decorum.

Who am I kidding? I take the dignified glass in one hand and the bottle in the other and head for the bedroom . . . alone. This feels sort of like being married to Alex, but worse.

⌒⌒

It's been a week. Thankfully, I was busy with the kids and work. I actually didn't see Alex at all. We were ships passing in the night . . . as it should be. Alicia has been hassling me about getting together. I know she's going to grill me about Jacob, who did finally text on Tuesday, like it was no big deal. I asked him to meet me for dinner tonight, told him that I needed to talk to him. I fully plan to give him a little piece of my mind for what the kids call "ghosting" me last weekend. But first . . . I needed to deal with Alicia.

I'm headed to meet her for brunch at a little rooftop restaurant in Santa Monica. She was irritated that I asked her to drive across town, but I had packed a bag and figured I'd end up staying at Jacob's, so I headed out to the Westside early. I'm sitting at a table waiting, sipping a mimosa, when I see her come in and chat with the hostess. Alicia is usually all business, but today her blonde hair is down in soft curls on her shoulders and she's wearing a Boho-chic, light floral jumper. She looks relaxed and I'm relieved. I'm also dressed casually, beachy in a sundress and hat.

"Hi," I say. I stand and reach out to hug her.

"I love driving one hour to go twelve miles on a Sunday morning."

"It's noon," I say matter-of-factly.

"It was the morning when I left," she says as she sits.

The waiter comes over and Alicia orders a mimosa. We're looking at the brunch menu in silence and it's making me uncomfortable.

"I'm sorry it's LA. What was Mark doing today?" I ask, trying to change the subject.

She looks up and shrugs. "I don't know, like going mountain biking or something." She squints. "Why?"

"I'm just wondering. Making conversation. Are you mad at me, Alicia?" As soon as the words are out of my mouth, I realize how childish I sound.

"Mad? No. But I know why we're down here. I know why I just drove an hour and paid forty dollars to park. I know it wasn't for the view." She gestures toward the semi-obstructed ocean view we have across the totally concrete parking lot below. "I know where Jacob's apartment is, we employ him occasionally."

"All right, let's talk about the elephant."

"This is like a woolly mammoth, Dani . . . tusks . . . extinct . . . the whole bit."

"Funny," I say.

"Do you remember the last time you thought things were getting serious with Jacob? Because I sure do."

"That's different. We were young," I say.

"He's not different though," she says.

I gesture for the server. "Can I get another mimosa?"

"Just bring a bottle," Alicia says.

"I don't want to get drunk."

I feel a pit in my stomach like I've been caught sneaking out of the house by my parents.

"We're not going to be drunk after splitting one bottle of champagne," she sneers. "But for the record, I know why you're even trying to stay sober right now."

"Because my car is here," I lie.

"Okay." She rolls her eyes.

"Alicia, the last three years of my life have been terrible. I've been horribly lonely and depressed. I'm finally feeling good—"

"You definitely look good, but that's not really the point. I'm worried about you getting hurt, that's all."

"He, like, really likes me."

"He, like, really likes cheeseburgers and puppies and sunshine. The guy likes *everything*. He's a happy-go-lucky, noncommittal man-child. You are a relationship addict and this was easy because you knew him. He's *not* looking at this the way you are."

"I think he is. I'm having dinner with him tonight." Even though I know there is a small truth to what Alicia is saying, I'm not listening. Jacob is into me. When we're together he seems enamored by me. He tells me I'm beautiful and successful and he makes me feel like a person, not a wife, not a mother. I'm getting tipsy. I'm having an early dinner with Jacob at five, so I feel like I need to rein it in and calm down. "Let's get some food," I say.

"Fine."

We order, talk about the overpriced menu, and then the conversation shifts back to dating.

"Why don't you date around? Instead of hanging out with an old flame?" she says.

"I don't think you understand, Alicia. All of my friends, except for you, are mommy friends. Either from baseball, elementary school . . . the freakin' church I went to that one time . . ."

"Yeah, that was weird when you did that." She laughs through her nose.

"It was for the boys," I say. "The fact is, I don't have people to go out with. You're married not only to Mark but to your job . . . and all those other women, I have nothing in common with them, other than the fact that we all have kids."

"I meant go on a dating app. Date a whole bunch of different people. That's what I would do."

"That's what every married person says."

"Now you're an expert on being single?"

I attempt to pour champagne out of the empty bottle. Three drops go in my glass. "That was fast."

"We'll take another," Alicia says to our passing server.

He arches his eyebrows. "Erm . . . okay."

"No, Alicia."

I reach out, waving him off. She swats at my hand. "Who cares, it's Sunday brunch."

The server is already on the mission. "How are you gonna get home?" I ask.

"I booked a massage and room at Shutters. I need the massage and peace and quiet to go through a deposition. What about you? How are *you* gonna get home?" she says in her snarky lawyer voice.

Shutters is a fancy hotel on the beach in Santa Monica. It's expensive and the spa is even more over-the-top. But Alicia can afford to drop hundreds of dollars on peace and quiet for one night.

"I don't know. I'll Uber," I say absentmindedly as the waiter fills my glass.

"So what's it like? Sleeping with him?"

"Jacob?"

"No, the pope."

"It's good, I guess. Let's not talk about it anymore." I'm bummed she's not being supportive.

She's exasperated. She takes a deep breath in and out. "I'm sorry I'm being a jerk. I'm seriously curious, though, I want to know what it's like."

"Dating him, or just the sex?"

"All of it. I'll keep my opinions about the situation to myself."

"Finally," I say. "It takes an entire bottle of champagne to get you off my back."

"Tell me everything." She's inhaling a plate of eggs Benedict. I've pushed mine around, annihilating the twenty-five-dollar eggs and hollandaise.

"It's fun . . . We do stuff . . . It's nice."

She stops chewing and looks up at me. "You are an Emmy Award–winning writer and that's the description I get?"

"Okay, fine. In bed, he's boring," I say, like it's a confession I've been holding on to for decades.

"Boring? Jacob?"

"Yes, he's robotic, like he's running on a treadmill or something. Just in and out, you know?"

"Really?" She's genuinely surprised.

"Yeah, and . . ." I lower my voice. "Like, missionary only."

"No!"

"Yes."

"Well, what are you like?" she says.

"I don't want to tell him what to do."

"You have to."

"No, I don't," I say. "I like spending time with him. Going to the beach, yoga, riding bikes . . ."

"So, like, *no* foreplay?"

"I don't think he knows where the clitoris is," I whisper. I feel almost evil saying it out loud. "It doesn't matter, that's not why I'm with him."

"Well, that's why he's with you!" she blurts out.

"Shh, quit yelling."

"I have a theory," she says.

"What?"

"If you've never been in a committed relationship, your sexual partners—which you barely know—aren't going to tell you what they like. They're not going to say, 'Right here, it's right here! I know it's not where you thought it was, but it's true, it's

RIGHT . . . HERE!'" She points to her crotch and continues. "'Look, honey, I can bend over in front of you and it still works,' or like, 'You can put your mouth on that!'" She's laughing almost to tears now and I am too. We're officially drunk.

"I know. He needs GPS directions. I mean, the last time we were together I tried to turn around, but he flipped me over onto my back and just started the old heave-ho. I think he knows, he just doesn't care. It's like going to the gym for him."

She's still giggling. "That sounds amazing," she says, rolling her eyes.

"I guess I took some things for granted."

"Like what?"

I'm not thinking before I speak. I'm really out of it. We're not even adding a splash of juice now. "Like the fact that in four minutes Alex could make me—" I stop myself.

Her smile turns from humorous to sympathetic. "You taught him well."

"Somebody else is probably enjoying the fruits of my labor as we speak," I say with one last little laugh. "A kid-cancer doctor, angel, model, perfect specimen . . ."

"Don't think about that," she says. "Everyone's different anyway. Alex is probably fumbling his way through uncomfortable experiences too."

"No, he's not," I say with a seriousness that is giving me a stomachache. "He was *always* good at it."

After about three hours of laughing, drinking, and then trying to sober up, we ask for the check.

"My massage appointment is at five and I want to check in first. I better get going. What are you gonna do for an hour?" she asks.

"Go walk on the beach . . . think about things."

We stand and start to head out of the restaurant, when Alicia turns to me and says, "You're divorced, Dani. You're single and you don't have to be a mom . . . now is the time for cocaine and threesomes."

"One never stops being a mom."

"You know what I mean."

"I'll be fine. I know he likes me. I am a relationship person. I don't want that other stuff."

We hug. She pulls away and says, "It's not so much about you not wanting it, it's about the way the world is. The world you haven't been a part of for more than two decades has changed."

"Okay, Lish. I *hear* you!" I give her a kiss on the cheek, say goodbye, and head for the boardwalk.

Before I know it, it's almost five and I'm walking into the restaurant to meet Jacob. I feel a bit windblown and disheveled, so I pop into the ladies' room first and clean myself up. Perfume, breath mint, and five Advils later, I head out to the front of the tiny seafood spot where I see Jacob standing against a pillar. Before he sees me, I take a moment to take him in. It's the first time I've really looked at him from a distance.

I wonder, if I didn't know him, would I be attracted to him? He's in great shape, but he kind of has one of those faces that's easy to forget.

He looks up, sees me, and smiles instantly. His eyes light up as he walks toward me. *He likes me.* I repeat the words over and over in my head.

"Hi, lovely." He leans down and kisses me on the cheek.

"Hi." I know there are things I want to say, but I'm holding my tongue for the moment. "You look like you got some sun."

"Yeah, a lot of sun," he says with a laugh. "Table's this way. Shall we?"

I'm reading into his response. Why did he laugh? It's irking me. I need to get it off my chest.

As soon as we sit down, I start in. "So, Costa Rica?"

"Yeah. You ever been?"

Does he not understand that I'm mad? "No, I've never been."

"You should go. I go a couple times a year . . . at least. Really consistent surf and just totally untouched land. It's gorgeous."

"Is that an invitation?"

"Huh? Um . . ."

I'm glaring at him.

"You said I should go. Are you inviting me?"

The nonplussed expression on his face is already getting old. "Well, Dani, I just got back."

I glance around the room and make it obvious that I'm irritated. A deep breath in and out and then I say, "I don't understand, Jacob. What is going on with us? I mean, you didn't even tell me you were leaving the country."

He jerks his back. Now he's clearly looking surprised. "I don't understand."

The waiter comes, pours us each a glass of wine, and leaves. The tension is palpable. I take two large gulps of wine.

"Why didn't you tell me you were going to Costa Rica?"

"Why *would* I tell you?"

"Are you serious?"

"Dani, I don't know what you think, but I'm sorry if you were under the wrong impression."

My chest is hot, my hands are twitching, and I'm positive my face looks like a tomato. "My impressions can't be wrong. They're mine and they're subjective. But let me explain something to you . . . when you are in a relationship, you tell the other person you are leaving the country."

His confused eyes widen piteously. His voice is low when he says, "We're not in a relationship, Dani. We hung out a few times."

"We slept together."

He arches his eyebrows. "Yes, we did. It was very nice. I really like you . . ."

"But?" I say. I'm fully prepared for him to dump me right now.

"But I'm not really the commitment . . . the, um . . ." He's fumbling his words, looking for the right thing to say.

"What, the marriage type? I don't want to marry you," I say before emptying my glass of wine down my throat.

"No, what I mean is, the monogamous type."

Something in my mind shifts. It's like I opened the blinds. *He dates many women.*

"Am I the Sunday night girl?" I say.

"No, it's not like that at all. I'm just . . . I don't know how to explain it to you."

"Is the girl you tagged in the Costa Rica picture your girl-friend?"

He's searching his mind. He doesn't know what I'm referring to. "Ohhh, Milena? No. I don't have a girlfriend, Dani. Milena surfs."

I'm not his girlfriend. It stings a little. Of course I'm not. I know I'm being ridiculous. It's humiliating. Still, I can't stop. "But do you sleep together, is what I'm asking."

There are four awkward beats of silence. I already know the answer. "Yeah, we do," he says.

"I don't mean sleep together. I mean, do you have sex with her?" I am pouring salt in my own wounds now.

He's finally losing his patience. "Yes, Dani, I have sex with her and with other women too. Not just you."

Tears flood my eyes. I stand up, feeling idiotic and confused. I want to go home. I want to go to my house, not the stupid apartment. I want to go to the house I made a home. I want to hug my children and remember what it feels like to be loved.

"Don't leave, Dani, please." I sit, but I'm still clutching my purse. "I thought you just wanted to have some fun. I thought you knew I wasn't really that type?"

"That type?" I say. "Have some fun? Sounds cheap."

"No, it's not cheap at all."

I'm having déjà vu. This is basically how it ended when we were in college. I stand up again. "You're just avoiding expectations."

"I'm intentionally avoiding them, because I can. I'm single and I like to do what I want, when I want."

"That's selfish," I say.

"No, it's not selfish, it's honest. You can call it whatever you want. It's normal to me and to a lot of other people. I'm sorry you got the wrong idea."

"Goodbye," I say as I finally leave.

I walk a mile and a half to Shutters and call Alicia. I get to her room, plop on the bed and cry into a pillow. I tell her I don't want to talk, and then fall asleep without another word.

~ᗢ

It's Monday morning, my head is pounding. Alicia is already gone. She left orange juice and a bagel next to the bed and a little note.

> Dani,
>   I'm sorry. I know it was for the best though. Give yourself some time.
>   Love you!—Lish

Back at the apartment, I spend all day writing and on work calls. Around eight, I finally drag myself into the kitchen. I heat up chicken soup and look for a record to play. *Devils & Dust* is still on the record player, so I put it on while I look for something else.

I'm back in the Cape Cod memory with Alex. We were lying in bed at the B&B. He rolled over to face me. He was propped up on his side. "What should we do today?"

"Do you want to rent bikes again?"

"Yeah, we can do that," he said as he brushed a strand of my hair back.

"Even though the hot girl that works at the counter was ogling you for ten straight minutes?" I said with a laugh.

The clerk at the bike rental place was a very pretty young woman who definitely made it obvious that she liked Alex.

"I didn't notice."

"How could you not?"

"I really didn't, Dani, I swear."

I believed him.

"Well, she was," I said.

"You're the only woman I want to be with. I love everything about you. I don't even see anyone else. And as far as looks, you blow them all out of the water anyway," he had said.

I feel myself getting emotional at the memory. The song is over, so I take the record cover and pull the blank sleeve out. I know Alex doesn't look at any of these, so I take a pen and scribble *I MISS YOU* on it before slipping the record and sleeve back into the cardboard.

It's true. It might be the first time I've been willing to admit it to myself, but I do miss him. Alex would have never treated sex as something so trivial and arbitrary, the way Jacob did. When we were happy, Alex could say things to me that would convince me that I had something special . . . that I was unique. Tonight I just feel like a typical aging divorcée.

21

what is "my type" anyway?

ALEXANDER

I really like Kate . . . as an employee . . . as a front desk clerk. I'm looking at her right now as she's talking to a patient. She's smiling, speaking slowly and calmly to the elderly woman. I'm bummed I don't have a permanent position to offer her, but I will be happy to have Jenna back.

Jenna had her baby. She took the regular six-week maternity leave and then I offered her another six weeks paid. She was surprised I was staying afloat, but Kate has been pulling her weight and more. I really wish I could offer her a job.

I approach her to hand her a file. "Thanks for organizing that. I can actually read the writing. It's above and beyond. Kate, I really appreciate it."

"Oh, you're welcome. I wanted to talk to you. Do you have a minute around noon? I just need to wrap up a few things." I glance at the clock. It's 11:45.

"Yeah, sure. You know my schedule," I say with a laugh. "I'll be in my office."

Kate comes in right at twelve on the dot. Very professional.
Kate is pretty, with brown hair that's always in a neat ponytail,
greenish eyes. Actually, I'm not sure what color they are. She's
usually dressed in a monochromatic, business casual outfit, but
today she's wearing jeans for a change and a floral blouse. I wonder if this is how she dresses when she's not at work. It's Friday
after all . . . and her last day. Kate is young, but she's mature. She
was a great fit and I'm dreading this conversation. I hope she's
not expecting me to offer her a job.

She knocks on the open door.

"Come on in, Kate," I say as I gesture for her to sit in the
chair across from me.

I wouldn't describe Kate as a bold person, not like Dani. I
would say she's more on the timid side. Less communicative.
I don't know that much about her. I've never asked and she's
never offered.

"Hi," she says.

"Hi." We stare at each other, blinking. I clap my hands together. "So . . . your last day."

"Yep." She nods.

I have no idea what she wants. "You've done a great job,
Kate. We just threw you in and you really knocked it out of the
park."

"Oh, thank you so much."

More silence.

"I really wish I could offer you a job—"

"Oh no, I didn't expect that at all. I always knew it was temporary. I actually have a job lined up that works out better for
me."

She doesn't want a job? Have I been underpaying her?

"Well, I'd like to give you a little parting bonus—"

"That's not necessary," she says.

"No, I insist," I say as I scour the drawer for the clinic checkbook. "So, what job do you have lined up?"

"Oh, it's a case manager position at a clinic right next to my kid's preschool."

I look up, eyes wide. *She has a kid?* "Wow, you're a mom? I had no idea. Why didn't you tell me?" I glance down at her hand. No ring.

"I don't know, I—"

"How old? Is the kid? Are you married? I don't think I even know how old *you* are. I definitely didn't expect you to have a kid." I'm speed-talking nervously for some reason.

She laughs. "Well, I was pretty young when I had him."

"Oh, you have a son?" I'm even more surprised now, since my kids have been in and out of the clinic multiple times. You'd think she would have brought up parenting boys.

"Yeah, it's crazy, it was my last year in college. If it wasn't for my parents, I would have never finished. He's six now. I'm not married . . . actually . . ." She looks around and fidgets with her hands in her lap. "Actually, Tristan doesn't even know his dad. He was just a . . . a mistake—I mean the guy, not Tristan of course!"

"I knew what you meant."

"I *chose* to have Tristan. He's my whole world," she says.

"I get it. Well, I guess I'm happy you found a better spot to work. It should make things a little easier on you." I'm scribbling my signature on the check. I don't even know how much to give her. I write it for a thousand dollars. Seems like a good amount. "Here you go."

She takes it timidly and looks down. "Oh my gosh, this is too much."

"No, Kate, seriously, that's fair. You did a great job. You're a single mom and you never asked for time off or to leave early . . ."

I pause. "Actually, why don't you take the rest of the day off? Go be with your son."

She laughs lightly. There is something I can't figure out, some disconnect. "Um, Alex . . . I, um . . . Actually, Tristan is staying at his grandparents' tonight. I didn't come in here to ask for a job, or a bonus . . . or to leave early." She laughs nervously again.

It hits me. She's flirting . . . kind of. I'm squinting and continually nodding my head. I don't know if I'm still her boss and I don't know what to do. "Kate . . ."

"You've been so great, Alex. I wanted to see . . . I know this might seem a little inappropriate or presumptuous, but . . ." She's biting her bottom lip. "Do you want to have dinner with me, Alex? No expectations, just dinner. I know you're at your apartment on Fridays and I'm gonna be alone tonight and it's my last day and . . ."

"Yes. Let's have dinner." Oh god. It just comes out. Why do I feel sick to my stomach saying that? It's been many months now since the divorce was final.

"Great." She stands up and heads for the door. It's the first time I have looked at her ass—she has a nice one. I can't help it, I'm human.

"Okay, Kate, I'll call you?"

"Sure, yeah. I'm not very good at this, Alex." She blushes.

What is wrong with me? I don't know what to say or do. "I'm not either, obviously. Text me your address and I'll pick you up? Like maybe around seven?"

"That sounds good."

"Do you like Cuban food?" I ask.

"I've never had it, but I eat pretty much everything. I'd love to try it."

It's weird to me that she's never had Cuban food, but then I do the math in my head based on how old her son is and realize

I'm almost twenty years older than her. *Am I a cliché?* I don't even *know* any people in their twenties, except maybe our neighbors.

I stand and smile. "Okay, then. You can go ahead and take off. I'll see you tonight." I wave like a moron.

She laughs and I'm relieved.

As soon as she's out the door, I sit back down in my chair and dial Brian. I need to talk to somebody. I have questions. Is the age difference okay? I know what Brian is going to say. He's gonna say just have fun with her, but I still have that sinking guilty feeling. I call Mark instead.

"Yo," he says.

"Hey, do you have a minute?" My voice is shaky.

"Yeah, what's up? You sound like you're being tortured."

"I am. Listen, you can't tell Alicia this, please, please, *please.* I know she will immediately tell Dani everything."

"I won't tell her anything. What's going on?"

"The temp . . ."

"The cute one?"

"Yeah, I'm going to dinner with her tonight."

"Awesome, I won't tell Dani. Anyway, do you remember that divorce you guys got?"

"I know, I just feel like it's really soon and Kate is young. I don't want Dani . . ."

"Dude, Dani's been dating her old college boyfriend."

I instantly feel woozy. "Jacob?"

"Yeah," Mark says in a flat tone.

I'd always hated the way Dani talked about Jacob. He was definitely her *one that got away,* even though she'd never admit it. She talked about him like she'd never had more fun with anyone in the world. I'm irritated, but I don't want to show it.

"Well, good for her, I guess. That basically erased any unnecessary, lingering guilt I had."

I should have slept with the hot doctor.

"You shouldn't feel guilty anyway. You guys did everything in order."

"What do you mean?" I say.

"Well, it's not like you guys ever cheated on each other."

"Well . . . Lars . . ."

"Did you really think they . . ."

"I don't know . . . I . . . Listen, um, will you still not say anything? I just feel like an idiot for talking about it."

"No problem. Enjoy yourself, man."

We hang up.

For the rest of the day, I try to distract myself with work.

It's late by the time I get to the apartment. I only have ten minutes to get ready. I shower quickly and am out the door. I can't stop thinking about Kate's age.

As I drive to her apartment in Pasadena, I'm reminding myself that this is *just* a date. The parking situation is horrendous near the old part of Pasadena where she lives, but finally, I find a spot. I'm fifteen minutes late, which is very unlike me.

I scan the tenant list for *Littlefield,* Kate's last name, find it, and press the button.

"Hello." It's Kate's timid voice.

"Hi, it's me, Alex."

She doesn't respond, just buzzes me in. The apartment complex is not a dump, but it's not nice either. It reminds me of a place a twenty-five-year-old would live. I realize I still don't know exactly how old Kate is. I'm assuming if she has a six-year-old she gave birth to her senior year in college, that would make her twenty-seven.

I see Kate up ahead, standing at the bottom of a stairway. *What is she doing just standing there?*

Boom! I freeze. All of the sudden the age difference hits me. It's never going to work. She was a school-aged child the year Dani and I got married. She could have been our flower girl. I hesitate on the path. Oh. My. God! The image of Kate as a little kid is playing over and over in my head. I want to run. I just stand there staring back at her. My mind is racing with exit strategies.

"I have some bad news," she says. I'm a distance from her but begin walking toward her slowly.

Yes! She's canceling. I'm saved.

"Oh?" I say.

"So my mom brought Tristan back here because she had to take my dad to the hospital."

"Oh no. Is he okay?" I say as I get closer to her. The sun is going down and the light is perfect right now. She looks ready for a date, but not overdone.

"He's fine. He had a bout of diverticulitis."

"Eek," I say.

"Well, he's not supposed to eat popcorn, but it's his favorite thing in the world." She rolls her eyes.

"I'm glad it's nothing major," I say.

"I'm sorry I didn't text you. I was scrambling and thought I could get one of the two sitters I use in this complex, but they're both busy. I was really looking forward to having a little freedom," she says with a light laugh.

She looks beautiful right now, in a natural, girl-next-door, Jennifer Aniston circa *Friends* kind of way.

"It's not a big deal, Kate. We can reschedule." As soon as the words leave my mouth, I see a little boy peeking his head through the banister at the top of the stairs.

"Hi." He waves.

"I think someone escaped," I say with a smirk.

"Tristan, go back inside," Kate says in an authoritative voice I've never heard. She turns to me. "I'm sorry—"

"Mom, I'm hungry. Is the man taking us to dinner?"

I arch my eyebrows. I want to ask her if lots of strange men take them to dinner. "Tristan, no! Go back inside!" She turns back toward me. "I'm so embarrassed. I'm sorry."

"Why are you embarrassed? That's how kids are. Remember, I have two?"

"Yeah, I know. I just . . . I'm . . ."

"Mom, I want to go to Applebee's." Tristan starts coming down the stairs. He's a cute kid. He's not really being obnoxious . . . yet. He's just curious.

"Hi, I'm Alex, you must be Tristan? I've heard a lot about you," I say and then shoot Kate a teasing look, since I literally just learned of his existence this morning.

"Yeah, I'm Tristan. Are we going to Applebee's?"

Kate is mortified. Her face is beet red. I smile at the kid and look up. "This begs the question, Kate . . ."

"What?"

"Do lots of men take you and Tristan to Applebee's?" As soon as I say it, I realize it's none of my business. Even though I'm teasing, I'm still being rude.

She laughs, thank god. "No, never." Tristan comes all the way down and stands next to her. I realize he's actually looking out for her in his own six-year-old way. He's a little too old to not be following directions, but it's clear that he wants to know why I'm talking to Kate.

"So, did your mom tell you she and I work together?"

"Yeah," he says. He's not smiling.

Kate looks at Tristan. "Listen to me, go upstairs before you're in major trouble. Grams will take you to Applebee's next time, okay? I'm just gonna talk to this man I work with for five more minutes and then I'll be inside." He follows her orders but doesn't seem happy about it. She waits for him to go back up the stairs and inside before she says, "Sorry about that. The story goes more like this, I have never been on a date before. At least not since I've had Tristan. Apparently, my mother decided without my permission to tell Tristan that 'Mom might start going on dates now and kissing boyfriends.'" She rolls her eyes dramatically. "I'm pretty irritated with the situation."

She takes a breath in and out and then smiles. She's charming and sweet and I feel for her.

"Do you normally get along with your mom?" I can't stop thinking about Irene.

Kate squints. "Yes, my mother is an angel, truly! She meant well. I shouldn't be mad at her. Tristan kept asking her where I was going and she didn't want to lie, so . . . I get it." She laughs, looks up at the apartment door and then back at me. "I just didn't expect to have to answer his questions before there was even the possibility of a kiss . . . you know?" She chuckles.

I lean in, brace the back of her neck, and kiss her. It just feels like the right thing to do, and I must be right, because she's basically melting in my arms.

When we pull apart, it takes her a second to fully open her eyes. "Oh, wow," she says, breathy.

I'm smiling, and it's not forced. "That's an encouraging response," I say.

"I didn't mean I expected to kiss you—"

"I knew what you meant. You were simply telling me about what happened today." Something comes over me. I decide I don't want to overthink everything anymore. I like her. "I know it's probably a little strange, but . . . Applebee's?"

She starts laughing giddily. "Are you serious? You do *not* have to do this."

"I want to. Unless you think it'd be confusing for him."

"No, I'm just going to tell him you were my boss and you want to take us out?"

"Great! But first, why Applebee's?"

"It's his favorite restaurant," she says.

My eyes widen. "*Applebee's* is his favorite restaurant? I mean, there's a million amazing restaurants in this area."

"He's six . . ." she says as her smile fades. "And it's just me. We don't have a lot of money."

"Shit, I'm sorry. I wasn't thinking." Oh my god, I feel like such an elitist asshole.

"It's okay. We can go anywhere, he'll be fine. I'll go grab him and our stuff. Do you want to wait here?"

I nod.

She goes up the stairs quickly. I'm thinking about how spoiled my kids are. Thank god, they're still somehow well-rounded. I hope . . .

For some reason, I feel compelled to expand this kid's palate, but I know it's not my place.

Kate comes down carrying a booster seat and a small backpack. Tristan is trailing her with a smile.

"He's still in one of those, huh?"

"Yep, age eight or eighty pounds. You're gettin' rusty."

Oh man, what am I getting myself into?

I get in the driver's side of my small Audi SUV. I don't care that much about cars. I don't drive a lot. Dani actually picked this car out. I would have never gotten black on black leather seats. It's always hot in this thing. I'm sweating already.

"This is a really nice car." Kate is looking at all the glossy finished surfaces and silver buttons.

"It's a lease," I insist on qualifying to her.

I'm about to tell her that I have an old Jeep Wagoneer, but I don't, Dani does. When we first met, I gave her crap about that car because it always broke down. She insisted on keeping it. Years ago she had argued, "It will matter later, I promise, Alex. No one has the old Brady Bunch station wagon anymore." She smacked the hood and said, "We're gonna fill this baby up with lots of memories, and always have them here for safekeeping." We took every road trip in that thing, most of our vacations, beach trips, driving up the coast with all the windows down. Of course I didn't fight her for it in the divorce. It was hers.

"Well, it's nice anyway," Kate says.

"Huh?" I'm out of it.

Inside Applebee's, I'm opening what can only be described as a multi-panel, trifold, presentation board menu, which once opened literally blocks 280 degrees of my view. Tristan is busy coloring the kids' menu. I lower my exhibition display. "Whattya gonna get?"

She's smiling. "Do you think the Four Cheese Mac & Cheese with Honey Pepper Chicken Tenders will be too ambitious? It says here it's 1,350 calories." She bursts out laughing and I follow suit.

"I mean, whatever you don't finish, I'll funnel down after I eat my Classic Whiskey Bacon Cheddar Clubhouse Prime-Rib Cheeseburger. What *is* this place?"

We're smiling at each other. The server comes over. She starts to give a spiel about the menu and Kate politely stops her. "That's okay. Tell her what you want, Tristan."

"I'll have the kid's quesadilla, French fries, and a Coke!"

"Sprite," Kate corrects.

"I can't have a Coke, Mom?"

"No," Kate says. "I want you to go to sleep sometime this

year." She looks back up to the server. "Also, can you bring him a little side salad so he can eat something green today? We'll take two Coronas and, um, a cheeseburger and a salad to split." The server starts to run down options and Kate interrupts again. "It's okay. You choose," she says. "We trust you. We've had a really long day."

Wow, Kate just took charge.

"Okay, no problem," the server says as she collects our giant menus.

Once she walks away, I say, "Well, okay, then."

Kate is overwhelmed. I remember those days with Dani and the boys. Parenting is exhausting, but Kate's in the homestretch. My kids are at the age now where I'd actually prefer to be at dinner with them over just about anyone else.

"Alex," Kate says, "I know you've eaten at amazing restaurants, and I know you're well traveled and well read, but I also know you're not picky. I've been ordering your lunch for the last three months, remember?" She leans in and whispers, "And to be honest, I'm not planning on camping out here, the lighting is already giving me a headache."

"Hey, I'm not complaining. I'm just along for the ride," I say.

"I know. I like that about you, Alex. You don't seem to really . . . care."

Time stops.

Whoa! For a moment it feels like I just put my hands on a hot stove. I'm tempted to argue with her that I *do* care. I remind myself that I wasn't going to overthink things.

"Thanks, Kate." I turn my attention to Tristan. "Hey, kid, sometime I'll make you a quesadilla that will knock your socks off, no restaurants required."

What the hell did I just offer?

They both laugh lightly and I'm relieved, but still surprised I blurted out something like that without thinking. Kate notices that I've gone completely quiet.

"Well, yes, sometime we'll come by the clinic and pick up one of your famous quesadillas."

We wrap up dinner and the lame conversation about chain restaurants. Tristan was a good kid, just happy to be at Applebee's. He's tired now and as we drive back to their apartment complex, I glance in the rearview mirror and notice that he's fallen asleep.

"He's out," I say.

"He always does that. He's a really easy kid, actually."

"To your credit, being a single mom can't be a walk in the park all the time."

We're talking quietly. "I'm used to it now. My parents help out when they can." Parking hasn't gotten any better around her apartment in the last two hours. "You can just drop us at the front, Alex."

"I'm not going to drop you off on the street with a sleeping six-year-old, a car seat, and a bag of stale French fries, Kate. I'll help you get him in."

It's quiet for a moment. I look over to gauge her expression. She's smiling serenely. "Are you sure?" she says.

"Of course."

"I just don't want you to feel weird—"

"I don't feel weird about it at all. It really is just a logistical thing," I say, and it's the truth.

"It's a kind thing to do, Alex. A *gentlemanly* thing to do."

I wonder what Kate is used to. I know she hasn't been dating, but does she hang out with people who drop her and her sleeping kid off on the side of the road at nine o'clock at night?

Once I finally find a spot, we get out quietly. When she

reaches in for him, I whisper, "No, I'll get him. I'm used to carrying two like this."

Tristan stirs a little but then rests his head on my shoulder and falls back to sleep. We get into the apartment without saying a word. Kate gestures for me to follow her to the bedroom on one side of the apartment. It's Tristan's room. I wait while she quietly pulls his comforter back. I lay him down, he stirs again, then he's asleep. I'm watching Kate remove his shoes and socks and tuck him in. We are lit only by a blue fish-shaped night-light lamp in the corner.

She looks up at me and breathes out with relief. Then she pantomimes tiptoeing out of the room like a burglar. I have to hold back from laughing. I'm having déjà vu. These days are familiar. Exhausting, but the sweetest.

Once we're in the hallway, she closes the door and motions toward the living room and adjacent kitchen.

"Phew. We did it! Thank you so much," she says. "He's tough to get down sometimes, he really pushes it. The car usually works, but I can't really carry him up the stairs anymore. I appreciate it so much."

"It's really no big deal," I say.

"Well, it's rare for me to get the opportunity to relax before I have to go to sleep."

I look down the length of her extremely good-looking body. I'm thinking about helping her relax. I shake the thought out of my head.

"Well, that phase will be over soon for him." She's staring at me, blinking, maybe mulling something over. I arch my eyebrows. "Well—"

"Would you like a glass of wine? It'll probably be gross to you though."

"Wow, you're really selling it, Kate." I smile.

"No, I mean it's two-buck chuck," she says with a shy laugh.

"I don't care what it is. I'd love to have a glass of wine with you," I tell her.

"Okay, have a seat." She gestures toward the couch.

Her apartment is what you'd expect. IKEA mostly, and a lot of photos of just her and Tristan. It's clean and tidy but void of personality. Dani is one of those people who likes eclectic but organized chaos throughout the house. She's a neat person, but she's also the type who will randomly stuff things in cabinets and then chime, "Outta sight, outta mind!"

I should stop comparing.

Kate returns with the wine, hands me my glass, and takes a seat next to me. "Your place is nice," I tell her.

"Thank you. It feels a little college-dorm-roomy for a thirty-year-old, but it works for us."

"You're thirty?"

"Twenty-nine, I'll be thirty next month."

"But I thought you had Tristan—"

"Yeah, I had him my senior year, but I was already on the six-year plan because I changed my major three times." She laughs at herself. "And when I had Tristan, it added another year. Then I decided to go back to school for what I'm doing now, so I guess I'm one of those people . . ."

"One of which people?" I say earnestly.

She shrugs. "I don't know, like fickle or something."

"You're only thirty. You have the schooling and you're raising a kid. Don't be so hard on yourself, I wouldn't call you fickle at all."

I glance around, looking for a possible music source.

"How 'bout some music?" I say.

"Music?"

"Yeah, like a Bluetooth speaker or something I can link to my phone." I'm not trying to be slimy by setting the mood, it's just unbearably quiet and Kate isn't a gabby person. There are a lot of lulls in the conversation. And, well, after so many years with Dani, I guess I'm just used to having music playing.

"Oh. I do have a speaker. It's in my room. Come on." She stands and holds out her hand. I hesitate for just a moment and then stand and follow her to her bedroom.

Inside her minimalist room, she hands me a small Bluetooth speaker. I sit on the edge of her bed, attempting to link my phone to it. She sits next to me, waiting for me to figure it out.

In an attempt to break the awkward silence, I gesture my head toward the TV. "What do you like to watch?"

"Everything. I'm kind of a TV junkie, but I also like to watch the great artistic films."

I nod and smile. Something about her doesn't make sense. It seems forced. "Did you ever watch *Litigators*?"

"For sure, I loved that show!"

"Dani wrote for that show for years."

"Who's Dani?"

"Danielle, my wife . . . ex-wife."

"Oh, yeah, of course. Maybe I did know that."

"She won three Emmys for it." People who were into TV knew who Dani was. Maybe this is Kate's way of subtly insulting Dani. I guess it's understandable. It's probably intimidating knowing I was married to her.

"Oh, right. I was wondering why her last name is different. Is it Brolin?"

Aha. She knows exactly who Dani is. "Yeah, she kept her last name because she was already established as a writer when we met . . . and also Danielle Atkinson-Lloyd is kind of a mouthful. Danielle Brolin just sounds better. The boys have my last name, though."

"Really? You'd think she'd want it. It actually sounds more writerly to me. She might have had more success with your last name."

I'm stupefied right now. "She's an award-winning writer. And none of it has anything to do with her last name. Let's change the subject, shall we? I don't think we want to sit here talking about my ex-wife, right?"

I can't decide if I should just stop talking altogether. I lift my wine to set it on the vanity for a moment.

"Oh no, I don't put drinks there. You can put it here." She points to a coaster on her nightstand. It's a wineglass, for god's sake. I stand up anyway and put it on the nightstand, and then reach for the Bluetooth speaker again. I'm finally able to link my phone and turn on the Miles Davis Spotify station. The sound is terrible on this speaker, but it's better than nothing.

"Oh, I like this, who is it?"

It's the song "So What" with John Coltrane. Possibly one of the most recognizable songs in existence. I know she's heard this song at least two hundred times, in at least two hundred lobbies or department stores.

"It's Miles Davis," I say.

"That's right."

There's not enough time tonight to teach her about jazz. I lean down and kiss her lightly on the lips. She pulls me down onto the bed.

We have sex the way people do in their early twenties. It wasn't unpleasant or awkward, it was . . . nice. It was sort of like Kraft Mac & Cheese. You know exactly what it tastes like, you know the texture and how you'll feel afterward, and you know on some level that you really like it. At the same time, you know there are countless variations of mac-and-cheese. There's gourmet, deconstructed, truffle oil, skillet fried, mac-and-cheese made from the finest aged Gruyére from a tiny, misty, green village nestled next to the Alps in Switzerland, where the cows are, in fact, happy . . .

I can't believe I'm comparing sex to mac-and-cheese. I'm getting dumber by the minute. It's not Kate. She's beautiful, sexy, smells good, moves well, and she definitely turns me on. It's just that I felt like if I closed my eyes, it could have been anyone. I guess despite what Dani thinks of me, I want more than something that feels so . . . predictable. I'm not being snobby about it. Sometimes I prefer Kraft over the fancy shit! I'm just saying, it wasn't memorable.

Kate is being sweet. Kissing my face. She's lying naked on top of me. "That was amazing, like mind-blowing," she says near my ear.

"Wow, thank you," I say.

"It was my pleasure," she replies.

Wait a minute. Was she saying she was amazing? It doesn't matter. It's been a very long time since I've felt this good, and I'm relieved it wasn't awkward. I'm going to enjoy this moment.

"Do you mind if I lie here for a bit?" I say.

"No, not at all. You can stay as long as you want. You can stay all night, if you want," she says flatly.

No, I don't want! I don't want that kid wondering what the hell is going on.

"Thank you, Kate, but I am going to go home tonight."

"That's okay. Did you know your phone has been blowing up for like half an hour? Are you gonna answer it?"

I can't hear that well and didn't turn the ringer on, which I usually do when I take it out of my pocket. "Yeah." I reach over and grab it.

Five missed calls from Dani and one text from a second ago . . . my heart is already pounding out of my chest.

Dani: The boys are alive and in good health, but this is an
emergency so fucking answer your phone, you shitbag.

"I have to call my wife. Ex-wife." I get up out of the bed and
wrap a throw blanket around myself while simultaneously dial-
ing Dani.

"Are you serious?!" She screams when she answers. She's
raging mad. "You have two children and you don't answer your
phone at eleven o'clock at night? I've called you thirty times!"

I feel like I'm having a heart attack. "What's going on, Dani?"

"I just pulled your son outta the back of a freakin' cop car. I'm
bringing him to the apartment! Be ready for him," she yells and
then hangs up.

"Oh no," I say to myself.

"What is it?" Kate says.

"I have to go. My son got in trouble. I have to go, I'm sorry."

My good ear is ringing, which is making me ten times more
anxious than I already am. Right before I lost my hearing in my
left ear, there was a loud ringing noise just like this. I'm going to
go completely deaf at the exact worst time in my life.

22

where are you?

DANIELLE

"Put your seatbelt on and shut up!"

I pull out of the driveway of the heavily littered strip mall that contains the Charminar Indian Restaurant, open twenty-four hours; a coin laundromat; a 7-Eleven; and, of course, the most impressive of them all, the headliner, the grand high poohbah, a Spearmint Rhino Gentlemen's Club.

I'm driving in the opposite direction of our house, trying to stop hyperventilating. I'm taking Noah to the apartment to face his father after almost being arrested for loitering and then mouthing off to a police officer at ten-thirty at night when he was supposedly at a friend's house doing thirteen-year-old boy things . . . whatever those "things" are that don't involve committing crimes.

"Where are we going?" Ethan says in a timid voice from the backseat.

"To *hell* if we don't change our ways!" I scream.

I'm shocked that Noah is managing to sit stoically in the passenger seat.

When we get to the complex, I pull Noah by his ear all the way from the car to the apartment front door. Ethan is traveling a safe distance behind us in an effort to separate himself from the criminal I'm dragging.

When we get to the apartment front door I use my key, open the door, and announce, "The juvenile delinquent is here!"

The apartment is dark and quiet so I flip the lights on in the living room and kitchen.

"Alex," I yell, not kindly. "Sit," I say to Noah, pointing to the couch.

I'm confused. Where is he? I go to the bedroom . . . empty.

"Hi, Dad!" I hear Ethan say in the living room.

When I walk out, I see Alex standing in the entryway, looking disheveled. He's sweating and breathing hard.

"Where were you?" I say in a calm voice.

Alex looks at me but doesn't answer. He looks at Ethan, "Hi, buddy." He then walks to the couch and stands over Noah, who is sitting with his arms crossed over his chest. "What happened?" Alex asks.

Noah is tongue-tied.

"Do you happen to know where Spearmint Rhino is?" I say.

Alex squints. "He was at a strip club?"

"That's a strip club?" Noah says. "I didn't even know."

"Deliberately obtuse, obtuse, *obtuse!*" I say.

Alex walks over to me. "Calm down. What did the police say?"

"The cop I spoke with said they believed the boys were in the laundromat to vandalize it, and then apparently when your son was confronted by the cops, he told an officer of the law to . . . and I quote . . . *'bite my shiny metal ass'*!"

Alex buckles over with laughter.

"Are you serious?" I say to him. "You're laughing?" Noah and Ethan are still silent, staring up at us.

"I'm sorry. I just can't believe he said that. It . . . actually sounds like something you would say, Dani."

"So this is *my* fault now?"

He breathes out and drops the smile. "No. I'm not saying that. What happened, Noah? Tell us everything."

"You guys won't listen because you believe that cops are always right."

"No, we don't, actually, but we believe in abiding by the law and respecting other people," I say.

"I still haven't heard what happened," Alex says.

Noah takes a deep breath. "Listen, the washer at Jose's house broke—"

"So you were doing their laundry at ten-thirty at night?" I say. "Bullshit! You don't even do your own laundry."

Alex looks at me. "They need to start doing their own laundry, it's getting really out of hand."

"Did you forget that we were talking about how your son got arrested?"

"I didn't get arrested, I wasn't even sitting in the cop car, I was leaning against it. Mom, you're exaggerating!"

"You were handcuffed," I say.

Noah shrugs, "They just did that for show."

"I don't care what it was for," I shoot back.

"Noah, tell the whole story, start to finish. Dani, stop interrupting," Alex says.

"Jose's mom, Suzanna, did her laundry earlier that day. She asked us to walk down to the laundromat, which is only two blocks from their house, and look for a sweater she thought she left in a dryer. When we got down there, we were going through all the dryers looking for the sweater, and the lady that works there freaked out and called the cops."

I'm breathing in and out, trying to listen. I think I believe him.

"Go on," Alex says.

"So the cop comes in right when we miraculously find the sweater. Jose has the sweater in one hand and his cellphone in the other. The cop tells us to come outside, so we do. He then starts grilling Jose about the cellphone and Jose is like, 'It's mine, I promise.' Jose tries to tell him what we were doing, but he wouldn't listen, kind of like what you guys were doing to me a minute ago," he says. *Smart-ass.*

"Keep going," I say. "And leave out the commentary."

"So, the cop is, like, pestering Jose. He's like, 'You steal those cellphones so you can get initiated into gangs or to talk with your gang boys,' and we're like, 'No, this is *our* stuff!'"

I look at how Noah is dressed. He's wearing shorts, flip-flops, and a T-shirt that has an atom symbol on it, with the words *Don't Trust Atoms, They Make Up Everything!* I mean, Noah is like the epitome of nerd in the best possible way, and I know for a fact that Jose won both the science fair and the geography bee three years running, I don't think he's petitioning to be in any gangs.

"So," Noah continues, "the cop was, like, obviously talking that way to Jose because he's Mexican."

"We don't know that," Alex says.

"Kinda sounds like it to me," I say under my breath.

Alex glances back. "What?"

"Nothing. Go on, Noah, get to the part where you told him to kiss your ass," I say. "And that other part where you were hand-cuffed."

"So, I say to the cop, 'Why are you hassling him? We're good kids, we're doing his mom a favor.' And he says, 'No one asked you. Why don't you keep your mouth shut, kid?' So obviously that's when I said, 'Why don't you kiss my shiny metal ass?' I feel like anyone would have done the same."

"No, Noah! People wouldn't say that to a *police officer*. Are you crazy?" I yell.

Alex is still standing there, quietly assessing the situation.

Noah rolls his eyes. "You would have said it, Mom."

"Anyway, so then he handcuffed you?" Alex asks.

"He told Jose to go home and then he told me something about how I was shaping up to be a felon. Before he called Mom, he handcuffed me and said, 'This is so you don't go trying anything while we wait for your mom.' Like I was really gonna take off wearing flip-flops. It was all for show, to scare me. Whatever."

"Would you have run if you were wearing Nikes?" I say through gritted teeth.

My hand is shaking and my ear is twitching. I know I'm reaching anger Defcon 3. Alex looks calm, which only fuels my frustration.

"You don't get me, Mom!" Noah says to my face, pointedly.

"Excuse me? I don't *get* you?! I *grew you* . . . in my body . . . like a mad fucking scientist! *I totally get you!*"

"Danielle," Alex warns. "Calm down. Let's talk in the kitchen and try to decide what to do."

He used my whole name. I'm in trouble. "Fine," I say. The apartment is small. We walk three feet into the kitchen. The boys can totally hear and see us. It's ridiculous.

I have my hands on my hips.

Alex is about a foot taller than me so he has to lower his head to talk quietly. He leans down and says, "I believe him."

"Why?" I want to know if Alex has even thought this through

or if he's looking for an easy way out. A way to stay in the kids' good graces. "How are you so sure?" I push further.

"Because he's just like you, Dani . . . Always getting in trouble for doing the right thing." He half smiles. There is something in his expression that looks almost like admiration.

"I would have totally done that, huh?" I say.

"Yes, you would have done the exact same thing. You're both entirely incapable of hiding how you feel about something."

"I hope it doesn't get him in actual trouble," I say.

"Look at him," Alex replies. I look back to see Noah setting up the chessboard to play Ethan. "He's not looking for trouble."

"Neither am I, but it seems I have no problem finding it."

"You're shaking, Dani." He takes my hands in his. It feels unfamiliar. That's how long it's been. I forgot how soft his hands are. They're big and masculine, but soft.

"I'm short-circuiting," I tell him. "My anxiety is through the roof! We still need to talk to him, Alex."

"I'll do the talking. Come on."

What? This is new. Alex is doing the talking?

"Noah," Alex says, "remember when your mom was in Salt & Straw with you guys that one day and saw that man mistreating the worker?"

"Yeah, I do remember, he was a jerk. How can a person be unhappy when they're about to get *ice cream*?"

"He implied that the girl was dumb, right?" Alex asks.

I huff. "Really? This is the analogy you're using?"

"Yes," Alex says with a hint of humor.

"Dad, he called her a 'dum-dum' right to her face."

"Right, Noah. It was wrong of him. But then your mom went outside and knocked his ice-cream cone out of his hand."

"Yeah, she did." Noah looks at me and smiles, as if to say, *Good job, Mom!*

"But what happened?" Alex says.

"Ugh, why are we dragging this out? What your dad is saying is that two wrongs don't make a right," I blurt out.

Alex looks at me with slight irritation. "I want him to understand that his behavior got him nowhere."

"I think the cop realized he was wrong for profiling Jose, so he had to use me as a scapegoat," Noah interjects.

"That's not the point. Never mind. Listen, Noah, you're not in trouble. Don't ever do that again. I'm glad you were defending Jose, but Jose got to go home and you got handcuffs. The man got a new ice-cream cone and Mom got banned from the Galleria mall. You see my point? I know you both do. We're all tired. We are not punishing you, okay? Let's call it a night," Alex says.

I agree, after feeling a little wounded that I was being reprimanded alongside Noah. It's almost 2 A.M. and I don't want to drive home. Part of me wants to ask where Alex came from earlier, but I don't.

"I'm gonna set up the blow-up mattress for the boys, and I'll just sleep on the couch."

"No, you can have the bed. I'll sleep on the couch," Alex says.

We're both strangely calm in this moment, even though this situation is uncharted territory for us. "Are you sure?"

"Yes, a hundred percent."

I commandeer the bathroom first. I brush my teeth, wash my face, and look for something to wear, but I don't have anything here, so I strip down and throw on a T-shirt that Alex left hanging on the towel rack. He won't care.

In the bedroom, he knocks and pushes the cracked door open as I'm getting into bed.

"What's up?" I ask. I feel modest with him for the first time in ages, maybe forever. I point to the T-shirt. "I hope you don't mind."

"No, of course not."

He sits on the edge of the bed. This is all so strange and I'm not sure what to make of what he's doing.

"I want to help out more, with the boys, with the household stuff, whatever," he says in a low voice. He hardly ever talks quietly because he is so hard of hearing.

"What is this? Are you implying that I'm doing a bad job because of what happened tonight?"

"No, not at all." He starts to get up to walk out. "I knew you were gonna get defensive."

"Sit down, please. What is this all about?"

He sits down and angles his body toward me. I can smell a woman on him. It's either perfume or some kind of soap or lotion. In this moment, I feel like the realization would be easier to accept if we said it out loud, if we came clean. He can say who he's been sleeping with, and I'll say I hooked up with my ex a handful of times, and then we can just move on. I'll leave out the part in which I felt dogged and disposable from the whole dating experience. He doesn't need to know that, he's probably having a good ol' time.

There have been many instances in my kids' lives when I've used the "ripping the Band-Aid off" analogy. I think it applies here, but Alex isn't like that. I can throw something in a closet and forget its entire existence, as if I have no sense of object permanence, but when it comes to people, my brain never stops. Alex can "out-of-sight, out-of-mind" actual *people*. So, in his case, he wouldn't want to know anything. My imagination, however, *lives* for the possibility of what people are doing at any given moment. In my head, I've basically already married Alex off to whoever's perfume this is. They have some kids, maybe three, and I'm wondering who I will be to those kids.

"Listen, Dani, I'm not bringing this up because of what happened, I swear. Other than this snafu tonight, the boys are doing great. You're an awesome mom, you always have been. It's not that. You just look tired all the time lately."

"Thank you very much. Everyone knows that *tired* is code for old and ugly."

"Dani, you are so skinny right now. And you're shaking from anxiety! You've also been a little forgetful lately and—"

"Okay, okay, enough!" I say. "I know. I've been stressed. I'm sorry. I'm not dropping the ball with the kids at all though."

"I know you're not. I just don't want to see you this stressed," he says. I cock my head and look at him. He's being sincere. He actually cares, which feels . . . weird. When my mother was dying and the rumors about Lars were flying, I was a nervous wreck, falling apart and emotionally depleted, but Alex barely seemed to look at me.

"I'm just worried about the show. I've been wanting my own show for so long and now I finally have it and I'm terrified."

He puts his hand on top of my foot, which is under the covers. He rubs my foot through the comforter. It's an old habit, muscle memory.

We used to be like this.

"The show is going to be great," he says. "You have a natural sense for this kind of stuff. Let me help out more . . . at least until the pilot airs. I'll do four days instead of three, okay? It's settled."

I nod, so he gets up to head out. "Alex?" He turns around near the door. "Thank you," I say, and I mean it.

"You're welcome."

"One last thing?"

"What?"

"I want to know when you have a girlfriend, okay? I know I don't have a right to know, but please just tell me. You know how crazy my mind is. I'll give you the same respect in return."

"Okay, Danielle. I don't have anything that remotely resembles a girlfriend right now."

"Okay. I went on three dates with Jacob, but that's done with," I blurt out. "I don't have much time for dating, but I'm sure we will both see other people at some point. It's just better to rip the Band-Aid off, you know?"

"Okay. I will let you know."

As soon as he walks out, I fall fast asleep. Sleep that comes easily requires a level of peace. There's peace in knowing another parent is there with you, even if they're in the other room. It's something I took for granted before.

~

In the morning, I walk to the kitchen to find a note from Alex. I look over and see the boys are still sleeping on the blow-up mattress.

> *Dani, I had to go into the clinic to do a makeup appointment and some paperwork with Jenna. She's bringing her baby, Sophia, with her if you guys want to come down and meet her.*

I feel something in my chest. I think it's happiness. For a long time after I had the miscarriages, I couldn't hold other people's newborns. Right now I feel unreasonably excited about meeting Jenna's baby. I decide I'm going to wake up the boys with some tunes.

The Doors' *Morrison Hotel* album is sticking out from the sideways stack on the shelf. *Perfect.*

I pull the record and sleeve out and read the writing on it. It's my dad's, but maybe I'll add to it today. I put the record on and move the needle to the fourth song.

Song 4: You're dancing in the kitchen, doing some variation of the Hustle to the song "Peace Frog"—wearing the green bell-bottoms, my favorite. You're eight months pregnant and still getting down. Dance your heart out, Irene.

She was pregnant with me. I set the record sleeve down, turn up the volume, and do the Hustle all the way into the kitchen. The kids are now awake and staring unamused.

"I'm gonna make you guys pancakes!" I yell over the music.

"What is this?" Ethan says.

"This is The Doors. Jim Morrison, baby!"

"You're so weird, Mom," Noah grumbles loudly.

"Pot-kettle, Noah," I say in a singsongy voice. "You're the weirdest of us all. Now go take showers, both of you!"

I'm a firm believer in messing up your kids just enough to give them a sense of humor.

23

does this feel like peace to you too?

ALEXANDER

Jenna's baby, Sophia, won't stop crying. Luckily, she was asleep when the patient came in this morning, because her screeching sounds like the last pterodactyl being murdered.

"She's the worst baby! I can't believe I had two perfect angel babies and number three is a fusspot. It's nonstop," Jenna says.

"It's not just fussy, she's, like, *wailing*. Are you sure there's nothing wrong with her?"

Jenna rolls her eyes. "There's nothing wrong with her, she's just colicky, which is some word doctors use to make you feel like it's normal that your baby cries twenty-four/seven. I am losing my mind. She won't stop."

Jenna is shooshing her and looking into her eyes, silently begging Sophia to be quiet. She's rocking and changing the baby's position multiple times. Nothing is helping. Jenna is a very down-to-earth person. She's not dramatic or whiny, so I know this is getting to her. She's lost all of the pregnancy weight and then some, and looks hollow, like she hasn't slept in a year. I feel bad for even asking her to come back to work, but she said she wanted to. And now I think I understand why.

"Do you care that I invited Dani and the boys to come meet her?"

"Do they want to see what a possessed baby looks like?"

I shrug. "She's really cute."

The door jingles and in walks Dani and the boys. "Hi," Dani says cheerily just before her smile disappears. "Oh no, unhappy baby on the loose." Dani is dressed differently. She's wearing a flowing skirt and a tank top. It's very Earth Mothery for her. Maybe this is what she wears on Saturdays now? She seems different, more relaxed today, despite the screaming baby.

Dani walks up to Jenna and kisses her on the cheek. "You look amazing," she says. It's a lie . . . the good kind.

"Can you believe this? I should know how to do this!" Jenna says. "I can't believe I'm having the hardest time with this one. The labor was fine, but once she was out, she wouldn't latch and then when she finally did, she *destroyed* my nipples, now all she does is cry all day." Ethan winces. Dani just listens and Noah and I are both focused on the baby. I'm hoping someone will get her to shut up soon.

"I'm about to start lactating myself," Dani says with a laugh.

"Gross, Mom." Noah frowns.

"Has she eaten?" Dani asks.

"Yes, more than enough," Jenna says.

"Noah was like this. He was my first, so I got it out of the way. When I had Ethan, it felt like a Sunday stroll in the park."

Ethan looks at Noah and smiles boastfully.

"I'm losing my mind," Jenna says, exasperated.

"Here, let me see that baby."

Dani has the baby in her left arm as she takes the blanket off the desk and wraps it around Sophia several times, very tight. Sophia is screaming bloody murder. Dani takes the end of the blanket and uses it to cover the baby's eyes. She then puts the wrapped-up baby burrito in the crease of her arm and holds the baby tight against her chest, rocking and making a clicking noise with her tongue every two seconds. Suddenly, I'm right back in those early days—and sleepless nights—with Noah.

Miraculously, Sophia stops crying. She makes a few mewling sounds and then she's quiet. Dani continues clacking and rocking her while Jenna stares in disbelief. Dani puts a finger to her mouth, and we all stand in silence for about three minutes until Dani slowly stops the noise and motion.

Once it's completely quiet and she's standing still with the baby, she whispers, "She's asleep. This was exactly how Noah was. It took me a couple of months to figure out."

"What did you do? Isn't she squished?"

"Not any more squished than she was in your belly." I'm basically reading lips now because Jenna and Dani are talking in hushed tones. "Sometimes their little brains aren't ready for all the stimuli and voices. If they can't see anything, then they can't be overwhelmed. And the clicking is like something to focus on that's consistent, like white noise, or your heartbeat, which was cozy to her. My old neighbor taught me this trick. I felt like I was abusing Noah or something by wrapping him up so tight and clacking at him, but it works. They sleep and so do you."

"Thank you, Dani. This is the first time I've felt that there is hope. I'm serious. It's like I'm seeing a light at the end of the tunnel." Dani laughs. Jenna is being a little dramatic. She walks up to me quietly and says, "I can't believe you divorced her. I'd marry her myself."

Dani is oblivious now, in her own world. She's sitting in one of the waiting room chairs, holding the baby. She's just staring at

Sophia lovingly and all I want to know is what she's thinking about at this moment.

I really believe that if it wasn't for the miscarriages, Dani would have had five kids . . . at least. It's bad enough to have one second-term miscarriage, but two? Absolutely crushing; it destroyed her for a very long time.

After the first, we tried again. Noah and Ethan were still toddler-aged, two and three years old. Dani got pregnant right away, but she kept it a secret. She didn't even tell me until after her doctor's visit when it was confirmed with a blood test and ultrasound. She saw the heartbeat, came home, and walked up to me at the kitchen sink as I was doing dishes. She had Ethan on her hip—I remember he was twirling her long hair around his index finger.

She leaned in close to my ear and said, "I'm pregnant." She seemed much more cautious than excited.

I turned around and said, "Really? That's great."

"Yeah. I bought a fetal doppler, it was eight hundred dollars. I hope you don't mind," she said with zero emotion. It was rare for Dani to be expressionless. You could usually tell within a few moments of being around her what she was feeling. If she wasn't dancing, cracking jokes, making funny commentary or kissing and hugging you, then she was probably yelling or crying. Occasionally, you'd get an even-keeled version of her, but it was rare. I think she took that side of herself to work, mostly. She's always been "love hard, fight hard" when it comes to the people in her personal life.

In the kitchen that day, I tried to make light of the situation, which was a bad idea. "Are you planning on checking the weather?"

Her expression stayed cold. "A fetal doppler is so that we can know if the baby is dead inside of me."

The way she said it felt so harsh. "Why are you putting that out there?" I asked.

"What?" Mad Dani was starting to come out. "You mean out into the universe? Like I'm capable of willing something to happen with my thoughts and fears? What a gift . . . and a curse!"

"That's not what I meant."

"So if this one dies, it will be my fault for buying a fetal doppler?"

"Dani, you're being terrible right now."

She broke down and started crying. Ethan noticed and frowned, so she went and set him on a play mat in the living room, then walked back into our bedroom. When I came in, she was curled up on the bed.

"I'm sorry, Dani."

"I'm sorry too," she said in a cracked voice.

"Noah's already sleeping. I'm going to put Ethan down and I'll be back," I told her. I came right back and curled up behind her.

We made love that night. It was slow and tender. She told me it was exactly what she needed to get her mind off the baby . . . to focus on our love and the family we already had. She was so affectionate and warm then . . . attentive in a way that made you want to reciprocate it instantly. At that time, I had never felt so close to a person. I haven't since, and to be honest, I doubt I ever will.

Two months later, she was looking for the heartbeat on the doppler. She called to me from the bedroom. "Alex, come in here, please!"

By the time I got into our room she was almost hyperventilating, standing at the vanity mirror and holding the wand to her stomach.

"What's wrong?"

"Let me lie down on the bed and you try it. I can't find the heartbeat!" she said, out of breath.

"Try and stay calm." She was lying on her back horizontally across the bed. She held her sweater up above her bra.

I moved the doppler in a grid slowly over her stomach, listening. The volume was all the way up. We picked up Dani's heartbeat. "That's me," she said.

"I know." I moved it to the lower part of her stomach, where an early baby bump was forming. I was still moving the doppler wand, but I already knew.

I remember so vividly Dani looking up at me, eyes wide, waiting to hear something. After a couple of minutes, tears began streaming down her face. She wasn't frowning. Her face wasn't scrunched up and she wasn't making a sound, but tears were pouring off her cheeks. This went on for the entire hour it took to get the kids to my mom's and for us to get to the hospital. A constant and steady stream of emotional pain.

When the doctor came in and did the ultrasound, we all saw the tiny baby, but no heartbeat. At that point, Dani was resigned. She was no longer crying, just numb. The doctor apologized and asked her if she wanted to wait to miscarry naturally or if she wanted a D&C to remove what the doctor described as "fetal tissue."

"Danielle, this is not an indication that you cannot have more children," Dr. Lee told her. "I know this is a painful process. We're going to check all your levels and do a thorough exam in a week or so, and then we'll make a plan for what's next. Most of the time a miscarriage is because the baby would not have been viable anyway. You understand that, right?"

Dani nods.

"If it's because of your body, or hormone levels, there are things we can do, but most often it's your body doing the exact right thing. You've proven you're capable of carrying to term and having healthy, natural births."

Dani looked exhausted and vacant behind her eyes. She was just nodding, indifferently. "Okay," she said.

"We can give you progesterone once you're pregnant again and it will help build up a more stable lining in your uterus. There are a number of things we can do."

Dr. Lee was young. She didn't have any children of her own. I think in Dani's mind the doctor couldn't possibly understand, so Dani showed her grace.

"It's okay. I understand. Thank you, Dr. Lee."

As they wheeled Dani out of the room, heading for the operating room to perform the D&C, I followed next to her bed as far as they would let me.

At one point Dani looked up at the nurse and said, "I want to know what the sex is."

The older female nurse nodded and smiled sympathetically. "Of course, honey."

Right before they took her in, I bent and kissed her forehead, but it was like she wasn't there. She was staring off into space.

They scheduled an appointment for a week later for her to see her OB-GYN. My mom was there to help her. At that point, Irene's symptoms were becoming obvious. We realized she had been suffering from early-onset Alzheimer's probably since around the time Ben died, so my mom started helping Dani a lot more and she took care of her after the second miscarriage.

When Dani came home from the hospital, she mostly just slept for that entire week.

The day of her follow-up appointment to plan next steps, I got a text message from a urologist's office. It was an appointment reminder that I had a vasectomy scheduled for the following Friday. This was news to me. We had never had a single conversation about a vasectomy or about not having any more kids.

I called Dani immediately. "Hey." I was gentle with her.

"Hi," she said.

"What is this appointment you made? We haven't even talked about this."

"Fine, then you don't have to do it. I'll go get my tubes tied. I don't want to be on birth control and I don't want any more kids. It's my choice. I'm happy with our two. I'm sorry I didn't tell you. I didn't think they would call you. I was going to talk to you about it tonight."

"Dani, do you think you should be making this decision right now?"

In a flat voice, almost monotone, Dani said, "I just thought since I spent years on birth control, I've given birth twice, unmedicated, and I've lost two babies . . . I thought maybe you could just go ahead and do this. It's a much simpler procedure for you than it is for me anyway."

I was stunned into silence. Dani made decisions easily, so I knew she was serious. She wasn't the type to act fickle or hem and haw.

"I'll do it, okay?" I told her.

It felt strange that she was essentially taking the decision away from me. *What about me? Do I still want kids?*

As if she was reading my mind, she said, "I don't think anything will happen, but if for some reason you end up with someone else, someone who wants to have kids, then you should consider that now, before you do it. I know I don't. I am a hundred percent certain I do not want any more children."

"How can you be so sure right now, Dani?"

"I'm sure right now because this feeling is fresh in my mind, in my gut, coursing through my veins. I don't want to get down the road, having forgotten this hellfire I am living in, and decide I'm strong enough to go through it again. I don't want to forget that I saw a tiny, dead baby girl the size of a fucking Yukon Gold potato wrapped in a blanket. Do you remember that?"

Right before the D&C was about to be performed, Dani's body started to deliver the baby on its own. She started to actively miscarry while in the operating room. They called me in to support her, but she didn't need it. She was drugged up and unengaged, but I stood next to her head anyway and held her limp hand. I guess because Dani asked to know the sex earlier, when the tiny baby came out, the nurse showed it to her and said, "Do you want to hold her?"

Dani was heavily sedated and just glanced at the baby for a second and then mumbled, "No. Cremate her."

That's what they did with the first one.

Dani shoved the box containing the ashes from the second miscarriage into the back of the hallway closet, next to the box from the first one. Out of sight, out of mind. We didn't talk about it until we were having the vasectomy conversation a week later.

"Of course I remember seeing her. I'm sorry. It was horrible."

"I'm just glad I didn't tell anyone except you this time. I don't want any more kids, Alex. I want to be a good mother to the two we have. I don't want to be a damaged, heartbroken person like this. I need to move past it."

"I understand. I'll get the vasectomy, Danielle. I know I'll never want kids with anyone else."

"We can always adopt." Her voice got higher, like there was a hint of hope in it. Looking back now, I realize it wasn't hope, it was surrender and relief. I know because I felt it too.

In the clinic waiting room, Dani is still holding a sleeping Sophia while the boys are sitting on each side of her, playing on their phones. I'm wrapping up paperwork on a patient and Jenna is working faster than I've ever seen her. It's that mom efficiency—she knows at any minute, Sophia is going to wake up screaming, so Jenna is utilizing the time.

When all the work is done, Dani puts Sophia in the car seat for Jenna, who's still watching in awe. "You're a miracle worker. Can you come to my house every day?"

"Just try that little technique. It feels weird at first, but it'll work. In a couple of months, the crying nonstop phase will be over and you'll be on to the next exhausting thing," Dani says, laughing with ease.

"I know, I know." Jenna looks back at me. "You gonna lock up, boss?"

"Yeah, I got it."

After Jenna leaves, Dani and the boys are waiting for me by the back door. "Dani, I'll take the boys tonight. I'll start doing four days this week."

Dani's just looking blankly at me. "Okay," she says in a low voice. I know what she's thinking right now. She's wondering what she's going to do with herself and this extra free time.

"Why don't you take advantage and get some writing in?" I say.

She frowns. "No, I don't want to work right now."

"Oh, hold on!" I run back into my office and dig through my desk drawer. A patient had given me a Burke Williams Spa gift card that I was going to give to Jenna, but I've decided Dani should have it.

I hand her the gift card. "What's this?" she says.

"It's a spa gift card. You can go get a massage or a facial, or whatever."

She's staring at it in her hand like it's a rare gem I just dug out of some dangerous mine in the Congo. She looks up. "Thank you." For a moment, she's earnest, and then her mouth breaks into a teasing smile. "This is uncharacteristically thoughtful of you, Alex."

I roll my eyes. "Dani, just say 'thank you' and be done with it."

"I did," she whines. "I'm excited. I'm gonna request a male masseuse." She winks.

"Mom!" Ethan gripes.

"What? They have stronger hands," she says, batting her eyelashes.

I can't help but smile.

It's been two months and I've been seeing Kate regularly almost every Thursday and Friday.

It's . . . nice.

Her kid is starting to treat me like I'm his dad and that's worrying me, but I let Kate know that she needs to be honest with him. Last night, she asked me what we were to each other and I didn't know how to answer.

She was naked, standing near her vanity. Tristan was asleep in his room and I was lying on her bed, fully clothed on top of the comforter. I showed up, as I often did, after I knew Tristan would be asleep. My goal was to not confuse him. Kate was just coming out of the shower when I got there. In her room, she dropped her towel unabashedly and was looking for something to wear in her dresser drawers, while I just laid there watching her.

"Can I ask you something?" she said. That is my least favorite question. It's rhetorical and has absolutely no point.

"Of course."

She was lifting a lace-embellished nightgown over her head to put on. "What are we to each other, Alex? You come over, we eat dinner, or we go to dinner when I can get a sitter, then we have sex. You make breakfast in the morning for Tristan and me sometimes, then you leave. If we're lucky, you spend the day with us. But we've never talked about what we're doing, exactly."

She came over and sat on the edge of the bed.

"Do we have to name it?" I ask.

"I'm in love with you, Alex." My stomach dropped. "Did you hear me?" she presses.

"I heard you."

"You're not going to respond?"

"I . . . I love you too, Kate." It was the worst. So obviously forced.

"Thank you for saying that," she murmurs.

It blew by her. Or she just wanted to hear it so badly, she didn't care if it was sincere or not.

The truth is that being with Kate is boring. There's no way around it. I'm just not imagining any significant future with her. A lot of guys would be into her. She's beautiful and sexy, and most importantly, she's sweet, but it would be like eating Kraft Mac & Cheese for the rest of my life. Our conversations are banal at best. It's like chatting with a patient and I *hate* small talk. Every time I go to her house, she tells me about some current event she read about or saw on the news and what she thinks of it. Or a TV show she likes. Or she talks gossip about her friends, whom I don't even know. Sometimes she talks about food or working out. The point is that she talks nonstop about nothing . . . and I just listen. We never have anything remotely resembling a profound conversation.

I believe Kate feels that because of my age, I'm getting the better end of the bargain in the relationship. Like she's a 10 and I'm an old 5 who used to be a 9 and wants to feel good about himself. I let her believe that because I like the more confident version of her, but what I know about Kate now is that she should be with someone her own age. She should mature alongside someone at the same stage in life. A person who has had similar experiences that she can relate to.

For now, though, the relationship is serving a purpose, as callous as that sounds. I knew I would have to be up-front with her eventually. But last night, instead of having a conversation about it, I avoided it. She started touching me, things were progressing. I got naked quickly before she began heading south.

About two minutes into what she was doing, she paused, looked up at me, and said, "Am I your girlfriend?"

"Yes, Kate, you're my girlfriend."

Now it's Saturday. I'm at the apartment getting ready to go to the house. I need to tell Dani.

I hear my phone buzzing in the other room, so I go to retrieve it. It's my mom.

I have a *Leave It to Beaver* family. My mom and dad are still married, going on fifty years, and they're happy and healthy—nothing to report. I have a little sister, Amanda, an occupational therapist who is ten years younger than me. She used to work at the clinic, but now she lives in Santa Barbara with her long-term boyfriend, Josh, who is a high school PE teacher. Everyone gets along. My mom and dad are both teachers still, and happy. I'm fairly close with Amanda, considering how far apart in age we are. She always seemed like such a little girl to me, and now it suddenly hits me that I'm dating someone younger than her.

I answer the phone. I figure talking to my mom about Kate first will make telling Dani and the boys easier.

"Hi, Mom."

"Hi, honey. Listen, for Thanksgiving we're gonna do it here. Your sister and Josh are coming down and they're staying the whole weekend. Amanda misses you guys. Anyway, your dad wants to show off the winter garden." She lowers her voice. "He never stops talking about it." I can almost see her eyes rolling through the phone. "Oh yeah, and guess what? We set up a TV in the garage so the boys can play those virtual murder games."

"It's Super Mario Kart, Mom," I say.

"Whatever, let's talk about the menu."

"I have something to tell you." I realize I haven't even asked Dani about the holidays.

"Well, go on, then," she says.

"I'm seeing someone. I have a . . . girlfriend."

I wish I could see her face, or maybe I don't. She loves Dani. "Alex . . ." She's quiet and calm. "Alex, that's really great." I don't believe her.

"Great?"

"Dani is bringing that delicious sweet potato casserole she makes and an apple pie. I thought you could bring some rolls?"

Rolls are reserved for the shitty cooks and she knows it. My mother is doing a very good job of changing the subject.

"Mom, I told you about Kate because I was going to tell the boys that I'm seeing her and introduce them to her son. She has a six-year-old." My mother is still silent. "I want to bring them to Thanksgiving."

I do not actually want to bring Kate and Tristan to Thanksgiving, but Kate asked if she could meet my family. She also said her parents would be out of town for the holiday—in Idaho, at her sister's house. I can't leave Kate and Tristan home alone on Thanksgiving. I don't know how Dani is going to react, but I figure in a week and a half I should have everyone prepared and accepting of the reality that I am seeing someone.

My mother huffs loudly through the phone, signaling that she's irritated with the conversation. "Okay, Alex, bring your new girlfriend and her kid. Have you cleared this with Dani?"

"I'm going to talk to her about it today."

"Who is this person anyway?"

"It's Kate, remember the temp at the clinic who was taking over for Jenna?"

I hear her laugh once. "Alex . . . isn't she like half your age?"

"No, not half." I already feel like an idiot about this whole thing, but I refuse to walk away from this conversation with my tail between my legs. "I deserve to be happy. Dani deserves to be happy too. Right now, Kate is making me happy and I want to bring her and her kid to Thanksgiving, and I expect everyone to be nice to them."

"Alex—"

"Mom, listen . . . can you please call Amanda and tell her and Josh and also let Dad know?"

"Okay, fine," she says in a low voice.

We say goodbye and I'm somewhat relieved that the first step is out of the way. I gather my stuff and head to the house.

Dani is rinsing off the driveway when I pull up, so I park on the street. "What happened?" I ask as I get out of the car.

"Louie Louie puked in the driveway after I took him for a run." It's still funny to me that we named our chocolate Lab Louie Louie and Dani is the only person who calls him by his full name. I think she just likes saying it. She looks so thin right now, it seems concerning that she's running.

"Why are you running?"

"Because I'm training for the Olympics," she says, while shutting the hose off and coiling it up.

When she stands up, I block her from going inside. "Funny, Dani, but seriously, you're so thin."

"This is how I was when we got married. I've been so stressed lately, fatigue from work and writing. I'm not trying to lose any more weight, I just want to get back in shape."

"Okay."

There's a long pause. She looks around as if to say, *Why are you still standing in my way?*

"Can I talk to you?" I ask.

"I'm all ears."

"Can we sit down?"

"Are you serious, Alex? No, just tell me. What, do you have a girlfriend or something?"

How does she always know things? It's a sixth sense. "Yeah, I do."

"Okay. And?"

"I'm going to tell the boys tonight. She has a son who is six. I'm going to take the boys to meet her and her son at Applebee's so they can all get to know each other."

Dani winces. "Applebee's?"

"Is that really all you have to say?" I ask her.

"No, actually I do have a few questions. Let's go inside. The boys are upstairs."

I sit down at the breakfast bar in the kitchen and watch Dani wash her hands. She comes over and stands across from me.

"Who is it?"

"It's Kate."

She looks to the ceiling like she's searching her mind. "The teenage temp?"

"She's thirty."

"Well, come on, Alex, do I have to pry this crap out of you? What is she like? You're obviously serious if the boys are going to meet her. So, she has a kid? Are you prepared to be a stepfather? Have you thought this through?"

"Quit talking down to me, Dani. We're not married anymore, you don't have a right to treat me like a child. You didn't then and you don't now. And no one said I'm going to marry her anyway."

She's staring, unemotional. She blinks a few times. "You're right. I'm still their mom though."

I raise my voice and say, "No one is saying you're not!"

"Goddammit, Alex, let me finish. This conversation is not about you and me. This is about the boys. About how they are going to take it!"

Out of the corner of my eye I spot Ethan in the doorway of the kitchen. "Take what?"

Dani looks up, startled. She then turns to me. That's my cue. "Will you go get your brother, please?"

"What's wrong?" Ethan asks. He looks concerned, his arms folded over his chest. Ethan is smart and mature, but he's still only twelve. He's wearing pajama pants with dinosaurs on them, for Christ's sake. It's starting to hit me.

How will *they take the news?*

"It's nothing bad," Dani says. "Just go get Noah so we don't have to repeat this."

After Ethan walks out, I say, "One last thing, Dani. I'm bringing Kate and Tristan to Thanksgiving at my mom's."

In true Dani form, she says, "Whatever, Alex. You better prepare Kate for the fact that your parents like me more than you." She laughs as she refills her coffee. The boys come into the kitchen and sit at the counter. It's silent. Dani is staring at me with wide eyes. "Well, I'm not gonna tell them, Alex. This is all you."

"Guys, listen. I've been seeing a woman."

Dani laughs through her nose once and I know it's because I called Kate a woman.

"Okay," Noah says. "So?"

"It's Kate from the clinic," I add.

"Okay, Dad. Can we go now?" Ethan asks.

"Listen, she has a son, Tristan, he's six. I want you guys to meet him and get to know Kate better tonight. We're going to meet them at Applebee's."

"Applebee's?" Ethan asks. He's not being condescending, he's actually confused.

"Yes, Applebee's!" I bark. "What is everyone's problem with it?" Dani is laughing to herself in the corner of the kitchen.

"Okay, whatever," Noah says as he gets up from the stool and heads for the hallway.

Ethan stands and walks over to Dani. Without saying a word, he wraps his arms around her for a hug, like he's checking in with her to see if she's okay.

"All this stuff probably feels a little weird for you guys, but everything will be good," Dani says to Ethan as he hugs her. "We're still your mom and dad and we're still here for you."

They're comforting each other. I feel guilt for the first time. It's hard not to when Dani is handling the situation and the boys with such grace.

24

i don't know how i feel

DANIELLE

It's Monday morning and I'm headed into the office. A writer named Mirabel has become my work BFF. She's standing near the outside of my office talking to Eli as I approach from the elevator. Work has been stressful, but it has also been a godsend.

"The lady of the hour," Eli says.

"What's going on?"

The pilot episode hasn't aired yet, but the studio has seen it, along with four other episodes also in the can, as they say. The actors are all unknowns so there's a lot of fear that the show will completely bomb. Mirabel is constantly reminding me that no one knew a single actor on *Grey's Anatomy* when it premiered, and that's gone like seventy-five thousand seasons.

They don't look concerned, they look happy.

"Well, first of all, good morning, lovely. I hope you eat a cracker today, you look too skinny," Mirabel says.

I wish everyone would stop commenting on my weight. "Come into my office," I say.

They both follow me in and sit down in the chairs. Eli starts, "Okay, things going on today," he says as he's staring at a schedule on his phone. "The writers and cast will all be in at nine for a table read, which is in twenty minutes."

"Great," I say.

"They scheduled the pilot finally," Mirabel says. "It's airing February 14."

"Ew." I'm cringing internally. "Why Valentine's Day? The show is like the antithesis of Valentine's Day."

"I don't think so!" Eli says.

"It is," I argue. "Are they trying to be ironic? The whole point of the show is that relationships don't have to look like they did in 1908! The point of the show is that different arrangements work for different people. It's not at all in line with some anti-quated, consumer bullshit holiday!"

"Calm down," Mirabel says. "You're shaking."

I take a deep breath. "I had too much coffee," I say.

"Maybe they *are* trying to be ironic," Eli says. "That would be sort of brilliant."

"Let's move on. What else?" I ask.

"That's it," Eli says as he starts to stand. "Oh, Lars might come in later."

The thought makes me happy. Even though I'm still a little angry at Lars, I do actually miss him. "Fine," I mumble.

Eli leaves the room. "So what's up, how was your weekend?" Mirabel asks.

"Okay, I guess. I found out my ex-husband has a girlfriend and he's gonna bring her to Thanksgiving." I'm trying, unsuccessfully, to sound indifferent.

When I look up, Mirabel is smiling. She's younger than me by a few years, not married, and has no kids. I actually don't even know if she dates. I know she's a workaholic, in good shape, a fantastic writer, but I've never gotten the sense that she has much of a personal life. It kind of feels like she lives at the office. We go to lunch a couple of times a week, but she mostly talks about the show and listens to me gab about my life.

"How do you feel about it?" she says.

"I'm trying not to care. I just don't want my kids to be affected, you know?" I notice how pretty Mirabel looks today. She has an Eva Mendes thing about her and now I'm wondering where her Ryan Gosling is. "What about you? You never talk about your life. Do you date?"

"No, I'm divorced. It's been seven years," she says matter-of-factly. "Since then, I haven't been interested."

I wonder for a moment if that's how I'll be in seven years.

"I had no idea," I say. You'd think she would have brought it up when I was talking about my divorce. "So, what happened?"

"What happened was that I didn't want kids and he did. That's basically it. I kind of let it go because I didn't feel like it was fair of me to keep him from having a family."

"You didn't talk about it before you got married?"

"I don't think I knew. I don't remember having a conversation about it with him," she says, "though if we did talk about it when we were first together, I probably would have said I wanted kids. But then I saw all my friends with their kids and . . . I knew it just wasn't for me."

"So, does your ex have a family now?"

"Yep, three kids, nice wife, the whole bit. But this isn't about me. Just now I was thinking how you're completely in denial about your feelings, Dani, and that's why I was smiling. I was there once. *Of course* it must irk you that Alex has a girlfriend and that he's bringing her to Thanksgiving."

"Would you be shocked to hear, though, that I *want* him to date? I want him to have a girlfriend."

"Why?"

"So he can see what he lost," I say, and it's the truth. I know Alex inside and out. I know our problems had nothing to do with personality. I know beyond a shadow of a doubt that he loved me. We didn't make it, that's all. I hope he'll at least be able to look back and not hate me. I hope he'll realize we had something special.

"Well, hello." I hear the familiar deep soulful sound of Lars' voice. He's in the doorway. Mirabel knows him from a show they worked on together years ago. She stands, hugs him, and says, "Hi, Lars. I'll leave you two for a chat."

He walks all the way into my office, but doesn't sit. Lars is a brilliant and attractive man—not in the universal way that Alex is attractive, more in how he carries himself. He's tall, with completely gray, longish hair. A dead ringer for Mads Mikkelsen. Despite how attractive he is, I was never personally physically attracted to him. Maybe my body already knew something my brain didn't.

"Hi," I say. "Are you going to stand there staring at me, or do you want to have a seat?"

"I'm cataloging this shot . . . this memory. The view right now with you standing next to *your* desk, in *your* office . . . *your* own TV show poster behind you, D . . . it's like I'm looking at a painting and it's moving me . . . You did it, you really did it."

"Always a way with words. Come here and hug me," I say. We hug, and for a moment we're back to ten years ago when we started working on his show. "It's good to see you, Lars. Congratulations on your marriage."

"Thank you," he says as he sits down. "Congratulations on your divorce."

"Touché." I sit down at my desk and say, "So . . . are you here to ask me for a job?"

"Eli pulled some strings and let me see an early cut of the pilot."

"You're kidding. I haven't even seen it. I've only seen the dailies. How is this possible?" I ask.

"I don't think he wants you to see it until all the garnishes have been added."

"Ahh, that makes sense. Smart man."

Lars better tell me what he thinks of the show before I have to ask. He knows whenever a writer has to ask, it's a bad sign. And he surely knows I'm holding it together on the outside, but inside dying to know what he thinks.

My office is bare bones. It's a writer's office, not a designer's. Aside from the poster on the wall, there are papers scattered and a few pictures on my desk. I have an open window that looks out onto the Warner Bros.' backlot New York Street. Lars looks outside and stares like he's in deep thought for moment before looking back at me.

"Is that where they shot *Friends*?"

I laugh a little. He's playing with me and I think I'm going to play along. "Yes, that's where the *Friends* set was. Do you remember the logline for that show?"

"Tell me."

"*It's that time in your life when your friends are your family.* Isn't that just brilliant?"

"Where are you going with this, D?"

With feigned innocence I say, "Oh, I'm just saying . . ."

I'm referring to the day that I came up with the logline for

Litigators, after Lars had written the pilot and we were about to pitch it to the studios. I had said, "I got it, *It's the only family of lawyers you actually want to know*." I remember Lars thought it was confusing and offensive, especially because the execs were probably all lawyers. I figured they would totally get the joke and think it was funny. I was right.

Lars and I are doing a dance right now. This is how we worked. He's putting it together.

"One person can't fulfill all your needs," he says.

I smile widely. He's guessing the logline for my show, *Yours and Mine*. He's spot on. I'm burning up. When is he going to tell me what he thinks?

"D?"

"What?"

"You were always right, especially about the logline for *Litigators*."

"Great."

I can't do this much longer.

"So . . ." he says.

He takes a deep breath and lets it out. His smirk is back.

"You're an asshole, Lars."

"The show is nothing short of phenomenal, it's absolutely brilliant. You're going to make superstars out of those eight actors and probably win yourself multiple Emmys in the process. You nailed it."

My eyes well up. This feels like a parent telling me they're proud of me. "You think so?"

"I know a thing or two about this business." Then, his expression turns serious. "I'm sorry about everything I did and everything I didn't do. I'm sorry I wasn't there for you when your mother was dying."

Now the tears are streaming down. "Lars—"

"Have you forgiven me enough to let me write you an episode?"

"Of course." I get up and walk around my desk. He stands and we hug for a long time. "Why didn't you tell me? You know I love gay people!"

"I was stupid, I don't know. I was still in denial, I guess. I feel terrible for what it did to you."

"It wasn't you, it was that cretin Beth Zinn," I say as I lean back against my desk.

Lars sits down again and glances over at the picture on the wall of the boys and me hiking Bryce Canyon. "Alex couldn't take it, could he?"

I shake my head.

"Does he still think—"

"Who knows. I think he's moved on. He has a girlfriend."

"I feel terrible. Like I should call him now, but is it too late?"

"To save our marriage?" I say with a wry smile. "Yeah, it's far too late for that."

"You know he called me at the height of it all. I didn't want to tell you. I didn't answer. He left me a voicemail."

"Alex and I were already having problems long before that. We didn't talk anymore, we only fought. There was pressure from every direction. Alex checked out. He stopped understanding, and I stopped trying to make him understand. My mother was completely out of her mind. She was horrible to him . . . to all of us. The Beth Zinn thing was just the final straw. We even stayed married for a while after that. I mean . . . we tried. But there was too much resentment and it was miserable for the boys. Things feel better now, for everyone."

"But you and Alex . . ."

"Me and Alex what?"

"I don't know, it's weird, D. I know things had gotten bad, but for so many years, you two were like a well-oiled machine."

"That's not exactly a romantic description of marriage."

"Well, okay, I get that. When I first met you, though, I was envious of what you and Alex had. It was like a secret you wouldn't let anyone in on. And you were a *sexy as hell* couple!"

"Don't make me sad, Lars. He has a *girlfriend*. All good things must come to an end."

"It's unlike you to use a trite line like that. Do you really believe it anyway . . . that it couldn't last?" he asks.

"I feel like the universe is testing me today. This particular topic keeps coming up and I'd really like to go back to how you were praising me about the show, and how I was making you grovel on your hands and knees."

"Well"—he stands—"my precious D, I *am* talking about the show, aren't I?" He winks and then takes my face in his hands and kisses my cheek.

"One person can't be your everything," I whisper.

He clears his throat. "I want the season finale. I want to write it with you, if you haven't already. What do you think?"

I blink. "What did the voicemail say?"

"The voicemail? Oh, Alex? He was drunk, but he sounded more sad than mad. He said there was no one like you. That you were one of a kind. And then he said, 'Lars . . . you can have that bitch. She's all yours!'"

"Wow," I say with a laugh. "A little harsh but that wasn't the first time he called me a bitch."

"I don't think he thought it through. I regret not calling him that moment and talking sense into him. He definitely meant what he said about you being one of a kind. I agree."

Silence.

"He should have told *me* that."

25

i am thankful for you

ALEXANDER

Why didn't it occur to me earlier that bringing Kate to Thanksgiving to meet everyone was a bad idea? Why now, when I'm ten minutes from my parents' house, is it finally hitting me? Maybe it's because Tristan is singing the *Paw Patrol* theme song over and over in the backseat and I'm about to lose my mind. He's singing over a Talking Heads song that's playing on the radio. I don't know how he's doing it, I'm actually sort of impressed.

My brain feels like it's malfunctioning because my single working ear cannot process the two different melodies, so I turn the radio down. Kate is quiet and staring out the window.

"Are you nervous?" I ask.

"No," she says.

I have to remind myself that Kate is usually nothing. "What are you thinking about?"

"Nothing."

"You'd be dead if you were thinking about nothing," I say with humor.

"I was just thinking about Thanksgiving and what a lovely holiday it is to be with family, sharing a wonderful meal. Do you think I'm dressed okay?"

"Yes," I say. "You look very nice." It's true. She always looks good, put together and neat in her jeans and sweaters.

My parents live in a beautiful old Craftsman house in the Historic Highlands of Pasadena. It's actually the house my mother grew up in. She inherited it after her dad passed away fifteen years ago. It's redone and beautiful and has this huge wraparound porch and large yard that my parents have made into a gorgeous garden. It's the kind of backyard you can take a stroll in and get lost.

When we pull up, I notice Dani's Jeep is parked crooked in the driveway. I shake my head.

"What?" Kate says.

"Dani's a horrible driver."

Kate ignores the comment. "We're here, Tristan! Be polite, okay, this is Alex's family we're meeting."

"I know, Mom, you told me. Are Ethan and Noah gonna be there?"

"Yes," I say with a sinking feeling. I don't want this poor kid to get attached to my family. I just need to get past this day.

I walk through the unlocked front door without knocking. Pots and pans are clanking, there's laughter coming from the kitchen. Kate and Tristan follow me into the living room, where Josh and my dad are watching football.

"Dad, Josh," I say. They both look over and stand up. My dad is basically the older version of me, and Josh is a tall, skinny, crunchy guy who always looks like he's smiling even when he's mad. They walk toward us. Tristan is partially hiding behind Kate's leg. "This is my . . . girlfriend, Kate, and her son, Tristan. Kate, this is my dad, Alex Sr., and Josh, my sister's boyfriend."

They politely shake hands. Everything feels awkward despite all the smiles. "Well, welcome," my dad says.

"How's the garden?" I ask.

My dad's eyes light up. Josh is just standing there smiling. He's a passive guy, sort of like Kate. He's . . . nice.

"You gotta see it, son. Go say hi to the girls and then come on out and I'll show you."

"Okay, Dad. Let's go in here," I say to Kate.

I lead Kate and Tristan into the kitchen. My mom has one of those swinging doors, so it's like as soon as you push on it, you're transported to another dimension, where everything is in motion. My mom is pulling something out of the oven, my sister is chopping celery at the center island, and Dani is standing at the sink with her back to us.

The kitchen is bright and full of life. It has butcher block countertops, white subway tiles, and a large, porcelain farmhouse sink. Every brushstroke on the light-yellow shaker cabinets was painted by my father, who also installed the countertops and refinished the old wood floors. There are always thriving plants on the windowsill, homemade bread in a bread box, and even though there are a ton of Thanksgiving dishes in the making scattered about, my mother still has a perfectly arranged bowl of fruit in an old yellow Pyrex bowl in the middle of the center island. There are oranges, apples, lemons, limes, and one magnificent yellow banana, without a hint of brown on it, lying over the top. It's like a still life I have seen a million times. I don't know how she does it. There's music playing from a speaker in the corner. It's some sort of hipster folk song that I know my mother didn't put on. It was either Dani or Amanda—who, by the way, are like sisters.

Since Amanda's so much younger, she met Dani when she was still in her early teens. Over the years she's often turned to

Dani for advice, and in many ways, they're closer to each other than Amanda and I are.

Dani doesn't love how, on holidays, only the women end up in the kitchen, so I'm usually in there with them instead of her, but today it looks like she had no choice.

"Hello!" I announce. They all stop what they're doing and look up at us.

"Alex, come here and close this oven as soon as I take the casserole out," my mother says. It would be a completely normal thing for my mother to say if Kate and Tristan weren't standing right next to me. I hope she doesn't ignore them all day.

As I walk over to the oven on the left, Amanda approaches Kate on the right. "Hi, you must be Kate? I'm Amanda, the little sister." Amanda is pretty in a natural, no makeup kind of way. All she and Josh do for fun is tent camp, hike, and hug trees. They're easy to be around and nonjudgmental, so that makes this part a little easier.

"Nice to meet you," Kate says. "This is my son, Tristan."

"Hello, Tristan." Amanda bends and shakes his hand. He politely smiles, but he's still quiet.

My mom walks over and puts her hand out to Kate, "I'm Brenda. Nice to meet you, happy Thanksgiving, and welcome," she says like she's rehearsed it a hundred times.

Kate smiles and says, "You as well, thank you for having me. You have a beautiful home and I'm grateful to be able to be here and spend this holiday with you."

My mom smiles, but I notice that she doesn't really acknowledge Tristan except for ruffling his hair a little. "Well, that's what it's all about today," my mom says.

I'm watching the exchange and so is Dani from the other side of the island, where she's now leaning her back against the sink. Dani smiles and throws up a motionless wave, "Hi, Kate."

"Hi, Danielle." No one except for me calls her Danielle and it's only when I'm mad. I know Kate said it because it's how I've referred to Dani now and then. She doesn't realize how it sounds to everyone else. My mother and Amanda are standing still and silent. Dani is actually the one who breaks the silence.

"Hey, Tristan, I'm Dani. You want to come here and check out some mollusks?" I laugh quietly to myself. Dani can do and say the most bizarre things, but usually it always ends up working, and sometimes it feels like fresh air. She successfully diffused the tension. I mean, who eats oysters on the half shell at Thanksgiving? But why not? Kate pushes Tristan's back, encouraging him to approach Dani. He walks over to the sink while Dani grabs a step stool and puts it next to her. "Hop up here, Captain."

Tristan giggles and stands on the stool.

I approach the sink on Dani's left side. "Are you shucking oysters?"

She looks up at me and whispers, "This holiday is stupid."

Dani always had an issue with Thanksgiving, but she still goes along with it to make the parents happy. I know the oysters are her way of trying to update the tradition.

She's shucking while we're talking. "Yeah, well, oysters will be a welcome change," I tell her.

"I think so," she says. "All right, Captain T, I have to do this part with the knife to open them up, then you set them on the plate."

"Gross. Are we gonna eat those?" Tristan says.

My mom chimes in from the other side of the kitchen. "I think oysters for a Thanksgiving appetizer is a great idea!" Dani can do no wrong in my mother's eyes . . . or my father's. Dani looks at me and winks. She's rubbing it in.

Tristan is holding a shucked, raw oyster in a half shell in his hand and staring like he's just discovered an alien life form.

"You debating?" Dani says to him. She always talked to our kids like adults too. She's a warm and loving mother, but she has this way of making kids feel like individuals, which they should.

"Should I try it?" Tristan says.

Dani shrugs, her face inscrutable. "It's sort of an acquired taste. Do you want me to give you a pointer?"

I turn around and notice Kate has stopped chopping celery with Amanda. She's watching the exchange between Dani and Tristan.

"Yes, please," he says. "I'll take all the help I can get." Now he's talking back to her like an adult. People used to marvel at Noah and Ethan's vocabularies. It's because Dani never dumbed anything down for them. She didn't baby them, and she gave them choices.

"Okay, listen, let me get some lemon." She turns back toward the center island, where the reliable bowl of fruit is. She looks at Kate and smiles warmly, then digs a lemon out of the bowl before turning back toward Tristan. She's essentially ignoring me, but that's okay. Dani cuts the lemon, then squeezes some onto the oyster Tristan is holding. He starts to lift it to his mouth. "No, not yet!" He pulls it away. "I haven't told you the trick yet." He's staring at it with disgust. "Watch me," Dani says as she slides one out of the shell and into her mouth quickly like it's second nature. She opens her mouth to show Tristan the oyster is gone. "The trick is, once you send it sliding off the bow of the boat, you chomp once, then down the hatch, Captain."

"Just chew once?"

"Yep. Exactly. It's the taste after you swallow the oyster that we're trying to get to. If you can do that, you'll be smooth sailing."

Tristan does exactly what Dani told him to do. He still looks revolted for a second, but then opens his mouth to show Dani it's gone. He smiles from ear to ear.

"You did it! Nice work. What did you think?"

"It was great!" I know for a fact Tristan didn't think it was great, but he wanted to.

"Well done," Kate says. I walk over to stand next to her. In a low, almost inaudible voice . . . for me anyway, Kate says, "I can't believe he ate that."

How is Dani being so normal right now? I don't think I could handle going to Thanksgiving dinner with her new boyfriend, but this situation doesn't seem to be fazing her. I'm guessing it's because she's already imagined it and prepared for it. That's just how her brain works.

Later, right before dinner, my mom comes up to me and says, "You gonna get a little red Corvette next?"

"She's thirty," I say back.

My mom shrugs, then continues into the dining room.

Everyone finds a seat. It's not an organized process and there's no hierarchy. It's sort of like throwing chess pieces into the air and seeing where they land. Except that Kate is clinging to my right and Tristan to my left. This part is awkward. I glance at Noah and open my eyes wide. He makes the exaggerated frown face, like he's sucking air through his teeth. I think he's empathizing with me.

Clockwise at the head of table sits Noah. The four chairs across from me, left to right, sit my mom, Dani, Amanda, and Ethan. Josh is at six o'clock. Then our side is my dad, Kate, me, and Tristan.

I'm directly across from Dani. I smile at her and she laughs. It's probably the first time I've smiled at her in years.

There's a little bit of conversation going on at both ends of the table. My mom seems to be engaging Noah next to her so she doesn't have to talk to Tristan across from her. She keeps touching Noah's hand. In a way, it seems like she's trying to let him know that Tristan isn't moving in on the boys. Food is getting passed around and everyone is talking either to the person next to them or across from them, except for me. I'm quietly taking it in. Amanda is making conversation with Kate, but it's piecemeal and uncomfortable for Amanda, I can tell.

"So you live in old town Pasadena?" my sister says to Kate.

Kate is spooning mashed potatoes onto her plate, so it looks like she's responding to the food. "Yeah, well, kind of. I live in the apartments across from that Jiffy Lube on Colorado. The last time I took my car in there, I think they messed it up somehow and now it's leaking oil. The manager at my complex has been hassling me about the oil in my parking space for weeks."

I'm looking at Amanda, who is dumbstruck. Everyone is quiet for a moment. I can tell Amanda doesn't know how to respond. I don't know if Kate gets nervous or what, but she does this thing where someone will bring up a topic and she'll respond with something totally off subject. Then she continues on and on while the other person is left dumbfounded. Kate is not always like this when we're one-on-one.

"How's work going, Amanda?" I say to fill the space.

"It's really good. I'm gonna be taking some time off—"

My mom clinks her glass with a fork. "Everyone have their food?" We say yes or nod. "Great, it's time! Everybody's favorite."

"Oh no," Amanda grumbles. My mom insists that before we start eating on Thanksgiving, we go around the room and say what we're thankful for. Everyone dreads it, but if we try to get out of it, she will pout all the way through dinner.

"Noah, why don't you start," my mom says.

I can feel Tristan next to me bouncing in his seat. He wants it to be his turn.

"I'm thankful for the Xbox in Gram's garage—"

"Hey, it's my garage too," my dad says teasingly.

Noah continues, "And in Gramp's garage. And I'm thankful for my family . . . even Ethan."

Ethan acts like he's going to chuck a roll at Noah, but he puts his arm down, smiles, and says, "Thanks, bro."

"Okay, my turn," my mom says. "Of course, I'm thankful for having all my children and grandchildren at the table . . ." Dani looks up and over at her. I wonder in this moment if Dani's thinking about her mom. "And I'm thankful for the winter garden, even though a certain someone won't stop talking about it," my mom says to my dad. "I'm thankful we all have our health." She holds up her wineglass. "Cheers. I love you all." After my mom takes a sip, she leans over and kisses Dani on the temple. "Dani, your turn," she says.

Anything like this is difficult for Dani. It will go one of two ways. She'll either turn it into a joke or she'll get sentimental and start crying. I'm on the edge of my seat wondering which Dani we'll get.

She clears her throat. So far, she's holding it together, but I notice the hand holding her wineglass is shaking. She sets down the glass. She's nervous. "Well, of course I'm thankful for my perfectly imperfect boys." A lot of kids wouldn't get that statement, but Noah and Ethan understand that Dani means it as a compliment. "All of you," she says, and glances around the table without making eye contact. "Thankful for the ones I love who are not pictured today, Alicia and Mark, Louie Louie, my mom and dad . . . Ben." Somehow, she's not crying yet. She's just smiling.

"Sparty," I say. She looks up at me and laughs.

"My goldfish, Herman, that I had in fourth grade." Now everyone is laughing lightly. "And . . . I'm thankful I got the show, and seriously, seriously thankful for that hot male masseuse at Burke Williams."

"Mom," Noah whines, but everyone else is laughing. I guess sitting here with my girlfriend gives Dani license to say that. We all know it's a joke.

"Yes, congratulations again on the show, Dani." My dad raises his glass.

Amanda starts talking without anyone prompting her. "I'm thankful for my family and Josh, everyone's health and happiness, and my new backpack from REI. Go, E."

Ethan sits up in his chair. "I'm thankful for my family and thankful that Noah finally discovered deodorant."

Everyone laughs except Noah, who rolls his eyes. "Go, Josh," Amanda says.

"I'm thankful for everyone here, especially you, my love," he says to Amanda, but she's not outwardly romantic, so she laughs it off.

My dad chimes in, which feels like an interruption but I don't think Josh cares. "Well, I'm gonna say it, I don't care what you all think, I'm thankful for the winter garden I have spent many arduous hours nurturing and cultivating and . . . well . . . I guess . . . I guess I'm thankful for all of you too," he says. "Especially my best friend over there who has to listen to me go on and on about the stupid garden."

My mom laughs and then smiles lovingly at him.

We all look at Kate. She hesitates for a moment. "I'm thankful for my son—I love you, Tristan—and my job and . . . for all of you being so nice, welcoming me and Tristan into the family."

FUUUUUUUUCKKKKKKK.

Everyone is quiet and still. Dani is nonplussed, but my sister looks like she's trying to decipher a very complicated flow chart. I can feel Tristan still bouncing beside me. He's been waiting for so long, so I use it to my advantage. I think I know how to recover while all the eyes are on me.

"I'm gonna let Tristan go, he's been really patient."

Noah rolls his eyes at me.

"I'm . . . I'm," Tristan is so excited he can barely speak. "I'm thankful for Dani!"

We're at zero oxygen again. Suffocating quietly. It feels like hours have gone by like this.

Finally, Dani says, "Thanks, Captain, I'm thankful for you too." She's oddly unemotional.

My dad clears his throat loudly. "Go ahead, son, your turn."

I don't have anything planned, I always go with the basics. "I'm thankful for my family, and for you, Josh, for putting up with that crazy hippie over there. Noah and Ethan, I couldn't have dreamt up better kids and awesome people. Cheers. Cheers." We all clink glasses and drink.

I realize I didn't thank Dani specifically. She was my family before, so I didn't think of it. I'm hoping she didn't notice.

This whole day has been botched. *Why didn't I see this coming?*

"Let's eat!" I say loudly, and the hum of conversation finally rises over the unbearable silence.

26

aren't we a cautionary tale?

DANIELLE

I'd be lying if I said I wasn't enjoying the spectacle of Alex digging himself a Grand Canyon–sized hole right now. His judgment must be clouded by all the amazing sex they're having. I can't *believe* he brought her to Thanksgiving. What was he thinking? When he told me at the house a week and a half ago, I was only a little surprised. Honestly, I kinda thought he was bluffing just to see my reaction.

The truth is that at first, seeing the three of them across from me—Tristan, Alex, and Kate, like the new and improved, more wholesome family—was making me nauseous. Now I'm thoroughly enjoying it because Alex has not stopped fumbling since he sat down. I wonder if Kate even noticed that Alex didn't say he was thankful for her or Tristan.

We're all eating, everyone is talking, and Alex has stopped digging, for now anyway. He's talking to his dad and Josh about the merits of composting. Amanda has given up on conversing with Kate, and Brenda is doing a really good job of pretending

Tristan doesn't exist. Later, she'll say it's because she's a kindergarten teacher and she needs a break from talking to little kids, though she never treated Ethan or Noah that way.

Kate is awkwardly working her way into the conversation. She's just shifted the topic from composting to bicycle riding, and Alex Sr. looks like he's running to catch up. Kate seems really . . . nice. I don't want to say dumb, but . . . she's dumb.

Even though Alex doesn't sit around philosophizing esoteric mumbo jumbo, I know he is intellectually present and capable of thinking deeply and of adding important or relevant statements to a conversation. I know the type of person Kate seems to be used to irritate him, but he's been more than tolerant of her this whole day. Maybe he's in love. No, he's not in love. Maybe he thinks he is.

I look from Kate to Alex. He's now sitting perfectly still and staring at me. He arches his eyebrows and mouths the words, "I'm thankful for you too."

My expression must be one of curiosity. I smile with a closed mouth. He's blinking like he's waiting for me to say something. "I know," I mouth back.

He laughs quietly and shakes his head.

Dinner is wrapping up when Amanda clears her throat and says without hesitation, "Listen, you guys, me and Josh are getting married."

"Josh and I," Brenda corrects her instantly.

"Well, it's about time," Alex Sr. says loudly.

Amanda and Josh are like Alex and me in that they're not into flare. Frankly, I thought they would never get married. They don't want kids, so what's the point? Anyway, as of late, aren't Alex and I a very clear warning about marriage?

"That's great! Congratulations," I say as I side hug Amanda.

"Congrats, you guys," Alex says. "So, when is this happening?"

"And where is your engagement ring?" Brenda adds.

"Mom," Amanda whines. "We're not doing that."

"Why not?" Brenda says like she's just sucked on a lemon.

"We got tattoos," Josh says in his dopey way. It was clearly a secret. Amanda jerks her head back and glares at him.

"Spill the details, Amanda!" Brenda barks. Everyone else around the table is silent.

"We're getting married on New Year's Eve in Vail. We want you all to be there. It's gonna be small, only our families and a few friends. Just get your flights and we'll cover everything else." I wonder if Amanda realizes that she's just invited Alex's fling . . . and the kid.

"Vail?" Brenda says. Her face is still puckered.

"It'll be beautiful. We wanted a winter wedding," Amanda whines.

"I think it's great, you guys," Alex says, trying to pull his mom off the ledge.

"Well, show us the tattoos," Brenda says.

"We're not showing you. We just got each other's names."

"Where?" Brenda is pressing and Amanda looks perturbed.

Amanda bursts out, "Near our *genitals,* Mother! We are not showing you."

"Oh, for the love of Jesus," Alex Sr. says.

Brenda picks up her glass of wine and downs it in one gulp.

"Speaking of Jesus," I say in a low voice, "I'm about to reverse Jesus you, Brenda, and turn that wine into water."

I was whispering, but Brenda directs her response to the whole table. "Am I being unreasonable for asking?" No one responds. Brenda resigns. "I'm happy for you guys. I knew eventually you would come around . . . but I just hoped . . . Never mind. It'll be great!"

Finally it feels like the table has settled.

"Dani, Amanda, will you girls get the pies and bring them out here?"

As Amanda and I both stand to retrieve the pies, Kate says to the whole room, "I'm excited! I've never been to Vail."

Alex is as white as a ghost. For a moment, I feel sorry for him . . . but the feeling passes quickly.

Inside the kitchen I'm alone with Amanda, gathering plates, flatware, and pies.

"I can't believe he brought her," she says.

"Well, he did. And you invited both of them to your wedding."

When I look across the center island to Amanda, I see realization finally shine into her eyes. "I did, didn't I? He'll never bring her, will he? All the way to Vail? On New Year's?"

"Are you asking me if I think Alex will bring her?"

"I don't think he would. Do you?"

"It's less than a month and a half away? If he's still dating her, he'll bring her. He won't be able to tell her no because he's still learning how to use his big boy words."

I hate insulting Alex to Amanda, but I'm exhausted by the whole situation. I'm tired of pretending to Alex's family that he's perfect, which is what I've always done, which is actually the reason they like me so much. Because I never put down their precious Alex. I know deep down they think the divorce was my fault, due to some affair that wasn't an affair at all.

"Whoa, Dani."

"Whoa what, Amanda? Bringing her here on Thanksgiving . . . with her kid? It's confusing for everyone. It's confusing for the boys especially."

"Maybe he's actually in love with her?" One thing that is undeniable about everyone in Alex's family is that they're loyal. Her expression isn't antagonistic, it's more inscrutable. Almost like she's playing devil's advocate. "Maybe he'll eventually marry her."

I'm just blinking across the island at Amanda, debating on how to respond to this. "I know this is hard to believe, Amanda, but you don't know your brother as well as I do."

"What? Of course I do. Look, Dani, I know this is hard for you." She pauses. Her expression changes from speculative to sympathetic. "I *know* Alex. I'm not sure what you meant, but I know this can't be easy for you."

"I'm fine. I really am. I just meant that I know he's not going to marry her . . . and I know he's not in love with her. I've seen Alex in love before, remember?"

Brenda enters the kitchen. "What's taking so long? That girl is on her own planet out there. I have no idea what she's talking about." We both know Brenda is referring to Kate.

"We were actually just talking about that," Amanda says.

"About why your brother has his head up his ass?" Brenda spits back. I'm shocked. She's never talked about Alex that way, and she rarely curses.

"Wow, Mom," Amanda says.

"Well, we all know Alex isn't serious about her. Why would he bring her to Thanksgiving? Just to confuse the kids?"

I look at Amanda and raise my eyebrows.

"I don't think Alex realizes," I say. "Maybe he does now, but I don't think he thought about it when he asked her to come." Not quite sure why I'm defending him.

Later that night, Alex offers to stay with the boys to give me a couple of extra days since he knows I'm slammed with the show. The clinic is closed for the long holiday weekend, so it makes sense anyway. He also made a point to mention that he'd be taking Kate home first. I don't really know how serious they are, but I know Alex doesn't want to push the envelope, which would be taking his girlfriend to our family home with our children. Though we've never said it, that house is off-limits. He knows that.

I'm at the apartment alone now. Even though I did a stellar job of looking like I didn't care, today has been emotionally draining. I've felt inside-out all day. Kate aside, Alex and I were still trying to adjust to being a divorced couple.

There are feelings and memories attached to every holiday. And those memories are compounding the loneliness I feel in the apartment right now. Usually on Thanksgiving, we always ended up having a late-night second dinner with the leftovers. When the boys were young, we'd put them to bed, steal off to our bedroom with a plate of pie, a bottle of wine, and we'd stay up late, feeding each other, talking, rolling around naked, laughing about family dramatics, kissing, exemplifying true intimacy . . . proving to ourselves once again that we needed only each other. I wonder if he's doing that with Kate right now.

I go to the record collection and pull an album out blindly. When I see the cover of Eric Clapton's *Slowhand*, I know there's a message written on the sleeve because I can easily remember writing it. It's not a holiday memory, but one I've held on to and thought about many times over the years. I remove the sleeve:

Song 2 "Wonderful Tonight"
   Tonight I was obsessing over my post-baby body. I cried at my own image in the mirror and then felt terribly vain for it later. Noah was sleeping. You put this record on, pulled me close, and we danced slowly in the living room.

Earlier that night, Alex and I were arguing about Noah and how to get him to sleep. He was only a couple of months old. I rocked him to sleep every single night in those early days and sometimes it would take two hours of rocking and shushing him. Afterward, I would be exhausted. Alex thought we should sleep train him and let him "cry it out" in his crib.

We put Noah in the crib and let him cry for fifteen minutes before I went back in and started rocking him. When I finally reemerged, Alex was sitting on the couch in the living room, smiling. "Quitter."

"I'll try again tomorrow. It's too hard."

He followed me into the bedroom, where I was changing out of a breast milk–drenched T-shirt into another shirt, which I knew would be in the same state in a few hours. I looked at my body in the mirror and cringed. Alex tried to wrap his arms around me from behind. I was shirtless and braless, wearing a pair of sweats. Pulling my arms up over my breasts, I tried to cover myself.

"Don't," he whispered. "You're beautiful." We hadn't been together yet since I had Noah, and I still didn't feel ready. I started crying. "What, Dani?"

"I'm so gross and ugly. I don't want to do this."

"I don't know what you're talking about. You're beautiful, even more beautiful now." It seemed like he understood. I believed him.

"I want to put a shirt on," I told him.

He let go of me. "Put a shirt on. Come out to living room when you're ready. Let's have a glass of wine."

"But—" I was about to argue that I was breastfeeding.

"You can have a glass of wine, Dani." He smiled and then chuckled, "Maybe he'll sleep better."

I laughed and it was a relief. "That's terrible. I'll pump and dump."

"Whatever you gotta do."

He walked out of the room. I took a two-minute shower and threw on the nicest pair of sweats I could find. I brushed my hair and put on a dab of lip gloss.

The song "Wonderful Tonight" was playing. "Come dance with me," he said, in a low, playful voice.

As we were dancing, my head on his chest, I said, "This part is harder than I thought."

"What part is that?"

"The part where I care about my body. I imagined that I wouldn't. I imagined I'd be proud of my stretch marks, you know? Like a stronger woman, not so shallow. I don't feel like a woman at all. I feel like a vessel that should be sunk out in the middle of the Pacific."

Alex's body shook with laughter. "Oh my god, Dani. You are not a shallow person. You're being so hard on yourself right now, and then you're being hard on yourself for being hard on yourself! It's only been two months. For the record . . . you look absolutely beautiful to me. I want you just like this. I don't care what you're wearing or how many stretch marks you have, or if your hair is done, long, short, makeup, no makeup, fat, skinny, none of it matters."

"How can you say that? You must have a preference."

"Because I'm in love with your brain, Dani. I actually really *like* you, which I think is just as important as loving you. You're funny and clever, smart, kind . . . loving. You're good at loving me and Noah. Truly, I think you have a rare gift for making people feel loved. You're exceptional at it."

The tears came again. I remember I was so emotional. Alex held me for a long time that night as we danced to "Wonderful Tonight." He said all the right words, and for that moment I believed him, and that's all that mattered.

It's two days before New Year's Eve. I've been absolutely exhausted lately. Getting ready for the premier of the show has been taxing on everybody, including the kids and Alex. They've all had to do their parts picking up the slack. I cannot *wait* to get some time off. There were a couple of weeks before Christmas when the boys were with their dad all but two days, while I was either at the office, the set, or in the apartment writing like a madwoman. Christmas came and went. The four of us spent Christmas Eve and Christmas morning together, and Alex and I got along well. He reserved Christmas night for Kate and Tristan, which was fine. I was just happy he didn't bring them to the house.

Now I'm packing for Amanda's wedding while the boys are golfing with their dad. For a while, I wondered if I should even go, but Amanda is like a sister to me and everyone in Alex's family said it would be weird if I didn't. Kate and Tristan are, in fact, going, as I predicted.

Alex and I are flying with the boys out of LA tonight and Kate and Tristan are coming tomorrow night because she couldn't get out of work tomorrow. Alex said she was irritated that he wouldn't wait for her, but he explained that he wanted to fly with his kids, and she'd just have to deal with it. I'm glad, because I think it's important for Noah and Ethan to see Alex making them a priority.

We are his family. *I* am his family still. Married, divorced, separated, or dead, I am still his family. She'll have to grow up and accept it.

27

are we good now?

ALEXANDER

Eataly is this giant three-story Italian food haven in Los Angeles with two restaurants, a cannoli bar, an espresso bar, a wine bar, a salami bar, a freakin' homemade pasta bar, along with endless rows of Italian imported goods. I could literally spend days here. Kate and I are roaming the aisles as we wait to be called to our dinner table

Earlier today, I golfed with the boys, then left them with Dani so I could do some damage control with Kate before leaving for Vail later tonight.

Kate is currently perusing a glass display housing a vast selection of Italian chocolate truffles. "Do you see something you want?" I ask.

"No, I'm just looking."

"Let's get some truffles. Pick out a few," I say.

"Am I getting apology chocolates?" Kate and I have never really argued.

She's very easy to get along with, not dramatic and overall low maintenance. However, she *is* irritated that I'm flying to Vail with Dani and the boys and not her and Tristan, and I'm not tolerating her silent tantrum well.

"Do I need to apologize for wanting to fly to my sister's wedding with my own children?"

She's not looking up at me as she talks. She's still bent over the display case. "I just don't understand why we couldn't all fly together."

"I already told you, Kate. Because I told my sister I would be out there first thing in the morning tomorrow to help Josh set up the ceremony area. Dani promised to help my mom with the flowers. It's not my fault you have to work."

"I just thought you'd wait."

Now I'm really losing my patience. "You were invited to the wedding," I say in a tone that makes it sound like I'm telling her she should be grateful.

She stands up straight and faces me. We're just inches apart. I'm looking into her narrowed eyes. "Do you not want me and Tristan there?"

"I didn't say that. Can we please not fight about this?"

"Is this our first fight, Alex?"

"I don't think it warrants a fight, but yes, I guess we are fighting." Neither one of us is moving, we're just staring at each other. "I want you there, Kate."

"I personally would go for the hazelnut truffles," comes a man's voice from behind us. I recognize it immediately.

I look behind me to see Lars standing there. I haven't seen him in years. Long before all the rumors about him and Dani started flying, he and I actually got along. "Lars," I say, without emotion.

"Hello, Alex."

"Lars, this is Kate, my girlfriend. I'm sure Dani told you that we're divorced now."

He nods. "She did."

"Kate," I say, "This is Lars, Dani's ex . . . colleague." Kate and Lars shake hands.

"Dani and I are actually working together again," Lars says.

The fucking nerve of this guy. "Of course you are," I say.

"Hello," comes another man's voice from behind Lars. He peeks his head around and waves to Kate and me. He's younger than Lars, attractive, and smiling widely. "I'm Neal." He reaches his hand out to Kate first, then me.

"This is my husband, Neal," Lars says.

I stand there trying to put together the events of my life over the past five years. "Nice to meet you," I say quietly. "Lars, were you always . . ."

"Gay?" Lars says. "Yes. I was always gay, Alex." He chuckles and glances over to Neal.

"But why—"

"Alex, can I have a word with you?" Lars says.

I look over at Kate, who doesn't seem fazed. "Sure."

We step to the side. Lars can be intimidating, but right now he looks apologetic. "I'm sorry, Alex." He shakes his head and looks away. "I could barely admit it to myself. I was living a lie. It's terrible, but I was waiting for my father to pass and—"

"You don't have to apologize. Honestly, your orientation or when you wanted to come out is none of my business, or anyone else's." I do wish I would have known, though, it might have stifled some of the arguments.

"I feel partially responsible . . . for you and Dani . . . you know. I just . . . I should have called you."

I'm blinking, expressionless, looking for something malicious in his eyes, but there's nothing. Just regret and remorse. "I know it seemed like a really big deal, but Dani and I were near the end already. I don't think it would have made a difference."

"Dani said the same thing, but I'm not sure I believe either one of you."

Does Lars really have the right to know the inner workings of my relationship with Dani?

"I love Danielle, I do. We were just not good at being married anymore. For a long time. We would still be together right now if this were only because she slept with you." I smile. "Honestly. I would have forgiven her for that. Hell, I did forgive her for that and it didn't even happen!"

He exhales out of his nose and shakes his head like he's exasperated. "It's a shame, because I like you both so much," he says.

"I appreciate you saying that. It's all water under the bridge."

"Yeah." He looks up at the ceiling in thought for a moment before looking back at me and smiling. "So, you went younger?"

"Well, it looks like you did too," I say lightheartedly. "It's fun, you know?"

"It'll do for now," he fires back with a wink. "No one is as fun as Dani though."

I nod and smile. He's not wrong.

We hug. I feel a tremendous sense of relief, not just knowing Dani never cheated, but also, oddly, because Lars and Dani are working together again. He's always been in her corner, and she deserves that support, which I hadn't been giving her.

"Our table is ready," Kate says behind me. We say our goodbyes to Lars and Neal.

"I'm so looking forward to a glass of wine," Kate says.

I'm not paying attention to her. All I can think about is telling

Dani that I know the truth now, and I also want to congratulate her on getting Lars on board for the show. They make an amazing writing team.

"Did you hear me?" Kate whines.

"No," I say. "Remember? I'm hard of hearing."

28

i can't be this person for you

DANIELLE

"We should have left earlier," I say as we inch through the security line. Noah and Ethan are quietly watching me internally melt down over the stupidity of the people in front of us who apparently have never been in an airport security line before. The TSA officer has repeated twenty times the instructions to remove shoes and belts before getting to the metal detector, and we seem to be the only people listening.

"Mom, it's fine," Ethan says. "You're shaking, like uncontrollably. Chill out."

I hear our flight being called. "Shit."

"We're going to make it," Noah says. "It's gate thirty-five, it's like twenty feet away. I can see it from here. Stop freaking out, Mom."

"'Scuse me," I say to the security agent. "They're calling us."

"Come on," she waves us over. She funnels us into a priority line and we're through security in a minute.

I hear our names again. "Let's just carry our shoes," I say as I begin jogging toward the gate.

When we make it to the jetway, the male gate attendant at the podium says, "Danielle, Ethan, and Noah, I take it?"

"Are we really the last ones?" Ethan asks.

"Yep. You made it by the skin of your teeth," the gate attendant says with a smile. We walk briskly down the jetway and onto the plane.

I can see Alex in an aisle seat toward the middle of the cabin. His head is back. He's sleeping already . . . *asshole*.

"There's one seat next to Dad, or one next to me all the way in the back. Who wants what?" I say. The boys hate making these kinds of decisions. They're sensitive and feel like they're in a constant state of choosing sides. They don't respond. "Eenie, meenie, miney, Noah you sit next to Dad so you can ask him about the skateboard decks in the garage."

"Okay," Noah says.

As I get to the aisle where Alex is, I intentionally bump his shoulder. He opens his eyes and looks up at me. "You're so late," he says. "They kept calling your name. I texted you a million times."

"A million times, huh? Is that a lie or an exaggeration?"

"Shh, we don't have time to fight right now," he says.

He stands to help put Noah's carry-on in the overhead compartment. "It must be nice to only have to pack for one person," I say.

He shakes his head. "You would have been late even if you were alone."

I smile condescendingly at him and he smiles back. "Your insults no longer bother me. Isn't that weird?"

"You better get in your seat before you get us all kicked off this plane. Why'd you book this insane flight anyway?"

"Because I had some work to do this morning. You could have gone with Kate," I say as I walk away. He is right about the flight. I wasn't thinking when I booked it. We're leaving LAX at 7:30 P.M., then a four-hour layover in Denver. We won't get into Vail until almost 1 A.M.

Alex and I haven't really been bickering lately, but it still annoys me that he has the nerve to criticize something I did for him as a favor. When I get to my seat, I text him.

ME: Alex, you could have booked your own flight, or offered to take the boys since you're not working at all this week. Or you could have gone with Kate. Any number of scenarios, but instead you let me take care of it and now you're complaining.

He doesn't respond. Ethan and I put our earbuds in and fall asleep on each other's shoulders.

I wake up as I feel the plane descending into Denver. "Wake up, Ethan, we're gonna land soon."

He yawns groggily and stretches his arms. "I'm starving," he says.

"We'll get something in the airport. We have four hours to kill."

As Ethan and I exit the jetway, we see Alex and Noah waiting for us. "I'm so hungry," Noah whines.

"Here." I start to get money out of my wallet and then stop. "Are you hungry, Alex?" It's a habit to ask about his needs and I wonder if I will ever kick it. It's like wanting a cigarette when I drink even though I haven't smoked in twenty years.

"No. I had a big dinner before the flight." He's expressionless.

I hand Noah forty dollars. "Get something for yourselves that's semi-healthy, please. Don't leave this terminal."

"What are you gonna eat?" Alex says.

Since when does he care? I turn to Ethan. "Grab me a sandwich or something, you know what I like," I say. The boys start to walk away. "We'll be right here," I say, and then look at Alex. "Well, I will anyway. You can go do whatever you want."

"No, I'll sit here with you."

"We have four hours," I say.

He points to the small airport bar behind me. "Wanna go have a drink?"

"With you?" I say.

He rolls his eyes. "No, by yourself."

"I could go for a glass of wine, I guess."

We walk over and find two stools at the bar. We're close enough to the gate that we'll be able to see the boys come back.

"This is a huge airport. Do they have their phones? Knowing Ethan, he won't stop until he finds exactly what he's craving."

"Yeah, they have their phones. They're fine, and they have plenty of time to dillydally," I say.

Alex smiles. "You've loosened up a lot with them."

I can feel a scowl forming on my forehead. "I was never a helicopter mom. Anyway, they're thirteen and fourteen now and Noah is an inch taller than me. I can't really boss them around anymore."

The bartender comes over. "What can I get you two?" he says.

"Separate tabs," Alex jokes.

"Are you serious? You're not gonna buy me a drink, Alex?"

"I'll have that IPA on tap and whatever she wants," Alex says.

"I'll have the most expensive wine by the glass, please," I say in a singsongy voice.

The bartender laughs. He's attractive, also probably almost

twenty years younger than me, but who cares, I'm still going to flirt with him.

"You two know each other, I take it?" he says.

"He's my ex-husband." I say the *ex* loudly and add a wink. The bartender laughs again.

Alex is smiling and shaking his head. When the bartender walks away, Alex clears his throat and sits up straight. It's a self-conscious movement, which is rare for him.

"I always imagined you'd go for a silver-fox type," he says.

"If you're saying that because Lars is all gray, that is ridiculous."

"I actually ran into him earlier today. He told me you guys are working together again."

I want to respond, but I also want to see where Alex is going. "Oh yeah?" I say.

"I met his husband," Alex says in a cool tone.

I laugh through my nose. "I didn't know either. Would it have made a difference?"

"I don't think so." He's looking right into my eyes.

"Me neither," I say. "So, where did you see them?"

"Eataly."

My knee-jerk reaction is to say, *You went there without me? That's* our *thing,* but I hold my tongue. I'm sure he went with Kate. "Nice."

The bartender brings the drinks over. "I like your tattoo," I tell him, but I actually don't. I'm trying to act like I don't care that Alex took Kate to my favorite place in the world.

"Thanks," the bartender says.

"What time are you off?" I wiggle my eyebrows and then burst out laughing. "I'm kidding, I'm sorry." The guy knows he's hot, so he's not offended.

He and Alex are both laughing now. "I don't know that I've ever waited on a divorced couple before. This has definitely made my day more entertaining, so thank you."

"Dani, always trying to get a laugh," Alex says.

My smile disappears. "Alex, always being the joke police."

Alex takes an audible breath and lets it out, before forcing a smile. "I'm sorry. I'm sorry about what I said on the plane earlier too. I wasn't thinking."

"It's fine. Clearly this *was* a dumb flight to choose. I just wanted to get as much done at home as I could. I figured we could sleep a little on the plane."

"It's fine. And I'm happy you're working with Lars. You guys make a phenomenal writing team." Alex glances to the bartender. "So, younger for you, Dani?"

"Pot, kettle, Alex."

"She's *thirty,*" he says.

"She was a baby when we got married," I ping back.

"Not a baby, a teenager," he says. "And she's not dumb."

I look behind me jokingly to see who Alex is talking to. "No one said she was?"

"Yeah, but I know exactly how you think."

I've already downed the glass of wine and motioned for the bartender to bring me another. "Oh yeah. Alex the mind reader? I don't think she's dumb. I don't care *what* she is. What I do know is that Thanksgiving was a little soon for that sort of thing, and I'm sorry, but it's *weird* that she's going to be at this wedding. I'm trying to be objective, I'm only thinking about the boys and her son. Believe it or not, I do want you to be happy."

He huffs and then settles into a slouch. It's resignation. "I know you do. To be honest, I wish I would have put more thought into the Thanksgiving thing, because that led to this."

I can't believe he's apologizing and admitting it was a bad move. I don't want to spoil his guilt streak by rubbing it in, he'll just get defensive. "I don't know about her kid, but through this whole thing, I know our boys will be fine. Thank god they're smart . . . and nice. They understand things that I didn't understand at their age. Things I didn't understand until I was forty," I say with a laugh.

"I know." He pauses and looks at me thoughtfully. "It's mind-blowing how much I've learned from them. You got exactly what you worked so hard for, Dani . . . smart and kind kids."

It's a nice compliment and it definitely lightens the mood. "That's not all I want for the boys though. What I really want is for them to know how to love, like *really* love. There's happiness in it, I think. That's what I care about. Their happiness."

"You think love equals happiness?" he says.

"No. I think the act of loving does, the skill, the ability in it—practicing and refining it . . . you know?"

He nods. "Yeah," he says in a quiet voice, but I know from his response that he's still not grasping what I'm saying.

"I want them to know how to love well. It will bring more meaning to their lives," I say. "I think we did for a long time, Alex. I think we still do, in many ways, it just looks different now."

He opens his eyes wider. "I know what you mean. You do love them well, Dani. There's no question about that. They've learned from you."

"You too," I say, and it's true.

"Thank you for saying that." His eyes are clear and pleading like he wants me to know he's being real. "Dani, sometimes I think we loved each other so much that we hated what we were put through with the same level of energy."

"Maybe." I'm starting to choke up. All I have to do is think about the fact that Kate will be at the wedding tomorrow and I snap out of it. "Let's enjoy each other's unique silence."

He nods. A few moments pass. Alex and I know how to be next to each other without talking.

He looks at his phone and begins texting someone. "So, I guess you and Kate are serious, then?" I already know the answer, but I want the satisfaction of hearing him say it . . . though I doubt he will.

"Thanksgiving was a mistake, I told you that. The wedding invite was a mistake."

"What are you saying?"

He puts his phone in his back pocket. He seems irritated. "I'm frustrated, Dani. With the situation. She told me she loved me."

I'm not surprised, but he's looking at me like I should be. "What did you say?"

"What was I supposed to do?"

"Be honest with her. That's what you should do. She's a single mom. The kid doesn't even have a dad."

As the bartender walks by, Alex says, "Can I get a whiskey?"

"That bad, huh?" the bartender jokes.

I laugh out loud, still slightly flirtatious.

"Subtle," Alex says.

I shrug. "When in Rome."

"I need to talk to Kate. It's not that she's acting jealous, but she's texting nonstop like she thinks I should be giving her a play-by-play just because you and I are together."

"Sounds like jealousy to me. What are you gonna say? She needs to get used to it . . . I'm not going anywhere."

"I don't know what to say. I have to think this over. She has a lot to offer someone. She's beautiful and very sweet . . . and honestly, *zero* drama." He opens his eyes wide to emphasize that part. It's clearly a dig at me.

"So, she's boring?" I say, knowing that sort of remark gets to Alex.

"What I'm saying is that she has a lot to offer someone!" he says loudly, drawing a few sets of eyes our way.

"Okay. Jesus."

"Just not me," he says in a low voice.

"Yikes. Looks like you got yourself into a little pickle."

"Dani, please. I'm going to have to talk to Kate and let her down and it's going to be hard. I don't want to mess with her head, or that kid's head."

It hits me that I'm having a conversation with Alex about breaking up with his girlfriend. I finish my wine in one large gulp and stand. "I'm sorry, Alex. I can't be this person for you. Thanks for the wine." I leave the bar, find the boys, and commit myself to protecting my dignity for the rest of the trip.

29

do you still think about us?

ALEXANDER

As weddings go, Amanda and Josh's was a standard small, intimate affair. There are about thirty people in attendance now at the reception. I'm sitting alone at a table in the back running over the events of the last twenty-four hours while I watch Kate dance with Tristan in a semicircle that includes my sister, her best friend, and my mother. Kate is moving in quickly and I feel like I'm suffocating.

Yesterday she flew in at 4 P.M. She and Tristan came with me to the rehearsal dinner because I was running late and didn't have time to take them to the hotel first. It's another thing I should have thought through. I'm guilty of letting Kate believe she's part of this family. Naturally, my entire family, along with many of Amanda and Josh's friends, know Dani, so she has a great time mingling and catching up. Kate just kind of stood around after we ate last night and waited for people to come up and talk to her, but no one did. Then later, when we were alone, she complained about everyone loving Dani more.

I was up late last night reassuring her that it has nothing to do with her personally, it's just a history that I cannot delete. And even if I could, I wouldn't want to. In one of the low points of the conversation, Kate said, "Why is she even here?"

I replied, "Because Dani is like a sister to Amanda. She's family and nothing is ever going to change that. Even if I got remarried, Dani would still be around." It was another failed attempt to explain something to Kate, only to basically light myself on fire.

"So, you do eventually want to get remarried?" Kate said.

"I don't think so," is how I responded, but I should have just said "no."

By the time the ceremony rolled around, Kate was over it. She put on a smile and didn't mention anything else to me. Tristan has been on his best behavior too and the guilt about stringing her along and confusing him is starting to get to me. I asked my sister to make an effort to include Kate, so now Amanda has Kate and Tristan at the center of the dance party. Noah and Ethan are dancing near them in a group with Josh and some of his friends and family. I haven't seen Dani in a while. Knowing her, she's probably off somewhere becoming best friends with some member of the hotel staff.

"Wanna go smoke a ciggie?" I hear Dani's voice behind me.

I look up and laugh. She's tipsy. "Didn't you give that up, like, thirty years ago?"

"Come outside with me. There's a heater out there."

I get up and follow her, hoping no one sees us. It would be an odd sight for us to be sneaking off together.

The outdoor area is completely empty. It's a large Tuscan veranda reminiscent of the Macaroni Grill, only we're overlooking a snow-covered golf course. There's little light below or in front of us, so the golf course looks like a large white void in the moonlight. There are hints of the snowfall from earlier on the concrete, but not much. It's still freezing. We find the one heater near the veranda rail and huddle around the base of it.

She has two cigarettes in her hand and holds one out to me. I take it. "Where did you get these?"

"From the DJ's assistant."

"Hanging out with the roadies again?"

"You know me. Can I get a sip of that?"

She points to my glass half full of bourbon. She takes a sip. "Holy shit. Is that just straight whiskey?"

"It's been a long day. I'll share."

"It's warming me up already. Remember when we used to do this?" she says as she lights her cigarette.

"Yeah, many long talks. Many cigarettes." I light mine, inhale, and blow out a ring of smoke. "Damn, that's good. I wish they weren't so bad for you."

"Yeah, me too. And I wish we didn't have to roll back in there smelling like 1976," she says. We laugh giddily. We're both drunk.

"I don't want to go back in at all," I say.

"This place is like *The Shining*. There's no one here. Let's go back in and look around. Come on." She finagles the cherry out of her cigarette and watches it fall into the snow near her feet. Dani pays attention to sounds, smells, and sights in a childlike way, like it's the first time she's seen fire get stifled by snow. She leaves the rest of the unsmoked cigarette on the base of the heater, so I do the same. As she starts toward the front entrance, I follow.

"Are we gonna go look for ghosts, or for Jack? Or is Jack technically a ghost now?"

She spins around on her heel so fast it creates a gust of wind.

She points her finger at me. We're mere inches apart. "Don't," she says in all seriousness.

Dani is the biggest scaredy-cat in the world. I'm convinced it has to do with her imagination. It's so vivid that scary ideas or thoughts are paralyzing to her. She probably has a three-dimensional image in her mind right now of Jack wielding an ax.

"Okay, okay, sorry. You're the one who mentioned *The Shining*," I say.

"Just don't, please."

She is so easily petrified that she won't even allow conversation about something scary to take place in her presence. She hates Halloween even more than Thanksgiving and she makes it known. Every October first, she breaks out the Easter decorations for their second appearance of the year. Dani's favorite holiday is Easter, and it's not because of Jesus. It's because of the chocolate and bunnies. Every year when Halloween rolls around, she says, "Chocolate and bunnies or rotten winter squash and flesh-eating zombies? You choose." As if we actually have a choice.

She does let the boys dress up, but she wants no part in it. I picked out all of their costumes when they were little, and I'm the one who has taken them trick-or-treating over the years. In the beginning, everyone fussed about Dani's nonparticipation in Halloween, but she would just say, "I'm sorry. I'll make up for it at Christmas." We're all used to it now, but it's still hard for me to refrain from teasing her at least a little bit.

"So, what are we looking for, then?"

"Snacks?" she says.

"Sure."

We find our way into the dark and empty hotel kitchen. There is no way we're allowed to be in here. There is a small white light over the industrial stove making it just bright enough for us to see where we are.

"I think that's the freezer. Come on."

"We don't want to get stuck in there," I say, and now I'm also having flashbacks from *The Shining*.

"Those don't lock that way, silly. That only happens in the movies." She yanks open the giant walk-in freezer door and a whoosh of freezing air hits us.

"I'm not going in there."

"Whatever," she says. She walks in and the door closes quickly behind her. The air suctioning mechanism turns on and the door is sealed closed. I have one second of worry and then I hear her joyfully yell, "Yessss!"

Less than five seconds later, she's pushing the door open from the inside with her foot. She's carrying a giant vat of ice cream.

I help her by pulling the door open all the way. "It's like you have an ice cream–locating sonar."

"Really, it's chocolate in general, but chocolate ice cream is even better." She sets the vat down on the stainless-steel counter and begins opening cabinets and drawers. "Where's the spoons?" She holds up a giant serving spoon. "This should give you an idea of how much ice cream I plan to eat right now. Come on, bring your whiskey. We'll use it as a chaser." She hops up on the counter and begins removing the lid from the vat.

"Are you just gonna eat it straight outta that thing?"

"At this point I've lost all sense of decorum in most areas of my life, Alex. Why start implementing protocol now? I'll leave a note if that makes you feel better. They can charge it to my room."

I shake my head. "Some things never change."

"Who would want them to?"

She's right. This is the Dani I fell in love with and I wouldn't want anything about her to be different. I hop up on the counter alongside her. She pries some chocolate ice cream onto the big spoon and tries to shove the whole thing in her mouth. We're both laughing. She's trying not to spit it out, but I know she has brain freeze. Some of the ice cream is running down her chin. She bends completely over and wipes her mouth on the underside of her dress hem.

"Dani, I'll look for a towel or a napkin."

"Oh my god, that's delicious ice cream. What is this thing?" She turns the vat around. "Häagen-Dazs. I should have known." She spoons up some more and hands it to me. "Your turn," she says while she sips the large glass of whiskey that we've barely made a dent in.

We sit side by side in silence, eating ice cream and drinking the whiskey.

She sighs. "This is nice. See, we *can* be nice." There's a noise outside the door. She jumps off the counter. "Hurry up, get down."

Now we're both on the floor, hiding behind the counter. We hear muffled voices having a conversation. It might be a while, so we both sit on the floor. "Smells like Lysol down here."

"Could be worse," I say.

"True. Who is this new glass-half-full Alex?"

"What are you talking about?"

"There's a reason why I've called you a grumpaholic for the last five years."

"I'm working on it," I say.

"So, what's new, Alex? What did you think of the wedding? Is everyone happy? Are you following me around *The Shining* because you're trying to avoid Kate?"

Dani's MO is rapid-fire questions before the other person has a chance to respond. "What's new? Nothing," I say. "The wedding was great. Amanda, Josh, my parents are happy. And no, I'm not intentionally avoiding Kate."

"Are *you* happy?"

"I don't know. At the moment, I'm drunk."

"Me too."

She giggles loudly. I shush her and she gets quiet. The voices are still outside the door, but it seems like they're getting farther away.

"Tell me something I don't know, Alex. Just one thing. Tell me a secret," she whispers.

Dani always asks this question and I know she means something personal. "Did you know that some cats are actually allergic to humans?"

"Fascinating," she snaps. "Tell me something I don't know about *you*."

Right now, I don't feel guarded or mad. I feel tired. Tired of pretending that everything always has to be right or a certain way.

"I still think about you when I . . . you know." I arch my eyebrows.

She doesn't get it at first, and then her eyes get big. She realizes. "You still think about me when you jerk off?" she says, laughing.

I smile. I give up. "Yes. It's true," I say in all seriousness.

She stops laughing. "Really?"

I nod.

"What do you think about specifically?"

"Dani—"

"Just tell me."

I take a deep breath. She's not going to let me out of this. "I

think about our fifth 'anniversary, when you were lying on that
big bed in the hotel in Maui. You were on your stomach, propped
up on your elbows, with your feet up behind you. Naked. Smiling at me. And then what you did next. That's what I think
about."

She's staring at me, blinking. For a moment, I think I've
made her sad. "I think about that night too . . . on the lanai
later."

I nod. "Yeah, that was a good night."

"Do you think about me when you're with her?" she asks.

I nod. "Yes, and I think she senses it."

"It's too late for us, Alex." Her voice is low and apologetic.

"I know," I say. She's right.

She blinks again, and then we're startled by the sound of loud
cheering coming from the reception.

"Oh, shit. It's midnight," she says. "It's New Year's."

"We never missed one," I tell her.

"Why start now?" she says, and then we're kissing. I'm not
sure who initiated it, but it feels so good.

People in their forties don't take their time when they're on
the floor of large industrial hotel kitchens on New Year's at mid-
night. I think it's been all of forty seconds and we're having sex.
I have her pinned against a wall. She's kissing me all over, and
god, she feels amazing.

We hear the door swing open, and freeze. Even though most
people would only catch a glimpse of Dani and me from the
waist up, where we are still clothed, unfortunately it had to be
Josh who caught us. Josh is six-foot-four. There's no hiding.

He looks shocked for a second, and then he smiles. "Wow.
Cool, cool. Happy New Year, guys!" he says. He holds up a fat
joint. "I was just gonna smoke a doob in here. Sorry." He starts

to turn around to head out. He still looks confounded. As he's walking out, he waves his arm absently in the air and says, "As you were."

"Oh my god," Dani says. "Thank god it was Josh. He's stoned out of his mind already. He'll think he was hallucinating."

We continue, and when it's over, we're giggling and stumbling and searching for more alcohol, until everything fades away.

~

I wake up in my clothes in a double bed, alone. It's my room and it's early morning, I can tell by the light. I roll over and see a sleeping Kate and Tristan. She opens her eyes and looks across at me. She points to Tristan's head and mouths, "Don't wake him up. We need to talk." She juts her thumb back, pointing at the balcony.

I'm not sure how much Kate knows, but I'm almost positive I'm in trouble. I've been horrible to her. We tiptoe out to the balcony and close the sliding door.

"It's freezing out here," Kate says. "Why did you come back here before midnight and just pass out without telling me? Were you that drunk?"

I'm putting the pieces together. Somehow, she thinks I was in the room the whole time.

"How late were you dancing?" I ask.

"We shut it down. I mean, Tristan fell asleep on a chair, but your sister, Dani, your mom, and a bunch of your sister's friends were basically kicked out of there at 2 A.M.," she says with a little laugh. She holds her hand to her head. "Ow, too much alcohol. I still wish you'd have told me you were going to bed. You're a lightweight."

"Dani was there?"

"Yeah. She's so much fun. She really comes to life after mid-night. She started a conga line and then she started the limbo with a broomstick . . . and then she stood on a chair and sang 'Love Shack.'"

"I'm not surprised," I say quietly. I quickly look down and realize my belt and shoes are off. I have a one-second flashback of Dani removing them and putting me to bed last night, I'm assuming right before she made her grand reappearance on the dance floor. Some things never change. Who would want them to?

30

i'm calling you

DANIELLE

"One of the producers asked about you," Mirabel says to me as we wait for an Uber outside of the studio.

"What do you mean? What did they ask?"

"He," she says. "He asked if you were dating."

"Oh, weird." I scrunch up my nose. "Which producer?"

"He has a unique name. I think it's Tré."

I know who she's talking about. "He's an associate producer," I say. "And he's young."

"Well, he asked about you."

I ignore her and continue staring at my phone. The little cartoon Uber car is going in circles two blocks away. "We're gonna be late."

A text comes in from Alex . . .

Alex: Congratulations! I watched the show and it was fantas-
     tic. About the wedding, Dani . . .

It's been six weeks and this is the first time he's mentioned it. I see bubbles on the screen. He's contemplating what to say, so I beat him to the punch.

> Me: Don't worry about it. It happens. It's common and we
> were drunk.
> Alex: Right. Well, congrats on the show.
> Me: Thank you.

"It's your party. You can be late."

"Huh?" I'm sidetracked, thinking about me and Alex in the hotel kitchen. I can feel a grin plastered to my face.

"Where'd you go? Who are you thinking about?"

"Nothing. Alex was texting me."

"Hmm. That's an interesting reaction to one of Alex's texts," she says.

"Oh, forget it, he was just saying the show was good."

The show premiered today. A few of us got together and watched it at the office, and now we're headed to a bar Eli rented out in Hollywood for the after-party. I'd already seen the pilot, I watched it last week, completely alone because I didn't want anyone to see me reacting to it. I was not overjoyed, but not totally disappointed either. The acting seemed disjointed and clunky to me. I know it's impossible to be objective about something you've written that has been brought to life by other people, but I do hope that, as the episodes grow, the acting becomes more fluid. I have to remind myself that most pilot episodes are shot when the actors barely know each other, and it takes time to develop an easy rhythm.

Finally, the Uber driver pulls up in a large black SUV with tinted windows. We hop in, and within a minute Maribel says, "So, do you want me to introduce you to Tré?"

"Not tonight. Tonight, I just want to thank everyone, have a couple of drinks, and stick a fork in it. I'm wiped."

"But it's Valentine's Day."

"Oh yeah, that's right, well in that case, definitely no. Why don't you go out with him?"

She shrugs. "He's not my type. Too young."

After two hours of thank-mingling, Maribel comes up to me and says, "I'm heading home. I just ordered an Uber. Do you want to go right now? Eli left with that hot young PA dude, and none of the other writers are here anymore. I don't know any of these people."

"Of course Eli left with that guy." I roll my eyes.

"How come Lars was a no-show?" she says.

"It's just not his style. He doesn't like building too much hype around something before the big reviews have all come out."

"I get that." She juts her thumb back toward the door. "So, you ready to leave?"

"My house is in the other direction. Go ahead and go. I'm gonna grab one last sip and then use the restroom before I head out."

"Okay." We hug each other. "See you tomorrow."

I go to the bar, order a whiskey neat, down it in one gulp, then head for the restrooms. There's a line. The woman in front of me turns around.

What? No! Beth Zinn.

"What are you doing here?!" I groan. She's trying to torture me.

"As far as I know, this place is public. What are you doing here?" she fires back.

"Celebrating. But you know that. There's a freakin' sign out front!"

"Right. By the way, bummer you got that terrible review in *EW*."

I intentionally avoid reviews for this reason. My hands are sweating and my stomach has dropped like I've ingested a cinder block.

"I don't read reviews," I tell her. "Sorry *Graceless* got canceled."

"It didn't get canceled, it just didn't get re-upped."

"It's the same thing . . . it's today's version of getting canceled. Why do you want to keep intruding on my life anyway, Beth? Like, what have I ever done to you?"

"I just don't get the hype around you. You got this show because of your connections. No one sees the coincidence that Eli was the one who put this together for you?"

"Wait, what? It was my pilot. Here you go again . . . trying to take something away from me. You've got problems, serious issues."

"That's what people say about you."

"Really?" I take a deep breath in through my nose and let it out slowly through my mouth. I really am done with this woman . . . and the whiskey is kicking in. "Do you know what they say in Eastern philosophy? They say to love your enemy. Your enemy will teach you more than your friends. Guess what? *I love you, Beth Zinn!*" I say, and a second later my fist is connecting with her face.

There's a scuffle of arms and legs and shouting, a little hair pulling, and the next thing I know I am being handcuffed outside of the bar. I'm not even sure how I got from the bathroom to the street, but I vaguely remember a giant bouncer calling me a bulldog as he was carrying me over his shoulder.

"I'm getting arrested?"

The female cop looks up to the sky for a moment and back down to where I am sitting on the curb in handcuffs. "What exactly did you think was happening?"

"Where is Beth Zinn?"

"Who is Beth Zinn?" the officer says.

"The woman I punched."

"Oh, her? Yeah, they're taking her to the hospital. For sure a broken nose. She was bleeding like a pig."

"What a gross way to describe it. But are you going to arrest *her*, is what I really want to know?"

"Ma'am, we have witnesses that saw you punch her."

I'm suddenly very sober. Sober me would never physically hurt another person. Beth has pushed me to the brink. I've never been arrested or even been inside of a jail before. I'm picturing something from *The Andy Griffith Show*. Actually, I'm hoping for that, but picturing something more like *Orange Is the New Black*.

I'm a criminal. I look down at my two-hundred-dollar jeans. *I'm gonna get shanked.*

"Is there any way out of this?" I say to the officer.

"Uh . . . no," she says as she pulls me to my feet and maneuvers me over to the police cruiser. She pushes down on my head, basically forcing me into the back of the car. I've seen this a million times on TV, but would never imagine it hurts this bad.

"Easy, my god."

"No more talking." She slams the door and then walks over to converse with another officer. They're getting statements from bystanders, as well as the burly bouncer. I'm done for.

There are a million things running through my head right now. One is, *How am I going to keep this quiet?* The officer gets into the car and we drive away in silence.

When we pull up to the Hollywood police station, I say, "Can you take me in a back entrance? Something a little less conspicuous?"

She looks at me in the rearview mirror. Her eyes are crinkled at the sides. I can tell she's smiling. "You're not that famous."

"That's not why! I just know a lot of people in this town."

"Maybe you shouldn't go around breaking noses, then."

"Listen, you don't know that woman. I bet you would have punched her ages ago. Anyway, she'll probably get a better nose after this. Her old nose was too pointy," I say.

"You should probably stop talking," the cop tells me.

The inside doesn't look like *The Andy Griffith Show* jailhouse or *Orange Is the New Black*. It's more like a hospital with bars. After they take my mug shot—for which I accidentally smiled—my fingerprints and basic information, they put me in a cell with no one else, thank god.

A few minutes later, a guard comes up and asks if I want to make a call. I nod and she takes me to the hallway where there is a phone attached to the wall. "Go ahead. You get one."

"Can I have my phone?"

"No."

It hits me that I don't know a single phone number by heart except for Alex's. This day just keeps getting better. There's a clock on the wall. It's 11:30 P.M. Brenda is watching the boys at the house because it's Alex's days at the apartment. He's probably at Kate's, lying in bed . . . naked . . . I'm *so* annoyed that I have to call him.

I dial the number. He answers in one ring. "Hello?" he says groggily.

"Hey. I got arrested. I need you to come and bail me out."

"What? Is this a joke?"

"Really, Alex? You think I would joke about this?"

"You got arrested?" he says, and now he's actually laughing. "For what?"

"I punched Beth Zinn in the face. Can you please just come and get me?"

The deputy guard is rolling her eyes and shaking her head at me.

"I don't know what to do," he says.

"Call a bail bondsman. They'll figure it out. Have you never watched TV in your life?"

"Well, I don't know how to find a good one. Is there like a section on Yelp with reviews?" He's teasing me.

"Call the one where that sexy Jesus spins a sign on the corner that says, 'Let God Free You!' I think it's on Highland. Look it up . . . Jesus Christ Bail Bonds."

Alex is laughing so hard he can barely speak. "How are you not laughing right now, Dani?"

"Maybe because I'm hungover, in jail, and there is a very tall and strong-looking deputy hovering over me. Just hurry up, please. I have to go. I'm at the Hollywood police station," I say quickly as the deputy is reaching to hang up the phone. I look at her and glare. "Wow, you guys are tough. It's like I'm being treated like a freakin'—"

"Criminal?" she says.

"Hey, wait a minute . . . innocent until proven guilty. I watch *Law & Order*, okay?"

She's smiling as she pulls me along toward the cell. "Did you get someone to take care of things for you?" she asks.

"Yeah, my husband. I mean ex-husband." She looks at me peculiarly. "It was the only phone number I knew by heart."

She laughs. "Well, I guess you can't call him 'good for nothin'' anymore, can you?"

"Funny."

It's been hours, I've been sitting here on a concrete bench staring at my hands. I don't think I regret punching Beth, which makes me sad about the whole situation. I've never disliked anyone so much.

The deputy comes to unlock the bars. "Come on. Your ex is here."

"Never thought I'd be so happy to hear those words."

We both laugh. "By the way, the charges were dropped. I guess no broken nose and no hard feelings. It was all a big misunderstanding." She lowers her voice. "Boy, oh boy, did you get lucky."

I don't think I would call it "luck," but I'll take it for now. As soon as we turn the corner, I see Alex. I sometimes forget how handsome he is. I realize more now that every once-in-a-while, you have to move away from a person to see why you were attracted to them to begin with. He's standing with his hands in his pockets, leaning against the wall.

When he looks up and sees me, he smiles. In the beginning, Alex and I were like two opposite magnets in a drawer. My north to his south. We grew closer and closer together . . . until we fused. It was then that we became the same, too alike . . . too close. We were so close, so similar, we started to repel one another. We lost our identities and surrendered to being a couple. To being a mom and dad with no singular identities, no separateness, no autonomy. Now I'm seeing him again from the other side of the drawer and there are so many things I want to tell him.

"Hey, slugger," he says.

"Hi," I say with a mock frown.

The deputy hands me my things and I'm free. I follow Alex outside and it feels natural to be with him. It's calming.

We get in his car and start driving out of the parking lot. I turn my body toward him from the passenger seat. "Thank you," I say.

"Of course, Dani. Do you mind if I stop at the Mobil gas station by the freeway? I'm on empty."

"Yeah, go ahead. Thanks for asking."

"Sooo, Rocky Balboa, I guess we're making this a family thing? We're like an organized crime family now . . . minus the organized part."

"Ha, ha, ha! I thought you'd be mad."

"I'm not mad. Are you kidding? This is the most fun I've had in ages. I mean, bailing your ex-wife out of jail on Valentine's Day? It doesn't get better than that."

"I'm not amused."

"Why was Beth at the premier party anyway?" he says.

"I don't know, probably to torture me. She must have come to her senses, though, because she dropped the charges. God, I don't know why I let her get to me. Beth is like Comic Sans, you know? No one really takes her seriously . . . why should I?"

"Comic Sans? The font?" he says.

"Yeah, exactly."

"What font am I?"

"You're definitely Wingdings, impossible to read," I tell him.

Alex laughs once and then begins fidgeting with the air conditioner. "Are you cold?"

"No, I'm fine."

"Do you want me to take you to the house? My mom will probably ask a million questions."

"No, can we go to the apartment? I have some clothes there."

"Of course. I'll sleep on the couch."

When we get to the apartment, we go in separate directions. I take a shower, put on sweats, and head back into the living room, where Alex is sipping red wine and sitting in the leather chair. The record player is spinning a Miles Davis album. "Wine?" I ask, surprised that he's drinking this late.

"I'm tired, but wired," he says.

"Me too."

He stands. "I'll get you some."

I sit on the couch. He comes back and hands me a glass, then sits in the chair directly across from me. "Was Kate mad that you had to leave?"

He squints. "I broke up with Kate weeks ago, Dani. I thought the boys would have told you."

I'm not surprised, but I do wonder why he didn't tell me himself. "How did she take it?"

He shakes his head. "It was . . . sort of mutual. Ended up being . . . unemotional. We both agreed that our time together was nice, but we were looking for different things."

"What were you looking for, exactly?"

"You." He blinks. I really can't read him right now. "Or maybe the opposite of you."

We're staring at each other. There is a subtle nuance about marriage that he's touching on right now. It's like the things that annoy you the most about your partner are also the things that make up what you love about them. He loved that I was spontaneous, creative, passionate, and intense, but he also hated it. And for me, it was Alex's loyalty, his steadfastness, and passiveness that drew me to him. But sometimes that passivity looked too much like indifference and I hated that about him.

"I get what you're saying. It was too soon for a serious relationship," I say.

"Something like that. Why didn't you tell me you were a poet?"

"What are you talking about?"

"Let's do something. For one hour, let's answer each other's questions with total honesty and agree we can never bring up the topic again if we don't like the answer?"

This is not typical Alex. Typical Alex does not like talking about his feelings. "Okay," I say.

"I snooped on your desk and was reading one of your yellow legal pads. I saw a poem on it. Was it about me?"

I deliver the same canned response when anyone close to me asks if a fictional character is based on them. "Everything I write comes from the people I know. The characters are amalgamations of many people."

"Was that poem about me, Dani?"

He knows it was different, not a characterization. It was more a question and a plea to him that I thought he would never read. It didn't matter to me if he read it because it wouldn't have changed the outcome of us getting divorced. I take a deep breath. "Yes, it was about you, Alex. Sometimes I write poems . . . just scribble them down on the yellow notepad, and they all eventually end up in the trash." God, that felt good.

"Why would you throw them away?"

"Because they're just for me . . . no one else."

"I'm sorry I snooped. But if you're still wondering, the answer is yes, I still love you." The room is quiet with the exception of the softly playing jazz. I don't know how to respond. "Your turn," he says.

I know Alex still loves me. That was never in question. It was more, does he *like* me? "Why did it take you twenty-something years and a divorce to be curious about me?"

He looks thoughtful for a moment before answering. "That's fair. I regret that I didn't ask questions about your writing . . . and about your feelings. As far as the snooping, in all honesty, I thought I was respecting your space. You said yourself the stuff you scribble on the notepads is just for you."

"It would have been nice to know you cared enough to snoop once in a while. It feels good to know a person is thinking about you when you're not there, even if they're being a little intrusive. I had nothing to hide. You would have known that if you looked harder."

"I'm sorry. I never thought of it that way, but now that you say it, it makes sense. I've also looked at some of the album sleeves since I've been in the apartment. I know that you named Jane after the Velvet Underground song. It was heartbreaking to read that, Dani. I'm sorry I wasn't there for you then. I'm sorry I wasn't looking."

"The first memory we made to that song was good and happy. Do you remember it? It was the first night in our house? I'd rather hold on to *that* memory."

"Yeah, I do. It was a great night, Dani. You were so fun and vibrant," he says.

"I still am. You're just too close to see it." I take a deep breath and let out an audible sigh. "It's impossible to want for something you already have, you know? That's the irony in marriage."

"Did you cheat on me when we were married?" he says.

"No. Did you sleep with that doctor woman here?"

"No," he says. "Why is your password *lovelove6* now?"

"It has been that for a long while. You're becoming a very good detective, Alex. I didn't know you had it in you."

"Well . . . why six?"

I feel a stabbing pain in my heart. "The two babies, Alex. The babies, the boys, you, and Louie Louie."

He looks pained by the realization. "Did you name her? The second baby?"

My breath hitches. Before I even begin to answer, tears are streaming down my face. He grabs a box of tissues off the end table and literally throws it next to me on the couch. "What is it? Tell me." He's frustrated. I should have told him all of this. We could have mourned together.

"Lucy," I squeak out, and now I can't breathe.

"That's a good one. Can't beat the Beatles." He's getting choked up. This is the extent of the emotion I've seen from Alex. "You know what's sad, Dani? Every now and then I imagine walking them down the aisle."

I blink and look closer. Alex is crying. I throw the box back at him. It's the first time I've seen him cry . . . ever. I'm shocked, which is a useful distraction from the conversation about the babies we lost.

"You should have told me that you were thinking about them too. We should have talked about it. What happened to us, Alex? Why couldn't we talk like this? What *happened*?"

He shrugs. "I don't know. I couldn't contain you, and I couldn't keep up with you, your emotions, your ups and downs."

"Why were you trying to?"

"I don't know anymore."

"You don't have to keep up, you just have to stay in the right place. A place where I can always find you. That's what home is."

"You still scare me sometimes, Dani. It scares me how much you feel and how much passion you put into everything. I was afraid of what you would do when you were so unhappy. I thought I was doing more by being silent. I didn't ask questions or talk to you about things because I was terrified of the answers. If I brought up the babies, I knew it would send you spiraling."

"You don't know everything thing about me. It's not spiraling, it's processing. I might lose it for little while, but I always come back stronger. It would have been worth it to me. Instead, you were silent, which made it seem like you didn't care. Months before my mom died, you went into a hole, Alex. You wouldn't even make eye contact with me."

"I couldn't look at you. I believed that the rumors about Lars were true."

"Lars took off and moved, and my mother died soon after. All of the bad was fading away, leaving an empty space for us. Why did we fill it with resentment and disdain instead of love and healing? We're both to blame." I look down into my wineglass.

"I checked out when I felt like I had lost control of my family, my house, everything. I hung on to things that weren't even true and I'm sorry. In retrospect, I should have been there for you when all the accusations were swirling and your mother was dying. I'm sorry, I understand how hurt you were. My vision was skewed. I was looking at us like this tangible object that had been broken beyond repair, and I saw you as the one breaking it. Now I realize that you were the one keeping it together, while I looked on in silence."

I'm surprised by Alex's introspection. "Alexander, are you waxing philosophical on love? How do you see it all so clearly now?"

"Something fluid surrounding us, something living in the ether. It's a scent, a sound, a taste, a feel, memories, laughter, it's an inside joke only you and I can understand."

"And we did for so long, didn't we?"

"We still do, Dani."

I nod. There were so many things I wanted to tell him. I knew I wanted him back. It wasn't just our past, it was that we grew and changed through everything and even though we were apart, the space made room for a bigger, stronger love. "At the wedding, I realized, out of everyone in the room, I only cared to talk to you. And at the premier party, I wanted to celebrate with you. We were so good at celebrating."

"We still are, Dani."

"At Thanksgiving, when you smiled across the table at me, it was like seeing the Alex of twenty years ago. I missed *us* so much," I say, and now I'm crying again. "Why do you think we're in this place now, Alex? Right here where we've landed, looking across at each other this way. In this room, finally talking and finally telling the truth?"

"I guess we had to get a little lost to find each other again. I know without a doubt that I am still in love with you, Dani, and I want to be with you more than anything. You are one of a kind and I don't want to change *anything* about you." He looks thoughtful for a moment, and then laughs. "You are my Times New Roman. The original, bold and classic."

I'm crying and laughing at the same time. I get up and walk toward Alex. "I don't think I've ever loved you more than I do right now."

We are kissing. Everything is right.

31

i'm here

ALEXANDER

I roll over and see her sleeping next to me in the apartment bed. It's been two months that she and I have been sneaking around like teenagers since the night she got arrested. There's something sexy about meeting her at the apartment. In a way, it forces us to be present. There's no life chaos swirling around us. We can be *still* here. There's nowhere to go.

She opens her eyes and looks at me. "Morning," she whispers.

I run my hand over her hip, caressing it. "Hi," I say.

"Coffee?"

I shake my head no and then lean in to kiss her. "We're not very good at being divorced, Dani."

"Why didn't we do this when we were married? Why didn't we take our time?"

"I don't know, but I do know we need to tell the boys what's going on."

I'm looking at Dani, thinking how beautiful she is. Her dark hair is draped over her bare shoulder.

"Have you told Brian?" she asks.

"He was poking around. I said I was dating someone."

"Ooh, scandalous. What did he say?"

"He said what all guys say to each other, 'Is she hot?'"

"What did you say?"

"I said 'yes' of course. Because it's true."

"Well, thank you for saying that. We need to tell him what's going on. I see him on the lot sometimes. Alicia and Mirabel know. I think Lars does too. I'm sure Alicia told Mark."

"Why do you think Alicia knows?" I ask.

"She said I seemed happy. It reminded her of our earlier years and I guess I reacted a certain way to that comment. She called me out specifically about you, but I ignored her."

"You're not very good at hiding your feelings."

She laughs, then leans over, puts her hands to my cheeks, and kisses me. "Let's tell the boys at dinner tonight. But can we keep the apartment for a while? I'll make it my workspace and we can just write it off. I love it here."

"I think that's a good idea." I lean in and kiss her again. "Let's stay in bed for a little while."

"Ow!" she yells. "Cramp, cramp." She's now bending forward and frantically massaging her calf. I can see her shoulder twitching as she's rubbing her leg.

"Dani, what is wrong?"

"Nothing. Just a muscle spasm."

I notice for the first time that I can see her ribs through her back. She's very skinny. "I'm worried about you. You're so thin."

"It's just stress. It's gotten better, haven't you noticed?" She takes a few deep breaths, lies back, and puts her head on my chest. "You feel good."

Life has changed in the last two months. I never thought I'd hear Dani say nice things to me again. We had created a vacuum, a black hole that we existed in for so long that it seemed impossible to get out of. We were both so closed off. I don't know how we made it back.

I run my hand over her shoulder and down her arm. I feel what I took for granted. Why didn't I want to stay in bed like this next to her? We both got into the habit of being complacent and I'll never let it happen again.

"Dani, I think you should go to a doctor and get checked out."

"I swear to you, Alex, this is literally work stress."

Leaning over, I kiss her neck and whisper, "Well, I can relieve your stress, then."

Dani and I are sitting across from Noah and Ethan at Umami Sushi, Dani's favorite restaurant. They're staring at us in a way that is making me feel like they're our parents.

"What's this all about?" Noah says.

Dani and I both ignore him. She waves a server over and then raps off an order for the whole table. Once the server is out of earshot, Dani shrugs and says, "What's this all about, you ask? Sushi? Well, it's fish. Some of it's raw, some of it's not. It's all delicious. Except for eel."

"You guys are such weirdos," Ethan says. "We know you're sneaking around with each other." He rolls his eyes dramatically.

"How did you know?" I ask.

"G-Ma told us. So you brought us here to tell us this big news we've known about for a month?"

I jerk my head back. "Grandma knows? How does she know?"

Dani smiles. "She's nosy, and they're right, we've been obvious. Well, I guess that's that, then. Where's my edamame?"

"That wasn't all we wanted to talk to you about," I say. "We don't . . . your mom and I don't . . ." I stumble over words.

"We don't want you guys thinking we're getting married again, because we're not. We're also keeping the apartment," Dani says.

Noah shrugs. "Cool."

About halfway through the meal, I look over and see her holding her neck. "Are you choking?"

She shakes her head no. She swallows. "That was a big bite. And my throat's been bugging me lately—maybe I have strep or something."

"You really need to go get checked out," I say.

"I will, I will!"

"What's wrong, Mom?" Ethan says.

"Just anxiety and stress about the show. It's nothing."

"So is, like, the house ours, and you guys get the apartment?" Noah asks.

"So, like, no, not a chance in hell," Dani replies.

Noah looks at Ethan. "I tried."

32

i need you

DANIELLE

I'm lying on my back, about to enter an MRI machine. The doctors have run a battery of tests on me. The weight loss, tremors, and difficulty swallowing could be a whole plethora of things, but they want to rule out all the worst-case scenarios.

"I need you to keep still," the tech says over the speaker.

"I'm trying," I say, but both of my hands are shaking. When the MRI is over, I scoot off the table, and the moment my feet hit the floor, everything turns to black.

"Danielle, it's Dr. Richmond," I look up into the eyes of Rob Lowe circa *St. Elmo's Fire,* minus the bad hair.

"Wow. I knew it. I knew my personal heaven would involve eighties' heartthrobs playing doctors in medical dramas."

"Well, I'm glad to hear you're speaking well. This isn't heaven, unfortunately, but it is Saint Joseph's Hospital in Burbank."

"How did I get here?" I'm genuinely confused.

"You were getting an MRI upstairs and you passed out, so they brought you down here to the ER."

"Did you say 'ER'?" George Clooney is going to walk in next. I'm crossing my fingers under the blanket.

"Yes, the emergency department. A neurologist and your primary are on their way here to talk to you about your scans. I'm just here to find out how you're feeling right now. Are you comfortable? We're giving you some fluids. You were very dehydrated."

It occurs to me that this doctor is acting strangely, and I'm thinking it's odd that my primary and a neurologist are rushing over when I seem fine.

"Is something wrong with me?" I say in a paranoid voice.

"Your doctors are on their way to talk to you about your scans," he repeats. He can't tell me anything. It hits me. *He can't tell me I'm okay, because I'm not.*

"Can you hand me my phone, please?" He does, then leaves the room. I dial Alex.

"Hello?"

"Come to St. Joe's. I'm in the ER department. I need you."

"Dani, what's going on? Are the boys okay?"

"It's not the boys, it's me. The doctors are coming to talk to me about my MRI. A neurologist, Alex. Something is wrong with me. I *need* you!" I shout, and then immediately hang up.

I suddenly feel lightheaded and sick to my stomach. "Nurse!" A nurse enters the room. "I'm going to throw up." She hands me a vomit bag and I heave into it, but there's hardly anything in my stomach.

Dr. Richmond comes back in and says to the nurse, "I just put the order in. Five milligrams of diazepam."

The nurse leaves the room while I'm still heaving. A minute later, she's back and messing with my IV. "What are you giving me?"

"It's diazepam. Just to calm you down a little bit."

And it does. I lie back on the pillow and close my eyes. Something is really wrong with me. What is going to happen to the boys? To Alex? Am I going to have to watch them watch me die? The thought is excruciating.

Time is imperfect in these moments. I feel Alex next to me. I open my eyes. He's standing by the bed with his hand over mine. My primary doctor is there, she's in her sixties, about to retire, and she's next to a man whom I assume is the neurologist. He's probably around the same age. All salt, no pepper. No more hopes for George . . . no more jokes. Nothing will be funny ever again.

"Hi, Dani, how are you feeling?"

"What's going on?" I ask.

"I'm one of the neurologists here at St. Joe's. My name is Dr. Miller." He reaches out and shakes my hand.

I feel droplets on my hand and look up. I can only see Alex's profile, but I can tell that the tears are his.

"What's wrong with me?"

"Danielle, you have amyotrophic lateral sclerosis. ALS."

My eyes go wide. Alex makes a mewling sound next to me. My primary doctor is just looking at me with sympathy.

Alex leans over the bedrail and buries his head in my chest. He's sobbing now, his body is shaking. "No. I just got you back," he whispers.

I still haven't said anything and I'm not crying. I must be in shock.

"I thought only men got ALS? I thought it was hereditary?" I say finally.

"It's more common in men, but women can get it. It is sometimes hereditary, but in your case, it doesn't look that way." Dr. Miller's voice is filled with empathy.

"Well, are you going to test my kids? They need to be tested.

Right now!" My brain is going a million miles an hour. Soon, I won't be able to communicate all the things I need to say.

Dr. Miller comes to my side and puts his hand on my shoulder. "We can do genetic testing on your children to see if they carry the gene. But right now, Danielle, you can go home and live your life. In fact, I urge you to resume as much of your normal activity as possible. We'll send a specialist to your house to talk to you about what might happen and how you'll be treated, but for now you're okay to go home and be with your kids. You're okay to work, if you want."

"I'm not going to work, are you kidding? I'm gonna charter a super yacht in the South of France. I'll spend my days snorkeling and my nights gambling in the Mediterranean casinos with James Bond."

Both doctors smile piteously. It feels like they're patronizing me even though I'm not joking, only exaggerating a little. I wonder if everyone will patronize me from now until the end. Alex still looks inconsolable. His face is buried in his hands and he's crying.

"How long do I have?" I ask, looking to Dr. Miller.

"It's hard to say right now. About seventy percent live three to five years after diagnoses; ten to twenty percent, ten years or more. Beyond twenty years is very rare."

Alex looks up from his tear-soaked hands. "But it is possible." Alex is not asking the doctor a question. He's making a statement. He looks at me. "That's what's gonna happen, Dani. Obviously. You are rare, and you're going to Stephen Hawking the shit out of this."

That's what has finally brought me to tears. The hope in Alex's eyes. The futile hope. This is going to be the worst part, watching the people I love be crushed by the fact that I'm dying.

"We'll leave you two alone. Let us know if you have any other questions. We're putting together a packet for you to take home. You'll be discharged in a few minutes." The doctors leave the room.

Alex watches them walk out. He's standing still, just staring at the sliding glass doors. He's in shock too. "Alex?" He looks down at me and starts to cry again. "Come get into bed with me," I tell him.

He doesn't hesitate. He lowers the bed rail and slides in as I peel the blanket back. Nothing matters anymore. Rules don't apply. He curls into my body as I cover him with the blanket. The nurse walks by and turns off the light, then closes the door behind her.

We lie, holding each other . . . hearts broken, terrified . . . glued together in pain . . . sobbing.

33

i'm right here

ALEXANDER

It's September now. Los Angeles is unbearably hot. This morning, Dani asked if I could move her chair into the garden again for the fourth time this week. She's been sitting there for hours. The peach tree she's next to is fruitless and the tomatoes have all come and gone, but Dani likes that spot. I think she spends a lot of her time now imagining chapters in our story that don't involve her having ALS. I think that's how she's coping.

We gave up the apartment a couple of months ago because we needed the money to pay for Dani's care. It's better for all of us to be together in one place anyway. Dani didn't argue with that.

I buried the girls' ashes under the peach tree and had some marble engraved and placed there. Dani chose the inscription, *Angel Babies—Jane and Lucy.*

When Dani and I told the boys that she had ALS, they went through all the stages I did. There was a lot of denial. Noah looked for alternative medicines and researched possible cures, while Ethan would repeat over and over to Dani, "You've got this, Mom! You'll beat this." It didn't matter that we repeatedly told him there was no way she could actually beat it, he still believed she could, because Noah and Ethan believe that Dani is superhuman. She has showed them how to solve every single one of their problems, except for this one.

Outside, in the shade, Dani watches the boys play catch or jump on the new trampoline while she sits in her chair in the garden, dreaming up Noah and Ethan's perfect futures that she's going to miss.

Her disease progressed much faster than we expected. Over the few months after she was diagnosed, we carried on the way we had been. Falling in love again, enjoying our lives, and trying to avoid the idea that we were going to lose each other. But it wasn't long before regular tasks started becoming more difficult for her.

Dani can still talk, but it's very hard to understand her. She can still walk a little sometimes, but that's deteriorating quickly. She has to be fed with a feeding tube connected to a port in her stomach, and most of her personal needs are assisted by a caretaker who comes in four days a week.

An ALS specialist came to the house yesterday and set up a system that would allow Dani to communicate on a computer since she cannot type anymore and her speech is also progressively getting worse day by day. The computer tracks Dani's eye movements as they move around a keyboard to select words. There is a very large learning curve and she has to train the computer to know her most common phrases. It's tedious, and for a woman who wrote as a career, sometimes ten thousand words a day, it's frustrating for her that it takes fifteen minutes to form a sentence. We are reassured by the specialist that Dani will get the hang of it. Privately, Dani told me that she'd rather not say anything at all.

I hear the doorbell ring, and I know that it's Dani's father coming for a visit. His first and likely his only. Jim isn't equipped for handling this sort of thing. If I were in his shoes, the worst part would be knowing I was the last member of my family to roam around this planet with none of the people I built my life with. But he's already been living that way since Ben died. I know this visit is an obligatory one.

I open the door. "Hi, Jim, come on in." He smiles, but doesn't say anything. He steps into the entryway and stands awkwardly with his hands in his pockets. I always wondered if he was shy. After two decades of being with Dani, I had barely spoken to him other than surface small talk. It used to be a point of contention. I thought he didn't like me. After living with Irene, getting to know the normal side of her during her lucid moments, it became obvious their family was more matriarchal. Irene ran the show in many ways, and Jim took a quiet backseat. I think when Ben died and they divorced, Jim just went through the motions of his life, as disconnected as one person could be.

"How have you been?" Jim asks.

"I'm okay. Dani's outside in the garden. I'll take you out there in a minute. Did you know the Emmys are on tonight? Dani's nominated twice."

"That's great," he says with a smile. I'm surprised he doesn't say he's proud of her, but I guess he never really has.

Jim is average height, looks a little like Dani, dark hair that's now completely gray, and light brown eyes. He's thin, like for twenty years he's only been eating to survive, and he always wears Levi's, a white T-shirt, sneakers, and an old Dodgers hat. He must have several of each because I've only ever seen him wear that outfit, except for at our wedding, when Dani had to rent him a suit.

Jim follows me to the back door and stops for a moment when we reach the shelves where the record collection is. He looks at them, then glances next to the shelf where Dani's hospital bed is set up in the living room. There are machines and trays with medications. It looks like a place where someone is setting up to die . . . and it is.

"She's outside."

He nods. I stay inside, he won't be here long. Dani has had an exhausting day and I don't want him adding to her stress by being so seemingly aloof.

She's still sitting in her motorized chair near the peach tree.

"Hello, Dani," Jim says to her. She smiles a crooked smile. When she talks now, she sounds drunk. In fact, when she was packing up her office to leave and I was helping her, some of the staff on the show, who didn't know Dani was sick, asked if she was drinking to celebrate the Emmy nods. Dani's reply to everyone was, "You know it!" She always said it with a smile.

"Hi, Dad," she says. She seems a little clearer today, but her smile is crooked and her eyes are a bit droopy from the medication.

"I'll leave you two alone," I say, and go into the kitchen to pour Jim some iced tea. I take my time so they can talk. It's only been about five minutes when I start to head back outside and see Jim walking toward me. "Iced tea?" I try to hand him the glass, but he doesn't take it.

"Actually, I'm going to head out." He takes an envelope from his pocket and hands it to me. "This is some of my bonus, if you could pass it on to the boys? For their college funds or if they want to buy a new bike or something." He smiles faintly and then his eyes well up.

"Jim—"

He cuts me off. "I got to go." His voice cracks, he looks at his feet, shoves his hands in his pockets, and walks toward the front door. I doubt I will see him again until the funeral.

After watching him walk out the door, I find Dani, in the same spot. She looks up and smiles at me. "When is . . . Alicia . . . coming . . ."

It's getting so hard for Dani to talk. "She and Mark will be here around five with the gang. What happened with your dad? Why was he only here for a minute?"

"Don't let yourself . . . don't let yourself . . . Come here," she says, and she's reaching her arms out to me.

I brace the arms of her chair and bend over so that we are eye to eye. "What is it, Dani? Tell me."

She puts her hands on my face. I know this is difficult for her physically. She pulls me close so we're mere inches apart. "Don't let this break you like . . . don't be broken like him. For the boys."

I nod. "I know, Dani. We don't have to talk about that."

"Yes, we do. While I still can."

"No, Dani, we're going to get that machine set up for you, where you can say anything you want. You have to try and . . ." I stop myself. I can tell she's getting irritated, and I don't want to piss her off.

"Listen to me . . . please," she begs. "I can't even cry. My tears hardly work anymore. I'm crying inside, it's so frustrating."

"I know," I say.

"I want to talk to you now, while I can." She's having one of her good talking days, which she knows are few and further between now.

"Okay. I'm right here. I'm not going anywhere. I'll listen," I tell her.

About thirty yards behind us, on the other side of the yard, Noah and Ethan are jumping on the trampoline, playing some sort of wrestling game. The springs are loud as they jump and

I'm relieved the boys are behaving like they should, playing joyfully even if the moments like this are fleeting lately. Dani and I are about to have a conversation. I'm not sure where it's going, but I know it's serious and I know it will take her some time to express herself.

I pull a patio chair over to sit next to her.

"My dad told me he loved me. He said he wished he would have gotten help for himself. He said he's felt like an observer of his life. Like he was watching it on a movie screen, because if it came to life, he'd have to walk around with a broken heart forever."

I nod. "I know, Dani. I think he does the best he can."

She smiles. "You can't be that way, Alex. You can't throw in the towel. The boys need you to show them how to *live*, not just exist."

"You've taught them a lot, Dani. What is this really about?"

"Find someone. Don't take forever either. The longer you wait, the harder it will be."

"What are you talking about?" I say, and now I'm irritated.

"Put me on your lap," she says.

I pick her up and set her on my lap. I'm on the verge of tears. Her body is deteriorating by the second. I doubt she even weighs ninety pounds anymore.

"Just say what you want to say, Dani."

"You're a relationship person. Find a wife, or a girlfriend at least. Make sure she's good to the boys—"

"Dani—"

"No, I won't stop. Make sure she's *intelligent*, not just nice, with a good sense of humor. And find someone with a good ass. You really got screwed out of that on your first go-round."

"I love your ass, Dani."

"You know what I mean." She laughs, and it's been a while, so it sounds amazing to me. I feel her body jerking with laughter.

"I don't feel like I have much more time, or many days where I can find words like this. I want to tell you my wishes and I want you to talk to the boys. I thought about writing them letters, but I don't think I can anymore, and I don't want to use that stupid machine."

"I understand. What are your wishes?"

I'm looking at her and thinking about how beautiful she is. How she's always been beautiful, inside and out. How she's the best kind of pain in the ass. How I'm going to miss being frustrated with her. How I'm going to miss everything.

"You're such a good-looking man, with a great job, and a good heart and soul, and you have these amazing kids that any woman would be lucky to know. Someone is going to be so lucky . . . I mean, Alex, you're really good in bed. You're, like, the best."

She laughs again and so do I. "Okay, Dani," I say, and roll my eyes. "What else?"

"I don't want to be buried in that weird family plot my mom is in," she says. It's starting to sound like Dani is getting tired. She's slurring, but I know she's determined to tell me what she has to say.

We never made plans for our wishes after death and I'm nervous about where the conversation is going, but she is right. We need to talk about it now before it's too late.

"What should we do, Dani?"

"I want to be cremated. Put a little bit of me in this garden. Then I want you to call Trevor Locks. The special effects guy on the show."

I can feel myself starting to smile because I know Dani is either about to tell a joke or ask for something ridiculous. Dani is still inside there. Even though her body is giving out, she's still in there. "Dani—"

"Listen. I want you to ask him to mix some of my ashes with

that firework stuff and then just shoot me into the air, like grand finale style. I mean I want to go out with a bang, you know?"

We both laugh, but I think she's serious. "You're kidding?"

"No," she says. "Why the hell not? Let the kids have a sense of humor. Don't take life so seriously. I wish I hadn't."

"No regrets," I say.

"We all have some. Definitely the ice-cream thing at the mall, but not the Beth Zinn punch."

I kiss her. "I love you so much, Dani. I don't know what I'm going to do . . ."

"You're going to do exactly what I told you. Watch some fireworks, find a new person who makes you laugh and is good to the boys, and live your life. One last thing, Alex?"

"Anything, Dani."

"Split the record collection up for the boys. We'll go through them. I'll help you choose who gets what."

"Of course, Dani."

"Who is going to be here tonight to watch the Emmys? I don't know how I'm going to feel in a couple of hours. I'm already pretty weak."

"You don't have to entertain anyone, it's just Mom, Dad, Josh, and Amanda. Alicia and Mark and Mirabel."

"Okay. Well, I wasn't planning on doing a song and dance. Don't make a big deal out of it if we lose, okay? Just serve cake or something so people don't feel uncomfortable. I don't care that much about the Emmy," she says.

"You must care a little."

"Maybe for Lars and Eli, but stuff like that doesn't matter when you're dying. The only thing that matters is how the people you love are feeling."

"Okay, Dani," I say quietly.

Later, when my mom and Alicia are at the house, they're

whirling dervishes in the kitchen, preparing platters and drinks while Dani watches them from her chair in the doorway.

"Alicia," she says. "Put some booze in my feeding tube."

"I heard that, Dani," I say from the other side of the kitchen. She shrugs. Alicia walks over and hands Dani a shot of tequila. "I don't think that's a good idea," my mother says.

"Thank you," Dani says to Alicia.

"I'll always have your back," Alicia says, and then she lets out the most painful-sounding exhalation, then buckles over and starts crying hysterically. I've never seen Alicia like this. Dani moves her chair closer to Alicia as my mom hurries to Alicia's side.

Dani starts getting emotional, but she's trying to play it cool. I can't imagine how hard it is to see everyone breaking down around her.

I go to Alicia and take her in my arms. "Dani's always been the strong one," Alicia whispers.

"I know," I say.

"I'm not dead yet. Jesus Christ, will you guys hold the crying until they're wheeling my corpse outta here?"

"Danielle!" my mother scolds, but Alicia and I are laughing now through our tears.

Later, we're all sitting around the TV—the boys, my parents, Amanda, Josh, Mirabel, Alicia, and Mark. Everyone is sort of positioned around Dani's chair, sitting on the floor or leaning against the couch.

Dani looks up at me. "It's the next award. Get the cake ready."

The lead actress of *Yours and Mine* was nominated for Best Actress in a Drama, but she didn't win. Dani's show is also nominated for Outstanding Drama Series and this would be the award Dani would accept as the showrunner. Tonight, Lars and Eli are there in her place.

"Here we go," Mirabel says.

Jason Bateman and Steve Carell are presenting the Emmy and when Dani heard this news, she was so happy. They're two of her favorite actors. They come out and tell a joke, then announce the nominees. Dani has moved her chair right up close to the TV. When the camera cuts to Lars and Eli, she touches the screen, as if she's telling them she loves them.

"And the Emmy for Outstanding Drama Series goes to *Yours and Mine,* Danielle Brolin, Eli Abrahms, and Gina Edwards," Jason Bateman says with a huge smile.

The room erupts. Dani is still just staring at the TV. "You did it, Mom," Noah yells.

I go to Dani's side. She looks up at me and smiles. "Cake and champagne," she says. "Quiet everyone!" she says to everyone else.

We watch the TV as Eli, Gina, and Lars approach the podium. Eli and Gina move aside so Lars can take the microphone. "If Dani could be here, she would say how grateful she is. But since we're here in her place, we get to say how grateful we are for her. This was her vision, her dream, her hard work, her boundless talent, her undeniable vivacity, her zeal, and her passion. She's a rare and precious gem and we're all lucky to have her in our lives. Like in her other speeches, Dani would stand here and attempt to thank every single person who worked on the show in any capacity and it wouldn't take long before the music would be rising and they would be shooing her off the stage. If Dani is any part of your life, you know you've been touched by a great, compassionate, and one-of-a-kind person who has more integrity than anyone I know. Love you, D, you deserve ten of these!" He holds the Emmy up, smiles, and then starts to cry as he walks off the stage.

There's a standing ovation from the audience and Dani is still watching the TV, sitting one foot away from it and just taking it in.

"What a great speech," Mark says. "Congratulations, Dani."

Everyone else hugs and congratulates her. We're all trying to hold it together. Dani's grateful and gracious, but I can tell she's worn out from the long day. She isn't saying much.

Once everyone leaves, I'm setting her up in her bed in the living room, where I sleep next to her on the couch. The boys are brushing their teeth upstairs. I lay Dani down and she dozes off almost instantly. As I'm moving around cleaning up, she startles awake with a scream. Something guttural . . . terrified.

I run to her side. "What is it?"

"I . . . couldn't breathe. I just got so scared."

"It's okay. You're okay," I say, holding her.

"Was I a good person, Alex?" She's emotional and terrified. She's looking face-to-face at her mortality and it's breaking my heart.

"Yes, Dani. You are a good person. You have always been a good person. You are beautiful and aware and in tune with people. You're compassionate and empathetic. You've shown me and the boys how to love. You've made loving people a priority and it shows. I have *always* felt loved by you. And I have always been entertained by you in the best possible way. Your shows might be a career legacy, but I think the real legacy is how people have learned how to care and love from you."

She nods. "Thank you for saying that, Alex."

"It's all true."

"You're the most loyal, reliable, solid person and best friend. You are so good through and through, and the one thing that is giving me any solace right now is knowing that the boys have you when I'm gone. Don't let them date dumb girls."

I laugh. "Dani . . ."

"You know what I mean," she says. "I just feel like it's so close and I'm scared that I won't get to tell the boys everything I want to tell them."

"You need to start using the computer speech program, Dani, and they're going to have to do the tracheotomy soon."

She shakes her head. "I don't want it. I want to die before that."

I step away from her bed and just look at her. There is no mercy in this, in making her suffer this way. She's serious and pleading, and I understand it completely. Dani would understand this if it were someone else.

"I knew it!" I hear Noah yell from the bottom of the stairs, where he must have been eavesdropping. "She wants to leave us. She's not even trying anymore."

He runs up the stairs and I can hear him telling Ethan something. Dani looks to me. "Call them down here, please."

"Dani, you are so tired. You don't need to do this right now. I will talk to them."

"Please." She starts to cry. "Bring me my boys." It's been a few weeks since she's been this emotional. She told me it was getting harder and harder for her to show what she's feeling and thinking inside.

"Noah, Ethan!" I yell. "Get down here!"

They come into the living room with their arms crossed over their chests. They're still in denial. There's no way to tell them how much longer Dani will have, but I don't think it's long now. We can all tell how quickly it's progressing. One of the doctors told me six months would be pushing it.

"Boys, listen to me. Come here, lie with me," Dani says to them in her slurred speech.

Noah and Ethan look at each other and then up to me. "Lie down with your mom, guys," I say. They both do, but it's begrudgingly, and obvious they're hurting inside. They're upset. Of course, they have every right to be.

As well as Dani can, she pulls them close to her sides. I sit down in a chair next to the bed and all four of us are crying. There is nothing we can do. No one can change what's going to happen and this is the first time all of us are acknowledging it together and accepting it.

After a few minutes Dani collects herself and says, "While I can, I need to talk to you both."

"Go ahead, Mom," Ethan says.

"I don't want either one of you or your dad to be sad for me. I have lived a full life. Think about it. I've gotten to live so many lives through the stories I've written. My own life was so full and rich too. I've traveled, I've experienced love and loss. I've had the privilege of being a mom to you two. I'm okay with how this story is ending. I need you to be okay with it too."

Ethan and Noah nod as tears pour from their eyes.

"You will learn everything you need to know about being a good man from your dad, I promise. I thought about making you a list of things I think are important in life. I thought long and hard about it and realized you both have everything you need already. Life is unexpected. There are no perfect rules, no instructions, no manuals I can give you. But there is one thing I know for sure, with absolute certainty . . . just one thing that is inarguably, without a doubt, going to make your life better, and you need to know what it is and you need to remember it every single day," she cried.

"What, Mom?" Noah says.

"I know for sure that loving your people well will make your life better, but you have to practice it every day. It's a skill to refine . . . a craft to perfect. Love yourself, love your friends, love your family, love each other, love hard, fight hard to love,

love your enemies, love all the great loves in your life and love them well, and you will be the richest men on this planet. Love is not selfish or perfect. You can love this experience of losing your mother and be grateful you get to say goodbye when so many people don't. Be the memory keepers for me from here on out. Okay, it's your turn. I love you so much."

Noah, Ethan, and I cannot even speak because we are crying so hard. This is her final goodbye. Our shirts are all drenched with tears, Ethan looks like he can't breathe, and Noah is sobbing loudly.

I don't know how much time has gone by, but we are all now quiet and depleted. The boys are asleep on Dani's shoulders. She's asleep too. I wake Noah and Ethan, walk them each up to their beds, and kiss them good night.

When I come back down, Dani is awake. "Come here, Alex."

"I'm here." I sit in the chair next to her bed. I lean my chin on the rail and hold her hand and just stare at her. She smiles and I smile back. "I love you," I say.

"I love you too, Alex. Tomorrow, will you start playing the albums for me, and read all the memories?"

"Of course I will," I say, and then I kiss her hand. I lower the rail, close my eyes, and lay my head on her bed.

"Alex?"

"What is it, my love?"

"We made it," she whispers.

I look up at her. She's smiling as best as she can.

"Yes, Dani, we did."

34

in your heart

DANIELLE

He's walking down the hall toward the stairs. It's 4:32 in the morning. I know without looking at the clock. The springtime light isn't yet piercing the horizon. There are no cars on the road; his will be the first. It's quiet out and peaceful in my heart and in my mind. I can't walk or talk but I can still think, and I can still feel.

Alex is shifting his 170 pounds from one foot to the other, down the stairs . . . loudly. I can hear him from my bed, downstairs, next to the window where I look out at the peach tree, where my girls are, whom I'll be with soon.

I can hear all the sounds he's making. The coffee beans grinding, his feet shuffling across the travertine, the clearing of his throat—it all sounds like beautiful music to me now.

He's getting ready to say goodbye to the caretaker for the day. He'll come back into this room and continue reading the memories of my life from the record sleeves. He'll play the songs.

He'll laugh and cry. The boys will pop in and out throughout the day. Noah is almost ready for his driver's permit. They're changing a lot and all in good ways. The one thing I have been feeling blessed about lately is that they've accepted my choice to die naturally, to stop all the medical interventions.

When I think about the last year of my life, I remember thinking about the brevity of Ben's life. If he had grown up too fast. If there was a predetermined time line for him. However the universe is at work right now, I know that I got to tell my dad I loved him and that I forgave him. I repaired my marriage by getting a divorce. I taught the boys the only thing I know for sure, to love their people well. I wrote my own show, got an Emmy, gave Beth Zinn a nice little present that I don't regret . . . I'm far from perfect. I told Lars, Alicia, and Alex's family how important they were in my life. Louie Louie got a permanent spot at the foot of my medical bed in the living room and I love it. I love that Alex and I realized we could be our own people and still be in love and it was better that way. That we could have autonomy and many loves in many different ways. We were not just a husband and wife, a mother and father, we were Dani and Alex. And Dani and Alex love each other.

The peach tree is flowering right now. It's reminding me of my little girls and it's making me smile, which is difficult to do these days. Believe it or not, I'm smiling inside. We all need something to hope for, especially when you're this close. I'm going to see the girls, and Ben in all his nineteen-year-old beauty, and my mother, lucid and kind, and eventually everyone else I love.

In a minute, Alex will come in here and start on the next section of records. He'll play one, then read me the memory I wrote on it and say, "Blink once if you want this to go to Noah or twice for Ethan." We're almost to the last section, about thirty more albums. I have to make it until we finish. *I have to.*

Alex drives my Jeep now, which I think is great. Out of character, but great. He also planted a huge jacaranda tree, already fully grown, on the other side of the yard. I asked him why the Jeep and the tree and he just said, "The Jeep has a million memories. I have to be the keeper of the memories now, along with the boys. And the jacaranda tree, well, that memory is for me." I didn't press.

Today, we listened to the last album. The last memory. It was Patsy Cline's *Showcase,* which featured "I Fall to Pieces." Before Alex even read it, I remembered what was written because I had added to it when we were newly divorced.

"I love Patsy Cline," Alex says. "Oh, you and your dad wrote on this one."

I want to tell Alex the story about how my dad pursued my mom for so long before she agreed to go out with him, but I think Alex will put it together.

"Your dad's writing says:

'Irene, you know how much I fall to pieces when you're around. Just say yes. Tell me you feel the same way.'

"Wow, Dani, after reading all these it's so obvious how much your dad loved your mom and you guys. It's sad he could never pull himself back together." Alex looks at me. "I won't let that happen. Oh, here your writing says:

'I'm sitting in the apartment. I've just left the house where Alex is with the boys. I don't think I will ever not fall to pieces when I see him. I don't think I will ever really get over him.'"

Alex looks up at me, his eyes misty. "No, we would have never gotten over each other, there was no point in trying," he says with a laugh.

acknowledgments

Thank you . . .

To the readers for believing in the magic of fiction. Thank you for allowing Dani and Alex into your hearts, and most of all, thank you for your support.

To my friends and family who have continued to champion my books and who constantly build me up on this writing journey, your love is so appreciated. I have the deepest gratitude to you for inspiring me to write about love, family, and relationships.

To the Roomies, who have stuck around for years encouraging me to keep writing, you are the very best readers and cheerleaders. Thank you.

To the wonderful authors Liz Fenton and Lisa Steinke, Kate Quinn, and Jill Santopolo, who were willing to be early readers and offer the most beautiful blurbs. Thank you.

To Julia Stiles and Molly Connors for your willingness to

read, your lovely words, and your continued support of my work.

To everyone at Dial Press who read and worked on this book, thank you so much.

To Emma, thank you for taking me on despite the somewhat jarring circumstances. Your enthusiasm was heartfelt and so appreciated.

To Carly for having the sharpness, wisdom, and class to navigate this business with the most grace and open-mindedness . . . and shrewdness. You are top of your class. I admire your desire to continue growing, learning, and teaching.

To Annie, your belief in me and this book changed the way I looked at writing and publishing in the best possible way. Thank you for seeing the enduring strength in Dani and Alex. I still feel you with me on this journey.

To Tony, I am always walking around with your humor in my pocket. That is truly a talent you have, but you are so much more than that. You get it! And I hope you continue to nurture your depth and understanding of the human condition. You can be a writer, but you also have to be an orthodontist.

To Sam for being your loving, hard-working, wise, and pragmatic self, and for inspiring me to continue learning. You are a dream of a son. Thank you for being you.

To Anthony for workshopping life with me, for loving me still, and for understanding this book . . . thank you.

this
used
to be
us

Renée Carlino

questions and topics
for discussion

1. What do you believe was the catalyst to ending Dani and Alex's marriage?

2. As a reader, were you more sympathetic toward Dani or Alex? Why?

3. At the beginning of the novel, Alex found Dani's passion to be charming. And later he found that same passion to be "bitchy, self-righteous, or braggy" (185). How did their perceptions of each other change over the course of the novel?

4. In the novel, Dani says, "I am the default parent . . . the mother" (15). A default parent (often mothers) is one that typically is "first in line" when it comes to child-related responsibilities. Do you think Dani's and Alex's responsibilities as partners were unbalanced? Why or why not?

5. What do you think Dani learned from dating Jacob?

6. What do you think Alex learned from dating Kate?

7. What aspects of Dani and Alex's relationship could you relate to?

8. In reference to Alex while they were separated, Dani says, "Married, divorced, separated, or dead, I am still his family" (285). Do you agree? In what ways does divorce affect the family structure? In what way does it not?

9. What surprised you the most in the novel?

10. What did you like most about the book? Least? Were there moments that you just couldn't stop thinking about?

11. Is there anything you would change about the story if you could?

12. In your life, whose phone numbers do you have memorized?

13. Discuss the following quote from the novel: "'You think love equals happiness?' he says. 'No. I think the act of loving does, the skill, the ability in it—practicing and refining it'" (297). Do you agree? Why or why not?

14. Do you believe that love is a choice and a practice? Do you think some people are better at loving than others? Why do you think that is?

a q&a with renée carlino and hannah sloane

Hannah Sloane: I would love to start by asking, what inspired you to write *This Used to Be Us*?

Renée Carlino: Well, I've written so many books about the new part of a relationship: the beginning, the lusty love affair, the first year of a relationship. And I was at a point in my own life, and also in my career, where I wanted to write about these people that probably had that experience of falling in love very dramatically, but then what happens twenty years later? Where are they at? What's going on? How do you maintain that kind of love and passion in a long-term relationship? What happens to people as individuals? How do they change? We say people don't change, but they do. Or they sort of become the single entity within their marriage. I wanted to elaborate on that a little bit more with this story and these people.

HS: I wonder if there's a key message that you hope your readers will take away from this novel?

RC: Well, I think that one thing I really wanted to explore is the fact that the idea of marriage has changed, and it should change because our world has changed. So why are we still hung up on these old ideals or rituals of marriage when it doesn't really work in the modern day? Just like gender roles, there are also marriage roles and I wanted to know what it would look like if two people in a marriage did something different from the roles they had assumed? And what if being married isn't the best thing for some people, and if that's the case, what does divorce look like? There's a line in the book where Dani, the protagonist, says that they've stayed together for the kids, but now they need to divorce for the kids, because there was just so much turmoil in the marriage. But what does parenting through divorce look like? How should it look?

HS: *This Used to Be Us* covers such a huge time span. We see Dani and Alex in love and how that love changes. I wondered if you found that time span challenging to write, and ultimately, how did you choose which scenes to show us?

RC: The book actually did not originally have those scenes, but there was a point in the editing process where we were talking about the "how." How did they get here? Why is it so tragic that they're getting divorced? Unless we see how in love they were, what it looked like in the beginning, it was impossible to really understand the tragedy of where they end up.

Dani touches on that at one point, their sort of relationship hubris, when she talks about how they thought they were untouchable. They thought we were the perfect couple. And I think everyone probably feels that way in the beginning of a relationship. I always have said, most people don't hire a skywriter to declare your love for someone if you have the intention of divorcing them in three years. I wanted to touch on how you can go from that place in your relationship where anything feels possible, you feel so invincible, and show the moments that gradually began to pull them apart.

HS: Yes, the vignettes work so well because they give us a strong sense of Dani and Alex, both as a couple as you said, but also as individuals with highly contrasted strengths. I'm curious how these characters blossomed in your mind and if one formed more quickly than the other?

RC: All these characters are amalgamations, but I think Dani is sort of the way I am. I voice my opinion a lot. I also wanted to portray her as sort of the "default" parent in the relationship and in her family. She's not a weak person or subservient; she's very strong. But I think she's been the person who has had to remember all the little details and hold everything together. She knows where the insurance cards are; she's the one who has taken the kids to the doctor when they're sick or stayed home with them. And when they break up, it shines a light on all the responsibilities she's taken on that Alex had taken for granted, and that shakes up their roles.

And for Alex, I wanted him to have the journey of feeling confident at first, almost bragging about how he'll be fine and he can manage everything. I think when you're in a very bad place in your marriage, you think once you're just going to go back to being yourself, or who you were in college, or whatever. But he realizes very quickly that's not the case.

HS: In thinking about these characters, I leaned toward sympathizing with Dani more. I wondered if you felt conflicted as you made these decisions for these characters, and if you felt proud of them for certain moments of personal growth?

RC: Alex is definitely an avoider. He avoids addressing things. He does not know how to communicate his feelings. Dani has always been the communicator in their relationship. But I wanted to portray Alex's struggle to address difficult moments head-on, how that impacted his marriage and how he comes to that realization once he and Dani are no longer together. I think we see that in his relationship with Kate. He knows it's not really working, but he just doesn't want to address it. He decides he'll cross that bridge when they get there, you know, and he even says, "I love you," just to appease her for a bit. I wanted him to learn by the end of the story his tendency to avoid communicating and eventually learn to recognize things. I think that's when I was most proud of him.

HS: Did external factors work against them, ultimately causing their divorce? Or do you think that they needed to separate in order to find their way back and ultimately love each other more deeply?

RC: I think there were certainly a lot of external factors. One of them being taking care of Dani's ailing mother: It's very difficult when your own parent doesn't know who you are, and Dani had compassion for her mother, despite the fact that she was sort of this nightmare of a person, especially to her husband. That created so much stress on their relationship. But I think it was a collision of those type of external factors with also those elements of their personalities, as we talked about. The fact that Dani felt that Alex wouldn't communicate his anger, avoiding the house and just letting everything fester, creating this sense of quiet turmoil that lead into this explosion. And then Alex feeling like Dani didn't protect their marriage as she should have. She forgot that you have to keep trying. Marriage is a verb. You have to keep working. You have to keep running, you know, and he feels she stopped.

But I also wanted their story to represent this idea of how a marriage is sort of like two magnets. In the beginning, you're sort of two opposites, two separate entities being pulled together, and you get closer and closer until you fuse. You're one and the same. But eventually, that sense of closeness can transform and you start to repel one another. You're so close to the other person that you can't see them clearly as an individual anymore. And you start to wonder, who was I when we fell in love? Who were you? It's like we need to be able to see our partners on the other side of the street again, from a distance. Dani needs to see Alex in his element, to see him working and being his charming self. She needs to see the person she met in the beginning of the relationship, versus the person with whom she only talks about the kids, the finances, the logistics of a relationship. At the beginning of the book, she hates how predictable Alex is; she thinks he's boring and hates that she always feels like she knows what's going to happen. But as they have this time apart, she remembers why she fell in love with how solid and loyal he is, how comforting that predictability is. I think the apartment gives them the opportunity to see one another as individuals again, to see one another on opposite sides of the street again, rather than always in lockstep. And it also allows them to go back to themselves, too, after twenty-five years of living with a spouse, children, sick parents. Who are they when they're on their own?

HS: I have a six-month-old baby, and, I have to be honest, the idea of having another apartment that we can take turns escaping to sounds wonderful right now. Another observation I had is that there are many comedic moments in *This Used to Be Us*, particularly for Alex and Dani during their reentry into life as single people. Was that intentional?

RC: Yeah, absolutely. With Alex, Dani always said how he was never a smooth guy, and I wanted us to see him just terrified to get back out there. First there's the doctor who was beautiful, a great conversationalist, but he focuses on her crooked toes. And we know that's not the reason it doesn't go any further; he's just scared, but I loved showing that through this somewhat ridiculous focus. And then, with Kate, he loves how she's the opposite of Dani, but he eventually has to realize through a series of missteps more about who he is in a relationship and how that's led him to where he's ended up.

With Dani, I wanted to show how when you're in a monogamous relationship for so long and then you start dating, things have changed and people date differently, but Dani just has no idea how to operate in this new frontier. She's like, you meet someone, he's your boyfriend, you go on some dates for two years, you move in with each other, you get married. That's how it works. And when she begins dating someone who shows her, you know, not necessarily, she's just, like, wait . . . what?!

I wanted them both to have this wake-up call. I think, at the beginning of the book, they both think the grass is greener. Dani even says "the grass isn't greener; it's a vitamin-rich waterfall." But, in their own ways, they both discover that's not really the case. It's a fantasy. And I think that's the product of the complacency that sometimes comes with a long-term, committed relationship. It's hard to want something you already have. You start to think there *must* be something better out there, but it isn't always that case.

HS: I think our fascination with the grass being greener is so interesting. I had a similar premise for the relationship in my novel, *The Freedom Clause,* about a young married couple who decide to open up their marriage. Initially, the husband, Dominic, thinks, "Oh, if only we had more sex, everything would be great," and then the reality is, be careful what you wish for, because when that wish becomes a reality, his wife becomes much more empowered and sexually confident. And he really struggles with that.

RC: Exactly! And it's very compelling to explore the space between our expectations and our reality.

HS: And you present that so well, with such sharp humor. At the same time, there are also a lot of painful topics in this novel. You know, we hear about the death of Dani's sibling. There's divorce, Alzheimer's, miscarriages, and then, of course, the ending. But

I felt like the tone of the novel never became too heavy, or too dark, which I applaud you for, and I wondered how you navigated that? How did you juggle these really painful topics but keep the tone uplifting?

RC: I try to reflect the way real life really is. Sometimes, you have moments that are very dark, but then, you know, there are also lighter moments. Something happens, like someone holds the door open for you, or some little tiny, positive thing happens in the day. That's how life is, I think, the human condition.

HS: Yes, the beauty and the tragedy of life go hand in hand. I was thinking about how when you're younger, you're told this lesson of like "work hard, do well in school. You'll get a good job, and then you'll be happy," and then you reach a point in life, and, at least for me, I realized, oh, happy is not a continuous state. I'm not going to reach the state of happy. I'm going to be happy and sad and sometimes somewhere in the middle. And that's normal.

RC: Oh, for sure.

HS: So I wanted to ask you about memories. In particular, Dani writes notes on the sleeves of record albums. It was an interesting plot device and one that I haven't seen before, and I wondered how this came about?

RC: I read somewhere that music and smells are the things that evoke the most emotion and memory, and I know that's true for me. I can hear a song and am instantly transported back to the cassette tapes we'd listen to on family road trips in our station wagon. And so as I was thinking about ways that you can revisit memories, I thought about music and how a record collection could become a tangible thing through which they could revisit their memories, the really good times, the sad times, and when they put the music on, they're right back in those moments. I was trying to think of a way to create a flashback that wasn't so direct. And I think those notes helped them remember all those moments, the times when they weren't at each other's throats, when they were crazy in love.

HS: And I think those notes do a great job of setting the stage for the emotional gut punch of the ending, which I was not expecting, and I was not prepared for. Did you always know that this would be the ending to Alex and Dani's tale?

RC: Well, I admit I really like really like making people cry, which probably won't surprise readers of my other books. But anyway, yes, I always knew that was going to be the ending. I really wanted Dani to have this full arc at the end, to realize how rich her life was. At the beginning, she's complaining about how much noise Alex makes when he's walking down the stairs and making coffee. And at the end, she's observing how beautiful, comforting that sound is. So he's kind of loud, sure, but he's the most loyal, solid, reliable, dependable, loving, sexy person, grinding beans for coffee at six o'clock in the morning. I wanted her to see the beauty in her life.

And I also know so many of us wonder about the end of our lives. How will everybody I love feel when they think about me? What will be my legacy? What will it do? What will happen? How will my kids feel? How will they move on? Dani's always been the one to solve her kids' problems, but she can't solve this one, and I wanted to see her negotiate that with herself. I think so many of us have those.

HS: I still get emotional thinking about it. You mentioned your previous books, and I want to talk about that a bit more, because this is your twelfth novel, which is amazing. So what is your writing routine? And do you follow it strictly? And can we all please emulate it? Because twelve novels is remarkable.

RC: You know, before I wrote my first novel, I thought it sounded like the most daunting and impossible thing ever. I never even wanted to write a college term paper. I had written scripts before, but not a novel. And what I've learned is, first, you just have to sit down and write. I feel like I stole that from Nora Roberts, because she's written like seven thousand books or something. But you just have to sit your ass in the chair and write. But what I've also realized is that you have to also get a little high off the process of writing, which I do. You get high off every single six-hour writing run you do, and you think, wow, I this is going to be good. And then maybe you look at it the next day, and you're like, Oh my God, what a piece of crap, delete half of it. But that's not the point. The point is that when you're in it you're in it, and you feel that sense of vitality from the work, the process.

It's such delayed gratification. You may never get published. Maybe no one will ever read your book. You might never make any money off it. So you have to love doing it and find the excitement from the work of it. Write what you would like to read. Is it something that you bottle up? Is it your guilty pleasure? Start with that and see if it brings you joy.

HS: That's wonderful writing advice, thank you, as well as life advice, as we should all be focused on what brings us joy in life! So for readers and writers alike who've been observing your career, you've reached peak author status. You've published several books, and one of them, *Wish You Were Here,* is being adapted into a movie. In fact, you co-wrote the screenplay with none other than Julia Stiles. What advice do you have for aspiring authors from your long and established career?

RC: I think you need to understand how truly subjective reading is. You're going to have bad reviews. Don't read them, first of all (but you probably will, because I did). And then, I'd say stick with it. If you really want to do it, make it a discipline. It is a discipline. It's not a romantic or glamorous thing; it is committing to writing every day. And then you'll have lulls. I've had years of lulls, and the only way I can really get back into writing a full book is to just force myself to write a first few pages, which is brutal. But then, my, I start thinking about it. I always imaging my scenes while I'm driving. Instead of your grocery list, try imagining your scenes, and that will help you get into them when you're writing.

HS: And how is working on a screenplay different from a novel?

RC: Well, I wrote screenplays before I wrote a novel. I went to film school and worked in development. And I've always thought of stories as movies before I thought of them as novels. With screenplays, I have to restrain myself from putting in too much description. It basically is just dialogue and a little bit of direction. Also, your screenplay is not the finished piece. It's just an element of it. Most of the time, no one will see a screenplay or read it; that's not the point. It's more like a guide, so it will change. Don't get too attached to anything. I think the screenplay for *Wish You Were Here* has been changed a million times. There's so many things that were thrown out or have been added. And when we make it, that will continue to happen, because we'll discover that there are things that don't come across well for the actors or won't work in the scene. And the last piece of advice I have is, don't get hung up on structure (three-act or otherwise). Just think about what you need. You need a protagonist. You need a problem. You need conflict. Don't worry about when things should happen; just get it down.

Hannah Sloane is the author of *The Freedom Clause*, a bold and sexy debut about a young couple who agree to open their marriage, but they soon discover that a little freedom has surprising consequences. Sloane grew up in England. She read history at the University of Bristol. She has dual citizenship and lives in Brooklyn with her partner, Sam, and their daughter, Dot.

PHOTO: © CHRIS WOJDAK

RENÉE CARLINO is a screenwriter and the best-selling author of *Before We Were Strangers, Swear on This Life, Wish You Were Here, Sweet Thing, Nowhere but Here, Sweet Little Thing, Lucian Divine, After the Rain, The Last Post, Shopping for Love, Blind Kiss,* and *This Used to Be Us.* Her books have been featured in national publications, including *Cosmopolitan, InStyle, USA Today, HuffPost, Latina* magazine, *Publishers Weekly, Redbook, Sunset* magazine, *Coastal Living,* and *The San Diego Union-Tribune.* The adaptation of her novel *Wish You Were Here,* with a screenplay by Renée Carlino and Julia Stiles, is currently in production. Carlino grew up in California and lives in the San Diego area with her husband, two sons, and their sweet pup, John Snow Cash.

reneecarlino.com
Facebook.com/AuthorReneeCarlino
Twitter: @renayz
Instagram: @reneecarlino1